MW01222546

Flight to Egypt

Based on the Gospels of Matthew and Luke

Stephanie Meier

To Varun,

with many thanks for
the good time you
gave me in India.
Happy Christmas,

love from
Stephanie

Mariam, Jossef and Jeshua share the fate of refugees
the world over and throughout the ages.
This book is therefore dedicated to all refugees.

Comadre de suburbio

There was no room in Bethlehem, there was no room in Egypt,
And there is no room in Madrid, for you.
Joseph will be forced into unemployment for many days ...
The Nile will daily waste away your skin and the beauty of your
anonymous hands ...
And the Child will grow up with no more schooling than the
lessons of the sun and of your word.

Pedro Casaldáliga, Brasilian Liberation Theologian, 1965

2nd Edition, December 2022

In 2018, I wrote a story based upon the biblical account of Mariam's visit to her Aunt Elisheva *(Matthew 1, 18ff and Luke 1)*.

Continuing the New Testament story, Mariam and Jossef are now married and have had to leave hastily for Bethlehem, Jossef's place of origin, to register for the census.

As in the previous story, I have followed the gospel accounts of Matthew and Luke. However, the two do not tally. For example: The Presentation of Jesus in the Temple forty days after his birth, to be found in Luke's Gospel, would not make sense if the Holy Family had to flee to Egypt, as described by Matthew. Therefore, compromises were called for.

This time I have elaborated on the biblical account far more than I did in my previous story 'Visiting Elisheva', as the gospel only mentions the Flight to Egypt very briefly *(Matthew 2, 13-15)*. The fictional elements hopefully also add interest to the story.

There are many legends preserved by the Egyptian Coptic Christian tradition surrounding the Holy Family's flight to Egypt, and I have tapped into these legends. However, I have been reticent about accounts of miracles performed by the infant Jesus.

Stephanie Meier, St. Gallen, 16th June 2021

© 2022 Stephanie Meier
Printed and published by: BoD – Books on
Demand, Norderstedt
ISBN: 9783754397619

PART I:

The Christmas Story

On the road again! The afternoon sun shone mercilessly from a cloudless sky. There was almost no shade here. The donkeys hung their heads and tottered over the plain behind Mariam and Jossef. They had been on their way for two days now. After leaving the busy town of Skythopolis that morning, they had crossed the bridge over the Jordan. Now they were approaching Pella.

Mariam pondered upon how different this journey was from the one nine months ago, when she had travelled the same route with Sarah and Shimon to visit her Aunt Elisheva, discovering on the way that she was pregnant. She was still pregnant, but this time she was accompanied by her loving husband Jossef, who was taking good care of her.

There were crowds of people on the road due to the census. Mariam had been walking beside Jossef and leading her donkey. Jossef had set a slow pace for Mariam's sake; nevertheless, she now felt tired and asked for a break.

«Can you make it to those date palms?» asked Jossef. «Then we'll have some shade.» Mariam nodded. After another hundred yards they reached the palm trees, under which Jossef spread a blanket. With her husband's help, Mariam awkwardly lowered her heavy body onto it. Jossef offered her the water skin which was fast becoming empty. Mariam took a swig and rinsed her dry mouth.

«Phew!» she sighed. «Walking's becoming difficult with my fat belly, and my back's hurting!» She lay on her side and pulled her knees up towards her stomach, to relax her back.

«Would you prefer to ride now?» asked Jossef, after their short rest.

Mariam nodded. She mounted awkwardly. At a somewhat faster pace they continued towards Pella, and Mariam allowed her thoughts to wander.

It had been about here, travelling with Sarah and Shimon shortly before Pella, that she had experienced the first nausea of her pregnancy. At the time, she had not actually been sure that she really was pregnant. However, it had soon become clear that the child was indeed already in her womb.

Mariam remembered how hard it had been not to share her discovery with Sara. It was not in Mariam's nature to dissemble, so she had felt wretched until she had finally found the courage to tell her friend about her pregnancy.

It had been even worse telling her mother and still more agonizing telling Jossef. She believed she had lost him due to this admission. But aided by an angelic visitation, Jossef had returned to his betrothed. As it turned out, this mutual experience had strengthened and cemented their relationship. Ever since then, they knew just what they meant to each other. More importantly: They understood the significance of the child Mariam was carrying, and they also knew from the angel that his name was to be Jeshua.

Shortly afterwards Jossef had come to bring home his bride. Accompanied by all their friends and relations, her girlfriends had crowed the whole of the way from her mother's home to Jossef's house with that typically Middle Eastern high-pitched, quavering ululation. Mariam and Jossef had been married in front of Jossef's house under a goat-hair tent, as had been the custom since the time of the Patriarchs. They each took the proffered cup of wine, and Jossef gave his beloved Mariam the marriage contract. The revelries continued into the early hours of the morning.

Jossef had built a beautiful new house for them both. Mariam felt completely at home there and was very proud of her husband's skills. Just as their life had taken on a comfortable routine, the decree of Emperor Augustus had been issued, ordering every citizen to travel to their place of origin for a census. This had not been at all convenient for Jossef and his highly pregnant wife, but there was no way of avoiding it. They had packed up supplies for their journey to Bethlehem and loaded them onto their two donkeys, preparing to leave their beautiful new home and set off on the arduous journey.

Mariam's mother, Hannah, had suggested that the couple contact Mariam's half-sister Salome upon arrival in Bethlehem.

«Do you remember her, Mariam?» Hannah had asked. «She's the youngest child of my beloved Joachim – God rest his soul – with his first wife, Shoshana. You only saw her twice, but you were still very young. Salome's a midwife. She moved to Bethlehem several years ago with her husband, Zebedee. She may be able to help you.»

Mariam had promised to call upon Salome if the need arose. She had found it upsetting to leave, hugging her mother with tears in her eyes and already longing to be home again.

However, they were still on their outward journey and glad to have finally reached Pella. The evening sun coloured the waters of the Jordan red, and the palm trees reached up like black shadows against the fading sky. The town was teeming with people like them, on their way to their places of origin to register for the census, so Mariam and Jossef had to make do with meagre lodgings.

After leaving Pella, they travelled south along the east bank of the Jordan for two more days, grateful for the proximity of water and the relative coolness of the valley. From Jericho, they would go up to Bethany and visit Elisheva and Zechariah. They hoped also to visit Sara and Shimon, and from there to continue via Jerusalem to the southern heights of Bethlehem – a further week of travel before reaching their destination.

As they started on the uphill path to Bethany, Mariam felt a dragging in her womb, and Jeshua gave her a hefty kick. Even riding the donkey, the journey had been arduous. She called for another break, so Jossef helped his wife to dismount. He made her comfortable on the blanket, fondly stroking her hair and laying his hand upon her belly.

«Too much bouncing about for our Jeshua, huh?» he said. Jossef's presence comforted Mariam. Leaning against her husband, she breathed calmly and deeply, and told him how glad she would be when they reached Bethany. From there, it would not be much further to Jerusalem.

Once Mariam had recovered, they tackled the last mile. Even the donkeys were glad to reach their destination. Elisheva came out to meet them, beaming happily, with little Jochanan in her arms.

«Mariam, my dear! And this must be your husband Jossef! Welcome! Come on in. You will stay with us for a day or two, won't you?»

«Yes please, Elisheva! I'm so tired from travelling. It was tough for me, although Jossef did show great consideration and took good care of me!»

Jossef went off to stable the donkeys. The two women entered the house which held so many good memories for Mariam. Little Jochanan reached for Mariam's belly and laid his tiny hand on it.

«Yes, my darling, that's where your little cousin Jeshua is!» said Elisheva with a broad smile. «You see, Mariam? He remembers!»

The two women maintained a companionable silence, while Elisheva prepared strong, sweet tea. She asked Mariam to tell her all that had happened since they had last seen each other. While Mariam was telling her about their wedding, Jossef and Zechariah joined them. Elisheva and Zechariah wanted to know how Rivka and Mordechai's olive grove in Nazareth was faring, and Mariam passed on Rivka's regards. Meanwhile, Elisheva had lit the oil lamps. Mariam could now hardly keep her eyes open.

«Right, you two, off to bed with you! You've

had enough for one day; you need your sleep, especially Mariam. We'll let you sleep in tomorrow. I'll go over to Sara and Shimon and let them know you're here. You can visit them tomorrow afternoon. I suggest you sleep another two nights here, as the day after tomorrow is the Sabbath. If you want, you can walk to Jerusalem with Zechariah the morning after, when he goes to serve in the temple.»

2

Even the little village of Bethany was teeming with people when Mariam and Jossef set off to visit Sara and Shimon after lunch the next day. They had both slept well in Mariam's aunt's house. Mariam was feeling fit again, and ready to meet the day.

Sarah embraced her friend Mariam, then turned to face Jossef, who introduced himself to her and her husband. Shimon greeted Jossef with a broad smile. The friends went into the house, where there were now three children playing!

«Ah!» commented Mariam, «this must be your youngest daughter! What's her name?»

«Her name's Mariam, we named her after you!» answered Sarah brightly. «She's a clever lass, just like you!»

Mariam beamed with pleasure and went over to the children.

«Martha, I swear you've grown in the half year since I was last here! You too, Elazar! And Mariam looks a healthy little girl.»

Martha picked up her sister and hugged her just like a little mother. She passed the tiny baby over to Mariam, who took her in her arms in wonder.

«My child will soon be born,» said Mariam.

«Yes I thought as much, since your belly's pretty large! What a time to have to travel!» commented Sarah.

«You can say that again!» answered Mariam. «Well, that's what comes of Jossef's being of the

House of David!»

Little Mariam loudly demanded a feed, so Sarah relieved her friend of her daughter and sat down to nurse her. Mariam and Jossef soaked up the comfortable family atmosphere and enjoyed their day with these good friends. By the time they returned to Elisheva's house, Jossef already felt he had known Sarah and Shimon for a long time.

A second night with Elisheva and Zechariah and the peaceful atmosphere of the Sabbath gave Mariam and Jossef plenty of time to recover, so that they felt refreshed and ready for the walk to Bethlehem, where they hoped to arrive towards evening. At break of day, they said the morning prayer after ritually washing. This they would do religiously every day, no matter how little time or water was available to them. Then they packed up and left with Zechariah, leading their two donkeys behind them. Zechariah took his leave of the couple at the temple gate, wished them all the best for their journey home and blessed them.

Mariam and Jossef descended from the temple mount, taking the road to Hebron. They were amazed at the number of people on the road there. Even at Bethany, there had been a great many travellers, but shortly after Jerusalem the crowds became quite overwhelming. The noise had also increased, giving Mariam a headache. She had been unpleasantly jostled several times, so she decided to ride her donkey again to give her protection. They took a short break at the roadside for her to mount, during which Jossef gave his wife a drink from the water skin. Then they set off again, going with the flow of the crowd.

It was not far to Rachel's Tomb[1], where they paid their respects along with all the other pilgrims. Near the tomb, an old man was selling fresh figs. Jossef bought a few figs to augment their supplies and chatted to the fig seller.

«Must be good for business, these crowds!» remarked Jossef.

«Oh they are!» answered the man. «It's wonderful for sales! But this isn't a good time for you to be travelling on these crowded roads, with your wife expecting.»

«You're right!» said Josef. «Mind you, we didn't come far today, only from Bethany, and we're only going as far as Bethlehem. But with all this noise and jostling, it's very taxing for my wife.»

«Know what? After the tomb, you could take the next turning on the left,» advised the old man, pointing in that direction. «As you can see, no one's turning off there. It's a longer route – you'll come out near Beit Sahour at the edge of the desert – but it's quieter! After that, you'll need to take the next right turning. You'll soon reach Bethlehem beyond the hamlet of Beit Sahour. Also, you'll arrive at the town directly in the vicinity of the only guesthouse.»

«Oh, thank you very much!» exclaimed Jossef, «that's valuable advice!»

---

[1] The matriarch Rachel was the second wife of Jacob and the mother of Joseph and Benjamin. She died near Bethlehem.

Jossef went back to Mariam and asked her whether she was happy to take the longer path. She was all in favour of the old man's idea. She turned to him, putting her hand on her heart and bowing her head in a gesture of thanks.

As they departed, they both waved to the old fig seller, then the donkeys took the slight incline at a trot. They found the left turnoff where the path evened out behind the tomb. After this, the path followed the outline of the hill, descending gently towards the east. Far ahead of them, a group of shepherds were walking along the same path with their flock of sheep and goats; otherwise, there was no one on this path. After about half an hour, the shepherds arrived at their field. The sheep and goats dispersed and began to graze the sparse, stony ground. The shepherds waved and called a friendly greeting to Mariam and Jossef, who stopped to chat with them at the edge of the field, telling them they had just come from Jerusalem and wished to continue to Bethlehem. The shepherds explained exactly where they would find the turnoff for Beit Sahour, and Mariam and Jossef walked on. In Beit Sahour, a small hamlet, they filled their water skins at a well and continued to Bethlehem.

This route had indeed been much less demanding, even though it was further. Nevertheless, Mariam was extremely glad to see the first houses of the town appearing on the horizon. There was still an hour to go until sunset. It was quiet on the outskirts of the town, but even from there, they could hear the noise emanating from the town centre. A man trundled by with an old handcart, empty but for a few leftover cabbage leaves – obviously it had been market day, which no doubt explained the crowds. They only needed to follow the noise to find the guesthouse. However, when they arrived, they saw people coming out, looking disappointed.

«Not very promising!» said Mariam. «But let's give it a try anyway. I really can't go much further!»

They entered the guesthouse, where the landlord gave them a sour look.

«Sorry! No room!» he bellowed over the heads of the guests and those who had been rejected.

So out they went again and stood in the street, completely at a loss.

«What do we do now?» asked Mariam.

Jossef frowned. He had no idea. They retraced their steps a short way towards the south, just to get away from the noise. Bethlehem was only a small town and only had this one guesthouse, as they well knew.

Whilst they stood there looking about them, Mariam's waters suddenly broke!

«Oh, Jossef!» she shouted in desperation, «It's starting! Our baby's coming!»

Jossef's eyes widened in horror; he acted fast, hammering on the door of the nearest house, but there was no answer. He tried the next house – no answer there, either! Desperately, he knocked on all the doors, until finally a young man responded.

«My wife's having a baby!» shouted Jossef. The

young man's eyes widened, his mouth gaped and he disappeared inside the house again. However, he had left the door ajar, which gave them some hope. A middle-aged woman came to the door with a puzzled expression.

«My son tells me your wife's having a baby, is that right?» she asked Jossef.

«Yes! Oh, please, help us! Have you got room for us somewhere where she can give birth?»

«I can only offer you the stable. I'll spread some fresh straw in there so that the poor woman can give birth on it.»

Jossef was in despair, because he could feel his wife's desperation, but there was no time to search for a better option.

«Right, in that case please show us the way,» sighed Jossef, «oh, and thank you very much, it's most kind!» he added.

Luckily, the stable was directly behind the house. Jossef supported Mariam who was panting and swaying slightly, whilst the owner brushed the floor clean and spread fresh straw, introducing herself as Tabitha while she did so. The stable had a homely smell of straw and dung. With Jossef's help, Mariam lowered herself onto the straw and moaned in anguish.

«I'm off to fetch a midwife!» said Tabitha. «You're doing fine! Breathe deeply, that's it!»

Jossef held Mariam's hand and wiped the sweat from her brow.

«Oh my, why did it have to happen right here!»

groaned Mariam through clenched teeth.

«Mariam, please tell me what to do,» begged Jossef.

«Yes, Jossef, go to the house and ask for water and cloths, then please go and find Salome!» ordered Mariam. Jossef went off, grateful to have something useful to do.

Mariam was shaken by a first contraction. Luckily she had been present when Elisheva had given birth and knew exactly what to do. Soon, the labour pains were coming in shorter intervals. Mariam knew the child was coming. She supported herself on a hay bale and pressed with all her might.

Jossef returned with the water bowl and the cloths just as Tabitha arrived with the midwife, so he left again to search for Salome.

«You're doing just fine!» the midwife encouraged Mariam, helping her into a better position for the birth. «Keep going, alright? Press hard!»

Hours passed. Mariam was fighting and suffering greatly. The midwife supported her with both voice and hands. When Jossef finally arrived with Salome, Mariam was visibly flagging. Salome went over to her half-sister, stroked her sweating brow and gave her encouragement, while Jossef, his face very white, disappeared to the back of the stable. Seeing his wife suffering like this was really upsetting him. He went out and fetched the two donkeys to take his mind off things.

The midwife commented to her colleague that Mariam appeared still to be a virgin, which fact was confirmed by an amazed Salome. Mariam's face was lit by a brief, enigmatic smile, before she continued pushing and struggling.

Finally, the baby was born without any great complication. Jeshua played his part, and soon issued his first lusty scream. After she had tied off the umbilical cord and cleaned Mariam up, Salome laid the child in Mariam's arms. Mariam fell back in the straw with a huge sigh and held her son close with an ecstatic smile. Deeply moved, she breathed in the fragrance of her tiny baby. This sweet, mystifying scent was the purest joy she had ever known.

Jossef looked with wonder upon the tiny child and stretched out a finger to him. Little Jeshua briefly looked up at his father with large, dark eyes. Mariam leant against Jossef, exhausted but happy, with little Jeshua in her arms. God had given them the most wonderful gift.

Thus, the Lord came into his world, a meagre world with little comfort, but with loving parents who gazed at him for hours with doting eyes and only found a little sleep towards the early hours of the morning. Salome remained with the family to support them, showing Mariam how to nurse her child.

Now and again, the donkeys' hooves stamped on the wooden stable floor. One of the goats bleated briefly. Otherwise, all was silent on the southern outskirts of Bethlehem. But for those with ears to hear it, the spirit of God was present in the soft sound of beating wings and rushing wind.

3

The shepherds in the field near Beit Sahour had also come from Jerusalem on the previous day, where they had been selling sheep and goats to pilgrims for sacrifice. They had hardly been able to get through for the crowds, and like Mariam and Jossef, had been glad when they reached the quieter path after the turnoff at Rachel's Tomb. After Mariam and Jossef had continued on their way to Bethlehem, the shepherds discussed this remarkable couple.

«Crazy! Fancy taking such a pregnant woman travelling!» the oldest shepherd exclaimed.

«Guess they had to, 'cause of the census,» answered a shepherd boy, proud to demonstrate his knowledge of the current situation. «Incredible number of people on the roads right now!»

«D'you think they'll find somewhere to stay?» asked the old man.

«No! Shouldn't think so!» they all answered at once. They fell silent and pondered the matter.

The animals were driven into the dry-stone fold. The shepherds then rolled themselves into their warm coats and lay down on the ground to sleep.

In the middle of the night, the shepherd boy heard a sound like beating wings and rushing wind. He sat up and looked about him, to see whether there was a flock of birds flying over, but he could not see any, just a very bright star twinkling in the southwestern sky. The sound swelled to a buzzing. He wakened his colleagues, who could hear the buzzing too!

Suddenly, there was a great light all around them, brighter than the day. The men fell to the ground with shock and lay there trembling. Each of them saw the young couple in their mind's eye, and in each of their hearts an inner voice spoke, telling them to get up and search for the couple, as they were very special!

The shepherds were filled with joy, and their hearts leapt; they all felt a great jubilation, as if they were hearing beautiful music. Slowly, the light and the buzzing faded, until they could hear only the soft beating of wings and the rushing wind, then nothing.

These men were normally practical types, but now they looked at one another in puzzlement. They glanced at the fold, but the animals had not reacted at all to the sounds or the light. All was calm, as though nothing had happened. They continued the inner dialogue as if it had been spoken aloud and as if it was the most normal thing to do so.

«We've got to go and search for them!»

«For sure! That's a sign, it's got to be taken seriously. Must be something to it!»

They decided amongst themselves who would stay with the sheep. The others would leave for Bethlehem as soon as day broke. None of them could sleep after that. They all lay awake thinking of the unbelievable experience.

In the first light of day, the group of shepherds arrived in Bethlehem and went to the guesthouse, although they did not hold out much hope of finding the couple there. The landlord had no recollection of seeing a pregnant woman; there had been far too much hubbub for him to remember any individuals. All he could say was that they were not staying at the guesthouse.

The shepherds now started to feel slightly embarrassed at their own enthusiasm. Had they been mistaken? They wandered aimlessly through the lanes on the outskirts of Bethlehem, having no idea how to conduct their search.

While standing in front of a private house, they heard a baby crying. They looked at one another. It could be anybody's child of course; after all what was the likelihood of the young woman having just given birth that night?

The baby's cries seemed to come from the back of the house. The other shepherds were sceptical, but the shepherd boy prowled cautiously round to the stable, following the sound of crying.

Once he had found the source of the noise, he knocked gently, opened the stable door a little and peered inside – it was them! It was the couple they had seen in their field! They gave him a friendly smile. He hurried back to the lane and beckoned the other shepherds to follow him. When they all came and peered through the door, Mariam gestured to them to come closer to the manger in which she had laid Jeshua.

Again they heard the sound of beating wings and rushing wind. The shepherds knelt and removed their caps in veneration of this tiny baby, which appeared to be exuding light.

The old shepherd explained to Jossef and Mariam that they had come because they had seen a vision. None of them understood why they, as humble shepherds, had been sent to see the special child. But they all felt that it was somehow right and fitting.

«Would you like a lamb?» asked the shepherd boy. «We've got a couple of nice one-year-olds, and we'd be pleased to give you one.»

«Thank you,» answered Jossef, much moved «but I'm not sure we can roast it anywhere here. Mind you, some meat would do us good, especially my wife, who needs to regain her strength!»

«Maybe you could roast it on your way home?» suggested one of the others.

The shepherds seemed so keen to give them a lamb that Jossef politely accepted their offer. They arranged that the shepherd boy would return with the lamb, and all the shepherds made their way slowly back to the flock in the field near Beit Sahour, full of awe at what they had experienced.

4

Far, far away in Persia, a group of astrologers were consulting a chart of the present constellations. There would soon be a very special aspect: the conjunction of Jupiter and Saturn which only occurred every twenty years. A new star had appeared, shining very brightly and building a trigon with this conjunction and Mars. They agreed that Jupiter symbolized royalty, and Saturn in Pisces symbolized the Jewish people. This suggested that there would be a new Jewish king. They had heard that the present king, Herod the Great, ruling by the grace of the Roman Emperor, was not popular with the people. Could a major change be imminent? After much discussion, they decided to leave for Judaea to request an audience with the present king and try to find out more.

Travelling south, they would often be passing through desert land. They had their charts, texts, and supplies loaded onto their camels by their apprentice, Aftab, together with gifts for the new king, should they be able to trace him.

Further constellations showed that this king would have religious importance, was possibly still very young, would grow up in poverty as had King David of Israel and would die a painful, early death. For these reasons they chose as gifts: frankincense for dignity, myrrh for the anointing of the dead, and gold for royalty.

Navigation was a simple matter for astrologers, and they made good headway on their magnificent beasts, mostly travelling in the early morning and late evening to avoid the greatest heat. Two weeks on the traditional caravan trade routes already brought them as far as Syria. They crossed the border into the northern province of Gaulanitis and made for Tiberias in Galilee, where they intended to spend the night and gain first impressions of Herod's reputation by speaking with the local population.

Tiberias was the new capital of the Tetrarchy of Galilee and Peraea. The streets of this town were crowded with people. The astrologers went down to the harbour, as one generally found all kinds of people in a harbour who were happy to talk.

They did indeed find a tradesman waiting for a boat with a bale of cloth at his feet, who was glad to while away his time chatting to these foreigners. The man was a lively narrator who spoke with much gesturing. At first, he waxed enthusiastic about the father of the present Tetrarch, Herod Antipater, who, he said, had found favour with the highest circles in Rome through his bravery and his diplomacy.

«He's obviously found favour with you, too!» interjected Makahn, the eldest of the three astrologers. «His reputation has even reached us in Persia. Mind you, we have also heard other things about him. But we have heard little about his son, the present Tetrarch, Herod the Great. What is your opinion of him?»

«Well, to begin with, he freed our country of the disruptive insurgents, who caused so much havoc in our lives. That was good, and he was respected for it. But he's brutal. He'd sell his own grandmother, that's for sure. And he's been known to kill members of his own family! He'll stop at nothing to further his own interests!»

«So he's a nasty type!» interjected Behnam in his challenging way. «Such acts can easily lead to insurrection, can't they?»

«Well yes, maybe – but I'm a peace-loving person and I'd never get involved in insurrection!» added the cloth trader quickly. After all, you never knew who you were talking to!

«No, I was not implying that you would,» added Behnam raising his hands in a gesture of peace. «But you must admit that a ruler like that can cause fear and distrust amongst his subjects.»

«Ye-es, that's certainly true,» admitted the trader, «under Herod one has to be ready for anything! One tends to be cautious.»

«Very sensible!» agreed Makahn, winking at his two colleagues, who grinned at the fellow's cautiousness. They could tell that the man was now on his guard, so they slowly ended the conversation and went to look for someone else who may be more willing to express his true opinion. But after talking to two even more cautious people, the three astrologers gave up and went to find lodgings for the night.

The town was very grand. After checking into their lodgings, they wandered around the lively streets, between palaces in the Graeco-Roman style, past the forum and the theatre, and on to the baths where they enjoyed the comforting warmth of the thermal waters. Afterwards, they got talking to a Roman functionary in a nearby tavern over drinks.

The functionary voiced his opinion of Herod: «He's a reliable ally for us, as he nips every rebellion in the bud.»

«But we've also heard that his morals are not what they could be. Didn't he have members of his own family murdered?» asked Makahn with a side-glance at his younger colleague Kamran.

«Well, it's not our problem what he does with his own family! We see to it that we don't get involved with such things. To be honest, there are a lot of Romans who despise Herod; nevertheless, we use his power for our own purposes. And at least he's equally brutal to everyone, there's no favouritism!» said the functionary and laughed loudly.

The three astrologers took their leave of their Roman drinking partner. Slowly, they were gaining an impression of this despot Herod, as they had hoped they would. The people trembled in awe of him, and that was useful to Rome, as it kept this corner of the empire quiet.

The astrologers decided that they would indeed travel on to Jerusalem and request an audience with Herod. It promised to be interesting!

Two days later they were standing in front of the rambling palace in Jerusalem. They requested an audience from the gatekeeper, who disappeared to discuss Herod's agenda with a clerk.

«You're in luck!» he said when he returned. «I've made an appointment for you for tomorrow at the ninth hour[2]. Report to the East Gate!»

After lunch, the astrologers discussed their strategy for the audience on the following day. Then they went sight-seeing in the well-known city. As they were not Jews, they were not allowed to enter Herod's famous temple, but they had to admit that whatever crimes Herod had committed, he had a good eye for grandeur and had created beautiful buildings.

The next day, they arrived punctually at the ninth hour in front of the East Gate. They were taken to Herod's Hall of Office, where the rather plump ruler sat on a raised golden throne, dressed in richly embroidered robes, awaiting them with a proud, cynical look in his eye.

The astrologers approached the king reverently and spoke the required phrases to flatter his narcissistic character. Herod's mouth formed an unnatural smile which did not reach his cold, hard, piggy little eyes. He did not offer his guests a seat. A servant brought them each a cup of wine and also presented one to the king.

«Your Royal Highness, we are astrologers from Persia,» said Makahn. «At present, there is a constellation which suggests that extraordinary things are occurring in connection with the royal line. For this reason we have travelled here to find out more. Should your Royal Highness be able to tell us more, we would be most interested. Alternatively, if your

---

[2] In the ancient world, the ninth hour was about 3 - 4 p.m.

Royal Highness should wish it, we could give you an account of the astrological interpretations we have made.»

Herod stroked his clean-shaven chin. This was not what he had been expecting! The three wise men left him time to consider, not wanting to rush things.

Eventually, Herod said: «Very well, tell me of the interpretations you have made, although I am sure I know all the facts already. What exactly have you seen?»

«May we please roll out our charts for you, your Majesty?» asked Kamran, bowing his head slightly.

«Yes yes,» answered Herod, «show them to me, if you feel it will help, but hurry – I don't have all day!»

Behnam stepped forward and rolled out the astrological chart in front of Herod. Next, the handsome young Kamran stepped forward and pointed to the conjunction of Jupiter and Saturn on the chart, in the south-western sky. Herod gave Kamran a piercing look, but Kamran did not allow this to deter him and said in a calm, confident voice: «Here, the two planets Jupiter and Saturn are in conjunction. Jupiter is a symbol of royal dignity,» Kamran bowed his head slightly towards Herod at these words, «and Saturn is the symbol of the Jewish people. Further constellations show that this king will have religious relevance,» Kamran pointed to another planet, «he may still be very young,», he pointed to yet another planetary aspect, «and, like King David of Israel, he will grow up in poverty. One can also see that this new king will die an early, painful death.» Here he pointed with a frown to a further aspect.

The three men had agreed not to say more, but to leave it up to Herod how he wished to continue the discussion, as they had broached contentious topics.

Herod stroked his chin again. There was a tense stillness in the room. At length he said: «You may leave me now. I wish first to discuss this subject with my scribes and high priests, after which I might call you again for a further audience.»

Bowing low before Herod, Kamran, Makahn and Behnam walked backwards to the door and left the king's presence. They refrained from speaking while they were still in the palace, but once they were outside, they let out their breath through their lips.

«Phew!» exclaimed Behnam, «what a pompous man!»

«True, but I believe he's a dangerous man,» added Makahn. «It's a good thing we decided to be cautious. Possibly we've already said too much. Now we just need to let matters take their course.»

«I wonder whether he really will call us back,» continued Behnam, «and if so, it'll be interesting to see how the discussion continues.»

It took another two days for Herod to call upon the astrologers for a further audience.

«This time, you may accompany us, Aftab,» suggested Makahn, «so that you can learn how to deal with a pompous narcissistic ruler!»

The seventeen-year-old apprentice smiled, pleased to be able to gain further experience on this trip, other than merely taking care of the camels and the baggage. He was eager to learn.

For the second audience, Herod had also invited his scribes, which indicated how important this discussion was for him. The three astrologers noticed that the scribes were looking very serious and quite tense. All participants in the discussion were wary, as a great deal could be at stake.

Herod opened the discussion: «My scribes and high priests are of the opinion that this so-called 'king' you are talking about will presumably be born in Bethlehem in Judaea. We will now read the excerpt from our scriptures which could be an announcement of this birth.» He stressed the word 'could'.

He gestured to his scribes, one of whom stood to read the excerpt: «Thus it is written in the book of the Prophet Micah:

> *But you, Bethlehem Ephrathah, though you are small among the clans of Judah, out of you will come for me one who will be ruler over Israel, whose origins are from of old, from ancient times. Therefore, Israel will be abandoned until the time when she who is in labour bears a son, and the rest of his brothers return to join the Israelites. He will stand and shepherd his flock in the strength of the Lord, in the majesty of the name of the Lord his God. And they will live securely, for then his greatness will reach to the ends of the earth.[3]»*

---

[3] Micah 5, 2-5

The scribe had spoken with much pathos. He took his seat again.

«Right, that's enough!» ordered Herod superfluously. The astrologers glanced at one another and risked a cynical grin.

«With respect, your Royal Highness, that seems pretty much to confirm our interpretations,» said Makahn.

«Yes, it could be true. That is why I also wish to visit this new 'king'. It is never too early to make the acquaintance of future rulers, particularly when they have been prophesied by our scripture and would therefore be important for our people. I therefore suggest that you go now towards Bethlehem and find this young person, according to scripture it could even be a newborn babe. Make extensive searches, find him! And once you have found the child, I wish you to return to me and inform me of the exact location, in order that I may also go and pay reverence to him. Is that clear?»

«Yes, your Royal Highness!» answered the astrologers obediently. The scribes sighed with relief. All had gone exactly as Herod had planned it.

The astrologers bowed low and left the hall, then the palace. This time, they were accompanied to the gate by the scribes, who called for someone named Enosh. There appeared to be some excitement. The astrologers acted as though they had not noticed the nervous excitement, whereas in fact they were taking exact note of all that was happening. The scribes appeared to be talking emphatically to Enosh about some topic and giving him detailed instructions.

The astrologers could not tarry any longer or their interest would become suspicious. On their way back to their lodgings they wondered out loud what the role of this clerk Enosh could be. They had marked his appearance very precisely and also brought Aftab's attention to the scribes' behaviour.

«They're up to something, Aftab. Did you notice that?» said Makahn. «We'll be on our guard, but there's no need to take any particular precautions. We'll just wait and see!» Aftab nodded eagerly.

5

The astrologers left their lodgings immediately after the audience. While Aftab was saddling up the camels, he happened to notice Enosh, the clerk they had seen talking to the scribes, coming out of the same lodging house and disappearing into a side-street. He told his masters of his observation. Then they set off on their way, their four camels taking them southwards with the typical graceful, swaying stride.

Sometime later, Kamran said to Makahn: «Have you noticed that the clerk we saw this morning, is following us at a distance?»

Makahn nodded. «He's actually doing it quite well, but he hasn't reckoned with our sharp powers of observation!»

«There's nothing to be feared from a tail we're aware of,» agreed Behnam.

Aftab turned round to see this 'tail' who was following them.

«Hey! Don't look back, Aftab!» ordered Behnam. «Act as though we haven't noticed!»

At Rachel's Tomb they could hardly get through, as the road to Hebron was so crowded. The astrologers bought themselves some figs, stopped to chat with the fig seller and were given the same advice as Jossef and Mariam. They also decided to take the detour.

Shortly before reaching Beit Sahour, they spotted a group of shepherds with their flocks grazing in a field. The shepherds appeared to be excited about something, not at all as indolent and taciturn as such herdsmen usually were. They even came over to the camels and greeted the astrologers.

«Peace to you, shepherds!» Makahn called down from his camel. «Have you something to celebrate? What has made you so merry?»

The shepherds were only too pleased to recount their wonderful experience: the bright light, the family and the special child in the stable which had touched their hearts so deeply.

«So small, but somehow great!» said the shepherd boy ineptly.

Kamran nodded. «I believe I know what you mean, boy. And I have a feeling we are searching for this very family!»

«You're looking for such a humble family?» asked the oldest shepherd. «What d'you want with them?»

«It's a long story, but this child is undoubtedly very special, much more than you can possibly know! Be grateful that you have been privileged to behold him!» said Makahn.

«Could you take us to this family?» asked Behnam.

Suddenly the shepherds became wary. Aftab also became uneasy at this question and looked back to see if their tail was already on the path behind them. However, there did not appear to be anyone in sight.

«We don't know anything about you. What if

you want to harm the family?» said the old shepherd.

«You are quite right to be suspicious. And should another man riding behind us ask after the family, you must not, I repeat not on any account tell them anything, for this man really does wish to harm the family, whereas we mean well. You may trust us. However, the man riding behind us comes from Herod!»

«From Herod!» said the shepherd boy. «Hah, we won't tell him nothing!»

The shepherds huddled together and discussed the situation, after which the shepherd boy came back to the camels.

«Know what? We promised the family a lamb, and I'm going to bring it right over to them. You can come with me! We trust you.»

«Very well, thank you very much! But we must move immediately or our tail will catch up with us!» warned Kamran.

So the shepherd boy went over to the fold, picked out a flawless year-old lamb and carried it to Bethlehem, walking next to the camels and showing the astrologers the way.

***

The tail, Enosh, had had bad luck. At Rachel's Tomb he had dismounted from his horse to put some distance between himself and the astrologers. He took a swig from his water skin, and he was just about to remount so that he could keep an eye on his prey, when a group of young men started a loud brawl. Right next to Enosh, one of the men went for another with a raised stick, screaming at him. Enosh's horse shied, stepped backwards over a small scarp and fell.

Enosh swore loudly and rounded on the men angrily, but they were only interested in their brawl and ignored him completely. He helped his horse to its feet and led it up and down at the edge of the crowd. Such a nuisance! The horse had gone lame on its right foreleg. He remounted briefly to see whether the astrologers were still ahead of him, but they were nowhere to be seen. Enosh cursed inwardly and dismounted again. Now he would have no choice but to lead his horse all the way to Bethlehem. Once there, he could attempt to heal the leg with a compress. He would have to find out where his prey had got to. This little accident could endanger the success of his mission and cost him dearly, since Herod had been known to punish such mistakes with death. If only he had not dismounted from his horse!

***

When the group arrived at the house, the shepherd boy went ahead of the astrologers, peering cautiously into the stable. Mariam and Jossef sat peacefully with their child, speaking quietly to each other. The shepherd boy gestured to the four men to follow him into the stable.

«Peace to you!» said the shepherd softly. «I brought you that nice lamb I promised you. And I've got visitors to see you, men of goodwill.»

Jossef looked sceptical but thanked him for the lamb and indicated that he should pass it to Salome, who placed at the back of the stable next to the two goats. There was some bleating, but soon the animals quietened down again, and the shepherd boy left.

The three wise men stepped forward. Aftab stayed by the door watching.

«Peace be with you!» said Makahn in his soft melodic baritone.

«And with you!» answered Jossef and Mariam.

Makahn continued: «We are astrologers. Based on certain planetary aspects, we have seen that a king of religious importance to Judaea will emerge. This king may still be very young, and will grow up humbly, like King David of Israel.»

«What connection does this have with us, sirs, and why have you come seeking us?» asked Jossef.

«A conjunction of Jupiter and Saturn brought us to Judaea. But in order to find out more, we spoke with King Herod.»

Mariam's eyes widened. Could they really trust these men? Were they really men of goodwill, as the shepherd had said?

«Herod's scribes cited your scriptures, saying that a new King of the Jews was to be born in Bethlehem,» said Kamran, quoting the passage in its entirety, for he had an excellent memory.

«The Prophet Micah!» said Mariam softly and with reverence. «Are you telling us this passage relates to us?»

«Does that seem so impossible to you?» asked Makahn gently.

«It is difficult for me to grasp,» answered Mariam, «but this child was indeed conceived in a very special way. And at that time, both my husband Jossef and I received messages. We called them 'the visits of the angel'.»

The three astrologers nodded reverentially. The concept of an angel was nothing extraordinary for a scholarly Persian.

«What was this message, good lady?» asked Kamran.

«I saw a gentle, loving countenance before me, and I knew immediately that I would bear a child. Next, I heard an inner voice saying the name 'Jeshua', and I knew that the child must be so named. I felt that the child would become great and important for the people of Israel, for the House of Jacob. And I knew at that moment that this Holy Child I was to conceive would be called the Son of God!»

As Mariam spoke these words, they all heard the soft beating of wings and rushing wind in the room around them.

«That sound!» said Jossef, «We both heard that every time the angel came to us.»

«Vibration!» said Makahn, «All is vibration, all is oscillation! The metaphysical becomes densified. We hear the waves of spiritual beings who wish to support us. We see densified spirit! Everything is ruled by the interaction of proportions in all things. Everywhere, things are mirrored by their opposites;

the processes of growth and decay, of world and cosmos. That which is applicable in our visible world, also applies in the invisible sphere, which is yet at work in our visible world.»

Mariam glanced at Jossef and raised one eyebrow. Jossef smiled. They understood each other without words. These words did not really seem to help. On the contrary: Exalted scientific explanations of such subtle things somehow disconnected the experience. They made them into an object of science rather than making them tangible.

Nevertheless, the men seemed to be sincere and obviously had integrity, otherwise they would not have been able to hear those now familiar sounds of the spirit.

Makahn, Kamran and Behnam held up their gifts. Makahn went down on one knee before the child. He took the frankincense and censed three times, passing the incense burner in a circle around Jeshua, who started to cough. Mariam laughed quietly.

Makahn spoke: «May your life be dedicated to your people, future King of the Jews.»

Next, Kamran knelt before the child. He opened a pouch, took out two *aurei*[4] and laid them on the edge of the manger, saying: «This gold represents your royal dignity, blessed child!»

Lastly, Behnam knelt before little Jeshua, anoin-

---

[4] Roman gold coins, one Aureus was worth about the monthly wage of a craftsman

ted his forehead and the palms of his hands with myrrh and spoke: «Blessed are you, o King, also at that time when you will pass into the Realm of the Dead.»

The three men remained kneeling before the child for a while, then they rose and faced his parents again. The sound of beating wings and rushing wind ceased abruptly. Mariam and Jossef saw the serious look in the eyes of the three men and were startled.

«I am afraid we have to warn you,» said Makahn, «for Herod has asked us to report back to him exactly where you are to be found. He said he wished to pay reverence to the new king. But he did not say this with an honest voice. There was calculation in his eyes. We do not trust him.»

«Indeed,» added Behnam, «he is not honest. He wishes to harm you so that he may keep his position of power. We believe he sent someone after us, to trail our every move.»

«Does this man know where we are?» asked Jossef aghast.

«Aftab!» called Behnam, «Did you see our tail again? Is he on our heels?»

«No,» answered Aftab. «Surprisingly, I haven't seen him since shortly before Rachel's Tomb.»

«So he does not know where you are,» said Makahn to Mariam and Jossef. «Aftab has a good eye for danger. Nevertheless, you should be cautious.»

«Now we will return to our homeland,» said Kamran. «You may rest assured that we will not go anywhere near Herod again.»

«Peace be with you, and blessings upon your child!» called the three astrologers as they walked towards the stable door.

«Peace be with you, too!» answered Mariam and Jossef, «We wish you a good journey home. Thank you very much for the gifts and for your kind words, also for your warning!»

6

«Do you think we're really in danger, Jossef?» asked Mariam some days later.

«I shouldn't think there's any immediate danger,» answered Jossef. «After all, Bethlehem's full of people. If the tail was unable to follow those men, he'll never find us in these crowds. He knows nothing about us and has never seen us.»

Mariam relaxed. «That's true!» she said with relief. «I wouldn't mind staying here a few days longer before starting out for home. And we still haven't registered for the census yet.»

«No, I thought we could do that tomorrow, providing you feel strong enough,» suggested Jossef.

«Certainly! I think I've had time to recover. I feel strong enough now. Let's do that,» assented Mariam. «Tomorrow we'll have been here five days, and the day after tomorrow is the Sabbath. If we stay another three days, we could have the circumcision done here.»

«Oh my goodness, you're right, we'll have to!» exclaimed Jossef.

Before leaving for the census next day, Jossef asked Mariam to sew the two *aurei* into the hem of his robe.

«Our nest egg for the journey home,» he said cheerfully. Both of them were looking forward to returning to their lovely home in Nazareth.

But first, they made their way to one of the stalls that had been erected in the marketplace for the purpose of the census. Mariam carried Jeshua in a baby sling, so that he was safe in the crowds.

It was extremely loud in the town, with people shouting and clattering about everywhere. Carts trundled over the stones of the Roman road to Hebron. Now and then, a donkey brayed, adding to the general cacophony.

Registration was quickly done. As required by the census, Jossef gave his and Mariam's full names, the names of their fathers, Jeshua's full name, their ages, hometown, profession, financial situation, and land ownership.

They now needed to find out where the mohel[5] of Bethlehem lived.

«Let's ask Tabitha,» suggested Jossef. «She'll probably know.»

On the way back to the stable, they bought fresh fruit and olives. Then they knocked on Tabitha's door. She did indeed know where the mohel lived and offered the couple some tea.

«I'm Mariam, and this is my husband Jossef,» said Mariam. «We're so grateful that I could give birth in your stable! Thank you so much!»

«How's the little one?» asked Tabitha. «My son saw you had visitors. Do you have friends here?»

«Mmm,» said Jossef quickly, so as not to arouse suspicion. «Our little one is fine; in fact he's doing very well. However, we'll have the circumcision without any guests. Is it alright by you if we hold the ritual

---

[5] The person carrying out the circumcision

in your stable?»

«Yes, of course!» answered Tabitha with a smile. «My son Yitzhak can help prepare everything.»

The next two days flew by. On the first day, they celebrated the Sabbath, and the following day was taken up with preparations for the circumcision and for the trip home.

The mohel came to the stable and gave Mariam and Jossef a dignified greeting. He sharpened his knife and circumcised little Jeshua, who screamed gustily at such treatment. Jeshua was ritually given his name. Mariam and Jossef beamed happily. Now at last, they could look forward to returning home.

Towards evening, Tabitha returned to the stable with a present for them – a skin filled with sweet Bethlehem wine. She wished them both a good journey, but with such a serious expression that Jossef asked her what was wrong.

«Yitzhak told me this evening that he got talking to a man in the tavern. The man looked well-to-do. Somehow, they got onto the subject of you, and Yitzhak told the man he'd seen the three gentlemen visiting you in the stable. This man showed an extraordinary interest in the fact and wanted to know where Yitzhak lived. Only then did Yitzhak become suspicious. Something didn't feel right, so he gave him our direction as vaguely as possible. I just felt you ought to know that.»

«Thank you, Tabitha. The three gentlemen told us they had been followed, but we don't know the man you're telling us about. We don't know why he was following them or why he's interested in us,» Jossef purposely remained vague, so as not to raise any suspicion, «but we've got a strange feeling about it all. It's good you told us! I think it means we'll have to leave for home very soon, to be on the safe side!»

«So where do you live?» asked Tabitha.

«In Nazareth, in Galilee,» answered Jossef.

«Ah. Well, I hope you have a good journey home. Take care of yourselves and your little son. Peace be with you!» said Tabitha.

«And with you and Yitzhak, and thank you very much for everything!» answered Mariam and Jossef warmly.

They lay down to sleep. Jossef was fidgety, tossing and turning. He eventually drifted into a dream in which a shadowy figure was following them to Galilee. They kept turning round to look behind them and saw the man in silhouette, high on his horse, brandishing a sword and shouting: «Death to the King of the Jews! Death to all children!» He came nearer and nearer, there was no escape … Jossef awoke, bathed in sweat.

«What's up, Jossef?» asked Mariam. «Did you have a bad dream?»

«Yes, I had a nightmare. But I'm convinced it was more than that. It's a warning! If Herod really has sent a man after us, he'll not rest until he's found us and killed Jeshua.»

Mariam blanched. «So you really take it that seriously?» she asked.

«After this dream, I'm in no doubt. Jeshua's in

danger. Mariam, my love, I'm afraid we can't return to Nazareth now. Herod will search throughout Galilee and Peraea until he finds Jeshua. I'm sorry, but I believe we'll now have to flee to somewhere outside his sphere of administration. We'll no longer be safe in Nazareth.»

«But Jossef!» exclaimed Mariam aghast, «What about our house and all our possessions? And we only have enough supplies to get us back home. Wherever do you think we should go to?»

«I'm so sorry, my darling. I've no idea where we should go. Let me just think about it for a while, and you go back to sleep. Sorry I woke you!»

Mariam cuddled up to her husband, but there was no question of going back to sleep. She listened to the donkeys and goats stamping on the wooden floor. It would have been warm and cosy, had this unexpected threat not surfaced and caused them such anxiety.

Jossef suddenly sat up and exclaimed: «I know! We can go to my sister in Ashkelon!»

«What?» said Mariam. «Your sister? I don't see how that will help.»

«Mariam, you don't seem to understand how serious this is! We really must escape! Every hour we stay here, we're in greater danger, and Jeshua too. Don't you remember the words one of the astrologers spoke as he anointed Jeshua with myrrh on his head and hands? He spoke of his death, and I already had a bad premonition. My love, please try to understand that we need to get as far away as possible from here without delay. For the moment, I believe my sister's place is far enough.»

Mariam stiffened at Jossef's words. «So you think we ought to start at dawn already?» she asked anxiously.

«Even earlier,» answered Jossef. «We need to be well away from here before first light. The more people who see us, the easier it will be for this tail to pursue us.»

Salome awoke and asked what was wrong. Jossef explained the situation. Salome blenched and needed a few moments to assimilate the news, then she offered to accompany the family.

«Zebedee is away from home and will only be coming back in about a month,» said the trusty Salome. «I'd be pleased to go with you. Mariam's inexperienced in handling her child, and she's still weak from the birth. She needs someone to help her on such a journey!»

Mariam's eyes glazed over. She was deeply moved and hugged her half-sister, thanking her and accepting her offer.

Mariam and Jossef started packing frantically, and Jossef loaded their packs onto the two donkeys. The lamb also had to be bound to Mariam's donkey for the time being. It bleated pitiably, but there was no other solution, as they needed to start at a good pace. The lamb would provide them a good first meal on their journey, as soon as they were far enough away from Bethlehem.

Under cover of darkness, they set out on the

road to Hebron. Mariam once again carried Jeshua in the baby sling on her belly. He slept on without a care. They passed Salome's house, where she quickly gathered a few possessions in a bundle before rejoining them.

Driven by their fear, the family started at a good pace along the valley from Bethlehem towards Ephrath. They filled up their water skins at a spring south of Bethlehem and walked on for a while within sight of Herod's aqueduct. After about an hour, they reached the right turn, which they could just about make out in the dawn light. The whole day long, their path wound its way up and down scrubby hills, now and then passing through a small village. As the sun sank towards the horizon, they reached another turnoff which took them into the valley of the Nahal Guvrin river bordered by rounded, tree-lined hills. Beneath the shade of a broad holm oak, they finally felt safe enough to stop for a small snack. Jossef released the lamb from its bondage, and it joined the two donkeys in grazing the scrubby grass, while the family rested their weary limbs.

7

After his tavern conversation with Yitzhak, Enosh had immediately begun to ask around. Next morning, he was finally able to discover where the lad lived. He made his way to Tabitha's house. Once he had taken up the scent, he was like a dog after a hare – he did not give up. He knocked aggressively on Tabitha's door. Yitzhak opened it, as Tabitha had gone to the well. Yitzhak tried to hide the shock he felt in seeing that Enosh had already found him.

«This is a surprise, sir!» said Yitzhak with a slight jitter in his voice. «If you're looking for my mother, she's gone out, but she'll be right back.»

Enosh was excited, as he was sure he had almost reached his goal. «We don't need your mother at the moment, lad!» he said imperiously. «You just show me to that family you told me about yesterday!»

«But sir!» exclaimed Yitzhak desperately, «maybe the family doesn't want to be disturbed so early in the morning. What do you want them for, sir?»

Enosh decided it was now time to exert his full power. The minor clerk loved to flaunt others' authority to inflate his own importance. Taking Herod's seal from a pouch, he held it up in front of Yitzhak.

«In the name of King Herod, I demand that you take me to this family!» he shouted. His eyes gleamed as he took a threatening step towards Yitzhak, whose knees began to buckle, his eyes widening in fear.

«Y-yes, sir.» Yitzhak acquiesced and led Enosh to the stable behind the house. He opened the stable door, lowering his eyes sheepishly to the floor and allowing Enosh to pass. Whatever had that friendly family done? It was his fault that they were about to be caught.

«There's no one in here!» shouted Enosh from inside the stable. Yitzhak started and went into the stable. He was amazed to see that there really was no longer any sign of the family! How could that be? They must have left incredibly early!

«But they were still here yesterday evening, sir, honestly!» said Yitzhak, who was inwardly rejoicing but showing no sign of this to Enosh. «They must have already left.»

«I can see that, can't I!» said Enosh angrily. «Where were they planning to go?»

«Don't know, sir,» answered Yitzhak.

«In that case, I'll just wait here and speak to your mother after all. Maybe she knows.»

At that moment, Tabitha came round the corner with a water jar on her head, which she put down on the ground upon seeing her son with Enosh. She spoke a friendly greeting to the clerk.

«Mother, this is the gent I told you about, the one I met yesterday at the tavern. He wants to know where the family's gone to, that was staying in our stable,» said Yitzhak.

«Aren't they there anymore?» asked Tabitha, astonished. «They must have left very early. They were planning to go back home.»

«And where is their home?» asked Enosh.

«Um, what did they say, now? Um … goodness, sorry, I seem to have forgotten!»

Enosh was quite prepared to adopt harder methods when the situation demanded it. He grabbed Yitzhak, who was only a thin lad, spun him round to face his mother and put a knife to his throat.

«Now – tell me, or you'll regret it!» he growled through his teeth. «Where does that family live? Where?!»

Tabitha instantly felt quite sick. She swallowed hard, opening and closing her mouth like a fish. Then she moaned: «Nazareth.»

Enosh let Yitzhak go. The shaken youth staggered and fell against the wall.

«In the name of King Herod, thank you for this willingly proferred information,» said Enosh looking ironically from mother to son. He hurried off and left them standing there.

Now he needed to find out as much additional information about the family as possible. Showing Herod's seal, he asked at all the census stalls until he finally found the one that had registered a young couple from Nazareth with a new-born baby. He noted the names, profession and the address of the family.

Enosh was satisfied. His horse had not suffered permanent damage from its fall. He would return to Jerusalem immediately. Although he had not found the family, it would now be easy for Herod's henchmen to capture them based on the information he would be able to provide.

***

Oblivious to how closely they had avoided a catastrophe, Mariam, Jossef and Salome walked on for another hour at an easier pace. The speed at which they had started out had put a good distance between them and Bethlehem. For some time now, they had seen almost no one, only a few shepherds, and they began to feel a little less vulnerable. At this slow pace, there was no longer any need to bind the lamb onto the donkey. It gambolled along beside them.

They spent the first night in the Guvrin valley, making their camp beneath the trees. The animals drank from the river, and Jossef refilled their water skins. A strong fragrance of mint filled the air. Jossef collected firewood and lit a fire on which Salome boiled a pot of water and made a refreshing mint tea. Mariam baked some flat bread upon a hot stone. After this sparse meal, they slept instantly, exhausted from the long march.

Next day, their path was monotonous, always following the river and with hardly a soul in sight. Whenever he saw any, Jossef collected firewood and tied it to his donkey. As the path was flat and followed the river, it was not a strenuous day. After the previous day's long, speedy march, they were glad of this, allowing their thoughts to wander, as there was no need to watch their footing.

By late afternoon, they reached Beit Guvrin. The small town had recently been discovered by the

Romans, and there was a great deal of building work going on. The Romans had renamed the town Eleu-theropolis. Some villas were already finished and awaiting the arrival of their new owners.

«We'd better stay well away from the town,» suggested Jossef. «Here again, the less people we meet, the more difficult it will be to track us down.»

Approaching the town, they noticed that far away on their left, there were tree-lined hills with limestone rock-faces. They decided to make for these rocks as they would offer them protection for the night. As the sun sank behind them throwing long shadows, they arrived at the foot of the hills. A small path wound its way between the rock-faces. They dis-covered a wonderful cave system, inside which the stone seemed to have taken on organic shapes, shim-mering white in the dusk.

«We can make a fire here without the smoke being seen from the town,» said Jossef. «This is an ideal spot for the night! Now it's time to slaughter the lamb. We're going to have a proper feast! After that long day, we really need a good meal.»

Mariam sat next to Salome, leaning on a large stone and nursing Jeshua who had become fretful.

Jossef sharpened his knife, spoke a prayer of thanksgiving, and slaughtered the lamb with a swift, clean cut. Soon the fire was crackling merrily in the darkness.

Salome filled a pot with water, put it on the fire and left it to Jossef to skin the lamb in the boiling wa-ter. He disemboweled it, salted the meat well, and roasted it over the fire for almost three hours.

Meanwhile, Mariam sang her baby a lullaby to an ancient melody, with words from the Book of Proverbs:

«When you lie down, you will not be afraid;
when you lie down, your sleep will be sweet.[6]»

As the last notes of the melody died away, the silence was only broken by the spitting of lamb fat and the crackling of the fire. An appetizing smell filled the night air.

The lamb feast was accompanied by Tabitha's sweet Bethlehem wine. After they had eaten their fill, they cut up the rest of the meat, salting the pieces again to cure them. Then they rolled themselves into their warm sleeping mats and slept soundly in the safety of their cave.

***

Next day, they caught sight of Lachisch, which they passed by to the north. Far away on their left, the ruins of the ancient town glowed yellow in the sunlight. Sometimes, Mariam rode her donkey to spare her feet and her back. They continued along this path for two days. Soon the path descended gently from the Judaean foothills towards the coastal plain. The landscape became sparser, offering them less protection. By the end of the third day, Mariam was extremely tired and felt a slight panic.

---

[6] Proverbs 3, 24

«Jossef, I can't take any more!» she groaned, as they rested in the unrelenting midday sun. «What are we doing here? How long will this go on for? I want to go home. Even if we're in danger at home, at least we'll be with all our friends and family. Can't we turn round and go back? I'm so sick of this travelling!»

«My darling,» answered Jossef, «I do understand, I really do. I'm no happier about this flight than you are, and I'd also far rather go home. But we must never forget what this is really about. It's not about us! We must protect our child – we must never lose sight of that reason for our flight! Even when it gets difficult, we must never give up. We're responsible for Jeshua, and we know what a special child he is. He's a holy child, that's why Herod is after him. Jeshua is in serious danger. We'll probably face a lot of adversity, and it won't be easy. But our God has set us this challenge, and that means he considers us strong enough to meet it.»

«I know, Jossef, you're right of course. But just now, I don't feel at all strong. I'm frightened, my love. I can feel my heart trembling. Right now, I can't see any future for us, or for Jeshua.»

«Don't give up hope, my darling! Tomorrow's going to be another day, and our God will provide us with new strength for our path, you'll see,» Jossef encouraged his exhausted wife with a look of understanding. He was tired too. If they could just keep giving each other renewed strength, they would be able to bear this difficult situation together. Soon they would reach Ashkelon, where they would at least be able to rest for a while. Afterwards, they would both surely feel better!

At the end of the fourth day, they finally caught sight of the high protective wall around the ancient town of Ashkelon. It was built in the form of a half-moon, and behind it they caught sight of the deep blue Mediterranean Sea gleaming in the sun. They had arrived! Now they only needed to find Leah and her husband Daniel and ask for their protection and hospitality.

PART II:

In Ashkelon

8

The nearer Mariam, Jossef and Salome came to the town, the more people, animals, and carts were on the roads. A paved road led them over the green levels towards the Jerusalem Gate, through which the family edged their way between carts, camels, and crowds. Jeshua, awoken by the shouting, the trundling of wheels over stone and the sounds of the animals, watched the chaos around him with huge eyes.

«Since Daniel is a boat builder, we'd better go to the harbour. We can ask there for directions to his workshop,» suggested Jossef.

The harbour lay in the south-west of the semicircular town. Towards the sea, it was protected by a pillared quay. From the harbour, a broad ramp led up to the fortified wall of the town. Ships of all shapes and sizes were bobbing in the harbour, and the air was filled with the smells of fish and salt water. Goods were being unloaded; sailors threw ropes to others on the quay mooring the ships. Everywhere people were shouting, engaged in loud discussions. The noise seemed deafening after the quiet of the last four days. No one took any notice of them.

To begin with, they simply watched all the action, while Jossef decided whom it was best to ask. He eventually approached a fisherman who was busy with the floundering catch on board his boat.

«Peace be with you!» he called out to the fisherman. «We're trying to find Daniel, the boat builder. Do you know where his workshop is?»

«Peace to you, too!» the fisherman returned the greeting. «Daniel, you said? No, sorry. The only boat builder I know is Zadok. You'll find him at the end of the harbour!»

«Thanks very much!» called Jossef and they made their way to the end of the harbour to find Zadok.

Zadok did indeed know where Daniel's workshop was. He even sent a young worker to show Mariam, Jossef and Salome the way. The workshop was huge, much larger than Zadok's, and set back behind two houses in the middle of the harbour area. Not only did he build fishing boats, but Daniel also had trading ships racked up for repairs. Jossef was fascinated. He walked around and breathed in the smell of wood with relish, realising how much he missed his own carpenter's workshop. Mariam and Salome waited outside the entrance with Jeshua and the two donkeys.

A young apprentice took Jossef to Daniel, who recognised his brother-in-law immediately.

«Jossef!» exclaimed Daniel, patting him on the shoulder. «It's been a long time! Whatever brings you to Ashkelon?»

«Oh, Daniel, that's a very long story!» answered Jossef. «My wife Mariam and her relative Salome, my son Jeshua and I are looking for lodgings for a short stay in Ashkelon.»

«Well, of course you must stay with us!» said Daniel merrily. «You're most welcome! Leah will be thrilled to see you again, and we've plenty of room.»

Jossef thanked him and promised to tell Daniel and Leah the whole story that evening. Daniel ordered another young apprentice to show Jossef, Mariam and Salome the way to Leah and Daniel's house situated in the centre of the old town.

The house was large and well cared-for. Daniel's business was obviously flourishing. Jossef knocked, Leah opened the door, let out a cry of surprise and pulled her brother into a warm embrace.

«Jossef, my little brother!» exclaimed Leah, who was much smaller than Jossef, but ten years older. «Let me take a look at you! Yes, you're looking well. Married life obviously suits you!»

Jossef took Mariam by the hand and drew her towards him. «May I introduce my wife Mariam and our little son, Jeshua!»

Leah embraced her sister-in-law and cooed over the child who stretched out his hand towards her. "Ah, he's so cute!" she gushed.

«He's only two weeks old,» said Mariam, «and he's already been on such a long journey! Lovely to meet you, Leah. May I also introduce my half-sister Salome?»

«Welcome to you, Salome!" replied Leah. «Have you come all the way from Nazareth with the little one?»

«It's far worse than that, Leah. Jeshua was born on the way here,» explained Jossef. «It's a very long, confusing, and quite unbelievable story. I think it's best if we tell it to you both, once Daniel comes home. He told us it would be alright if we stayed with you for a while. Is that okay with you too, Leah?»

«Of course it is, lad — I'm thrilled to have you here for a while!» beamed Leah. «I'll show you where you can sleep.»

Mariam was tired from the journey and from all the impressions of the last few days. Jeshua had also started to cry. Once the donkeys had been stabled and the baggage brought in, Mariam gave Leah the remaining pieces of the lamb as a present, after which she lay down with Jeshua to rest. Salome also went to rest for a while.

Leah and Jossef stayed in the living room. Leah told him of life with Daniel since they had last seen each other five years ago. In the meantime, Leah's only child Jael had married a Jewish functionary.

She also told him that Daniel, who until recently worked for Zadok, had established his own company a year ago, and that the business was doing well. Daniel had soon been able to extend it to include ships, which meant he had more and more customers.

Jossef said how much he had enjoyed looking around Daniel's workshop, so Leah suggested that Daniel could give him a detailed tour of his works.

«Speak of the devil ...!» laughed Leah, as Daniel came through the door. He sat down next to Leah and Jossef in the living room, stretching his long legs out in front of him, and sighed.

«It's been a strenuous day!» he groaned. «Two weeks ago, I lost two members of staff who have moved away from Ashkelon. They've left a huge gap! We can hardly keep up with the orders.»

«Oh, poor Daniel, I'll bring you a beer!» said Leah, after giving her husband a kiss. «Want one too, Jossef?»

«Yes please!» he answered.

She went into the kitchen and came back with two foaming jugs of beer.

Meanwhile, Salome and Mariam reappeared with Jeshua. They had recovered from their tiredness, and Jeshua was content after feeding. Now that the whole family was together, Jossef and Mariam began to recount the incredible story. Jossef trusted his sister and his brother-in-law implicitly, and he left nothing out. Even the description of Jeshua's conception was recounted truthfully and received unbelieving looks from Leah and Daniel.

«Jossef!» exclaimed Leah, «Is this really my brother talking? The one who was always so down-to-earth? And now here you are talking about angels and dreams. Do you remember when we were children, I told you I'd seen an angel, and you laughed at me and said they didn't exist, or only in fairy tales or in the far-off days of the Patriarchs?»

«I know, Leah. In that respect I certainly must have changed,» said Jossef. «Mind you, it took a dream to convince me that what I'd experienced was reality. Or was the dream reality, too? I quite honestly can't say.»

«The main thing is: it's all about Jeshua and about his importance for our people, Leah,» added Mariam. «The angel told us that our child comes from God and belongs to him – in my case, it was more through an inner voice. My aunt in Bethany also recognised the importance of the child. When I was pregnant, I visited her, and as I arrived, she asked me how it could be that the 'mother of her Lord' had come to her – that's how she expressed it. I'll never forget that greeting.»

«Yes, and in my case, it was more dreams or visions,» interjected Jossef. «The angel told me that the child would be the saviour of our people, who were like sheep without a shepherd. Jeshua would save them from their sins, and all this would occur so that the Word of God was fulfilled, as proclaimed long ago by the Prophets. Those are portentous messages! I can tell you, it took us some time to digest it all.»

«All three of us, Elisheva, Jossef and I,» continued Mariam, «always heard a sound like beating wings and rushing wind whenever the angel brought us a message, and also whenever anything great occurred. Later, we heard the sounds again when three astrologers from Persia visited us after Jeshuas birth. While I was telling them of Jeshua's importance for our people, they heard the sounds too.»

Jossef frowned. «It's strange,» he said. «These wise men with so much knowledge stopped by on their way and visited King Herod. They told him of a new king. They may understand a lot about oscillation that densifies metaphysically and about the waves of spiritual beings who wish to support us and blah-blah, but why couldn't they exercise a bit of common sense and keep their mouths shut, rather than endangering our child?»

Mariam smiled. «Yes, you've hit upon a sore point there, Jossef!» she said. «Mind you, they didn't know how brutal King Herod is, and couldn't have judged what effect their disclosure would have upon him. And if they hadn't spoken to Herod, they probably wouldn't have been able to find us.»

«That wouldn't have been such a great loss,» murmured Jossef peevishly.

«By the way, there were some shepherds who also came to visit us in Bethlehem to worship our child. We happened to meet them on our way there, and they also received a message from the angels saying they should come and find us. It was they who brought the astrologers to us, and we also have them to thank for the lamb, some of which I gave you earlier on,» said Mariam.

«On the subject of lamb – time to eat!» said Leah and went into the kitchen with Mariam and Salome, where they prepared a light meal which the family enjoyed by the light of the oil lamp, together with the rest of Tabitha's Bethlehem wine.

9

Mariam was woken the next morning by the un-accustomed sound of seagulls. She did not immediately know where she was. Then she remembered that they had spread their mat on the floor of a proper house last night for the first time in a month.

The day was already well advanced. The sun was high in the sky. Daniel had left early for work, and Leah had allowed her relatives to sleep in, as they were obviously exhausted; particularly Mariam, who in addition to the journey, had endured the strains of giving birth. She was at the end of her tether, and Leah was sure it would not be enough for her to rest for just a few days, as Jossef had suggested the previous evening.

While she was preparing a small lunch for them, Leah therefore suggested they stay in Ashkelon for at least a month.

«You're safe here,» said Leah. «Ashkelon is outside the sphere of Herod's administration. Ashkelon also has a tradition of sanctuary. From ancient times, refugees have been given protection here. Make the most of it, enjoy some peace and quiet and replenish your strength!»

«That's very kind of you, Leah,» answered Mariam, «but we don't wish to be a burden on you!»

«A burden! That's no burden!» exclaimed Leah. «I'm thrilled to have you here and to be able to spoil my little brother! Don't worry your heads about it!»

Thus, it was decided, and if she was honest, Mariam truly was grateful for this hospitality, since she was well aware that the exertion had drained her.

Leah suggested to Jossef that he go to Daniel in the workshop that afternoon, as she was looking forward to a friendly chat with Mariam and Salome. She picked up some darning and began to offer Mariam helpful tips for her new-born baby. Salome confirmed her suggestions and gave further advice. Mariam rocked Jeshua on her knee and said it was high time she took the Mikwe[7], having given birth. Jossef smiled as he watched the women chatting so comfortably. Leah returned his smile but shooed him away, so he happily returned to the workshop.

Although Daniel was very busy, he immediately stopped what he was doing when he saw Jossef and showed his brother-in-law around the workshop. He explained every process in detail, pleased to have such an interested listener.

«Know what, Daniel? I'm itching to lend a hand here!» said Jossef. «I don't know the first thing about boatbuilding, but I do have the experience of a master carpenter which should be helpful. What do you think? Could you use me?»

Daniel spread his arms wide and beamed.

«Jossef!» he exclaimed. «You're the answer to my prayers! I don't need to think twice about it. Here, take a leather apron – I'll call over the master of apprentices; he can show you the basics. You'll soon get

---

[7] Ritual cleansing bath

the hang of things with your craftsman's skills, I've no doubt!»

Out of the blue, Jossef had employment and was as happy as a sandboy to be putting plane and lathe to wood again. That afternoon, he learnt how to make the planks pliable with water and heat, after which they had to be bent into form, requiring a great deal of strength. This was a completely new and exciting process for him. Daniel's workshop used holm oak and cypress wood from the hinterland; each piece of wood was chosen for its qualities and needed to be completely free of knots. Here, they respected the wood and worked with its characteristics rather than fighting against them.

Leah and Salome had accompanied Mariam to the mikwe, where she had been able to recover and as a result now looked and felt much fresher. When the two men arrived home that evening, Leah noticed with relief that the worried frown had disappeared from her husband's brow. He looked quite relaxed.

«Leah,» said Daniel, «I've found a new member of staff! Things are looking up at last!»

«Really? Who's that?» asked Leah, already guessing the answer.

Daniel grinned. «Your brother Jossef started his apprenticeship with me today!»

Everyone laughed in relief, and the evening turned into a proper celebration. Now, Mariam also felt better about staying with Leah and Daniel for a longer period, knowing that Jossef could contribute something towards their keep.

Since Jossef had been instructed by the angel not to sleep with his wife until she had given birth to Jeshua, Mariam and Jossef slept together for the first time that night. Lingeringly and completely at ease, they explored every curve of each other's body, finally coming together in the most deep and intimate union. Suddenly, the world seemed more colourful and very, very sweet. They slept peacefully, awakening occasionally to seek each other again, then drifting away into beautiful dreams. For them, this night could not be long enough!

***

Leah had told Jossef, Mariam and Salome that she had recently made friends with a young Egyptian girl named Merit who often visited them and had become something of a surrogate daughter to her. Merit's mother was Jewish, and her father was Egyptian. The family lived in Baltim on the Mediterranean coast of Egypt. Leah explained that Ashkelon had a large Egyptian community, and a strong Egyptian culture. Merit's father Meketre had come by ship to Ashkelon with ceramics from his pottery works and had brought Merit with him. Since that day, Merit sold her father's fine pottery in a small shop in the centre of Ashkelon. She was the ideal saleswoman, as she was bilingual, and this shop in her mother's old hometown was doing well. However, Merit did miss her family greatly.

Leah was a little worried about Merit, as she

had started a relationship with a Roman centurion. Who knew what that would lead to? The life of a centurion was hard and left little time for relationships. Leah had taken a great liking to her young friend and always tried to give her good advice.

On the first Sabbath after their arrival, Mariam, Jossef and Salome accompanied Leah and Daniel to the Ashkelon synagogue, and there they met Leah's young friend Merit.

After the service, a man delivered a political speech in the pillared vestibule in front of the synagogue. Daniel explained that his name was Judas the Galilean, and that he was hoping to recruit new zealots for his insurrections.

Merit looked concerned, and Leah invited her to come and join them at their house for the Sabbath meal. After the meal, they sat cosily in Leah's living room. Merit told them all about her partner, Lucius Antonius Cicero, who was a centurion in the tenth legion and often had to quell such insurrections as those led by Judas the Galilean. Right now, he was engaged in quelling riots on the borders of Phoenicia. It was obvious that Merit was very worried about her lover.

«Roman legions never attack unless they're quite sure they'll win, you know that, don't you, Merit?» said Daniel.

«Yes, of course, Daniel. But right now, they're fighting in inaccessible, confusing territory in the Beit Kerem valley, and, well, you never know ...» answered Merit despondently.

«Oh, Lucius'll do fine, love, with his experience,» said Leah. «if you get the jitters at every skirmish he's involved in, you'll soon have grey hair!»

«Ah well, at least he only has to serve for another five years,» said Merit. «After that, he can settle down in a civilian profession.»

«Will you hold out that long, though?» asked Leah, honestly worried about her young friend.

Merit looked sheepish. «I hope so,» she said doubtfully. «For his century, this is the first serious battle they've been involved in for three months. I hope it'll take that long again until they're involved in another.»

«You shouldn't have made eyes at a centurion,» said Daniel somewhat tactlessly, with a wink.

«I can't help it if we fell in love!» replied Merit, piqued. At present, she was not to be envied. On the other hand, when Lucius was not involved in a fray, she and her partner were able to enjoy their life together. He would take her out to the theatre or to the thermal baths, enjoying his free time with her.

«You just need to take life as it comes,» said Daniel smugly.

«Stop it, Daniel!» exclaimed Leah. «You can talk! These inane phrases are of no help to Merit!»

The conversation moved on to less delicate topics, restoring the peaceful Sabbath atmosphere.

10

Now that she had met Merit, Mariam wanted to visit her shop and see the pottery. She took Jeshua with her in his baby sling, and Salome accompanied her. The shop was located on the northern fringe of town, not far from the Jerusalem Gate.

On the way there, they passed the Buleuterion in the town centre, the assembly building of the senate. Two huge columns flanking the entrance were decorated with reliefs of the winged goddess of victory, Nike. Mariam stepped through the portal and caught a glimpse of the magnificent columned hall containing statues of various gods – the Syrian goddess Derceto with the body of a fish and the face of a woman, the Greek gods Pan and Hermes and the goddess Aphrodite. On the right, through the columned arcade, she caught sight of the Temple of Apollo. Then she saw that an official was approaching her, so she retraced her steps to the exit and they carried on through the busy streets of the town.

With the help of Leah's directions, Mariam and Salome soon found Merit's shop, a quaint little house with flowering plants in baskets and pots around the door. Merit was pleased to see Leah's sister-in-law again and showed her all her fine products with pride. She had placed small bowls of lavender around the shop, making it smell fragrant. Her range of pottery was extensive: small round-bodied jugs with delicate handles, and jugs with rounded bottoms and a wide handle on either side for looping onto one's belt.

Merit also had large clay ewers for storing wine and beer, which she mainly sold to taverns and inns.

Jeshua surveyed his surroundings and all the pots and jars with wide eyes. Salome put a small jug in his hands for him to feel, quickly retrieving it before he dropped it on the floor. Little Jeshua was very advanced for his age and always showed a great interest in all that was going on around him.

As Mariam looked around the shop, she asked Merit about her hometown. Merit was happy to talk about Baltim and about their sea voyage almost one year previously, during which she had been miserably seasick, vomiting frequently throughout the three days of the journey. Now she could laugh about it, but at the time she had not found it at all funny. Her father, who had excellent sea-legs, had laughed at her and kept taunting her about it, which had made the matter even worse.

«I do miss Baltim, but if ever I return home, it certainly won't be by sea!» said Merit with conviction, adding that she could swim like a fish – in water, she felt completely at home, just not on water.

«Do you think you'll be able to marry Lucius?» asked Mariam.

«I don't think so,» answered Merit. Mariam could tell that the subject made her uneasy. «Leah's warned me that as a solder, he's not permitted to marry. She reckons he may just be amusing himself with me.»

«I beg your pardon, Merit. I didn't mean to pry. It's none of my business,» Mariam hastened to reassure her.

«That's alright,» answered Merit. «It remains to be seen where our relationship is going. Lucius thinks we may be able to live in Cohabitatio[8]. I believe we'll just have to wait and see.»

Mariam bought two belt jugs and they returned to Leah's house. Hearing Merit talk of her insecure situation made Mariam feel very grateful for her stable relationship with Jossef, who had been as steady as a rock during their present danger and flight, always ready to protect her and Jeshua.

Several days later, Merit turned up in Leah's living room again, beaming with joy.

«Lucius is back!» she exclaimed. «They won the battle, and now they're back in the main camp.»

«Oh, thanks be to God!» said Leah, hugging her relieved young friend. «Now you can relax and enjoy life again!»

Merit's wish was fulfilled. Lucius' century really did not have to fight again for several weeks. Now he sometimes accompanied Merit to Leah and Daniel's house. He was a tall, well-built man and it was easy to see why Merit had fallen in love with him. Whenever his eyes rested on Merit, his expression made it clear that he was just as much in love with her as she was with him.

---

[8] Common-law marriage, a stronger bond than concubinage, but less strong than marriage

Merit was quite prepared to wait until the end of his term of service, since she was certain that they would find some way of living together at the end of those five years. Apart from his love for her, Lucius could also offer Merit a good life: Their children would be Roman citizens, and his salary of 18'000 sesterces per annum would offer them both a life of luxury. Until that time, they would enjoy the periods of leisure between Lucius' battles and peace missions. Merit's nerves had begun to bear up better during his engagements.

When Jossef had been working for Daniel for five months, Jeshua began to babble his first Aramaic words, and once he had started, he only stopped talking to breastfeed or to sleep. Salome had noticed that the child was very intelligent, way ahead of other children of his age.

One day, after Mariam had nursed Jeshua and he was waking from his post-feeding sleep, Salome got up to go to the kitchen. Jeshua said: «Salome kitchen!». Salome returned to the table with a glass of water each for herself and Mariam. Jeshua said: «Water!».

«Mariam, have you noticed how well Jeshua is already speaking, and that he usually says words in the correct context?» she commented to her half-sister.

«No,» answered Mariam, «I can't say I have. I thought that was normal and all children did that.»

«Salome's right, Mariam," attested Leah, "not all children can do that! Our Jael took about a year before she was using words in their correct context. Your little Jeshua is a very talented child – and just look how he's following our conversation! He looks at us when we're speaking. It won't be long before he starts trying to join in our conversations. Will it, my little sweetie?»

Jeshua giggled as Leah chucked him under the chin. From that time on, Mariam did start to notice how often her son tried to join in conversations. Leah and Salome were right, Jeshua was a gifted child.

Life in the extended family unit had taken on a pleasant routine. Sometimes Lucius was also part of this. Once, during supper, he told them about some gossip which was being shared in his legion. His Signifer[9], who had gone to Jerusalem on business, had passed on to him something he had heard at Herod's palace. Lucius' contempt for Herod was most obvious in the way he told the anecdote. He said that Herod seemed to have become more than naturally alarmed about some child who was apparently regarded as a future King of Israel.

«It seems one of his henchmen has infiltrated an olive plantation in Nazareth as a seasonal worker, so that he can sound out the locals!» explained Lucius. «Imagine that! When Herod becomes edgy about anything, that's when he's most dangerous. He won't give up until he's found this so-called 'king' and had him assassinated. In the past, Herod's been

---

[9] Carrier of the legion's banner, who also acted in an administrative and financial capacity

known to kill his own children and his wife, because they may have been involved in intrigues against him. He won't hesitate to do the same to someone else's child.»

Leah and Daniel had not said anything to Merit about the special importance of Jeshua for the people of Israel, and they had certainly not mentioned it to Lucius. They therefore tried to look unconcerned, and casually asked Lucius for further details. However, he did not know any more, so they changed the subject.

As soon as Merit and Lucius had left, they looked at one another with worried expressions.

«Herod's discovered our link to Nazareth,» said Jossef. «Luckily, we're safe here in Ashkelon, but I don't like the fact that people are still talking about us. Herod will stop at nothing; he may even find a way to trace us here. We know he already has blood on his hands.»

«No, Jossef,» interjected Leah, «he can't do that. Although Herod was born here and has a preference for Ashkelon with all the palaces, baths and wells he's built, he has no control here. This is a free town.»

«I still don't like it,» said Jossef. «He doesn't act according to any moral code, all that means nothing to him. He's capable of anything if he feels even slightly threatened.»

«But how can he find out from Nazareth where we are now?» asked Mariam. «My mother Hannah certainly won't say anything.»

«Hannah has no idea what's happened to us,» said Jossef. «She must be beside herself with worry, poor thing. But on no account must we take up contact with Nazareth, that would be far too dangerous.»

«True,» answered Mariam. «This henchman of Herod's is working undercover as an olive picker. He'll be keeping his eyes and ears open, in case anyone inadvertently gives anything away. On the other hand, it's very unlikely that anyone even knows of the existence of Leah apart from my mother.»

«I did once mention to Rivka that Leah couldn't come to our wedding because her own daughter was getting married in Ashkelon,» admitted Jossef sheepishly.

Although there did not appear to be any immediate danger, they had lost the carefree feeling of life in Ashkelon, and their daily routine no longer offered them the same comfort. Suddenly, they were once again aware that they were fugitives and that even here, they did not have a safe home. Jossef and Mariam began to think about moving on again – but where should they go?

11

Two weeks after this, Lucius had had to march away again to quell further Jewish insurrections, but by now, Merit had become fairly cool about this. She no longer trembled with fear or thought continuously about what might happen to Lucius. She filled her days with work. The shop was doing so well that she had been able to employ an assistant, who turned out to be so competent that he took a great deal of weight off Merit's shoulders and allowed her to visit Leah and Daniel even more frequently. There was hardly a trace left of her previous nervousness. Now Lucius had returned to the main camp, and Merit was looking forward to seeing him again.

«I know I shouldn't,» said Merit, on one of her visits to Leah and her family, «but I keep imagining what life with Lucius will be like. However, we still have another four and a half years to go, so I must learn to be patient.»

«That's quite understandable, Merit,» said Mariam. «You're so looking forward to it, it's only natural that you should daydream about life with him. As long as you keep your feet on the ground, you're not hurting yourself or anyone else.»

There was a knock at the door. Daniel went to open it. An unfamiliar legionnaire stood outside, asking for Merit, who went outside to speak with him. They could hear quiet voices and then Merit's voice rising until she was shouting frantically.

In the living room, the family looked at one another. Leah stood up and went outside. Merit flew into her arms and sobbed loudly, her head upon Leah's shoulder. Leah supported the poor girl, who had turned pale and could hardly stand, taking her gently back into the living room. Daniel went out to the legionnaire and asked him what had happened.

«Lucius Antonius Cicero was found this morning outside our main camp with his throat cut,» answered the legionnaire.

Daniel's draw dropped. He composed himself and asked for further details. The legionnaire informed him that Lucius had been the victim of Jewish insurgents hiding in ambush to assassinate him. The watchmen had seen the insurgents running from the scene of the crime, and there had been a woman with them. As Lucius had been of high rank, there was to be a detailed investigation into the case. Since she had been close to Lucius, Merit would be questioned by the Tribunal in two days' time. The legionnaire did not conceal the fact that Merit was under serious suspicion of being involved, as she was of Jewish descent and had been present during the speech of Judas the Galilean in front of the Synagogue. Daniel was appalled.

«But those two loved each other!» he said entreatingly.

«There's no point telling me that, my good man,» said the legionnaire, «I've got nothing to do with the proceedings. I'm just the bearer of this dispatch.»

Daniel took his leave of the legionnaire and returned to the living room. Merit was still sobbing, and Leah was trying to comfort her, her arm about her shoulders.

«One thing's for sure: you're staying here tonight,» said Leah. «On no account should you be alone right now.»

Merit nodded gratefully. All at once, she had no future; without warning, the rug had been pulled from under her feet.

Daniel beckoned Leah to come into the kitchen, and Mariam took over Leah's position as Merit's comforter. Daniel told his wife what the legionnaire had said to him. Leah gasped in horror. It was far worse than she had suspected. How could anyone suspect Merit?

«Well, the authorities seem to have got wind of the fact that Judas the Galilean gave a speech at our synagogue recently, and we were there; Merit was there too,» explained Daniel.

«But there were about a hundred other people there too – do they suspect all of them, including us?» asked Leah angrily.

«But only Merit had a relationship with Lucius,» explained Daniel softly.

It was appalling, and now Daniel and Leah needed to break the news to Merit that she was under suspicion. She needed to know what danger she was in. At a single blow, her glowing future had been turned into a nightmare.

Merit was horror-stricken when Daniel told her she was suspected of having been involved in the assault. In addition to the loss of her beloved Lucius, she now had to deal with this accusation. The pure horror of this exceeded even her grief. The Romans would be quite prepared to sacrifice Merit to satisfy their sense of justice and to ensure peace, unless she could prove conclusively that she was not involved. But how was she to do that? Her love for Lucius alone would not help her, as love could not be proven.

Merit suddenly declared decisively: «I want to go back home! There's no future for me here now. The thought of having to stand trial before that Tribunal is appalling. Lucius told me they're not at all squeamish in the way they deal with suspects. I wouldn't be able to stand up to torture. Lucius would be the first to advise me to f-flee …,» her voice gave out, and she wept bitterly.

«Why don't you sleep on it, Merit?» suggested Leah. «You need to think carefully before taking such a step!»

«Leah, my best of friends, it would be good if I could do that, but there's no time left. I'll miss you all terribly and I'll be so lonely. But rather that, than being sentenced to death by the Tribunal.» Merit trembled at the thought. «I'm so frightened!»

«If you really do go away, we'll miss you too, more than I can say, Merit. But how will you get home on your own?» asked Leah, «by sea?»

«No,» replied Merit, «I'll travel by land. Firstly, I get so terribly seasick, and secondly, when they do start to search for me, they'll expect me to go by sea.»

«That's very dangerous though, travelling all alone by land,» said Daniel with a worried frown.

«Well, maybe I can join a caravan,» suggested Merit, «at least as far as the el-Qantara[10] straits. The caravans usually turn off to the south there, in the direction of Arabia.»

Merit's shoulders slumped. She was emotionally exhausted. Leah laid out a mat for her on the living room floor. The others also went to bed, although no one now felt like sleeping.

Towards morning, Jossef finally drifted into sleep. He had a vivid dream, in which he again saw the angel he had seen over a year ago, when he had roamed the fields and hills of Nazareth in an attempt to assimilate the news of Mariam's pregnancy.

In this dream, the angel commanded him: «Arise, Jossef! Take Mariam and Jeshua, and flee with them to Egypt, for Herod now knows of your sister in Ashkelon and will seek you out here.» Awakening from this dream, he lay for a while staring into the darkness. Slowly, the soft sound of beating wings and rushing wind faded.

Mariam also awoke, sensing her husband's tension, and asked him what was wrong.

«Mariam, Lucius had already given us a warning that Herod was searching for us in Nazareth,» said Jossef. «I just had a dream in which the angel told us

---

[10] El-Qantara means "The Bridge"

to flee to Egypt, because Herod has now found out about Leah and knows where to look for us. We had a feeling this would happen. The time seems to have come to move on, and I now know how – we'll accompany Merit!»

PART III:

The Flight to Egypt

12

Even before Leah and Daniel were awake, Mariam crept into the living room, woke Merit, and suggested they travel to Egypt together with her.

Merit looked at Mariam sceptically. «Why do you want to go to Egypt?» she asked.

«Merit, we're also on the run,» explained Mariam, «and it seems Herod has found out we could be in Ashkelon. He'll send his henchmen to find us. You remember what Lucius said about the child Herod was looking for? That child is Jeshua! And they won't hesitate to kill our boy if they find us. That's why we can't stay here either.»

Since Merit had been dreading the thought of undertaking the long journey alone, it did not take long to convince her that travelling together would be a good plan. However, it was clear that they would need to leave the next day already. This was very abrupt, but they had no time for further planning.

Once before, Merit had travelled this route by land together with her parents, when they went to visit her mother's family in Ashkelon. The fact that she was bilingual would prove to be a great advantage for all of them.

After the morning prayer, they explained to a very distraught Leah that they were all planning to leave for Egypt together. Leah was now losing two beloved people at the same time, her brother and her young friend. She had also become quite attached to Mariam and her baby. Life seemed very unfair, and

Leah bemoaned the fate that was tearing them all apart.

«Flight's never pleasant,» said Jossef. «We would also far rather stay with you, or if we had to leave, then to travel home to Nazareth. But sadly, that's not our reality.»

«Yes, I do understand,» agreed Leah, «and it would be far more painful if anything were to happen to you or your child. I'd also rather lose Merit this way than through death.»

Leah turned to Salome who had been listening from beside the hearth with wide eyes. «Will you be going with them, Salome?» asked Leah.

Salome approached the family. «It's hard to travel with a baby. Would you like me to accompany you?" she asked.

Mariam and Jossef considered their situation carefully, then Mariam shook her head. «We'll have Merit with us,» she replied. «She'll be a great help to us. Your husband will have returned home ages ago. Go back to him. I'm sure we'll manage. But thank you so much for everything, Salome!»

When Daniel came home for lunch, Jossef explained to him what they were planning, and thanked him for giving him employment.

«I've learnt so much from you, Daniel – and who knows whether that may not stand me in good stead sometime in my life?» said Jossef.

«I've also profited from your work, Jossef! You'll leave a huge gap at the boatyard, and at home too!» answered Daniel. «Now I'll need to find myself a new boatbuilder.»

After lunch, it was in a despondent mood that the little group took their leave of their hosts and of Salome. Daniel and Jossef embraced, patting each other on the shoulder. Jeshua stretched out his tiny hand towards Salome, and his face puckered. Mariam had tears in her eyes as she kissed her sister-in-law and her half-sister goodbye.

Merit had gone to the potter's shop in the morning to fetch her donkey and had brought it to Leah's house. Finally, everyone was ready to leave, and the bitter moment could not be put off any longer. Merit and Leah both cried piteously as they said goodbye to each other. Leah, Daniel and Salome stood in front of the house, waving to the group as they disappeared around the corner.

In the next street, a neighbour was standing outside the door of her house and waved them a friendly greeting, asking Merit where they were off to. Merit answered nervously that they had something to deal with in Gaza. She kept the conversation as short as possible and they headed southwards.

At least physically, it would not be a hard day. They would stay the night in Gaza Town, and the coastal road behind the dunes was flat and easy.

Mariam drove her donkey on, groaning: «More travelling! When will we ever be able to settle down?» Although they had spent half a year in Ashkelon, it felt to Mariam as though they had only just arrived after their strenuous journey from Bethlehem. Jeshua seemed to sense his mother's unhappy mood; he was agitated all afternoon, crying more than usual.

At dusk, they found lodgings in Gaza Town. No one took any particular notice of them. So far, of course, the search for Merit had not begun, as her interrogation before the Tribunal was only due to take place the following day.

That night, Mariam lay awake for hours, unable to sleep. She stretched out a hand to Jossef, who took her in his arms in his sleep. Mariam snuggled up to her husband and sighed deeply.

Then she heard Merit start to whimper, so she untangled herself from Jossef's arms, went over to her friend and put her arms around her. At that moment, Jeshua began to cry for milk, so Mariam fetched her child, put him to her right breast and put her left arm around Merit again. It seemed to Mariam that she had two children in her arms. Merit was indeed still very young, hardly more than a child. As she held both of them tight, Mariam prayed to God that he would protect Jeshua and Merit, and that Merit would find inner peace again, once she reached her home.

Despite their lack of sleep, the little group of refugees set out early next morning, as they hoped to reach Raphia that day. Again, the road following the coast and was flat and scrubby, but this time they had further to go. Once they reached Raphia, it would no longer be far to the Egyptian border.

At midday, Jossef suggested they cross the dunes and go down to the beach for lunch. As everyone was quite hungry by this time, nobody objected to this. They found a good, unfrequented spot and Jossef collected driftwood for a fire. Mariam removed Jeshua's clothes, allowing him to play naked on the beach. He watched fascinated, as the water formed little rivulets in the sand. Merit squatted next to him and showed him how to build little dams of sand to block the water and reroute it. Jeshua laughed and scooped vigorously at the sand with his little hands. Merit's face relaxed as she concentrated on the boy. Mariam watched them and smiled, feeling confident that Merit would conquer her despair.

Mariam rose and began to prepare salted, dried fish with olives and shallot onions she had bought at the market the previous day. She cooked the fish slowly over the fire, adding the finely chopped olives and onions. She also made some flat bread. Jossef spoke the blessing over their meal: «*Blessed are You, Lord God, King of the Universe, through whose word all things are created.*» After the meal they all sighed contentedly, agreeing that the simple fare had been surprisingly delicious.

Now they had new strength for the remaining miles to Raphia and arrived just as darkness was setting in. Caravans of camels were arriving and departing, carrying spices and frankincense between north and south. The refugees felt quite safe from discovery in all the commotion, and satisfactory lodgings were soon found in a side street.

They marched on for two more days before reaching the Egyptian border near the Brook of Egypt[11], where crowds of people and animals were waiting to pass the checkpoint. Far away, they caught a glimpse of the long shallow beach which made landing a ship impossible here. They tried to look as inconspicuous as possible and to mix in with the crowd. Now they were at the border, they felt extremely tense. Just in case the border officials had already received the order to search for them, they gave false names and hometowns. Mariam noticed that one of the border guards was looking intensively at Jeshua, or so it seemed to her. She could feel her heart beating all the way up to her throat. She held her breath, but in the end, he said nothing and eventually allowed them to pass.

As they entered Egyptian territory, they breathed a huge sigh of relief. At least they had made it through that ordeal. Here, the country was very green. They noticed that water was being channelled via a canal system into the fields to irrigate them.

The next night they spent at a town named Rhinocolura[12]. Jossef asked Merit if she knew where the strange name came from. She explained that in times gone by, Ethiopian prisoners had been brought here after having had their noses cut off as a punishment.

«Or so they say,» she added, «but whether that's true or whether it's just a legend, I can't say,»

---

[11] Wadi el-Arish

[12] Greek for 'cut-off noses'

and she tweaked Jeshua's nose with two fingers. He giggled, acting the clown, then he wanted to 'cut off' Merit's, Mariam's and Jossef's noses too.

Mariam and Merit smiled at each other. Mariam noticed with relief that the dark shadows beneath Merit's eyes had all but disappeared and she had begun to regain some of her usual liveliness.

Merit had noticed that whenever she held Jeshua in her arms, she had a feeling of calm, as if she had cast away her worries. It was remarkable; when she was not with Jeshua, the worries plagued her again and the anguish returned. She was at a loss to understand this phenomenon. Jeshua was certainly a sweet child, but it was more than that.

Now they were away from Israel, they were able to relax a little more. There was no longer any immediate danger. The road followed the Mediterranean coast, and it was comfortably warm.

They soon arrived at the Serbonian Salt Lake. It was a huge body of water, only separated from the sea by a narrow sandbank open to the sea at one point, a kind of lagoon. Curlews were searching the reed beds for food. Their melancholy call lingered in the air. Merit felt homesick for the Burullus Salt Lake near her home, which looked very similar to this lake.

One day later, they arrived at the town of Pelusium, where they decided to stay for a few days, as next day was the Sabbath, and they would soon be leaving the Sinai Peninsula to tackle the el-Qantara straits. After that, they would pass through the ancient biblical land of Goshen, where they would mostly have to sleep outdoors.

As they approached the town from the east, they passed a large amphitheatre. The flags of the Roman legions fluttered from the top tiers, and they could hear the shouts and applause of the audience; there was obviously a popular play being shown. A quarter of an hour later, they reached the town, which was protected to the south by an earth wall like a long hill. On their right, the sea glittered dark green in the distance.

13

In Pelusium, they found lodgings in a richly ornamented three-storey building. Next door, they discovered a thermal bath. Jossef took Jeshua to the bath as soon as they arrived. The warm water soothed their tired limbs after the long march, and the little boy screeched loudly with the joy of playing in the water.

There was a pleasant atrium in their guesthouse, with a fountain and fine-leafed bushes which rustled softly in the breeze. Here, the four travellers sat and spent a few comfortable hours after a copious meal, enjoying the evening air.

«Oh, this is lovely!» said Mariam. «A bit of indulgence now is going to fortify us for the exertions ahead.»

Merit had taken Jeshua upon her knee and was playing ride-a-cock-horse with him. Jeshua beamed at her, as she lovingly stroked his dark curls.

«Mariam, it's a strange thing, but whenever I'm holding Jeshua, I feel so good! It's as if all my worries and my grief are wiped away. But afterwards they do return,» admitted Merit. «I don't understand it. Jeshua's a wonderful child, but it's more than that. It's as if he exudes a certain power …»

Mariam and Jossef exchanged meaningful glances. Should they tell Merit? After all, they were all in the same boat now, sharing the fate of refugees together.

«Merit, your feeling's actually quite right,» said Mariam, «Jeshua really is a special child. We've received messages telling us he's been chosen to play a special role in the fate of our people.»

«Messages?» asked Merit.

«Yes, messages, visitations from God. We call them the visits of the angels,» explained Mariam.

«Sometimes it was a dream, sometimes it was a vision, but sometimes it was more just listening to an inner voice,» added Jossef, «and always accompanied by the sound of beating wings or rushing wind. Spirit, you see …»

Merit said nothing for a moment, trying to assimilate this information. They were all silent, Mariam and Jossef giving Merit time to think.

Jossef proceeded to tell Merit the whole story of Herod and the astrologers. Merit stared unbelievingly, when he said the astrologers had told Herod that Jeshua would be called 'King of the Jews'.

«I see!» exclaimed Merit. «So that's why Herod's looking for him, and that's why you're fleeing from him. I did wonder,» she said. «But he's only a child, and you're just ordinary, humble people!»

«Yes, we found that astonishing too. However, we realised that God often uses humble, lowly people to do his will in the world. David was a humble shepherd, yet he became king of our people,» answered Mariam.

«It's all very mysterious, I can't really fathom it out,» said Merit. «On the other hand, I can certainly sense something about Jeshua, and what you're telling me explains that.»

Their talk had made Jeshua sleepy. Merit passed him over to Mariam, who gave him a kiss and began to sing him a lullaby. He soon fell asleep. They stayed talking by the fountain until the evening air became too cool, after which they went back to their rooms.

Merit was glad Mariam and Jossef had taken her into their confidence. Now she fully understood why they had had to take flight; before, she had not quite dared to ask. The child was indeed special, she had sensed that, and she was glad to have had her feeling confirmed.

That night, she dreamt of Lucius. The dream was very realistic, and quite cheerful. Lucius told her how much he loved her and how relieved he was that she was travelling in such good company. He embraced her, and she awoke with the feeling of still being in his arms. The dream had been comforting, but nevertheless she wept, as he had been so near. She could still feel his chest against hers, so she laid her hands on her chest to preserve the feeling. Merit sighed deeply, then she rose and went to the dining room to have breakfast with the others. She kept the dream to herself – like a jewel to be treasured.

After breakfast, they enjoyed the quiet of the Sabbath. Once again, they sat in the atrium. Often when they had rested under way, Mariam had recited scripture, psalms, and the Torah for Jeshua. As a descendant of the House of Aharon, she had learned the scriptures by heart as a child, and she still loved to recite them at every opportunity, even more so for Jeshua, who listened far more attentively than was to be expected in a child of his age. It seemed to Mariam that she could see the light of knowledge in his eyes, as if he recognised the words.

Now she told him the story of Exodus, as their journey would soon take them to one of the places on the route of the Israelites' flight from Egypt. She sang the song of God's deliverance of the people of Israel at the Red Sea:

> *«I will sing to the Lord, for he is highly exalted.*
> *Both horse and rider he has hurled into the sea.*
> *The Lord is my strength and my defense; he has become my salvation.*
> *He is my God, and I will praise him, my father's God, and I will exalt him.*
> *The Lord is a warrior; the Lord is his name.*
> *Pharaoh's chariots and his army he has hurled into the sea.*
> *The best of Pharaoh's officers are drowned in the Red Sea.*
> *The deep waters have covered them; they sank to the depths like a stone.*
> *Your right hand, Lord, was majestic in power.*
> *Your right hand, Lord, shattered the enemy.*
> *In the greatness of your majesty, you threw down those who opposed you.*

You unleashed your burning anger; it consumed them like stubble.
By the blast of your nostrils the waters piled up.
The surging waters stood up like a wall; the deep waters congealed in the heart of the sea.
The enemy boasted, ‹I will pursue, I will overtake them. I will divide the spoils; I will gorge myself on them. I will draw my sword and my hand will destroy them.›
But you blew with your breath, and the sea covered them.
They sank like lead in the mighty waters.
Who among the gods is like you, Lord?
Who is like you — majestic in holiness, awesome in glory, working wonders? [13]

God truly worked a great miracle in saving our ancestors, my little Jeshua,» said Mariam. «That's how our people were able to survive. But we must always stay faithful to our Lord; He wants us to be his people, do you understand?» – Jeshua beamed enthusiastically – «And you, my darling, are also a miracle! You also belong to our Lord!»

Jeshua was all smiles, as though he had been given a special gift, which indeed, in a way, he had.

Mariam lifted her son high in the air and rhythmically recited the last words of a Psalm:

---

[13] Exodus 15, 1-11

«Let the words of my mouth be acceptable,
the thoughts of my heart before you,
Lord, my rock and my redeemer! [14]»

«Lord!» shouted Jeshua loudly. They all laughed and beamed at Jeshua, who beamed back at them like the little sunshine that he was.

The days in Pelusium were a blessing. The travellers had time to recover from their exertions and to prepare for the next stretch of their journey. They admired the elegance of the town, marvelling at the noble Egyptian and Roman buildings. Statues of Roman goddesses stood side by side with Isis, Horus and Ptah; indeed, it was all rather confusing.

«I don't really understand what the people here believe in,» commented Mariam.

Merit smiled. «Yes, I can see that's not so easy to understand! The Romans are very tolerant in religious matters, you know. They have a relaxed view to religion. Egyptians are the same, not at all narrow-minded!»

«Strange religions,» answered Mariam, «they aren't really religions at all.»

«They certainly don't have such a close relationship to their gods as we Jews have to our God,» said Merit.

«Do you consider yourself Jewish, Merit? Not Egyptian?» asked Jossef.

«Yes, from my mother's side I'm Jewish. The Jewish faith and culture mean a lot to me,» answered

---

[14] Psalm 19, 14

Merit. «My father's not interested in religious matters. But I'm an Egyptian citizen, of course.»

They were all tired and went to sleep early, as they intended to continue their journey next day and needed to get up at dawn to reach Lake Zarou by evening.

Mariam and Jossef were already up before sunrise. Mariam dressed Jeshua for travel and carried him on her belly in the baby sling.

Jossef said a morning prayer:

«My God, the soul you have given me is pure. You created it, you formed it, and You breathed it into me.

You guard it while it is within me, and one day you will take it from me, and restore it to me in the time to come.

As long as the soul is within me, I will thank you, my God and God of my ancestors,

Master of all works, Lord of all souls. Blessed are you, Lord, who restores souls to lifeless bodies.»

He fetched the three donkeys from the stable, by which time Merit had also awoken and made ready to go.

«There's already a lot going on in the stable,» said Jossef. «Two caravans are preparing to leave for their journey south. I spoke with a trader of spices and frankincense – they're on their way to Ma'rib in Sheba with spices, after bringing frankincense northwards. He told me they'd even gone as far as the border of India – makes our journey look very short in comparison!»

«Ah yes,» pointed out Merit, «but they're on camels! They're far quicker than we are, on foot with the donkeys.»

«That's true, and in the desert, camels are un-demanding and sure-footed,» added Mariam.

In the meantime, Jossef had loaded their baggage onto the donkeys. The previous day, he had removed one of the *aurei* from the hem of his robe and exchanged it at an official booth for a few denarii and many sesterces. Once he had paid their rooms, the small group set off southwards in the cool light of dawn. They were walking directly behind the first of the caravans consisting of fourteen camels, the animals snorting and bellowing as they had yet to find a comfortable pace. The route took them between a rocky desert to their left and a marsh area to their right. The caravan had soon moved far ahead until the camels were mere dots on the horizon, but a second caravan overtook them shortly afterwards. Mariam squinted against the rising sun, gazing up at the silhouettes of the men on their tall, proud beasts. One of the men greeted the little group cordially as he passed them by; the other men ignored them.

Soon, the group of travellers had found a good walking rhythm. All three felt strong and well-rested after the pleasant days in Pelusium. They kept up a good pace until midday when they passed the el-Qantara straits, seeing Lake Manzala shimmering in the distance behind them. After this, they urgently needed a break, as they had been walking for six hours.

They stopped at the edge of a small lake, the first of the Ballah Lakes, which were connected to each other by a canal system. In this area, the farmers had even managed to drain the swamp sufficiently to be able to work small fields of vegetables and grain.

The water of the lake was brackish. The donkeys walked to the lakeside, lowered their heads to drink, then raised them again swiftly with a disgusted expression, and refrained from drinking. At one point, the group caught sight of the back of a small crocodile swimming past just below the surface. In the shade of a group of palm trees and acacias, they enjoyed a light lunch while the donkeys grazed the lush grass contentedly. Jossef heard the sound of water trickling nearby and went off into the bushes to find out where it was coming from. He came back smiling.

«There's actually a spring right near here,» he said, «but it's only flowing sluggishly. I'll take the donkeys over and water them. Afterwards, we can fill the water skins.»

He led the three thirsty beasts to the water, where they quenched their thirst. As Jossef returned with the donkeys, he swatted at a mosquito pestering him around his neck. The three donkeys also shook their heads to rid themselves of the insects.

«These pesky nuisances!» exclaimed Jossef.

«I know!» said Merit. «They're always annoying in swampy areas. Let's eat up and move on quickly!»

«Mosquitos or no mosquitos, I'm afraid I still need a little more rest,» objected Mariam.

They remained under the palm trees for the hottest part of the day. During their break, Merit taught Jeshua a few words of Egyptian, as she had often done when they halted for a while. Mariam and

Jossef began to learn the language passively, by listening in to Merit's playful lessons, which was an enjoyable way to learn.

At about the ninth hour, they set off again and travelled a further three hours to their day's destination, Lake Zarou. The lake was enormous; they could hardly see over to the opposite shore. As the sky turned orange and then red, they saw several fishing boats approaching the shore with their catch. The curlews could be heard calling from the reed beds. Jeshua pointed to a strange, grey and white bird with a dark, curved neck flying overhead – their first sighting of an ibis!

Jossef lit a fire, which helped to keep the mosquitos away. The little group huddled around the fire, rolled themselves into their mats and dozed off immediately from exhaustion.

Next morning, they set off early after a deep, refreshing sleep. Around midday, they met a number of caravans travelling along the el-Qantara straits, so they branched off onto a smaller, shadier path through the swamp, to avoid this traffic. They only made a short stop for lunch and a rest before continuing their journey, in order to reach Lake Timsah by evening. This lake was even larger than Lake Zarou; it was like being on the coast of the sea.

It was here that they crossed the path taken by the Israelites during the Exodus from Egypt with Moses. But 1500 years earlier, the Israelites had been travelling in the opposite direction: Coming from

Wadi[15] Tumilat they had turned south at Lake Timsah towards the Bitter Lakes, whereas Jossef, Mariam and Merit were coming from the north and going west into Wadi Tumilat.

While Jossef lit a fire, Mariam told the entire story of the Exodus again for the benefit of Merit and Jeshua, who were a grateful audience. She also told the story of Joseph, who had been sold by his brothers to Midianite slave-traders 500 years before the Exodus. These slave-traders had carried him off to Goshen. Joseph had risen from slave to high office in the service of the supervisor of the pharaoh's bodyguard, even becoming vizier. Joseph's father and brothers had later joined him in Egypt due to famine in Canaan. The Semitic tribes had settled in Egypt, until a new pharaoh had begun to subject the Israelites to hard slave labour, which was the reason why they had followed Moses out of Egypt in the Exodus and wandered in the Sinai Desert for 40 years.

Merit added that they were now already in the ancient land of Goshen where Joseph had been taken by the Midianites, and Mariam contributed the fact that their own route from Ashkelon had been the identical route the Midianite slave-traders had taken with Joseph.

«May I please interrupt your discourse?» called Jossef from the fire, which was now only burning

---

[15] Wadi: Valley or riverbed only carrying water after heavy rainfall

weakly. «Mariam, love, how about making us tea and something to eat before the fire's burned down?»

Mariam lifted Jeshua from her lap, passed him over to Merit, and set about her work, while Merit repeated a few expressions from the story of Joseph in Egyptian for Jeshua.

After the meal, which barely sated their hunger, they soon fell asleep. But once the fire stopped smoking, the mosquitos came back to disturb their sleep.

Feeling less than fresh, they set off early next morning, hoping to be able to cover half the distance to Belbeis, since their supplies were already getting low and they would be able to stock up again there.

But after walking for three hours, Jossef started to stagger. He shook his head which felt as if it was filled with cotton wool. His gait became more and more sluggish, and he had to put a hand on the croup of his donkey to stop himself from falling. He could tell he was getting a fever; he started shivering with ague and his teeth were chattering audibly.

Mariam came to walk next to her husband and asked him what was wrong. It was clear that he would not be able to go on much longer, so she called Merit over.

«Merit, Jossef's sick. We'll have to try and get him onto his donkey somehow,» she said. «Take Jeshua quickly, please. I'll take off some of the baggage and put it on my donkey so that Jossef has room.»

Merit took Jeshua with a worried frown. She reckoned she knew what was wrong with Jossef, and it bode ill for him. He presumably had the dreaded malaria, from which people often died.

As soon as Jossef's donkey was ready, Merit sat Jeshua under a palm tree, leaning him against the trunk, then she helped Mariam to get Jossef onto the donkey.

Their path followed the northern shore of Lake Timsah and continued along the same line towards the west. Merit headed the group, travelling as quickly as possibly along the valley. The flat land had a covering of shrubs and small trees. Far away in the south, they could see the rocky desert shimmering in the light of the sun between the trees.

Mariam walked next to her husband's donkey to support him whenever he threatened to fall off. They had to make many stops, as Jossef needed time to rest and to drink large amounts of water.

Merit suggested they may be able to find more protection in the higher ground to the north, but to do this, they had to leave the valley and the water course. As evening fell, they finally found a hill with rock caves to their left. Mariam thought it would be a good place to camp. She made her husband as comfortable as possible in one of the caves.

Now she needed to light a fire, which had always been Jossef's task. Mariam had trouble with the flintstone and the tinder to begin with, but after quarter of an hour's concentrated work and several failed attempts, with a shout of «Ha!» she had the brushwood burning at last.

She cooked a watery broth with a few dried vegetables, to give Jossef strength. She also baked flat bread upon a hot stone. That was almost all they had left to eat. She supported Jossef's head as he drank the broth, then she gave him some water and wiped his brow with a wet cloth. All the time, he was alternating between shivering and sweating, and he was clearly in a very bad way. Sometimes, he even became delirious and thought he had to go and visit a customer.

It was quite clear that they would not be able to travel next day. Mariam was very worried about her husband. Merit tried to comfort her, but her words lacked conviction, as she herself doubted whether Jossef would soon be well again – if ever. Jeshua sensed the adults' despondency and looked in confusion from one face to another, trying to understand what was wrong.

Mariam stroked his head. «Your father's very ill, Jeshua,» she explained, «so we're going to have to be very patient. We'll pray to our Lord to make him well again.»

Late in the evening, as the fire had burned down to embers and the last birds were singing in the shady trees, Mariam recited the reassuring words of Psalm 130:

> «*Out of the depths I cry to you, O Lord!*
> *O Lord, hear my voice!*
> *Let your ears be attentive to the voice of my*
> *pleas for mercy!*

*If you, O Lord, should mark iniquities, O Lord,
who could stand?
But with you there is forgiveness, that you may
be feared.
I wait for the Lord, my soul waits, and in his
word I hope.
My soul waits for the Lord more than watchmen for the morning.»*

She went to her husband and blessed him before lying down to sleep.

They stayed four days in the cave, during which
time Jossef's condition became steadily worse. He
vomited frequently and complained of pains in his
limbs. In his ague, no blanket could alleviate his shivering, and no amount of cool water could bring down
the fever. Mariam already feared the worst.

«Tomorrow I'll ride to Bubastis to fetch provisions,» said Merit on the evening of the fourth day.
«It's not quite so far as Belbeis. If I leave before dawn,
I should be able to get there and back by evening. I'll
just take a bag and some money, so that I can ride
quickly.»

«Thank you, Merit,» answered Mariam in relief.
«I'm grateful if I can stay here with Jossef. You're
right, there's nothing else for it. We've got almost
nothing left to eat and drink. But please promise to
take good care of yourself!!»

While they were speaking, they did not notice
Jeshua crawling off to the cave. He crawled over to
his father's mat and stared at his father's arm lying
shivering on the ground next to his body. Jeshua laid

his tiny hand gently upon the broad, hairy arm and remained for a while with Jossef. Slowly, the shivering stopped. His father breathed in deeply, then breathed out raggedly. All was quiet. Jossef felt a deep sense of peace. He felt Jeshua's hand on his arm, opened his eyes and looked at his son, who was smiling up at him. Jossef smiled back, took his little son in his arms, and kissed him. It seemed to him at that moment that there were thousands of loving beings in the cave; he could also hear the soft beating of wings and rushing of wind, and the air of the cave shimmered with a soft, golden light.

By this time, the women had noticed that Jeshua was missing. They came to the cave, stood at the entrance and wondered at the improvement in Jossef's condition and the peaceful atmosphere.

«Oh thank God, I do believe the sickness has passed!» exclaimed Mariam and ran over to her husband and her child. «Jossef, oh Jossef! I've been so very worried! You were miles away – you weren't even able to answer us anymore. I've been praying fervently for you, but I began to think I'd lose you! Ah, my darling, darling Jossef, you're looking so much better already! Praise be to the Lord, our God! Now you're going to be well again.»

15

Jossef slept throughout the night– a deep, healthy sleep. It would have been good for him to have stayed another day in the cave to recover, but he did not want Merit to have to ride all the way to Bubastis and back alone, so they set off the next day in the cool of the dawn. Mariam had baked bread with the last of the flour as their only provision for the day's journey. They ate a little of this before they left. Water was also going to be in short supply. They would need to ration both bread and water carefully all the way to Bubastis. The only small stream was a mere trickle here, hardly sufficient to water the donkeys.

Mariam had loaded all the baggage onto her own donkey, so that Jossef could ride. To begin with, he attempted to walk, but soon realised that he was still too weak after his serious illness. For a sick man, the day's journey was long. They made slow progress and were hungry, thirsty, and exhausted when, towards midday, the gigantic statues of the old town of Bubastis came into sight. The people of Bubastis worshipped Bastet, a cat idol, so the old temple complex was teeming with cats, which greatly pleased Jeshua. He crawled over to the animals and stroked them. He picked up a tiny kitten, but its mother hissed him an angry warning. Jeshua laughed, turned his back on the mother cat and showed his mother the kitten.

At that moment, they heard an angry shout from the edge of the temple complex. A man was coming for them with a raised staff, swearing loudly at them. Mariam and Jossef could not understand what had made him so angry, but Merit understood his dialect and explained: «We need to get away from here quickly! He's accusing us of trying to steal the holy cats. Jeshua, put that kitten down, please!»

Merit took the kitten from Jeshua and put it back with its mother, which hissed at her again. Mariam picked Jeshua up quickly.

Merit approached the agitated man, who was standing beside a large well, and began to explain that they had not understood the situation as they were from Israel. She had started to ask whether they could have water and somewhere to stay, when he interrupted her gruffly and told her that Jews were not welcome there, and that they would most certainly not be given any food.

«Please,» begged Merit, «can we at least have some water from the well? This man here has been very ill and urgently needs to drink.»

«Get out of here!» shouted the citizen of Bubastis angrily. «We don't want you here, and you can take your diseases with you! Now get lost, all of you!»

Behind him, other men appeared. They did not look any more well-disposed than their colleague. With heavy hearts, the little group of weary travellers beat a hasty retreat. Merit stopped at the edge of the temple complex, turning back to the men and shouting furiously in Egyptian: *« Whoever shuts their ears to the cry of the poor will also cry out and not be answered! [16]»*

Suddenly, the earth began to quake. A large statue of Bastet came crashing down, breaking in two as it hit the ground. Further statues, columns and obelisks disintegrated in clouds of dust before the earth finally became still again.

The angry men chased after Merit, who made a run for it and caught up with the others. As soon as they could be sure the men were no longer in pursuit, they slowed their pace and turned their heavy steps towards the south.

«What do we do now?» asked Mariam. «We can't possibly even survive the night without water, let alone walk to Belbeis.»

They sat down under a palm tree to rest. They were now too tired and thirsty even to think. No solution occurred to them. There was nothing to be hoped for with such hostile people. Merit said that as far as she knew, there were no more springs between Bubastis and Belbeis, so they had no chance of finding any water. Their situation was hopeless indeed.

They were just standing up to leave, when a young girl appeared on their path carrying a large pitcher on her head. She waved to them as she approached.

«Here,» she said, «we heard what the elder said to you, and it's quite true: You would not have been given anything by these people. But at least I've been

---

[16] Proverbs 21, 13

able to bring you a jug of water. Please drink and fill up your water skins!»

«Oh, thank you so much! You're a real god-send!» exclaimed Mariam, as the girl put the pitcher down on the ground before them. Mariam and Merit filled the water skins. They gave Jossef a drink first, then they quenched their own thirst. After this, they refilled the skins.

Jossef offered the girl a sesterce, but she declined. Merit thanked her again in her own language for her kindness. She and the girl had a long conversation which was unintelligible to Mariam and Jossef. Merit therefore gave them a summary of what had been said: The girl, whose name was Amunet, had come in search of the travellers at her father's wish. Amunet explained that they were all invited to spend the night with her parents to the northwest of Bubastis. Her father, Kulom, had witnessed the scene with the men of Bubastis and wished to let them know that they would be made welcome in his home. However, he had also told Amunet to explain to them that his wife, Sarah, had been seriously ill for some time, and would therefore be unable to offer them any assistance. Merit discussed the situation with Mariam. They were reluctant to accept the hospitality of a family which was already suffering. On the other hand, Jossefs condition forced them to do so. as they would clearly not be able to stay in Bubastis, and Jossef was unable to continue the journey to Belbeis without more water. So they accepted the offer with thanks.

They travelled for another two hours before reaching Kulom and Sarah's house. Jossef rode the whole way. He was still very weak but no longer felt ill. Thankfully, their route was quite shady, passing under a row of trees next to an almost dried-out brook. Jossef had required a large amount of water to slake his great thirst so that despite Amunet's kindness, their water supplies were once again dwindling.

They took a rest beneath a mulberry tree. Merit had managed to collect a few berries on her way, providing them with a small, refreshing snack from which they regained some strength.

It was dusk by the time the little group arrived at Amunet's parents' house. The short journey had further weakened Jossef, so Mariam was glad they had decided to come here rather than to Belbeis.

Amunet invited the family and Merit into the house, which was already so dark that they could hardly make out anything by the sparse light of the oil lamp. However, Kulom was aware that this was the same family he had witnessed being chased away from the town by the men of Bubastis, as he had been standing nearby at the time.

«Welcome to my house!» said the aged Kulom. «I'm very sorry my poor wife Sarah is unable to serve you, but she's been suffering from a severe lung disease for many years now. Lately, it's become even worse.»

As if to confirm this, a dreadful, incessant cough came from the next room. Amunet hurried to her mother to give her a healing draught.

Kulom was just as kind and helpful as his daughter. He gave the travellers a drink, after which he showed them where they were to sleep – in a cave near the house where the goats were stabled, as the house was too small for guests. Thanks to fresh straw and the presence of the goats, the simple lodging felt warm and inviting. Merit helped Mariam lay out the mats. Jossef lay down immediately and fell fast a-sleep. The others returned to the house to partake of a light meal with Kulom and Amunet

Mariam carried Jeshua to Sarah's room to introduce herself to her. Sarah was lying on a mat on the floor, grey of face and with stertorous breathing. She was hardly aware of Mariam's presence, so Mariam returned to the family, put Jeshua down and helped Merit and Amunet to prepare the meal.

Unnoticed by anyone, Jeshua crawled back to Sarah's room, laid his hand on her arm and remained there, until her stertorous breathing began to quieten and deepen Sarah slowly opened her eyes and looked in amazement at the small child next to her. She took a deep breath – the pain appeared to have been swept away! Jeshua looked at her with wide eyes and smiled. The smile was mirrored in Sarah's own face. The old woman sat up and placed the unknown child on her lap.

«You little darling!» said Sarah, «Whoever are you?»

Putting Jeshua down on the floor, she attempted to get to her knees. Very slowly, she stood up, took a first wobbly step, supporting her-self on the wall, blinking and reeling slightly. Her second step was more successful. Carefully, she picked Jeshua up and went to join her family in the living room. They all immediately fell silent and looked at Sarah and Jeshua with wide eyes.

«Sarah!» exclaimed Kulom, dumbfounded, «You're standing up! That's amazing! It's the first time for months you've been able to get out of bed!»

Sarah beamed, went over to her husband, and embraced him, still holding Jeshua in her arms. «Exactly, Kulom,» she said, «It's incredible! I can hardly believe it myself. This tiny little lad crawled up to my bed, touched me, and I immediately felt better!»

Mariam's eyes widened. Was that a mere coincidence? How could her son's touch once again have had such an effect? He was still only a baby!

The overwhelming joy of Sarah's sudden recovery made Kulom and Amunet almost forget Mariam and Merit's presence. Mariam took Jeshua from Sarah and the two women returned to their cave. They were exhausted from the incredible occurrences of the day and wanted nothing more than to sleep.

Next day, there was a festive meal to celebrate Sarah's recovery, during which Kulom asked the reason for the travellers' journey. They answered reticently, but while they waited for the main course, they told of their experiences during the last few days. Jossef described his remarkable recovery following Jeshua's touch. Jeshua, who was sitting on Jossef's lap, smiled up at his father, laid his head on his father's chest and fell asleep. Mariam and Sarah nodded repeatedly as Jossef told of his recovery.

«Yes», said Mariam, «our little Jeshua appears to have specials powers. It was amazing how his touch had a similar effect upon Sarah yesterday. Small as he is, he's been of so much help!»

Sarah and Jossef smiled at one another. «It's true,» confirmed Sarah, «For me it was just the same as it was for you, Jossef! I'm so glad you came to us!»

«Yes», said Jossef, «Although we met with nothing but aggression in Bubastis, at least it did lead us to you. And it's a good thing Merit didn't ride alone to Bubastis yesterday. Just think – those evil men could have harmed her, and she certainly would not have been given any provisions.»

The evening ended on a lighter note. Amunet served up a delicious pigeon pie, and the two families talked and laughed together until Sarah began to tire and they all went off to bed.

The travellers stayed several days with their friendly hosts. Sarah's sickness did not reoccur, and both Sarah and Jossef became stronger every day. The sojourn had been a blessing for them all.

***

After leaving Kulom, Sarah and Amunet, the group travelled south for one day, reaching Belbeis towards evening via the Roman fort to the north of the town. They saw hundreds of legionnaires just returning from a mission, marching in through the main gate. Jeshua was fascinated by the colourful flags fluttering in the wind and the breastplates gleaming in the sun. This was his first sight of an entire Roman legion. The flags of the legion were flying atop fortifying walls of yellow stone. In a large round tower of the same stone, the evening guard stood sentinel.

The travellers followed the walls of the fortification, going south in the direction of the old town. After half an hour they could see the houses of the pretty little town ahead. The warm yellow stone shone in the evening sun. Between the houses, the inhabitants had created well-kept gardens with spreading trees. The travellers had the impression they were going to like Belbeis and drew further hope from this.

They encountered a funeral procession, and Merit respectfully asked one of the mourners where they could find a guesthouse. The man directed them to a pretty little house in the centre of town. A friendly, middle-aged man opened the door and said that he would be pleased to accommodate them. First, the landlord showed Jossef where he could stable the donkeys, then he brought the travellers to their rooms which were simple, but clean and homely. There were brightly coloured fabrics hanging on the walls, creating a cosy atmosphere. Inside, the walls were of clay in the same honey-colour as the stones outside, making the rooms even warmer.

«If you want something to eat, you'll find a good eating house in the next street offering excellent food,» suggested their landlord and left them to relax and rest.

«He's no Egyptian,» commented Merit, «maybe he'll tell us where he's from. He seems nice!»

«Yes,» agreed Mariam. «I believe we'll be able to get some rest here and recover from our exertion. I wouldn't mind staying here for some time.»

Jossef was very much in agreement with this suggestion, as he still urgently needed more time to recover completely. Although Merit was longing to reach her hometown, she understood that this was important for Jossef and also agreed to a longer stay.

16

The four friends got up early and were given a light meal by their landlord, who told Merit he was from Judaea, from a small village between Jericho and Jerusalem. Merit grinned and told him that all four of his guests were of Jewish origin, and that Mariam and Jossef came from Nazareth. They laughed heartily at the trouble Mariam and Jossef had taken to speak Egyptian with their landlord; the couple were much relieved to be able to speak to him in their mother tongue, Aramaic, from then onwards.

The landlord, Ahab, called his wife Dinah, who was equally pleased to know they had guests from their own country. Ahab explained that there had been a strong Jewish community in Belbeis for some decades. They all met at a house which had been converted into a synagogue, and sometimes had guest speakers who were passing through on their way to Babylon, making a halt in Belbeis.

Ahab offered to show his guests around the town and left Dinah in charge of the guesthouse while he did so. First, they visited the synagogue which looked unassuming from the outside. But inside, it was much like the synagogues at home, with an ark for the Torah scrolls. Tiles decorated with Hebrew lettering covered the walls. The house had an atrium with benches for the congregation to rest under the mulberry trees. Ahab explained that discussions and lectures were often held out here.

He introduced the old synagogue caretaker, Jehuda, and said they should ask him if they ever had any questions about the building or the community, as he was well informed about everything and was familiar with all members of the community.

The next street they visited was the craftsmen's and trader's street, most of whom were carpenters or wood carvers. Obviously, Jossef wanted to spend time here and take a good look at everything. He explained that he was himself a carpenter by trade and arranged to go back and visit the woodworkers the next day, taking Jeshua with him, as it was not particularly exciting for Mariam or Merit.

Their first day in Belbeis passed pleasantly. By the evening, all four of them had the feeling that they had known Ahab and Dinah for ages. The couple were plump, friendly individuals with rosy cheeks, who looked rather alike – they could almost have been brother and sister. As Mariam told them the story of their reception in Bubastis, Ahab and Dinah looked at one another and shrugged.

«Mariam, the people of Bubastis think they're something special, merely because their town is so old,» explained Ahab. «They still worship Bastet, the ancient cat goddess. In Belbeis; we also have old cult places from that time dedicated to the god Bes, who has the look of a grinning satyr and is much loved by children for his mischief. That's why our town's called Belbeis or Belbes. Some say these gods were first introduced from Mesopotamia. The people of Bubastis themselves have become rather like cats. They defend their territory with more than necessary aggression against any outsiders or believers of other faiths. But I've never heard such a terrible story as the one you've told us! What swine! Refusing to give travellers water!»

They soon got used to life in Belbeis, which took on a pleasant routine. Jossef, Mariam and Merit were treated as members of the family, and as to Jeshua: He was really spoiled by Ahab and Dinah and learned to play on their warmth! He soon had them wrapped around his little finger, only having to look at them with his sweet eyes and angelic smile, and they melted before him like wax. They did not have any children of their own, so Jeshua became their golden boy. The fact that he took his very first wobbly steps under the shade of the mulberry tree in their own atrium, filled them with pride and joy. And from that day onwards, there was no stopping Jeshua!

Jossef often visited the carpenters, sometimes helping out when they were a man short. Sometimes Jeshua accompanied him. The boy made friends with the son of one of the wood carvers a little older than himself, who showed him how to carve a bird out of wood. The older boy actually held Jeshua's hands and guided them, but Jeshua still had the feeling he had made the bird himself. He ran to his father and proudly showed him what he had made. Jossef praised him and said he would make a good carpenter one day. Jeshua beamed, took his bird home with him and showed it to Mariam and Merit, who were helping Dinah in the kitchen. All three women clapped their hands gleefully over the little wooden sparrow and said what a clever boy Jeshua was.

On the Day of Preparation for the Sabbath, there was the usual hectic atmosphere in the kitchen and around the house, in order to have everything ready for the evening meal and the required Sabbath rest.

On the Sabbath day itself, they all went to the synagogue. While they were walking there, Ahab told them there was also a synagogue and a strong Jewish community in the small town of Babylon on the Nile, whose name reflected the fact that five hundred years previously, the prophet Jeremiah had been deported to this part of Egypt by the conquerors invading Jerusalem from the eastern kingdom of Babylon. The family were intent on visiting that community, should they reach the town.

It was like being back home in Nazareth. Mariam sat with Merit and Dinah in the women's section which was open to the main hall. After an opening silence, the Sh'ma Israel was recited: *Hear, O Israel: The Lord our God, the Lord is One*. Mariam listened to the familiar words of the Torah. She felt homesick for Nazareth and her mother, Hannah. How was Hannah coping with not knowing what had happened to her daughter? When would they finally be able to see and hold each other again?

Suddenly, Mariam was besieged by a great fear that she would never see her mother alive again, and a tear slowly trickled down her cheek. She sent up a fervent prayer to heaven that an angel would let her mother know she was alive and well.

«Lord, you have delivered us from great danger and brought us to these wonderful people,» prayed Mariam within her heart, «you will surely continue to hold your hand over us and over my mother.»

Their time in Belbeis did them all good. They made many friends in the Jewish community with whom they celebrated the lovely Shavuot Feast of Weeks, and it would have been pleasant to stay longer. But after a month, Merit began to feel restless, as she longed to get home, so they decided to set off again.

They took their leave of all their new friends. Jossef went to the woodworkers and said goodbye to his colleagues; Jeshua made his little friend a present of the carved bird he had made shortly after his arrival in Belbeis. As the boy took the bird in his hands, he thought he could feel its wings flutter beneath his fingers. He smiled at Jeshua and politely wished him a good onward journey.

The donkeys had led a lazy life in Belbeis. Now they found themselves being loaded with baggage and knew it was time to travel again.

All four found it hard to say goodbye to Ahab and Dinah. Who knew when they would be with such friendly folk again? Dinah did not want to let little Jeshua go, but they finally set off, with a warning from Ahab to take good care of themselves.

«Thank you for everything, and peace be with you!» the travellers called out, as they slowly disappeared towards the western horizon.

Dinah wiped away a tear and went back into the house. «Oh, Ahab, if only we'd been able to have children!» she exclaimed.

«My pet, it was God's will for us. We don't know why, but that's just the way it is,» answered Ahab. «However, we still have each other, and that's a valuable enough gift, isn't it?»

«Of course, pet!» said Dinah, kissing her husband, who put his arm around her broad hips. «That is indeed a priceless gift!»

17

By taking the north-western path, the travellers managed to avoid Bubastis, as they did not want to provoke another confrontation with the cat worshipers. To begin with, the path was flat and very green, criss-crossing brooks and streams over small wooden bridges. This meant they always had an ample water supply. There was a pleasant freshness in the air. The rainy season was not far off, and the banks of the Nile would soon be flooded.

They came to a region where farmers had rerouted the water from the streams through canals by means of waterwheels, to irrigate their small fields of grain. Most of these fields had already been harvested. The path circumvented the fields, and many other paths crossed their own, making it difficult to find the way. But Jossef always kept his eye on the sun, so as not to lose his orientation.

Now and then, they passed through small villages and hamlets. The landscape offered little protection, so at dusk, they decided to ask for lodgings in one of the villages. A friendly widow offered them accommodation and even a simple egg supper, for which they were very grateful as it spared their supplies. Jossef paid the woman for her hospitality before they set off again the following morning.

They continued for two more days through this area. The landscape became more fertile and the fields larger. These fields did not belong to small farmers, but to prosperous landowners who had many slaves working their land, kneeling in long rows, reaping the grain in these huge fields with sickles. On circular stone threshing floors, other slaves were occupied with separating the wheat from the chaff. The slaves worked next to the threshing oxen, throwing the wheat into the air to separate it from the chaff. The wheat was emptied into a huge granary through an opening in the roof. The slaves were supervised by overseers, and there was a general feeling of agitation about the work.

Near the threshing floor, the air was full of fine dust. As the travellers passed by, some grain dust got into Mariam's nose, and she started to sneeze. The travellers bowed their heads, plodded on and attempted to get away from the dust and the agitated atmosphere as soon as possible.

There followed a refreshing stretch between lush meadows beside a stream bordered by willows. After about two hours, they once again found themselves between the grain fields of prosperous landowners, which were also being harvested by slaves. About a hundred yards ahead, in a small depression in the land, they heard voices and screams. As they came nearer, they saw to their horror that three young slaves were being cudgelled by the overseers. One of the slaves had already collapsed, but the overseer continued to thrash him. All three lads were already covered in blood. Two of them were still screaming and attempting to protect themselves from the blows. The third had lost consciousness.

The travellers looked at one another. «We need to intervene!» said Mariam anxiously.

«No!» warned Jossef, «we've got no right to! These are slaves. Their owners can do whatever they want with them. We can't do a thing. Let's walk on!»

But Merit's eyes flamed angrily. «Not only do we have the right to, we have an obligation to intervene! They're human beings, and even animals have a right to be treated properly!» she shouted. «Come on, Mariam, we've got to do something!»

Mariam passed Jeshua over to her husband with a fiery look, and the two women marched resolutely over to the group in the depression. Jossef called out to them again to keep out of it, but his calls fell upon deaf ears.

«What do you think you're doing, thrashing these lads like that?» Merit asked one of the overseers, who raised his brows and looked at her in amazement. «Leave them be immediately! Can't you see you're nearly killing them?»

«What's that got to do with you?» asked the overseer. «What does it matter to you? They're useless tykes who only understand one language – the language of the stick!» and he lifted his staff again to thrash at the whining figure of misery before him.

«No!» shouted Mariam in Egyptian, «please no!» Then she had to change to Aramaic. «No one has earned such treatment! Have you got children? Would you want your children to suffer like this? These poor souls are also the children of some mother! Please, have mercy on them!»

Merit quickly translated what Mariam had last said, and the overseer did indeed lower his staff.

«Alright,» he said, «if these 'children' are worth so much to you, take them! As workers, they're complete duffers anyway. They scoff more grain than they harvest, just a load of dim half-wits. We'll be glad to be rid of them, they drive us up the pole! Go on, take them if you want, and welcome!»

The overseers actually turned their backs on Mariam and Merit and walked away, leaving the young slaves to the mercy of their rescuers.

Mariam and Merit called Jossef over, who rather sheepishly led all three donkeys down into the depression, after putting Jeshua on his own donkey.

«Now, that could have turned nasty,» he complained sullenly, «Fortune favours fools!»

«Jossef!» said Mariam angrily. «Whenever someone's in need, we have an obligation to help. Just look at them! First of all, we need to care for their wounds. Don't just stand there complaining, do something, come on! Give me the water skin and a few cloths!»

Jossef passed one skin to Mariam and the other to Merit. The women took the cloths and began to clean and soothe the lads' terrible weals. The patients moaned and winced with pain but did not say one word. They were on their last legs.

«So what d'you think you're going to do with them now?» asked Jossef. «We certainly can't take them with us!»

«Why not?» asked Merit feistily. «We can put them on our donkeys for now. We're most certainly not going to leave them to their fate here.»

Jossef groaned and rolled his eyes. «For heaven's sake! I hope we won't meet a lot more suffering beings, or we'll soon be a caravan!» Nevertheless, he helped the women to get the three slaves onto the donkeys, after they had been given a drink. The unconscious slave was laid across Jossef's donkey, so that he could support him. The whole cavalcade set off slowly on its way. It was hard going, but they kept on until the sun sank towards the horizon.

The place they had reached was not at all bad as a camp, so they spread their mats under the shade of an acacia tree. Mariam and Merit saw to it that the three boys were lying reasonably comfortably. They were so thin that all three had room on the one mat. Now, all three were conscious again, but looking fearful and exhausted. They had still not spoken one word. As the crickets began to chirp, Jossef lit a fire and Mariam cooked a nourishing broth with dried vegetables and a little dried meat. After they had all eaten their fill, Mariam, Merit and Jossef sat with Jeshua by the fire and discussed their new situation, while the boys, who had only eaten a little of the soup, had already fallen fast asleep.

«Maybe they've got family somewhere,» suggested Mariam, «and we can take them back to their relatives.»

«We must ask them tomorrow morning,» said Merit, «but I think we should continue our journey as planned. Once they've recovered strength, they won't be such burden and can maybe even help us.»

«You're quite right of course, and it's admirable the way you stood up for these three,» admitted Jossef, «but your safety, and most particularly Jeshua's safety, has always to be our top priority. I don't want something like that endangering you.»

«Hey, Jossef!» shouted Mariam, «'Something like that'? They're needy people who are just as endangered as we are, even more so, in fact!»

«Yeah, yeah, yeah,» answered Jossef, «you know exactly what I mean! No need to act 'holier than thou'! And once again: Our first concern must always be for Jeshua.»

«Of course, but the one does not exclude the other,» said Mariam. «We must never close our eyes to injustice. God has given us Jeshua, and God also gave us this situation. Don't you think it was strange the way those overseers gave up so quickly? I had a feeling we were being aided by divine power. And if that's the case, God will continue to help us.»

«Well, let's just hope so,» said Jossef dryly.

They grew silent and stared into the fire. Jeshua snuggled in his mother's lap. They began to relax, and soon became sleepy. Mariam raised her beautiful voice in a familiar lullaby, while Merit hummed along softly.

18

At sunrise the next morning they caught their first glimpse of the silvery curve of the Nile sparkling in the distance. In less than one day, they would be crossing the Nile by ferry, and reaching the town of Sebennytos[17] by evening.

Merit sat with the three boys and patiently attempted to draw their story out of them, while Mariam and Jossef loaded the donkeys. The boys were extremely uncommunicative – it was like getting water out of a stone. However, it was really not surprising, considering the unbelievable treatment they had been subjected to as slaves.

As children, they had been captured by slave traders and taken from their home, an oasis in the Libyan desert west of Wadi Natrun, to the landowner of a large farm, where they had been doing forced labour under the worst of conditions ever since. Strangely enough, they had hardly a word of complaint against the life they had led; they just seemed to accept it as inevitable. Merit asked whether they would like to return to their home, but the three boys just shrugged listlessly. Family life was presumably a thing of so distant a past that they were no longer able to picture it. It was, however, an incredible coincidence that their home village lay in the same general direction as Merit's hometown. Surely this was a sign!

---

[17] Today: Samanoud

They set off, with Mariam and Merit in front leading the donkey carrying Jeshua, the three boys in the middle, and Jossef following behind. As they walked, Merit recounted the boys' story to her friend. Mariam's eyes opened wide when she heard of the child-snatching by the slave traders.

«Oh, those poor boys!» she exclaimed. «No wonder they're so sullen! Let's hope they can recover in our company, and start to open up a little.»

«Yes, I hope so too,» said Merit. «The amazing thing is that their home is a little to the south-west of my own hometown!»

«That's got to be fate!» exclaimed Mariam.

«Just what I thought. We can take the boys back to their family. Mind you, they can't yet feel any joy at the thought, as they don't really remember life in their village. But their parents are bound to be thrilled to see them!»

They had to diminish their marching speed, since the boys were not yet strong enough to be travelling so fast. For this reason, it took them the whole day to reach the Damietta branch of the Nile, where they could at last board the ferry. The Nile was flanked by a reed bed where water birds swam and gnats danced. In the golden light of evening, a large reed boat with a high prow and a red sail passed them by, creating a wide backwash in the water. The ferryman waited for this large boat to pass before rowing the ferry towards them. He stood at the stern and wielded a single large oar from side to side behind the ferry, to propel the craft forward. As the ferry approached, the soft splash of water from the oar broke the stillness of evening.

The ferry only just had room for the group, which had now grown to seven people with three donkeys, so the boat was lying low in the water. As they cast off, Jeshua hung his arm over the edge of the ferry, dipping his hand into the water and feeling the pull of the water against his skin.

«Mind out, Jeshua!» warned Mariam, «Jossef, can you please hold onto him?» Jossef secured his son by hooking a finger under his belt, whilst looking up at the magnificent buildings on the opposite bank.

«Sebennytos must be about the size of Jerusalem,» he commented. «Let's go directly into the town centre and look for lodgings! I can share a room with the three boys, and you and Jeshua can sleep in the same room as Merit, Mariam.»

At the other side, Jossef paid the ferryman. They let the three boys disembark first, so that Mariam, Jossef and Merit could help the donkeys clamber out. Mariam passed Jeshua over to one of the boys, but he held him clumsily and Jeshua shouted in Egyptian: «Put me down!» The lad smiled, the first smile they had seen from any of the three, and set him down awkwardly. Jeshua jumped up and down, excited by the short ride in a boat.

«This evening,» said Jossef to the boys, «as soon as we've eaten, it would be good if you three could tell us a bit about yourselves – at the very least, we want to know your names!» Merit translated this request into Egyptian. Now the three boys were at least forewarned and could decide how much they wished to tell.

Jossef and Merit went on ahead to find the way to the town centre. Mariam followed behind with Jeshua and the three boys. They decided upon a modest guesthouse, where the three boys would not be so conspicuous, with their dark faces full of bruises and swelling from the thrashing they had received. They really did look rather dubious characters!

After they had settled in and the donkeys had been stabled, they all went off to find an eating house. They found a suitable place in a small side-street and sat down to enjoy a meal. The three boys displayed a good appetite for the Nile fish with vegetables and flatbread – the first time they had eaten properly. They had obviously only been used to frugal meals, as they were thin as rakes. No wonder they were unable to pull their weight as slaves. The eating house was pleasantly quiet, just right for the conversation they hoped to have with the lads.

«Right, now!» Jossef encouraged the boys, «Please tell us what your names are, and a bit more about yourselves, if you can! We're curious to know!»

Merit translated Jossef's request. At first, all three remained silent, looking down at their hands in their laps. Eventually the darkest-haired youth, the one who had held Jeshua so awkwardly at the quayside, said: «My name's Hemire.»

«Hemire, right, thank you. Welcome!» said Jossef in Egyptian.

«And you?» Merit asked the boy next to Hemire, who had slightly lighter-coloured hair.

«Hesire,» he answered curtly without looking up.

«And now you?» Merit asked the third boy, who had a broader chin.

«Hepire,» said the third boy.

Mariam, Jossef and Merit looked at each other and stifled a laugh.

«I guess you're brothers, huh?» asked Jossef.

«Yeah,» answered Hemire curtly. Starting a conversation with these three was very hard work!

«Right, Hemire, Hesire and Hepire, you're all very welcome in our little travelling group,» Jossef kept trying. «Have you any brothers or sisters?»

«Dunno,» answered all three boys in unison.

«And how old were you, when you were captured and taken from your home?»

They all guessed the answer:

«Dunno.»

Jossef gave up trying to get more information out of these three.

«Right, listen: We're going to take you home. Merit tells me your home is to the west of Wadi Natrun. What's the name of your village?» This sentence required translation by Merit, as it exceeded Jossef's Egyptian vocabulary.

They all waited in suspense for a further 'dunno', but Hemire was proving to be a real chatterbox compared to his brothers. He replied: «Kalya.»

«That's very good, Hemire. Now we'll be able to find your village and restore you to your parents,» said Jossef, and Merit translated again. No reaction from any of the three boys. Ah well, at least they now knew what to expect, and no doubt they would relax and open up a bit after a while.

Jossef mopped his sweating brow and Mariam smiled in amusement. «Hard work, isn't it?» she said in Aramaic.

«Phew! You're not kidding!» answered Jossef and smiled back at her. «But at least we now know what to call those three.»

Jeshua pointed at Hemire. «He!» he shouted; pointing at Hesire: «He!» and finally at Hepire: «He!» Then he laughed – He-He-He!

Mariam and Jossef laughed out loud and nodded. «Yes, you're quite right, Jeshua!»

The three boys managed a tired, rather crooked smile of response. They found the joke at their expense embarrassing. After all, they could not help the stupid names they had been given and their parents' lack of imagination. However, they were not going to be rid of this collective name any time soon. From now on, whenever the travellers wished to attract the boys' attention, they called out «He-He-He!»

19

The travellers spent two whole days in Seben-nytos, as the next day was the Sabbath. On the first day, they stocked up on provisions at the lively market. The market women chatted with Merit and Mariam, showing great empathy for their situation, offering them tea, and even lending Mariam a large granite bowl in which to knead the sabbath bread. The travellers returned to their simple lodgings, freshened up at the well outside, and prepared for the sabbath.

On the second day, in the evening after the Sabbath, Merit and Jossef planned their onward journey, while Mariam got Jeshua ready for bed. To begin with, they would travel northwards along the Damietta fork of the Nile. They would turn off and travel west until they reached another fork of the Nile which flowed directly into Lake Burullus, from whence it was not far to Merit's hometown of Baltim on the eastern edge of the lake, on the Mediterranean coast. Merit insisted that they would all be welcome to stay for as long as they wanted with her family, including the He-He-He, since the support Merit had received from them on the journey had been quite beyond price and her parents were sure to want to repay them in some way.

«Merit, it's really you who have helped us and brought us this far – whatever would we have done in Egypt without you?» amended Jossef. «But obviously, it would be wonderful for us to stay with you for a while, and we're looking forward to meeting your family.»

That night, the He-He-He slept so deeply that they could hardly be woken the following morning. While Mariam, Jossef and Merit were packing up and preparing to load the donkeys, the three boys just stood there rubbing their eyes. They had obviously never learned to help upon their own initiative and were presumably used to receiving orders for even the smallest task. This was neither Jossef's nor Mariam's way, but as soon as Merit realised how things stood, she decided henceforth to take upon herself the authoritarian role in the lives of the He-He-He.

«He-He-He, jump to it! Each of you take a bag and tie it to the donkey, look – like this, you see?» she called. This was the kind of language they understood. They immediately seized a bag each and attempted to tie them to the donkeys, but they did this so ineptly that Jossef had to check and retie each knot. Well, it was at least a start! The three boys had had a better connection to Merit from the start, so she automatically became their commander.

As they left the town, they looked with wonder at the impressive villas and palaces of the prosperous citizens. At the edge of the old town stood an ancient temple dedicated to the local war-god Anhur-Shu. His partner, the lioness-goddess Mehit was also depicted in a black granite relief. The temple was very busy when they arrived there as the local officials and citizens were engaged in sacrificing to both deities. The travellers were aware that, as outsiders, they were unwelcome there and soon left.

Whenever the group was travelling, the young He-He-He followed behind at a short distance. So far, they showed no sign of their reticence thawing. They remained uncommunicative and self-contained. Jeshua especially tried repeatedly to coax them out of their shell, but there was no response other than an occasional weak smile. It was rather depressing, and Jossef almost felt a certain degree of understanding for the slave drivers' treatment of them, even though it had been far too brutal – or at least for their vexation!

Mariam adhered to her opinion that they would have to have a great deal of patience with them, as they had had appalling experiences and were traumatised to the depths of their souls.

At least the three of them had now become somewhat stronger and could maintain the accustomed marching pace of the group. Thus they made good headway along the west bank of the Nile during the days that followed. Mariam, Jossef and Jeshua were amazed at the amount of traffic on the river. Now and then, they saw large sailing ships travelling up or down the Nile at great speed. They saw many small fishing boats, out of which the fishermen threw their nets with a dexterous sweep of their arm, and there were also small papyrus rowing boats for private transport, crossing the Nile from bank to bank, some of them with sails and some without. It was amazing that all these boats managed to pass each other without a collision!

Sometimes their path passed between irrigated fields of vegetables and grain, where ibises foraged for food. Jeshua watched a man knock a crow out of the sky with a throwing stick, after which he would hurl a piece of wood at any bird he saw flying past. However, the birds were in no great danger from his attempts!

From time to time, they passed the landing stages of wealthy landowners. One of them had built himself a large granary right next to his landing stage, and its high walls were decorated with hieroglyphs at the top and Latin below, advertising himself and his goods. Merit commented that that was rather over-doing it, since hieroglyphs were now really only used for religious inscriptions.

At one point, they saw a landing stage with a large ramp leading up to a river temple. The forecourt was open to the river and was supported by pillars, between which they could see paintings of deities and pharaohs on its walls. Just then, a funerary boat approached the landing stage. The prow and stern of this boat were raised high and decorated with carved, curving symbols of the sun and the moon. Out of the foreward, rounded deckhouse the voices of professional mourners could be heard wailing their lament. The aft deckhouse was larger and oblong in shape to provide sufficient room for the large coffin and the censing priests. As the boat reached the landing stage, the ten side rowers and the two aft rowers guided the craft carefully until it came alongside with a hollow impact.

As the travellers continued along the west bank, Jeshua turned round on his donkey and looked back to see the priests and their assistants lifting out the large coffin on two poles and carrying it up the ramp to the temple, followed by the wailing mourners, until they all disappeared through the forecourt of the temple.

«Imma[18],» asked Jeshua, «what will they do with the dead person now?»

«First there will be a ritual in the temple,» answered Mariam, «then the deceased will be placed in his or her grave. They will have rubbed the body with salt and ointments for many days and bound it in bandages to preserve it. They believe they can prepare the body for its journey to the realm of the dead by placing food and rich offerings in the grave.» Mariam was really not too sure about the subtle details of the Egyptian belief in the afterlife.

«Hm,» said Jeshua and pondered this in silence for a while.

Suddenly, Merit shouted: «Here it is! This is where our path leaves the Nile and turns west!»

Their path followed the south bank of a stream which branched off from the Nile to the west. Both banks of this stream were bordered by palm trees. To the left of the path were small fields of vegetables, irrigated by channels branching off from the stream.

---

[18] Aramaic for mum

The farmers were busy harvesting their crops before the rains came and flooded their fields.

Three hours later, Jossef suggested it was time to make camp for the night, as it would take them two more days to reach Lake Burullus.

While Jossef lit the fire, Mariam busied herself with cooking and the He-He-He sat sullenly to one side. Merit picked Jeshua up and put him on her lap. She immediately had the usual comfortable feeling and contemplated the uniqueness of this child she held in her arms. She had already experienced many instances of it: The healing of Jossef and Sarah, his intelligence, self-confidence, and inquisitive mind.

However, the story Mariam had told her at the beginning of their journey, the story of his conception, excelled all these. How could a human being be conceived by pure spirit? That would mean he was not only human, but also divine. Was that what Merit could sense in this child? – she asked herself, as she rocked Jeshua gently and felt the touch of his hair upon her lips. She wondered whether Mariam sometimes asked herself the same questions. It was no doubt a tremendous responsibility for Mariam and Jossef to bring up a child consecrated to God. Just the fact of having to flee from their home country, must be a great burden, a burden that Merit could well appreciate, as she was now herself a fugitive.

It occurred to her for the first time that Roman officials or the militia may already have discovered where she was from and may also be searching for her there. Deeply startled at this thought, she gasped loudly. Jeshua turned round and looked at her inquiringly.

«It's alright, poppet, nothing's happened! Something just occurred to me,» Merit reassured him. Jeshua put his little arms around her neck and snuggled up to her. The little darling! How she was going to miss him when Mariam and Jossef travelled on with him! Merit's eyes filled with tears. Right now, her life seemed to consist of harsh partings.

Mariam called everyone to eat. Merit took Jeshua by the hand and went with him to the fire, served herself a portion of soup thickened with wheat from the bubbling pot, took some hummus and sat opposite Mariam and Jossef by the fire. Jeshua sat next to his mother and was also given a portion of soup. The He-He-He received their portion and disappeared into the background. Jossef blessed the frugal meal. The conversation rippled along with the sharing of memories of all they had seen and experienced during that long day. But the sadness of parting and the fear of imminent danger remained with Merit the whole evening. This time, even Jeshua's touch could not dismiss them.

PART IV:

The Mediterranean Potter

20

Dark clouds appeared in the sky as they loaded their baggage onto the donkeys next morning, and a cool wind blew their shawls about their faces. They set off at a quicker pace, in the hope of reaching their destination before the rains started. There was a certain excitement in the air which was mirrored in the faces of those they met upon their way. The Egyptian farmers were convinced that their gods would be good to them again this year; the rain, which promised life and prosperity, was not far off.

Jeshua wanted Merit to carry him for a while. He too was aware of the tension in the air and could also sense Merit's own tension.

«Merit,» asked Jeshua, «what do the Egyptians believe happens to people after they've died?»

«Well, Jeshua, that's quite complicated!» replied Merit. «Before you go to sleep tonight, I'll tell you all about it. But for now, suffice it to say that the Egyptians have a very different view to death than the Jews. They believe the human soul is made up of many parts, and that the corpse of a deceased person needs to be preserved, so that one certain part of the soul can visit it every night during its journey to the realm of the dead. The Egyptians put an awful lot of work into this journey to the realm of the dead – they need to sing certain songs and recite special formulas, they have to mummify the corpse and place food with it, so that this certain part of the soul can strengthen itself for the journey.»

«How many parts does the soul have?» asked Jeshua, fascinated.

«There are eight parts, Jeshua – shall I tell you their names?»

«Yes please!» shouted Jeshua excitedly.

Merit put Jeshua down and began to count on her fingers. «Right! They're called Ka, Ba, Ach, Shut, Chet, Sah, Ib and Ren. There's even a nursery rhyme, so that children can learn and remember their names,» and Merit sang the nursery rhyme about these names.

«Ka, Ba, Ach, Shut, Chet, Sah, Ib, Ren!» Jeshua sang along and hopped across the path as he did so. Merit picked Jeshua up again, and both of them continued to sing the rhyme for a while, while Mariam and Jossef laughed gaily, and even the He-He-He could not keep from laughing.

They were travelling along a very monotonous, flat and dusty stretch. In the first few hours they passed through several small, squalid hamlets. But from midday onwards, they never saw a soul. The wind blew ever stronger, stirring up the dust on the path, and the going became tougher. They were for ever brushing dust from their eyes and their faces.

Jossef became concerned that they would not find suitable cover for the night, to protect them from the wind and possibly also from the rain. A hollow in the ground would have offered them protection from the wind, but if it started to rain, they would soon have been wallowing in water, so they pressed on. As the sun sank towards the horizon, they reached a group of palm trees, which Jossef considered to be better than no protection at all, so they made camp between these trees. There was no question of lighting a fire in such a high wind, so a little hummus and water had to suffice as an evening meal. Even conversation was impossible, as they could not hear one another above the howling of the wind. They lay down and attempted to sleep, but even that was impossible due to the wind.

Towards morning, they felt the first drops of rain upon their faces, and although they knew the rain would make the going difficult, they could not help but enjoy the refreshing feeling of the cool water. After all the dust of the previous day, it was a feast for the senses. They quickly loaded up their donkeys, to prevent their mats and provisions from getting wet. While they did so, Jeshua raised his face to the sky and allowed the rain to flow over him. Soon, all seven of them were doing the same.

Although they had not slept, the travellers were feeling elated and set off at a good pace for the last day of travel to Baltim. After an hour they reached a granary with a covered forecourt. Since no one would be working here in the rain, they were able to stand under the roof and enjoy a small snack before continuing on their way. They also brought the donkeys under the roof so that their baggage did not get too wet. A strong smell wafted from the warm, steaming flanks of the wet beasts.

The rain was no longer falling quite so hard as they set off again. Jeshua jumped happily between, and sometimes in, the puddles. In the distance they could hear the hoarse calls of ibises and herons – the wet weather promised them a rich prey in their hunt for fish and crayfish. The birds were congregating in a tree on the bank like huge fruits. As the travellers passed beneath the tree, Jeshua threw a stick at them, but the stick did not even reach the bottom branches. His father put him on the donkey.

By midday, the sky was black, and it began to rain even harder. Soon they were wet through, but it was still quite warm, so they kept moving, only eating a quick snack whilst walking. Jeshua asked Merit how far they still had to go to Lake Burullus. He had to scream to make himself heard.

«We still have at least another five hours!» screamed Merit in reply, but her voice was drowned by the sounds of the wind and the rain.

Only another five hours before she was back with her parents again – what a thought! But Merit was unable to feel any real excitement, as the fear of Roman officials searching for her at her home shut out every pleasurable thought.

Since she was unable to share her fears with her friends due to the noise of the wind, her thoughts kept revolving around this subject without finding any solution to the problem. What would she do? Run away again? It was an appalling thought! And if so – where could she run to?

They reached the spot where the small river flowed into the middle fork of the Nile which would lead them directly to Lake Burullus, flowing on into the sea near Baltim. The waters of the Nile had already risen a little and were considerably rougher than they had been at Sebennytos. In spite of this, they needed to cross the Nile by ferry again. The ferry here was considerably smaller than the one in Sebennytos, so the travellers had to split up into three groups. Each group took one of the donkeys with them. Jossef also took Hemire and Jeshua, Merit took Hesire and Mariam took Hepire.

The entire procedure took three quarters of an hour, since each group had to wait until the ferry returned from the other bank. Merit felt seasick from this short crossing and became quite pale. Even though it was not cold, Mariam was shivering by the time she reached the other bank, so she walked on immediately with her donkey. The others trotted after her, and soon everyone had warmed up again.

The rain fell relentlessly all afternoon. Now, no one was interested in the landscape. They plodded on with their heads down against the rain, longing to reach their destination. The rain could surely have waited one more day!

The long procedure at the ferry meant that they were about an hour later than they had expected. It was almost dark when Merit finally shouted: « Over there in the distance is the ocean! Can you see it?»

They looked hard. Indeed, they were just about able to make out the Mediterranean Sea, shimmering in the dusk with a silvery glow.

Merit was no longer able to hold back a shout of joy, and despite her fear, she marched ahead with accelerating strides. She was nearly home, and whatever lay ahead of her, she could hardly wait to hold her parents in her arms again.

The travellers finally reached the enormous salt lake where waves were being washed through the reedbeds towards the bank. In this weather, there was not a soul about; they were all safe and dry in their houses. The travellers circled the eastern bank of the lake and saw the lamps of the little town of Baltim twinkling in the distance. Merit led the group impatiently towards her parents' house, where a light was burning in the window.

«Would you mind if I had a quick word with my parents first, please?» begged Merit. «It won't take long, then I'll come out and fetch you.»

«Of course, Merit!» exclaimed Mariam. «You have been separated from them for so long now! Take your time! A few more minutes of this rain won't make any difference to us now!»

Jossef led the donkeys over to the wall of the house and tethered them there, so that they were slightly protected. Merit knocked on the door; her heart was hammering right up to her throat. Then she entered.

Her parents were sitting in the living room. They stared at their daughter with open mouths as if they had seen a ghost. In an instant, they were in each other's arms.

«Imma, Imma!» sobbed Merit, «I've missed you so much!»

«Oh Merit, my darling, my one and all, so have I missed you!» said her mother. «You're really here! I can hardly believe it!»

After they had kissed and hugged each other for a while, Merit asked nervously: «Father, have Roman officials come here searching for me?»

«Sit down please, poppet,» said her father gravely. «Yes, there have indeed been Roman soldiers and officials here looking for you. They told us what you were accused of. We know what happened, but what we don't yet know, is where you've been!»

21

Merit was now shaking all over, but despite her fear, she had not forgotten her friends waiting outside in the rain. «Father, I haven't travelled here alone. I've been escorted by wonderful people who've given me so much support. They're now waiting outside. Can I please invite them in?»

«Of course!» exclaimed Meketre animatedly, opening the front door. «They're more than welcome! The poor things are going to be soaked through, ask them in, by all means!»

«We're all so wet, that we really can't get any wetter!» said Merit and beckoned to her friends.

«Come on in, please!» she called into the darkness, «my parents say you're most welcome!»

The travellers entered the living room, dripping all over the floor. Merit introduced each of them to her parents and said: «This is my father, Meketre, and my mother, Judith.»

They all greeted one another, then Judith went into her room and brought towels, so that the travellers could dry off a little. There was a fire burning in the hearth, and the travellers settled in a semi-circle around it, whilst Meketre began his explanation.

«Merit, it took about a month for the Roman officials to find out where you come from. It definitely wasn't the assistant in your shop who told them; he kept mum as he realised you must be in danger. But the Romans are incredibly tenacious and artful in finding out information. Anyway, they found out somehow. Maybe Lucius had even mentioned to a comrade where you came from. We had no idea anything was wrong, since we had had no deliveries to Ashkelon during that whole period, so we hadn't been in contact with your shop.»

Merit sat completely still at her father's side, with eyes wide open and hands trembling, listening tensely to her father's every word.

Meketre continued: «One day they turned up here, four of them, knocking angrily at the door and ordering us to tell them where you were! You can imagine what a shock that gave us – I believe they noticed immediately that we weren't bluffing but genuinely had no idea about anything!»

«Oh father!» interjected Merit, «I'm so sorry you had to go through that! It must have been a terrible shock for you!»

«Yes,» admitted Meketre, «it certainly was. But in a way, it was better that we hadn't heard anything. If you don't know anything, you can't tell them anything. We feared greatly for your life, as they told us you had indirectly admitted your guilt to Lucius' assassination by fleeing. They told us you would be executed without trial as soon as they found you!»

«Oh father, I thought as much!» groaned Merit, tears pouring down her cheeks. «Whatever am I going to do now?»

«Now, Meketre, don't keep her in suspense,» interrupted Judith entreatingly, «please tell her!»

«My darling, you've no longer anything to fear,» said Meketre. «Two months later, the real culprits were caught, including the woman that had been seen with them. They even tortured all those involved, in the hope that they would also testify to your guilt. But of course, they knew nothing about you, so it soon became clear that you couldn't have had anything to do with it. We only heard much later that you were no longer wanted.»

Tears of relief now poured down Merit's face, and she threw herself into her father's arms. Then she hugged her mother and sobbed loudly, her head resting on Judith's shoulder. Judith stroked her daughter's head and said: «There, there my little one! Everything's alright, you're with me now, my baby!»

«Judith,» Meketre said insistently, «I believe we ought to give these poor people some dry clothes, don't you?»

«Goodness me, of course, how right you are,» answered Judith, stroking Merit's cheek once more before detaching herself gently from her daughter's hold and going to her room.

Meketre took his daughter in his arms again and comforted her lovingly, while Judith distributed dry clothes to all. The three boys were given some clothes from Merit's brother, Moses, who now lived with his own family. Judith showed them all where they could sleep. Mariam, Jossef and Jeshua were given a guest room, while the He-He-He slept in Moses' old room. And they would not be sleeping on mats here, but on proper bedsteads with legs and thick, comfortable bedding!

It was a large house. Apparently Meketre's pottery business was doing well. Behind the house, the stable had a large, flat-roofed porch, under which Judith hung the travellers' wet clothes on a line to dry off. Jossef stabled the donkeys, and they all gathered around the fire again. The exhausted travellers sighed with relief at the comfort of being in dry clothes at the end of a long, hard day.

It was now the turn of the travellers to tell their story. Mariam gave a summary of their flight and explained the reason for it, while Judith translated for Meketre, who did not understand enough Aramaic. Meketre found it most strange that Herod should make such a thing out of a small boy who could surely be of no danger to him, but Jossef explained that he was a despotic king who had had several of his own children murdered and who would stop at nothing. And because he had heard that Jeshua was born to be King of the Jews, he had developed a real thing about it and was determined to have Jeshua killed.

«This little lad – King of the Jews?» interjected Judith. «He's just a poor boy, however could he become King?»

«That's just it,» agreed Mariam, «that's exactly what we've always said. We don't really understand it either. But the Lord, our God appears to have decided that it is to be so. In his omniscience, he will know why. We can merely accept that it is so.»

«And these three boys who are travelling with you,» said Meketre, «they're Egyptians. They're not from Israel. How do you come to be travelling with them?»

Since Merit was still not able to speak, Mariam told them how they had met the He-He-He, and when she had come to the end of her narrative, Hemire surprised them all by telling them something about their life as slaves!

«We were only small, when we were taken by the slave-traders from Kalya,» he said, «hardly able to hold a sickle. We were kept like animals, got practically nothing to eat, kept getting beaten. We wished we were dead. It was awful. These people here are the first ones in all our lives who've treated us kindly.»

Mariam's eyes welled up with tears since she knew how hard Hemire found it to converse. This sad little account of a life filled with suffering summarized an existence lacking all hope or perspective. At that moment, Mariam was so glad she and Merit had had the courage to stand up for the boys.

«That's terrible,» concurred Meketre. «Slavery is now more widespread in Egypt than it has been for a long time! Mind you, particularly in the country, people have become so poor and fettered by these severe poll taxes, that they now all live like slaves. The poll tax was only introduced twenty years ago. Those living in the country must pay the full poll tax, which amounts to a whole monthly wage per year! Here in town, we only have to pay a reduced tax, and Romans, Greeks and priests are all completely exempt from tax. Incidentally: Jews are also exempt, which means they're often plagued by Egyptians out of spite and envy. My Judith and I could tell you a tale or two!

Life in Egypt under Roman rule is not as good as many think, although the Romans have a real craze for everything Egyptian. Apparently, they've erected obelisks in Rome decorated with hieroglyphs, and the people copy our fashions. But here, they keep us under their thumb and they're bleeding our country for all it's worth. Our entire grain crops are being shipped to Rome. I've heard that 135,000 tons of grain are being exported to Rome every year; that's a third of what the population of Rome consumes! It's a disgrace. And all this thanks to the hard labour of such slaves as these boys here. By the way, what are your names, boys?»

The He-He-He told Meketre their names.

«Well, Hemire, Hesire und Hepire, I don't need to tell you what it's like, do I?»

The three boys shook their heads silently but energetically.

«However, I must say I can't complain, » continued Meketre. «My business is doing well. Everyone always needs pots and ceramic goods.»

«And where do you get your clay from?» asked Jossef with interest. «Can you find your raw materials here easily?»

«Oh yes, and how!» exclaimed Meketre in his sonorous bass voice. «You see, as soon as the floods start to sink around October, there's wonderful clay to be found in the residual silt! We just have to help ourselves. That's why pottery is the ideal profession in these parts, it's very lucrative. Why don't you come over to my workshop tomorrow or the next day and take a look around! I hope you'll be staying here a while?»

«We don't want to become a burden,» answered Mariam politely, «but Merit did suggest that we could stay with you for a while. So if that's really alright by you …»

«It most certainly is, isn't it, Judith?» exclaimed Meketre passionately, «You've brought my girl safely home all the way from Ashkelon, so that's the very least we can do, and it's a pleasure to have you here!»

«Yes, absolutely!» agreed Judith. «Please stay as long as you like. We'd be thrilled, honestly!»

Merit smiled at Mariam and Jossef, pleased to hear her own words confirmed. She was honestly relieved that her friends could stay with her for a little longer, particularly Jeshua.

Thus, the matter was decided. Judith served everyone a nourishing vegetable soup, together with freshly baked, warm flatbread which smelt most appetizing, and a sweet new wine.

«*Better a small serving of vegetables with love than a fattened calf with hatred!* [19]» Judith quoted, as she placed the dishes on the table.

Merit grinned. Her mother loved to quote from the Book of Proverbs at every possible opportunity.

They sat cosily in the warm living room, while the rain pattered on the roof. The warmth and the

---

[19] Proverbs 15, 17

feeling of security relaxed the travellers, who were soon fighting to keep their eyes open.

As soon as they had finished their meal, they said goodnight to Meketre and Judith, going straight off to bed and sleeping immediately.

22

Next day, no one felt like doing much. Meketre went to his workshop, and the others just lazed around the house. Judith washed the still damp clothes and hung them up on the line again. She refused Mariam's help, telling her to rest like the others. The rest was indeed doing their tired limbs a world of good, as the long march in wet clothes had made their joints ache.

Jossef had noticed the previous evening that Mariam's donkey had gone slightly lame, so that also made it a good idea to remain in Baltim for a while. Jossef made a compress for the donkey's leg and fed it a few treats for comfort.

In the afternoon, while Mariam was sorting out their possessions and putting them away in a cupboard, Jeshua came and sat on Merit's lap. The pattering of rain on the roof was now very loud, and it was almost as dark as night.

«Merit, will you please tell me more about the Egyptians' realm of the dead?» he begged. «Will you tell me about Ka and Ba and all the other parts of the soul?»

«Oh, you've remembered that very well, bravo Jeshua!» Merit praised him. «It's like this: Ka returns to the dead body every night. Ka is a person's life force. Ka tries to reach Earu, the afterworld, and whenever it becomes too strenuous, the food in the grave is there to help him. Tiny Ushebti figures are also placed with the mummy to help Ka reach Earu.

But more importantly, the name of the deceased has to be written on the coffin, as Ka can't reach Earu without a name. On no account does Ka want to land in hell, because it's miserable there, except during the hours when the sun passes through the under-world on its night-time journey. Egyptians are ex-tremely afraid of death; that's why they've thought all this out. There's also a book with detailed instruc-tion on how Ka is to reach Earu. It's called the 'Book of the Dead' and gets buried together with the corpse, because dead people can't remember these things so well!

But all these things are only carried out for the dead bodies of people in high positions, such as phar-aohs and priests, since poor people can't afford them.»

Jeshua laughed. «Why do the Egyptians believe all these things, Merit?» he asked.

Merit thought for a while, then she said: «Well, the Egyptians have a god named Osiris. He was the brother and the husband of the goddess Isis. Osiris had a brother named Seth, who was envious of Osiris because he was so handsome and clever, and be-cause Isis loved him. So Seth killed his brother Osiris and cut him up into 14 parts. Isis was sad and wanted to bring him back to life, because she couldn't live without him ...»

Merit's voice failed her, as she was aware of her own desperate wish to bring her beloved Lucius back to life. Tears welled up in her eyes, but Jeshua demanded her to go on: «And what happened next, Merit? Could she bring him back to life?»

Merit pulled herself together and continued: «Yes, she could, because she was a goddess. She heard that she only needed to collect the 14 parts and put them back together for Osiris to come back to life, and that's just what happened! She was able to collect all parts but one, and Osiris came back to life.»

«Great!» rejoiced Jeshua. «And did they live happily to the end of their days?»

«They lived happily ever after, Jeshua, for they were god and goddess,» answered Merit, «and this fact, the fact that Osiris was brought back to life, is the reason why the Egyptians believe they'll also rise to new life, since they also believe there's a divine part of the human soul. That's the part which is called Ach. Would you like to hear an Egyptian song about death, Jeshua?»

Jeshua always wanted to hear a song, so Merit began to sind:

«The west is a land of sleep,
of dense darkness,
the home of those who lie there,
sleeping in coffins.

Concerning death, her name is: Come!
All who are called to her,
Come straight to her.
Their hearts quake for fear of her.»

Jeshua was so quiet on Merit's lap that she though he must have fallen asleep. But then he said:

«Merit, I'm glad I'm not an Egyptian!» and Merit had to laugh.

«Yes, Jeshua, I'm also glad I'm of Jewish descent like you, and that I believe in our God! The Egyptian gods have always to be placated with magic formulas and rituals. Wouldn't that be tiresome?»

«Yes,» agreed Jeshua. «But do you know any other stories, Merit?»

«I know a myth, but I'll tell you that another time, because I'm tired now and I need to lie down for a while.»

«I'm tired too,» said Jeshua. «Can I come and lie down with you?»

«Of course,» said Merit, gratefully taking Jeshua by the hand and disappearing into her room. She clasped the child to her and felt his special power driving out her grief for Lucius. Slowly, she relaxed, and the two of them dozed off until Judith called them to supper.

Although they had hardly done a thing all day, the travellers went to bed early and once again slept deeply until well into the morning.

They awoke refreshed, and finally felt ready for new ventures, so they decided to go with Meketre to the workshop and see his pottery being made, donning thick capes of untreated wool over their clothes against the rain. They hurried through the wet streets to the potters' workshop, a long brick building with a flat roof and a high brick chimney for the kiln. They entered the workshop through wide double doors. Inside, there was a grey, earthy smell – the smell of wet clay, which was being thrown by the potters on wheels distributed throughout the room. Pots were being produced by the minute and placed on long racks to dry, from whence other workers carried them on large boards to the kiln.

There was an amazing transformation in the He-He-He, as soon as they entered the workshop! Within seconds these dull fellows had turned into alert, interested young men with a light in their eyes that no one had ever seen there before. Hemire and Hesire went from one potter to another, watching how the edges of the pots were pulled up with a finger, while Hepire followed the men carrying the boards of dried pots to the kiln and watched them slide them in.

Meketre was aware of this transformation and watched the boys closely, but he did not say anything. He showed the group everything in the workshop including the storage room for wet clay, where the smell was even stronger. Jeshua wrinkled his nose and sniffed at the strange smell.

«Smells funny!» he commented.

«Yes,» said Meketre, «that's an unusual smell, isn't it, lad? I don't suppose you've smelt that before, have you?»

«No,» said Jeshua, «It's not bad!»

«For me, it's the best smell in the world!» gushed Meketre, who was a potter with his whole heart and soul.

Hemire sidled over nervously. «Meketre, how d'you become a potter?» he asked shyly.

«In my workshop, you can do an apprenticeship for half a year. After that you're a potter,» replied Meketre. «Why do you ask? Are you interested in becoming a potter, Hemire?»

«I think so, yeah,» he answered. Meketre did not push the point, leaving Hemire time to feel the wish growing inside him. Hemire returned to his brothers and told them what Meketre had said.

Meketre winked at Jossef. «I think I may have found three potential potters,» he said.

Jossef raised his brows and smiled. «That wouldn't be at all bad,» he said pensively.

The day passed quickly at the workshop. They were all fascinated by the processes being demonstrated. Merit felt proud of her father and the family business, in which she had played an important part with her little shop in Ashkelon.

«Now you know where my workshop is,» said Meketre, before they returned home, «you can look in any time you like. Jeshua, here's something for you! A lump of clay for you to make something out of, when we get back to the house.»

«Thank you, Meketre!» gasped Jeshua, thrilled, and he kept smelling the clay all the way back to the house.

Once they were home, Meketre showed Jeshua that he needed to keep wetting the clay to be able to mold it. It turned out to be more fun making the clay so wet that his hands became completely grey and slushy, like the potters in the workshop. He held up his grey hands towards his mother who threw up her hands in mock horror and shouted: «Eeew!» Jeshua laughed cheekily.

He formed a little sparrow from the wet clay, like the one he had made with the son of the wood-carver in Belbeis. But it was easier with clay, and you didn't have a sharp knife-edge to be careful of.

Meketre thought Jeshua had a talent for using his hands, and Jossef agreed that his son would make a good craftsman some day.

«If he has time, next to his day-job as King of the Jews!» said Meketre with a wink, and Mariam laughed.

That evening they all stayed up late, telling stories of their life and work. The He-He-He stayed up even later, and while Mariam and Jossef were putting Jeshua to bed, Hemire wanted to know when they could start their apprenticeship with Meketre. All three of them were serious about this. Hemire and Hesire said they wanted to become potters, and Hepire said he would like to learn to tend the kiln.

«Oh, I'm very pleased to hear that! You can start tomorrow morning,» said Meketre, «but in an apprenticeship, you learn everything, from pottery to firing and in November, how to extract the clay from the ground and transport it back here. If you exert yourselves during the apprenticeship and if you're attentive, you'll be trained potters in half a year. Then you can have a job here, or anywhere else you wish to work.»

Never had the three boys smiled so broadly!

23

Yet another boring rainy day made Jeshua into a very bad-tempered boy by the evening. Nothing suited him, and he threw a proper tantrum, which was something he seldom did.

«Come here, Jeshua! I've yet to tell you the myth of the two brothers I promised you,» suggested Merit.

Jeshua instantly lost his grumpy expression, beaming at Merit and climbing onto her lap to listen.

«But afterwards you must go to sleep like a good boy,» said Merit, before she began her story. «Once upon a time there were two brothers ... – you don't know what that's like yet, do you, Jeshua, not having a little brother yourself!» Merit gave Mariam and Jossef a cheeky, meaningful look, and they laughed at the obvious jibe. «Anyway, where was I? Ah yes, one of the brothers was named 'Truth' and the other's name was 'Falsehood'. Falsehood was jealous of Truth, because Truth was handsome and clever, whereas Falsehood was ugly and mean.

So Falsehood dragged his brother before the divine court under the accusation that Truth had not returned a knife that had been leant to him. The blade of this knife, said Falsehood, was Jal Mountain, the handle was the Trees of Koptos and the sheath was the Tomb of the Gods. Of course, Truth was unable to produce such a knife, so at Falsehood's request, the divine court demanded that Truth be blinded in both eyes and set to work as the gatekeeper at Falsehood's house.

One day, the beautiful Princess Charity was out walking and caught sight of the blind gatekeeper Truth, in front of Falsehood's house. Charity longed for Truth, as he was still a handsome man. She had her servants bring him to her own house and made him her own gatekeeper. That night, Charity lay with Truth, and after a while, a son was born to them, who was also handsome and very clever. The son eventually wished to know who his father was. Charity explained that he was the blind gatekeeper at her door.

Her son became angry and shouted: ‹May the crocodile take your whole family!› He had good food brought to his father and had a house built for him. Then he swore revenge for his father.

‹Who had you blinded?› the son wanted to know of his father.

‹My younger brother, Falsehood, did that,› explained Truth and told his son the whole unpleasant story.

The son found a bull with a beautiful coat of a special colour, brought the bull to Falsehood's cowherd, and asked him to take care of the bull until he returned.

While the son was gone, Falsehood came and asked his cowherd for the beautifully coloured bull. First of all, the cowherd did not want to give him the bull, but Falsehood told him: ‹You've got so many bulls, so just give me this one!› And thus Falsehood gained possession of the bull.

When the son returned and asked for his bull, the cowherd offered him any of his bulls, but explained that that particular bull had been taken by Falsehood.

The son dragged Falsehood before the divine court under the accusation that he had stolen a bull from him which was so large that when it was standing on Amon's meadow, one horn lay upon the western mountains and the other horn upon the eastern mountains. The great river was his resting place, and he sired 60 calves every day.

The gods discussed the case and came to the verdict that no such bull could possibly exist. The youth then said to the gods: ‹Is there a knife whose blade is Jal Mountain, whose handle is the Trees of Koptos and whose sheath is the Tomb of the Gods? Now judge between Truth and Falsehood. I am Truth's son, and I have come to claim revenge.›

So Falsehood was blinded in both eyes and was made gatekeeper at Truth's house. Thus, the youth revenged his father, and the argument between Truth and Falsehood was resolved.

At the end of the story, as in all Egyptian myths, they say: it has come to a good end.»

«But I don't think that's at all good!» exclaimed Jeshua. «At the end, they're both blind!»

«Yes, of course, you're right there, Jeshua. But doesn't it remind you of another story I've told you?» asked Merit softly.

«The story of Osiris and Seth. But in that story, at least Osiris could be brought back to life. Why couldn't Truth get his sight back again?»

«That would indeed have been an even better ending to the story, you're right. But this story is very old and has been told just this way down the ages. I'm afraid we Egyptians are a rather vengeful people! Aren't you tired, Jeshua? Will you go to bed now?»

«Bit tired,» said the boy, his eyes drooping almost shut. «Merit, if I go to bed now, will you sing me a lullaby?»

Merit picked up the tired little boy and carried him to his bed. She tucked him in, stroked his black curls, and sang him an ancient Egyptian lullaby:

«Heaven has carried the night,
heaven has born the night.
The night belongs to her mother.
Mine is the ease of health.

Night, give me peace,
and I will give you peace.
Night, let me rest,
And I will let you rest.»

Jeshua was already fast asleep as Merit sang the last note. She looked down at the child, and tears welled up in her eyes. Soon she would have to say goodbye to Jeshua forever. Would she ever have a child of her own? As she went to her room and climbed into bed, she thought of all that might have been with Lucius. Then she cried herself to sleep.

24

After a week of continuous rain, there followed a few days when the rain eased off a little. Merit, Mariam, Jossef and Jeshua took advantage of these days to ride out to the lake on their donkeys. The lake was enormous. In the far distance, a narrow, white strip of land could be seen, separating the lake from the sea, with a gap through which the sea flowed in and out, giving the lake its salt and tides. It was very similar to the Serbonian Salt Lake they had seen at the beginning of their journey.

The lake was shallow. Most of the banks were bordered by reed beds with many different birds, such as ducks with rust-red heads and grey backs, moorhens and lapwings, and both grey and white herons, all on the lookout for food.

The lake contained a number of islands. Upon one of these islands, there was an imposing Egyptian temple surrounded by large cedar trees. As they gazed at it, the sun broke briefly through the clouds, bathing the yellow walls of the temple in light.

They came to a wide sandy beach. Solitary fishermen were standing near the water's edge with nets. From time to time, the circular nets were thrown with an elegant sweep, landing flat upon the surface of the water. They allowed the nets to sink, gathering them up again and pulling the fish to the shore. Jeshua stood for a long time next to the fishermen, watching the simple but efficient method of fishing with fascination.

Other fishermen were out on the lake in flat-bottomed sailing boats from which they cast their nets. Both fishing methods appeared to be equally effective.

These days out and about in the fresh air were just what they needed after a full week of recovery, as their bodies had become used to permanent activity during their months of travel. Mariam's donkey's leg had also had time to heal during the week of rest, and the donkey trotted along happily with the others. After these outings, they all felt more balanced and calm, also sleeping better at night.

Then the rain started again, and they were once more restricted to the house and to the town. Merit and Judith showed their visitors all the sights the little town had to offer, but that was soon accomplished. After this, they had all the time in the world for talking, discussing the scriptures, politics, and philosophy. Judith told them about life as a Jew in Egypt, which was not always easy, and how she had met Meketre in Ashkelon twenty years previously and come with him to live in Baltim.

One evening, they got to talking about the future and how long the visitors would stay in Baltim. The He-He-He had undergone quite a transformation during their pottery apprenticeship. They were now quite self-confident young men and able to take part in a conversation.

«Do you three want to stay here?» Meketre asked them. «I can certainly employ you in my workshop if you wish.»

«It's great here, and on the one hand, I can well imagine staying here» commented Hemire.

«On the other hand,» continued Hepire, «you originally talked of taking us home, Jossef. We've not forgotten that.»

«Yes,» interjected Hesire, «we've been thinking it might be possible to establish a pottery in our village. But our big worry would be: Where would we get the clay from? It's very dry there. We have no silt, from which we could extract clay.»

«Listen,» answered Meketre, «You won't only find clay in the silt of the Nile delta. Clay may also be available where you live – you just need a reliable supply of water to create clay from the sandy soil. I'll show you how you can test your soil to see if it's suitable for clay ...» and the three apprentice potters put their heads together with Meketre, to learn all the details of clay testing. When Meketre heard that their home village was west of Wadi Natrun, he also suggested the lads should visit the glass factory near Baltim harbour, as it might be possible to produce glass with quarz and sand in Kalya, using salt from Wadi Natrun.

«When you're in Wadi Natrun, you must speak to the glass manufacturers, as there as several factories there!» suggested Meketre in conclusion. «And don't forget to pick up some salt while you're there – you too, Jossef – as salt is always a good means of exchange, especially in areas that don't have that precious commodity themselves.»

«On the subject of exchange,» said Jossef, «do you know where I can exchange my one remaining *aureus* into sesterces, Meketre?»

«Ah, now, you'd better go and see Senenmut. He also lives near Baltim harbour. He's a friend of mine. Give him my regards, and he'll give you a good exchange rate!»

«It's good to have friends!» said Jossef with a smile and a wink. «Thanks, Meketre, I'll do that.»

«As long as the rain's not too heavy tomorrow, we could all ride over to the harbour,» suggested Meketre. «We can kill three birds with one stone, because you can visit the glazier, and I can also show you our ship, with which we deliver our goods to Mediterranean harbours, Ashkelon being one of them.»

They all agreed that this was a good plan. The weather was indeed fairly bright the next day. As Meketre decided to look on the outing as part of the He-He-He's apprenticeship, it was no problem for them to be away from the workshop for the day. Merit decided to come too.

They had not seen such a large harbour since leaving Ashkelon. It was busy, the traffic was impressive, and soon their heads were swimming from the hullabaloo caused by sailors, traders and fishermen.

Meketre showed Jossef where to find Senenmut and explained how he could get from there to the glazier's workshop. Jossef did indeed get a very good exchange rate for his *aureus*, undoubtedly thanks to Meketre's greeting!

Afterwards he joined the others at the glazier's workshop, where the foreman was proudly showing the group around and describing all the processes. The glaziers produced an incredibly wide selection of products, from milk-glass windows for the baths in Alexandria to beautifully decorated vases, drinking glasses, plates, and small items of jewellery. The foreman explained how the different colours were created using various minerals. The He-He-He showed a particular interest in all the processes and asked intelligent questions about them. Jeshua and Jossef were also interested listeners, but the foreman soon noticed that Mariam was only showing a perfunctory interest in the work and obviously becoming bored. At the end of the tour, he gave Mariam and Merit a small gift each of a pretty little brooch in the form of a lizard, made of green glass with a red eye. «For your patience!» he said with a smile, and they thanked him warmly.

They returned to the harbour, where Meketre invited them to board his magnificent white ship. Prow and stern were both elevated in typical Egyptian style. The name of the ship, 'Naunet' – primordial waters – was painted in red on one side of the prow in demotic[20] script, and on the other side in Latin.

Merit stayed safely on the quayside, looking up and waving to them. «I feel much happier on firm ground!» she called merrily.

---

[20] A more recent Egyptian script than hieroglyphs, used for mundane texts

Jeshua asked Meketre whether they could go for a trip on the sea, but Meketre's crew were not in Baltim at present. «They'll be back about a week before they're due to set sail for the next Mediterranean trip – then we can see whether they have time to take you all out before they leave!» answered Meketre.

It had been another eventful day, and they had learnt a lot, particularly the He-He-He.

The following day the rain started again, meaning many more days in and around the house and town, and plenty of time to talk politics, to plan the future and to philosophise. They had now been in Baltim for a month. The rainy season would last another two and a half months, during which there was no question of setting out on their journey again, as their route would still be under water. Mariam and Jossef therefore decided to wait until the He-He-He had finished their apprenticeship before setting off again, as the three boys had decided they would indeed attempt to start their own pottery in Kalya. It had become important to Mariam and Jossef to bring the three boys safely home, as they had both come to feel responsible for them. Those three were still so young, and although they had developed greatly in character and as craftsmen, they would hardly be able to deal with the problems and dangers of such a journey on their own.

Meketre considered that the three apprentices would already be able to take their test at the end of December as had they shown great promise as potters. After the rainy season had ended, Mariam, Jossef and Jeshua would only need to wait one more month in Baltim before setting off on the next leg of their journey. They all agreed that this would be a good solution. Life with Meketre and Judith was extremely pleasant, but Mariam and Jossef could not impose upon them indefinitely.

Merit, for her part, was only too pleased that her dear friends, and most particularly Jeshua, would stay with them for another few months.

25

By the end of October, the rainfall slowly began to ease off. A great deal of rain had fallen, and the Nile delta was under deep water. The floods would once again ensure a rich crop this year. Mariam and Jossef were glad they had decided not to leave until January, as the ground was still very soggy.

Jossef also sometimes helped out at the pottery by carrying dried pots to the oven, bringing the potters their clay and other small unskilled tasks, as he had become heartily bored around the house. Mariam helped Judith and Merit with housework, but Merit was often in the shop, selling the goods from their workshop. Baltim town market did not reopen until January, and there was not even much business in the shop during the rainy season. However, it gave Merit a change.

During the months spent in Baltim, Mariam and Merit had taught Jeshua to read. Mariam had recited the well-loved passages from the Torah and the Psalms to him, and Merit had told Jeshua further myths and legends of ancient Egypt; she also taught him a few words of Latin. In Judith's presence, Jeshua automatically learned quite a few verses from the Book of Proverbs! In Spring, he would be two years old. For his age, he was extremely advanced and was proving to be a really gifted child.

One day, Jeshua asked his mother why they were in Egypt. Mariam had long expected this question and considered what would be her reply.

So she said: «Well it's like this, Jeshua: When we left Judaea for Egypt, some very nasty people were trying to hurt us. They wanted to hurt Merit too, that's why we all fled from Israel together.»

«Why did they want to hurt us, Imma?» asked Jeshua, astonished. «We didn't do anything to hurt them?.»

«No, Jeshua, of course we didn't. But some people do evil things because they're afraid, or because they're envious.»

Jeshua glanced over to Merit. «Like Falsehood in the myth, and like Seth who killed Osiris?» he asked her.

Merit came over and sat with Mariam and Jeshua. «Exactly, Jeshua,» she replied. «For you it was exactly like that. For me, it was a little different.»

«How was it for you?» Jeshua asked Merit.

«The Romans in Ashkelon believed I had killed one of them,» she said quietly.

Jeshua opened his eyes wide and shook his head vigorously. «No,» he said, «you could never do that, kill someone. You're a good person!»

«Thank you, Jeshua,» said Merit, «and you're quite right, but these Romans didn't know me, so they couldn't know that.»

«I'm glad we all ran away together,» said Jeshua, «otherwise I wouldn't have got to know you, Merit!»

«Oh, you little darling!» exclaimed Merit, lifting Jeshua onto her lap and hugging him. «I also think it's very, very good that we got to know each other!»

For the time being, that was enough. Jeshua would be sure to want to know more, but first he needed time to assimilate this new information.

Soon, a number of employees of the pottery would be setting off to dig clay out of the Nile silt and bring it back to Baltim. Meketre explained the process to the He-He-He. In Kalya, they would be using a different procedure, but there was no harm in also learning this method in case their future turned out differently. Jossef decided to accompany them, as he was interested to see with his own eyes how clay was extracted from the silt of the Nile.

At the end of November, Meketre considered the time to be ripe for the silt to have the right consistency. The oxen were put to the huge ox cart, Meketre divided his men into three groups, and these groups took their place on the platform of the cart.

Jeshua had been watching the preparations and begged Meketre to be allowed to go with them. This time, though, Meketre stood firm.

«No, Jeshua, I'm sorry, but it's far too dangerous! We'll all be so busy that we won't be able to look after you. This time you must stay at home.»

«But I can look after myself!» begged Jeshua.

«No, Jeshua, it's not possible!» said Meketre in a resolute voice. Jeshua pouted and watched sadly as his father climbed onto the platform and joined Hesire's group. The heavy vehicle rumbled off. The women stood with Jeshua at the entrance to the stable and waved to the men, as the cart disappeared round the corner in the direction of the Nile.

Meketre and his men took four days to extract enough clay for the coming year. They lodged at a guesthouse near the Nile and started work early every morning. Working only in loincloths and standing up to their knees in silt, they soon looked like living tin soldiers, covered from head to toe in grey, slippery clay! The work was extremely hard. For this reason, they always took a long lunch break, as they would not otherwise have been able to last the four days.

Meketre demonstrated the technique with the special digging tools, much like peat cutters, for the four new men. The process was quite similar to peat digging, but far more laborious, as the substance was so much heavier, wetter and stickier.

While he worked, Meketre also kept an eye on the new men to see that they had understood the process, sometimes intervening to correct them.

The lumps of clay which had already been extracted were placed on a tarpaulin, then Meketre called his men to lunch.

They all went down to the riverbank, jumping merrily into the water and washing the sticky, grey-green clay from their bodies. The relief of having a three-hour break put them all into high spirits. They joked, exchanged banter, and pushed each other into the river like children. As soon as they had dried off and put their clothes back on, Meketre conjured up a meal of pasties and a large bowl of hummus. There was ample water to drink, to rehydrate their bodies after all the hard sweat. The men found a comfortable spot under the palm trees on the bank of the river and immediately fell into an exhausted sleep, while Meketre kept watch.

When the three hours were up, he woke his men, who stripped again, donning the loincloths which had meantime dried in the sun, and returned to work for a further four hours.

Four days later, they had extracted enough clay for the coming year. The piled-up lumps of clay were placed on tarpaulins on the platform of the cart, covered with further tarpaulins and secured with ropes.

After one last bathe in the Nile, the men dressed for the journey home. Tired as they were, they had to walk the whole distance back to Baltim, as the platform was now full of clay. Each man carried his clay digger over his shoulder.

They arrived in the late evening. As soon as they had finished the nourishing meal Judith had prepared for them, they fell onto their beds and slept, happy in the knowledge that they would now have three days off as a reward for all their hard work.

26

The feast of Chanukka was a joyful celebration in Meketre and Judith's house. Every evening, Judith lit one more candle of the Chanukkia[21], and even Meketre, who had a very laid-back attitude to all things religious, joined in the celebrations for his wife's sake. The light spread a warm, homely atmosphere, and everyone was relaxed and happy, including the He-He-He, although the boys remained in the background during the celebration, since the Jewish religion was alien to them.

After Chanukka the weather was dry and sunny, and the wind picked up. Meketre announced that the crew of his ship were back and preparing the 'Naunet' for the Mediterranean trip in about a week's time so, if they felt like it, they could now consider going for that pleasure trip. Did they ever feel like it! Jeshua could hardly contain his excitement, but he could not understand why Merit did not wish to come too.

«You see, Jeshua,» she explained, «I get really sick on ships. And you don't want me to feel bad, do you?»

Obviously, Jeshua did not want that, but he found it rather lame that someone could have anything against a journey on a ship, even though he had never been on a ship himself. From the outset, he was quite convinced he would have good sea legs.

---

[21] Candelabra for Chanukka

On the day of the pleasure trip, the family went on board, including the He-He-He who had been granted a day off to come too. The sailors cast off and rowed out of the harbour. As soon as the ship was on the open sea, they hoisted the red sails with an eye painted on them, the canvas flapping loudly in the fair wind. The ship gathered way and seemed to fly before the wind. Jeshua shrieked louder than the seagulls overhead, ran to the stern and watched the backwash foaming aft in a great V-shape. A real adventure – at last, after so many weeks of idleness!

As Jeshua had sensed from the start, the swell had no bad effect upon either himself or his parents. They thoroughly enjoyed the exciting trip along the coast. But the He-He-He held fast to the railing, looking quite sick. Far to the west, Meketre pointed to a large city with magnificent white buildings.

«That's Alexandria over there!» he called above the noise of the sea and the wind. «Ever since the time of the Ptolemy[22], it's been the most magnificent town in Egypt!»

They all went to the portside of the prow and looked with awe at the town, which became more and more distinct as they came nearer. They saw the lighthouse at the harbour entrance, the island of Pharos which lay before the town, the town walls, several tall obelisks, and the Gate of the Sun to the east of the town. When the ship was lying directly before the town, the family were amazed to see that the streets

---

[22] The last Egyptian-Hellenistic dynasty before Roman rule

were all arranged perpendicularly to each other in a grid.

«The town used to be named Rhakotis, but it was far smaller in those days, only taking up the western part of today's town. Alexander had the old town demolished and designed this new town according to the Greek ideal. See that temple over there with the Grecian columns? And that palace, and behind it the Academy of the Arts? Impressive, aren't they? Alexander transported the obelisks from Heliopolis, and he also built an Isis Temple to gain favour with the Egyptians. He was a cunning man!»

The sailors brought the ship about and sailed upwind, gathering way for the home port. To Jeshua's mind, the trip had been all too short, but the He-He-He were rather glad to disembark and feel firm ground under their feet again. Jeshua laughed and fooled around, as the firm ground now felt as though it were rocking beneath his feet!

When they arrived home, Jeshua told Merit and Judith all about their day. He was over-excited, and they had to listen to everything three or four times!

«Right, time to eat,» said Judith, «Sit down and stop fidgeting, Jeshua! *When words are many, sin is unavoidable, but he who restrains his lips is wise!* [23]»

The sea air had given them all an appetite, and they served themselves large portions of Judith's nourishing pigeon stuffed with green wheat. After the meal, those who had been on the sea required a

---

[23] Proverbs 10, 19

short nap, having become sleepy from the fresh air and the many new impressions.

Towards evening, Jossef turned the conversation towards the right time for their departure. He sat together with Meketre and the He-He-He to make plans. They would require one week just to reach Wadi Natrun, and another day from there to Kalya. Meketre sketched on a piece of papyrus the approximate route they would need to take.

The He-He-He told them that their village was an oasis in the Libyan desert, but that the road to it was difficult, as it was hot and sandy. Meketre added that Kalya was on the border between the Sketis desert and the Libyan desert, which was an eastern extension of the Sahara. Since the path from Wadi Natrun to Kalya would prove to be so hot, he recommended they travel at night. However, it would mean timing their journey so that they could use a full moon for this stretch. They decided to depart one week before the January full moon. Meketre passed his sketch to Jossef, who thanked him and rolled it up.

The remaining week went by too quickly for Merit's liking. Mariam was already sorting through their few possessions and preparing for the journey.

At the end of December, the He-He-He passed their final apprenticeship test with flying colours. Meketre organised a small celebration in the workshop, to which he invited a few of his friends. The celebration was both for the three boys' successful test and also served as a farewell party for these friends he had come to hold so dear.

Meketre, Judith and Merit put on their finest clothes. The travellers had no fine clothes, so Judith saw to it that each one of them was given good clothes from their wardrobe. Mariam wore one of Merit's dresses in deep burgundy red, and Jossef was given a robe of Merit's brother Moses to wear. The He-He-He looked quite noble in girded tunics of fine linen out of Moses' coffer. Merit wore a white dress with a red floral print which hugged her figure, becoming fuller towards the ground and with only one shoulder strap. The other shoulder was bare. She looked stunning; it was a crying shame that Lucius could not see her now!

Meketre gave a speech, praising the diligence of his three apprentices, not forgetting to thank Jossef for his assistance, and wishing them all the best for their future.

«We've found true friends in you, and we're going to miss you very much!» he concluded and embraced each one of them with genuine warmth.

Jossef also thanked their host and his wife for the wonderful time they had had with them, and even the He-He-He gave a short speech. A very pleasant period of security, friendship and peace was slowly coming to an end, and they were all feeling a little melancholy. Only Jeshua had not yet realised the full consequence of this.

***

On the day of departure, Jossef fetched the donkeys from the stable and loaded their baggage onto them. Meketre called the He-He-He to come with him to the stable, where he showed them a mule already loaded for the journey with potter's tools. He explained that this was his parting gift to them, as they had worked only for board and lodging and had done a very good job.

Tears welled up in the eyes of all three boys and they embraced their master affectionately.

«That's the first present we've ever been given in our whole life! Thank you, Meketre, we appreciate it more than we can say!» said Hemire, his voice husky with emotion. Hesire and Hepire just nodded, as they were too emotional to speak.

They all found parting difficult, but as they began to take their leave of Merit, Jeshua looked up at them in confusion.

«But Merit's coming with us, isn't she?» he asked. «She's always been with us!»

Mariam squatted down in front of her son and said: «Not this time, my darling. Merit's staying here, it's her home; whereas we have to travel on.»

«No!» shouted Jeshua desperately. «Merit's got to come too! Merit belongs to us!»

Merit hugged Jeshua. The tears poured down her cheeks and into his curls. «Oh Jeshua! I'm so sorry we have to part. But I'm afraid it's true. I'm staying here with my parents.»

«Merit, please come with us, at least as far as the village where the He-He-He live ...» begged Jeshua, and his voice broke on a sob.

«Jeshua,» said Jossef gently, «I'm afraid that's not possible, or else Merit would have to come all the way back to Baltim on her own. That would be far too dangerous for her.»

Jeshua sobbed desperately and was quite beyond comfort. Mariam and Jossef embraced Merit, Meketre and Judith, wishing them farewell, but Jeshua turned his face away when Judith tried to embrace him. «I want Merit!» he screamed and did not stop screaming, even as his father placed him on the donkey and the little group moved off on the next stage of their journey, with the He-He-He and their mule following behind.

Meketre, Judith and Merit stood in front of the house, watching the travellers as they marched off, becoming ever smaller in the distance. Merit saw Jeshua turn round on his donkey and stretch out his arms towards her, still screaming. She also felt like screaming – it almost broke her heart.

27

On the first day of their journey, they circled the south bank of Lake Burullus, which only served to remind Jeshua of all the places they had visited with Merit on their carefree outings over the last few months. He sat huddled in silence on his donkey, crying now and then when things reminded him of her.

Jeshua was learning for the first time in his two years on earth that the loss of a beloved person was part of life, and he was struggling with this fact. Mariam saw his pain and blamed herself for not having better prepared him for parting from Merit. But if she was honest with herself, she had really thought he had long since understood that Merit would not be travelling on with them anymore. Ah well, it was too late now, the damage was done.

The He-He-He made repeated, touching efforts to distract Jeshua by means of games or jests, but not once were their efforts successful, so in the end they gave up. Nevertheless, as they set up camp in the evening on the bank of the lake and Jossef lit a fire, Jeshua went and sat silently with the boys. Mariam noticed this and let him stay with them while she cooked supper, hoping he would come over and join her for the meal.

But Hesire stepped up to the fire to collect his portion and also carried a portion back for Jeshua, who thanked him briefly and ate his supper silently and listlessly sitting beside the boys. A tear wandered down his cheek whenever he thought of Merit.

Mariam rubbed her face with her hands and said to Jossef: «Our poor little Jeshua! I'm worried. We should have handled that better!»

«Yes, I agree. He really is a poor lad!» agreed Jossef. «But I believe time will heal. We must be patient with him. He'll sort himself out, Mariam! He's a strong child, I'm sure he'll cope!»

Jossef laid his arm around Mariam's shoulder, pulled her gently to him and lovingly kissed her forehead. «Don't despair, love!» he said. «The Lord will help him, and us too.»

Mariam nodded, gazed into the fire and sighed deeply. For the first time, she found the burden of responsibility for her child hard to bear, because a small rift had occurred between herself and Jeshua. She loved him more than her own life, but she did not know how to heal this rift and restore the previous bond between them. Then she thought: Jossef's right, I've got to be patient, I mustn't try to force anything, hard as that is.

When they lay down to sleep, Jeshua stayed with the He-He-He. Mariam snuggled up to Jossef and allowed her tears to flow freely.

***

At daybreak they set off again after a light breakfast. First of all, they needed provisions. They continued along the south bank of the lake until they reached a small village, where Mariam asked a farmer for water and food. Jeshua immediately asked Jossef for a drink, but Jossef told him to be patient. Jeshua stamped his little foot, screaming loudly and throwing a proper tantrum. The farmer, who had not intended to help the family anyway, angrily sent them packing. Jossef put his screaming son on the donkey, and the travellers left again empty-handed.

One mile on, they met a man who had just reached the shore of the lake, coming from the south. They asked him where they could find food. He advised them to travel south to Sakha, from whence he had come, as the people of Sakha were more obliging than those living on the lakeside. So they turned left and carried on thirstily to the south until they reached the village. Jeshua was dehydrated and exhausted from screaming, so Jossef lifted him from the donkey and put him down on the ground while the travellers looked about them. As Jeshua's foot touched the ground, Jossef saw water come gushing out from beneath his foot. Jeshua lifted his foot and the spring came bubbling to the surface even more strongly. Jossef gave a cry of joy, called Mariam and the He-He-He over, and they gratefully filled the water-skins. Jeshua was finally able to drink his fill.

A villager had been watching the scene from a distance. She came up to the group and invited the travellers to come to her family for a rest and a meal. They were glad to accept her invitation and were given a meal fit for a king. The family invited them to stay the night, which they were very pleased to do.

Strengthened and well-rested, they set off again next day and soon reached the western-most fork of the Nile. They would be walking south on its west bank for five days before taking a right turning towards Wadi Natrun and walking for another day along that path.

After the rains, the landscape was lush and green. Jossef bought fresh fruit and vegetables and stocked up on grain. The farmer who sold him the grain also milled it for them. There were wells aplenty so that they never lacked water. On this stretch, the Nile meandered in many serpentine-like curves. This made their journey somewhat longer, but they stayed by the river, so as not to lose their orientation.

These would have been pleasant days of travel, had it not been for Mariam and Jossef's morose son! Jossef tried to draw his attention to the birds and animals of the Nile, but he hardly even looked. Mariam once tried taking him in her arms to comfort him, but he refused her comfort and struggled free.

Even the Sabbath did not have the usual peaceful atmosphere. Jeshua briefly lost his morose expression as Jossef read the week's scripture passage, but then he returned to his unresponsive and inaccessible state.

On the sixth day, Jossef consulted Meketre's sketch, checking for a sign that they had reached the turn-off. The Nile branched, forming an island, upon which a village had been built, and sure enough, they soon found the turn-off to Wadi Natrun. Several caravans were travelling to buy salt or bringing goods to the Libyan desert in the west.

For a while after the turn-off, their path remained green, then the landscape became more and more sparse the further they walked from the river and the nearer they came to Wadi Natrun. They glimpsed some rocky hills on the horizon, which was where the huge depression with the salt lakes lay. But the sun was already sinking behind those hills, colouring the sky first orange, then red, then lavender-blue, so the travellers realized they would need to spend another night outdoors before reaching Wadi Natrun.

Jeshua had stopped crying, but he remained morose and silent. He still often sat with the He-He-He, but at least he now slept with his parents again. However, that evening he came straight over to Mariam and asked her to sing him a psalm. Mariam looked down at her son in delight and promised him she would do so as soon as they had eaten. The evening was cool, and they all stayed sitting around the fire after their meal. Jeshua leaned against his mother, who began to sing:

> «The Lord is my shepherd; I shall not want.
> He makes me lie down in green pastures.
> He leads me beside still waters.
> He restores my soul.
> He leads me in paths of righteousness for his name's sake.
> Even though I walk through the Valley of the Shadow of Death,
> I will fear no evil, for you are with me;
> your rod and your staff, they comfort me.
> You prepare a table before me in the presence of my enemies;
> you anoint my head with oil; my cup overflows.

Surely goodness and mercy shall follow me all the days of my life,
and I shall return to the House of the Lord all my life.[24] »

«Imma,» asked Jeshua, «where is the House of the Lord?»

«That's the temple in Jerusalem, my sweet,» said Mariam, «and we used to go there often, when we were still able to live in Israel. One day, we'll have a home in Israel again, and we'll go with you to the temple to present you to our God, as our first-born. We should have done that after your birth, but then we had to flee.»

«Is it like the temple here, with lots of different gods in it?» asked Jeshua.

«No, in Israel that's quite different,» explained Mariam. «In the whole of our country there's only one temple, and our God is worshipped only there, sacrifices are only made to him, not to any other deities! That's why we call it the House of the Lord.»

«Was Merit in Israel too?» asked Jeshua with a nostalgic little sigh.

«Yes, my sweet, Merit was with us when we were in Ashkelon. She's also been to the temple in Jerusalem a few times. But now we're all here in Egypt and can't worship our Lord in the temple as we should. It's like the story of the Israelites, when they had to go into exile long, long ago. There's also a

---

[24] Psalm 23

psalm from that time that shows how sad they were that they'd lost their temple.»

«Will you sing that psalm too, please, Imma?»

Mariam did not need to be asked twice for a psalm, and she immediately began to sing:

«By the waters of Babylon,
there we sat down and wept,
when we remembered Zion.
On the willows there we hung up our lyres.
For there our captors
required of us songs,
and our tormentors, mirth, saying,
Sing us one of the songs of Zion!
How shall we sing the Lord's song
in a foreign land?
If I forget you, O Jerusalem,
let my right hand forget its skill!
Let my tongue stick to the roof of my mouth,
if I do not remember you,
if I do not set Jerusalem
above my highest joy! [25]

You see?» concluded Mariam, «That's how important Mount Zion is to us, upon which Jerusalem, our holy city is built!»

«When can we go to Israel?» asked Jeshua, «I'd like to see Jerusalem and the temple!»

«We don't know yet, my sweet. As long as this king is still searching for us, we have to stay in Egypt.

---

[25] Psalm 137

But one day, we'll be able to go back, I promise you that!»

Hopefully this promise will soon come true – thought Mariam. Inwardly, she thanked God that Jeshua had opened up to her again. She took him in her arms, kissed him on the head and pulled the cover over him. He was asleep before she had lain down next to him.

28

Next morning, the travellers were woken by the glistening light of the desert. They were in no hurry that day, as they would be able to accomplish the remaining distance to Wadi Natrun in half a day. They ate an ample breakfast before loading up their donkeys.

They had long left behind the lush green of the Nile region. Now they made their way over stones and sand which was billowing around in the air on the wind. The midday sun burned remorselessly down upon them. Jeshua dismounted from the donkey and walked beside it, sheltering from the sun in its shadow. They were all glad they had decided to walk the next stretch at night. This would give them time to take a look around Wadi Natrun, and to buy some salt. For the He-He-He, it would mean they had plenty of time to view the glass factories in the area.

Their first glimpse of the salt lakes caused them to gasp in wonder. The whole of Wadi Natrun was a gigantic depression, about 60 miles in length and 10 miles wide, lying more than 90 feet below the Nile. In this flat-floored valley lay the salt lakes which were fed by underground water from the Nile. As the group drew nearer, they could smell the sulphur from the lakes. Now, in early spring, the lakes glowed in yellowish-green, whereas in summer they would shimmer in reddish-blue. They were slowly drying out since the rainy season had not long ended. But salt workers had already started to rake the salt together to form large, conical piles. These piles lay in the little remaining water about 50 yards apart from each other. In a few weeks, once the lakes had completed dried out, the piles would be standing on dry land and could be filled into sacks. The salt was renowned for its purity and for containing other valuable minerals which made it suitable for mummification, as well as for the production of glass, which was why there were several glass factories in the area.

Between two of the lakes, they spotted a small town with a magnificent granite gate. Jossef suggested they take a look at this town, as it might have a guesthouse. A broad path led down into the flat-floored valley.

On the plateau there had been a light breeze, but down in the valley, it was a good deal warmer and there was no breeze, so they were pleased to find a guesthouse with an attached bath. The saline bath had a noble-looking façade of frosted glass which had been produced at a local glass factory.

Upon arrival at the guesthouse, they were invited by the friendly landlord to take tea with him in his garden.

The He-He-He took the opportunity to ask him about the nearest glass factory, and the landlord told them the way, saying that they would have to ride for about an hour to reach it. Jossef therefore suggested that the He-He-He also take the family's donkeys in addition to their own mule, which would enable them to get there and back in one day. In the meantime, the family would find plenty to interest themselves in the area, and if not, they could spend the time relaxing prior to the night march.

The landlord mentioned that there were fossils nearby showing traces of gigantic animals from prehistoric times. Jeshua was fascinated by this and said he wanted to see the fossils next day.

There was still a little time before supper, so Jossef, Jeshua and the boys went to the saline bath. After their bath and some supper, they felt like new and slept deeply in their comfortable beds.

***

The He-He-He arose very early next morning and rode off at speed, so that they would still have time for a rest after their visit to the glass factory.

Jossef, Mariam and Jeshua slept long and took an ample breakfast before setting off to find the fossils, which turned out to be near the edge of the town. Jeshua went from one fossil to another. He was amazed to hear that these creatures, dinosaurs and molluscs, had lived here long, long ago. The fossilized tracks left by dinosaur feet were so huge that the animals themselves must have been an unbelievable size. It was almost impossible to imagine that there had once been such large creatures roaming the face of the earth.

In the afternoon, they walked to the bank of the nearest salt lake and watched the men raking the salt from the rapidly evaporating water, increasing the size of the existing piles. They discovered a storage house in town where they were able to buy a sack of salt, and also bought two smaller empty bags in which to distribute the salt, one for themselves and one for the He-He-He. The salt would serve Mariam and Jossef both as a means of exchange and for preserving foods. They returned to the guesthouse garden to await the return of the He-He-He, who arrived in the late afternoon and excitedly recounted their experiences and insights from their visit to the glass factory.

The three boys were hungry, so they were provided with a good meal, while Jossef groomed and fed the tired animals following their fast ride.

After four further hours of rest, they loaded up their beasts and paid the landlord, who explained where they could find the steep upward path on the other side of the valley in the direction of the Libyan desert. They set off on the night march by the silvery light of the rising moon.

Travelling by night was a new experience for them all and held a special fascination. They heard unfamiliar cries of animals, and generally quite different sounds to those heard during the day. As soon as they reached the top of their rocky path out of the valley, a cool wind blew softly over the sand, raising it in swirls around them. Once, a desert mouse scurried on its long legs across their path; later they saw a sand-coloured snake wriggle quickly after its prey. They met a caravan going in the opposite direction, also travelling by night to avoid the heat of day. The calls of the men and the grunting and bellowing of the beasts faded slowly into the darkness behind them.

The He-He-He were feeling very excited, as they would shortly be seeing their family for the first time in ten years! It was a huge moment in their lives, even if they had practically no memory of the family.

All night, the travellers had hardly seen any plants other than the occasional terebinth or thorn bush. Early in the morning, as the sun bathed the desert in a deep golden light, they saw before them a group of buildings and palm trees sitting in the limitless sand as if they had fallen out of the sky.

«That's Kalya!» shouted Hepire. «I recognise it!»

«Me too!» shouted the other He-He, and all three of them started to run.

Jossef suddenly had a feeling of foreboding that this village, which had managed quite well without the three boys for ten years, may not be quite as welcoming as they expected. He also started to run. Mariam walked slowly on with Jeshua behind them.

Everything was quiet, since the villagers were still sleeping, but the He-He-He knew immediately which hut to go to. Only when they arrived in front of the hut did they suddenly come to a halt, looking at one another rather doubtfully.

Jossef, who had just caught up with them, called out breathlessly: «He-He-He, listen! You will take things slowly, won't you? They haven't seen you for ten years – they may not even recognise you!»

There was some movement in the hut. Someone had heard the newcomers. The door opened slowly and a wrinkled old face with leathery skin appeared.

«What d'you want here?» asked the old woman.

«Grandmother, it's me, Hemire!»

«Hemire?» asked the old woman in astonishment, «Hemire, Hesire and Hepire? Here?»

«Yes!» said all three, almost jumping into the air with excitement.

The old woman did not look at all pleased, however.

«Wait,» she said, «I'll go and wake the others, but they'll be very surprised to see you.» It was obvious she did not mean this in a positive way.

The He-He-He looked at Jossef doubtfully.

«Just as I said,» commented Jossef, «they'll have been taken unawares.»

In the meantime, Mariam and Jeshua had caught up with them. There was some low muttering in the hut, but it took almost a quarter of an hour before someone appeared in front of it: a man of about forty years, but with the same leathery, wrinkled skin as his mother.

«So,» he said, «you're back – after such a long time. Did you run away, or what?»

«We didn't exactly run away, dad. These people saved us from being killed by slave-drivers! You know how we were victims of slave-traders who took us by force to the east. Did you know where we were?»

«Mm, well, that wasn't exactly by force – they did pay us for it,» said their father, his eyes fixed on the ground.

«Paid?» said Hesire aghast, «You sold us?»

«Well, what were we supposed to do? We had nothing more to eat! We couldn't afford your keep any more. There was only just enough for the three of us,» said their father entreatingly.

The He-He-He's jaws dropped. They had built up a false picture of life in this village during the months of their journey. This picture had now been demolished with one blow. Hard reality now stood before them in the person of their father, who was nervously chewing at his lip.

«Did mum know about this?» asked Hepire.

«It was her idea,» said their father bluntly, going back into the hut and slamming the door on them.

«I don't believe it!» screamed Hemire.

«So that's all?» shouted Hesire. «Come out here at once, you cowardly dogs, and look us in the eye! We've been thrashed to a bloody pulp for ten years – was that just so you could fill your bellies? I don't believe it!»

The door opened again, and their father came out with the mother. «Just fetched your mum,» he said morosely.

Jossef and Mariam now understood where the initial taciturnity of the He-He-He had come from. These people were unbelievably coarse and monosyllabic.

«Well, how about it?» Hesire asked his parents, «can we move back in with you or not?»

«Ahah! So you've just come back to eat us out of house and home again, have you?» answered their father, while their mother just shook her head.

«No room,» their mother added. Their parents went back into their hut and closed the door again.

The He-He-He just stood there, looking crestfallen and confused.

«He-He-He, come on,» said Jossef, «let's find a place at the edge of the village to sit down and discuss what's to be done. You're not going to get anywhere this way. Your situation doesn't look too bright right now, and one thing's for sure: as long as you don't know where to live or whether you can stay, we're not going to leave you.»

They sat next to one another on a low wall. Jeshua sat opposite them on the ground playing with small pebbles.

«I think we must have begun to idealise our home and our family in our memory lately,» said Hemire. «You see, you were all so friendly and kind to us that we began to forget how hard the world can be! I think we started to block out the reality of it.»

«Our family's even nastier than we remembered them,» added Hepire. «I just can't believe they actually sold us! If we'd known that, we'd never have considered coming back here.»

«Don't be too hard on your family!» countered Jossef. «They probably only acted that way because they were starving and saw no other way out of their dilemma. And now they're probably acting so repellently towards you because they have a guilty conscience.»

«No,» retorted Hesire, «they're evil people, there's no getting around the fact.»

«Alright, maybe it's a bit of both,» conceded Hepire. «They've certainly never been nice people but admittedly, they were suffering. Life was, and still is, hard out here in the desert, and having us three to support …»

«Well what are you going to do now?» asked Jossef. «Maybe there's somewhere else in the village you can live. As soon as other people start waking up, we can ask around.»

«That's actually quite possible,» commented Hepire. «Even when we were small, people had started to leave the village to go and live in the Nile valley. I can still vaguely remember that.»

«Something could be made of this village,» said Hemire. «It's right on the caravan route. I'm convinced that a pottery could be profitable here!»

«Yes,» agreed Hesire, «our villagers were never ones to show initiative. Everyone always just complains. We could show them!»

«Excellent idea!» said Jossef. «Constructive solutions are called for here!»

«Whatever happens to us now,» said Hemire, «I'd just like to say thank you. Without you, we'd probably be dead by now, or at least inwardly dead. You saved us! Most of all I'd like to thank you, Mariam, for first standing up for us as you did, but you too Jossef, you were always committed to helping us. Never before have we experienced such loyalty. It's helped us so much in making something out of our lives, and we're not going to give up now! We're going to go on fighting!»

Hesire and Hepire nodded resolutely and agreed with Hemire, adding that they were also grateful from the bottom of their hearts and that they would never forget Jossef, Mariam, Jeshua and also Merit.

Jeshua had interrupted his game now and then to look up at the adults, trying to make something of this rather complex discussion. He asked the He-He-He: «Did your parents really sell you? Like they'd sell vegetables or meat?»

«Yes,» nodded Hesire, «they really did!»

«You see, they were very hungry, Jeshua,» added Jossef, «but even so, they shouldn't have done that, it was very wrong of them.»

Jeshua turned back to his pebbles with a frown. Adults could be such strange creatures sometimes!

A young couple with a small child came out of one of the neighbouring houses. They had heard voices, they said, and wondered who had strayed into their village. Hemire explained the situation and asked whether there was anywhere to live in the village.

«Oh, you're those people's children,» said the young man. «Well, I'm sorry to have to say this, but they're not well-liked in the village. Maybe you're already aware of this or you'll have suspected it.» The

He-He-He nodded. The young woman also nodded and continued: «It's as you say, there are houses in the village which are no longer inhabited. The previous owners left their homes to go and live in the Nile valley. Come along with us! We'll show you which houses are free. You'll need to put in quite a bit of work to make them habitable, though.»

There even proved to be two houses directly next to each other. They were collapsing in places, but the roofs were still intact.

«They're perfect!» shouted Hepire. «We can use one house to live in, and the other can be converted into the pottery»

«Oh, you're potters?» asked the young woman, smiling. «That'd be really good for our village! So welcome home!»

«Thank you!» answered the He-He-He with a smile.

Jossef and Mariam were pleased to see that there were other young people in the village, meaning that the He-He-He would not be left alone. Things appeared to be looking up!

«Maybe with time, you'll be able to forge a better relationship with your family, once you've shown what you're capable of!» Jossef said to the three boys who were already looked much happier.

«We hope so too,» said Hemire, «but if not, we'll just leave them be. We've tried, and we can't do more than that.»

29

The travellers used the unoccupied houses as a camp, as it was a cold night. The He-He-He spent one last evening together with their friends as they would take their leave of them the following evening and begin their new life in the village. Before they slept, the three boys were already putting their heads together to plan their pottery. Jossef and Mariam no longer had any scruples about leaving the three young entrepreneurs here in their village.

What suddenly made them feel a little uneasy, was the thought of travelling all alone in Egypt for the first time. After a short discussion, they decided to head for Babylon and find the community Ahab had told them about. Meketre's sketch only showed the route as far as Kalya. Jossef therefore suggested to Mariam that they first return to Wadi Natrun, and from there back to the Nile valley the same way they had come, as they already knew the route. Mariam considered this the only sensible solution, but she suggested they travel to Wadi Natrun by night again.

Jossef was able to spend the following day using his carpenter's skills to help the He-He-He with their plans for the renovation of the two houses. They were talented potters, but they knew nothing of woodwork or building. He even carried out some of the more challenging building work for them, particularly such jobs as required his carpenter's tools. He described all the further steps in as much detail as he could. After that, they would be on their own.

In the early afternoon, the young neighbour's wife came over with a dish she had cooked for her own family, having made enough for the newcomers as well. They accepted this offering with thanks. Jossef lay down to sleep and recover from his hard work, until the moon rose on the horizon.

They loaded up their donkeys, wished the He-He-He luck with their formidable endeavour, and took their leave of them. After so many months together, it was another emotional parting of the ways. Jeshua cried a little as he said goodbye to his three friends, but he had not developed the same connection to them as he had to Merit, so his tears soon dried again. As the family set off, the He-He-He stood in front of their new home and waved until their friends were out of sight.

Walking alone in the night felt slightly uncanny. To banish this feeling, Mariam sang an old folk song, taking her son's hand to give both herself and Jeshua courage. After a couple of hours, the strange feeling of travelling without their friends had left them. They soon became accustomed to the smacking rhythm of only three pairs of sandals, to the sounds of the desert at night and to their own company.

After descending the now-familiar steep path to the valley floor, It was all the more comforting to arrive at the guesthouse in Wadi Natrun and to see the familiar face of the friendly landlord, who was able to offer them the same room. He gave them a good breakfast, after which they fell upon their soft bed and slept for a few hours until the afternoon, which they spent in the garden with the landlord, telling him the incredible story of the He-He-He's arrival in their village.

«Those three boys will find their own way in life, with or without their parents!» said the landlord. «But it's unbelievable that people can treat their own children like that! Where are their hearts?»

«I believe the hardship of their lives robbed them of their hearts long ago,» commented Mariam. «What a terrible existence that must be, without a jot of warmth or friendliness. There's only malice and resentment left!»

«Jeshua, you must be glad your parents are not like that!» said the landlord. He asked them how they had met the He-He-He in the first place. Mariam told him the whole story from the moment when they had saved the three boys from being thrashed to death by their slavedrivers, up to the present day. The landlord fetched a bottle of sweet wine from a cupboard, and the conversation continued comfortably until darkness fell and the oil lamps were lit.

Only one of the travellers slept that night, and that was little Jeshua. Jossef took his wife in his arms, kissed her fragrant hair and her soft lips. Together they enjoyed hours of sweet, sensuous intimacy which had become rare enough during the last few months and which they had sorely missed. It was the first night of travel in Egypt which they had spent alone without friends, and they savoured this intimacy. Nestling close to Jossef, Mariam thought back to the moment in Baltim when Merit had teased them about Jeshua not yet having a brother. She wanted more than anything in the world to give Jeshua a little brother or sister, but while they were still on the road, it was undoubtedly better if she did not become pregnant again. The journey to Bethlehem had been enough for her, heavily pregnant as she had been!

In the morning, Jossef asked the landlord how long they would take to reach Babylon. He said they would take about five or six days to walk there if they kept to the banks of the Nile. Jossef suggested they stay in Wadi Natrun until after the Sabbath. This sabbath was more harmonious than the last one, and Jeshua's smile showed that he had now overcome the pain of leaving Merit.

Before leaving, they paid the landlord and bought some provisions from the market. Then they ascended the broad path out of the valley, heading back towards the east.

It was a relief to reach the Nile again after the dust and heat of the desert. The palms swayed gently in the breeze, and the reed-beds were alive with storks, herons, and ducks. Everywhere, farmers were busy sowing seed for the new cycle of another year.

Soon it would be the Feast of the Passover, by which time Jossef hoped to have reached the Roman fortress town of Babylon so that they could celebrate with the Jewish community there. They had been unable to celebrate the last Passover properly; now Mariam and Jossef wanted Jeshua to experience his first Passover within a community.

As the path was straightforward and easy to follow, they were able to look around them, savouring the verdant landscape. They saw a number of trade ships, which were travelling up and down the Nile between Lower and Upper Egypt. The nearer they came to the large town of Heliopolis, the more people, boats, and animals were to be seen on and around the Nile.

Jossef spotted a pile of clay bricks drying on the floodplains, which reminded him of the exertions of clay digging with Meketre's men in November. What a rich plethora of experiences they had had during the long period of their flight from Herod! This flight had turned out to be both a blessing and a curse, the more so as they had not yet seen or heard any sign that they had been traced to Egypt. However, homesickness often raised its distressing head, casting a shadow over their adventures. He well knew that his wife suffered far more than he did from homesickness, but Jossef longed to be working again. He also missed his home, and most of all he longed for security for little Jeshua.

On the fourth day they made a halt in the village of Matariya, where they took a light snack and rested beneath the spreading branches of a tree. Mariam leaned against the trunk and felt strength emanating from the old tree. She soon felt refreshed and glanced over towards Jeshua, who was messing around in the silt and looked almost as grey as Jossef had done when he was clay-digging!

«Jeshua!» called Mariam, «Stop that! Come here! What do you think you're doing? You can't arrive in a big town looking like that!»

She looked around and discovered a nearby spring. Without further ado she dipped her son into the water, clothes and all, rinsing the silt from his clothes and his body. Jeshua crowed with pleasure at the coolness of the water. As they walked on, he and his clothes dried in the warmth of the sun in no time.

In the evening, they crossed the Nile by ferry and reached the old town of Heliopolis, situated on a hill on the east bank. The black silhouette of a tall obelisk soared high before them against the pale-yellow sky. After passing through the gate in the town walls, they were surrounded by once-grand temple complexes and palaces to both left and right, which were now in disrepair. The Temple of the Sun contained a monumental statue of pink granite so large that it towered above the walls of the temple complex. They also saw empty spaces where obelisks and sphinxes had obviously previously stood, and they learned that these had been transported away by Queen Cleopatra four decades earlier. This put them in mind of the obelisks in Alexandria which, according to Meketre, also originated from Heliopolis. After the quiet of the country, the noisy crowds unnerved the family. All they needed now was rest. The first guesthouses looked too upmarket, so they carried on to a more suitable guesthouse. Exhausted as they were, they went early to bed and were asleep in no time.

PART V:

Passover in Babylon

30

Since it was not far from Heliopolis to Babylon, the family slept late the next day, before loading their donkeys and travelling southwards down the east bank of the Nile. After a short rest in the small town of Harat Zuweila, they carried on towards the old town of Babylon. Jeshua was the first to spot the points of pyramids far away in the west and wanted to know what the strange buildings were. Jossef explained to him that they were the burial sites of ancient pharaohs.

It was still early afternoon when they reached Babylon, so Jossef and Mariam decided to make straight for the Ben Esra synagogue in the hope of finding someone from the Jewish community there.

They were in luck: The young caretaker was busy cleaning the synagogue and was pleased to give them information. First, he gave them the address of a Jewish-run guesthouse, then he began to tell them the history of the community, which was the oldest in Egypt. In days gone by, the Jeremiah synagogue had stood upon the same spot. According to legend, when the prophet Jeremiah had been deported to Egypt, he had found the mortal remains of the patriarch Moses there. Some members of the community believed implicitly in this story, whereas others were sceptical.

Jossef explained to the friendly caretaker that they were intending to stay in Babylon until after the Feast of the Passover, so that they could celebrate in a community with their young son. The caretaker said he looked forward to seeing them in the synagogue on that occasion. He returned to his work and the family went to find the Jewish guesthouse.

The house was run by a young couple who gave them a friendly welcome and showed them where they could sleep, in a rather cool, dark room. Their own two children appeared, a boy of about Jeshua's age and a girl a little older. The children stood outside the room and peered inside, as their parents invited Mariam, Jossef and Jeshua to join them in the living room for a cup of tea. However, Mariam and Jossef first wanted to unload their things and stable the donkeys.

«Jeshua, you can go outside and play with the children until we've finished in the stable and in our room!» said Mariam. The three children were quite content with this arrangement and went running out into the garden together.

«We'll be happy here,» said Mariam, as they led the donkeys into the stable, «even though the room is rather dark. But the people are friendly, and it's wonderful for Jeshua to have some friends of his own age to play with.»

«Yes,» agreed Jossef, «I've got a good feeling here too. During the weeks leading up to Passover, we can get to know the other people in the community. Maybe we'll stay even longer, we'll see …»

As soon as the donkeys and baggage had been dealt with, they went into the landlord's living room. The landlord introduced himself: «I'm Gershon, and this is my wife, Esther. Please take a seat. I'll call the children, then we'll bring you your tea.»

The children came running boisterously into the room and went to sit with their parents.

«Imma,» said the little girl, «Jeshua's been on the sea in a big ship!»

«Oh, is that right, Jeshua?» asked Esther. «That must have been very exciting!»

«Yes, it was great!» exclaimed Jeshua. «And now Tirza wants to go on the sea in a ship too.»

«So your name's Tirza, is it?» asked Mariam, «and what's your little brother's name?»

«I'm Benni, and I'm not so very little!» said the small boy.

«No, you're not, in fact you're a bit taller than our Jeshua!» Mariam reassured him.

Mariam and Jossef, in their turn, introduced themselves and told the couple where they had been travelling. They explained that they were on the run, but that they had so far not seen or heard any sign that they had been traced here.

«It's good that you've come here. But please be very cautious! We've heard news from the community in Belbeis that Roman officials have been asking around there about a Jewish family from Israel. I hope you're not that family!» said Gershon.

«Really?» said Jossef, alarmed. «We did actually visit Belbeis, but that was about ten months ago.»

«Yes,» said Gershon, «these enquiries were also made some time ago. But probably all the fuss has died down by now, as they obviously haven't found anything out.»

«Let's hope so!» said Jossef with a sigh. «It's rather worrying, I must say. But no-one's been asking after us here, have they?»

«Well, no-one's asked me,» replied Gershon, «but you'll maybe want to ask around in our community.»

«I'll certainly do that, once we've become more familiar with the folk here,» said Jossef.

Gershon showed Jossef an old map marking all Jewish communities in Egypt. Jossef made himself a rough sketch on a piece of papyrus found in their room, upon which he noted the names of many such villages and towns.

Since the next day was the Day of Preparation for the Sabbath, they would very soon get to know the community. Mariam helped Esther in the kitchen and around the house, so that everything was ready in time. After Jossef and Gershon had been to the synagogue together, they all celebrated the Sabbath meal in warm fellowship. The table was laid, the Sabbath bread lay ready beneath a napkin by Gershon's place, there was a large goblet of wine next to it, and in the middle of the table stood the candelabrum with the Sabbath candles.

Esther checked that all was ready, then she lit the candles, lifting her hands towards them and reciting the blessing of the light. Gershon greeted the Sabbath and sang the Kiddush over the raised goblet, which was passed around for everyone to drink a sip.

He broke the bread and distributed it. Mariam loved singing the well-known songs with the others, and in conclusion everyone sang:

> «When the Lord restored the fortunes of Zion, we were like those who dream.
> Then our mouth was filled with laughter, and our tongue with shouts of joy;
> then they said among the nations: The Lord has done great things for them.
> The Lord has done great things for us; we are glad.
> Restore our fortunes, O Lord, like streams in the Negev!
> Those who sow in tears shall reap with shouts of joy!
> He who goes out weeping, bearing the seed for sowing,
> shall come home with shouts of joy, bringing his sheaves with him! [26]»

Mariam and Jossef felt truly blessed to be celebrating the Sabbath with such friendly folk, and Jeshua also sensed the ceremonial atmosphere and the blessing of fellowship.

***

The synagogue was an impressive building with an open vestibule bordered on three sides by colonnades. Inside, the hall was also framed by

---

[26] Psalm 126

colonnades. At the front where the Shrine of the Torah stood, there was a platform with a large menorah[27] on each side. On the Sabbath morning, the room was full to bursting. Mariam accompanied Esther and Tirza to the separate section for the women, while Jossef and Jeshua stayed with Gershon and Benni.

The Torah Scroll was taken from the shrine and carried in a ceremonial procession around the synagogue before the weekly Torah portion was read. After the collective prayers had finished, everyone met up around the fountain in the vestibule.

«Excuse me for a moment, please,» said Gershon to Jossef and Mariam, «I see someone standing over there between the columns who's never visited us before. I'll just go and greet him!»

Gershon approached the man and spoke to him for a while, but the man just waved his hand about, turned on his heel and went towards the exit. Gershon returned to the others with raised brows.

«Well! What a strange fellow!» he said. «When I introduced myself and asked where he was from, he didn't answer, he only gesticulated and left without a word! I wonder if he could have been a Roman.»

«Well he certainly looked like one, with that short hair and the curls on the top of his head,» said Jossef. «I could well imagine him in a legionnaire's uniform.»

---

[27] Seven-branched candelabra, an important symbol of Judaism

«Yes, so could I,» agreed Gershon. «Whatever did he want in our community? Well, I appear to have unintentionally scared him off with my greeting!»

At home, they all sat down to the main meal, a chicken stew with chickpeas, taro, beans, and wheat, which Esther had cooked the previous day. In the afternoon they recited the Minchah[28], and Gershon read from the Torah. As soon as it was dark, he lit the Havdalah candle. Jeshua, as the youngest child, was allowed to hold the candle while Gershon blessed the goblet of wine and the spice holder. Everyone received a sip of wine and a sniff of the spices to bestow strength for the coming week. They all held their hands up to the candle, spoke the blessing over the candle and wished one another a good week.

The Sabbath was over. Now Esther got to work dealing with all that had been put off for its duration, and Mariam helped her before they went to bed. It had been a long, exciting day and Jeshua did not want to sleep, so Mariam sang him a lullaby, then another and another, until finally his eyes closed, and he drifted off into dreamland.

---

[28] Jewish afternoon prayer

31

The great house-cleaning started a week before Passover. The house was swept from top to bottom, to ensure that there was not a crumb of dough left in any corner. The day before the first evening of Passover, every last bit of raised dough was removed from the house. As their neighbours were Egyptian, Gershon and Esther had been able to give them some bread and cakes beforehand. The rest was burnt in the garden.

Next came the baking of the unleavened bread. The dough was only briefly kneaded, to ensure that it did not rise. Each child was given a lump of unleavened dough and beat the dough until thin, then pricked it with a fork. The thin flatbreads were baked until crisp in the oven. This was a symbol of the fact that at the time of the Exodus, the bread had become crisp from the desert sun.

There was no more leavened bread for the whole of the eight days of the Feast of the Passover – as a reminder that the Israelites had had no time to leaven their bread before leaving Egypt for the Exodus.

As with all Jewish feast days, the Feast of the Passover began on the previous evening. Esther, Gershon and the children decorated the table, laying out cushions around it. The family went to the synagogue in the early evening for the opening Passover service, followed by the Seder celebration in the family home.

Everyone washed their hands thoroughly before meeting around the table. They settled themselves on the cushions, reclining on their left side, leaving their right hand free to receive the goblet. The door was left wide open for the coming of the prophet Elijah[29]. Gershon opened the family ceremony with a blessing and sang the Kiddush over the large goblet of wine in the middle of the table. Next to that were more goblets and the Seder platter with the symbolic foods in memory of the bitter experience of slavery, and a small leg of lamb as a symbol of the lambs sacrificed at the Exodus. All these dishes and the unleavened bread were consumed ritually during the evening. A piece of unleavened bread was dipped twice into a paste of fruits and nuts, and a goblet of wine was passed round as far as the youngest child. In between, Gershon read the story of the Exodus.

The youngest child, in this case Jeshua, had the task of asking the four questions, which were each answered by Gershon:

> «Why is this night different from all other
> nights? On all other nights we eat leavened
> and unleavened bread, why do we only eat un-
> leavened bread on this night?»
> «Long ago, the Children of Israel had to flee in
> the middle of the night with no time to finish

---

[29] It is believed that Elijah is present at every circumcision. His coming at Seder shows all male participants to be circumcised.

making their bread, so they were only able to take unleavened bread with them.»

«On all other nights we eat all herbs and vegetables, why do we only eat bitter herbs on this night?»
«The bitter taste of the herbs reminds us how bitter and hard the life of the Children of Israel was during slavery in Egypt.»

«On all other nights, we don't dip our food even once, why do we dip it twice on this night?»
«This dipping reminds us of the many tears of despair shed by the Children of Israel in slavery. The Charoset[30] dip reminds us of the clay for the bricks made by the Children of Israel during slavery.»

«On all other nights we eat sitting or reclining, why do we only recline on this night?»
«Reclining is a sign of freedom. Only free people can eat reclining, whereas slaves always have to be ready for service. God led the Children of Israel out of Egypt and with a strong arm, he made them free.»

Mariam had practiced the four questions diligently with her son, and he recited them without once hesitating. This animated the other children to

---

[30] Paste made of apples, figs, dates, nuts and wine

ask questions about the traditions of Passover and of their faith, all of which Gershon answered patiently.

At the end of the ceremony, the last piece of unleavened bread was broken and shared amongst all those present, and the last goblet was passed around. They sang a hymn of praise, after which the great meal could begin. Esther had prepared boiled chicken with vegetables which they ate with much laughing and joking.

After the meal, the two families sat comfortably together, discussing the meaning of the Exodus for themselves in their time.

«I think we're better able to sense the full meaning of the Exodus now that we ourselves are refugees in a foreign country,» commented Jossef. «When we were safe at home and still able to visit the temple whenever we wanted to, the Passover was more just a remembrance of the history of our people, but now it's gained a new relevance and vibrancy for us.»

«I'm sure that's more so for you than for us,» added Gershon, «since we were all born here in Egypt for at least two generations back – many of us no longer even understand Hebrew – whereas you really have been driven out of your home country.»

«No, Gershon, that's not quite true,» countered Esther. «Don't forget, that was the same for the Israelites in Egypt! They'd also been there since the time of Joseph, so we're quite like them, whereas Mariam, Jossef and Jeshua are more like those exiled from Israel to the eastern Kingdom of Babylon, who really were torn from their homes and had to worship God without a temple.»

«True,» added Gershon, «but the Israelites in Babylon had also been there in the second or third generation before they were finally able to return to Israel and build a new temple.»

«One thing's for sure,» interjected Mariam, «and this also applies to the people back home: none of us is really free. We're all living under the foreign rule of Rome. We may not notice it so much in everyday life, but it's still a fact we're all subconsciously aware of. I reckon that still makes the Passover a living experience for all of us, even for those who can sacrifice in the temple in Jerusalem at Passover!»

Jeshua was dosing on Mariam's lap. The conversation went back and forth, eventually touching on the real reason for Herod's search for the family.

«Why exactly are you wanted?» asked Gershon.

«It's a difficult tale to tell,» answered Jossef, «because even for us, it seems completely preposterous that we've had to flee because of Herod. But you know what Herod's like. If he gets a bee in his bonnet, he'll go to all lengths to protect his own power.»

«Yes,» replied Esther with an ironical smile, «that fact has even reached us here! But why should you present a threat to Herod? It seems unbelievable.»

«Well, it's like this:» continued Jossef, «When Jeshua was born, astrologers in Persia discovered a special constellation in the skies, so they visited

Herod and told him about it. Together with his scribes, Herod interpreted the prophet Micah to mean that a new King of the Jews would be born in Bethlehem just at the time our Jeshua was born there.»

«Micah – so it's about the Messiah!» said Gershon, impressed. «In that case, I can well imagine Herod becoming nervous.»

«And they think Jeshua is this king, the Messiah?» asked Esther.

«Not a king, not Messiah …» murmured Jeshua sleepily. Mariam smiled and stroked his head.

«We actually already heard we were wanted when we were still in Bethlehem,» explained Jossef, «so we left in the middle of the night and fled. Since then, we've been on the run. First we went to my sister in Ashkelon and felt safe there for a while, as Ashkelon is a free town which is outside Herod's jurisdiction. We were able to stay there for half a year, but then we heard that Herod had traced our family background to Nazareth and had heard about my sister in Ashkelon. From that moment on, we were no longer safe there and fled over the border into Egypt.»

«That's the craziest story I've ever heard,» said Mirjam, «and you've been travelling through Egypt ever since?»

«Yes,» replied Mariam, «we've been travelling most of the time, often sleeping out in caves. I've always been aware how vulnerable we are. But for Jeshua, it's all quite natural. Apart from a stay in Belbeis and another in Baltim, he's never known anything other than being on the move. We stayed in Belbeis for some time and were in contact with the Jewish community there. That was a good time, they were so supportive, just like you are here!»

«Yes, we know the Belbeis community slightly,» said Gershon, «who were you staying with?»

«We stayed with Ahab and Dinah,» said Mariam.

«Oh yes, they're good people!» affirmed Gershon, «they'll have looked after you well!»

«Yes, they did,» agreed Jossef. «The fellowship of that community really gave us new strength for our further travels.»

Towards the early hours of the morning the conversation slowly petered out. Mariam carried Jeshua to their room and covered him up. Although she was tired, she was unable to sleep, as she felt too troubled. Sometimes, when they were in good company, she was able to forget the danger for a while. But the danger was real, always menacingly present in the background and threatening the most important thing in her life – her beloved son.

PART VI:

The Plot Thickens

32

Once the eight-day Passover celebrations were over, Esther needed to go to the market to stock up on provisions. Mariam, Jossef and Jeshua decided to go with her. They met many friends from the community at the market who, like her, required fresh food supplies after Passover.

The Jewish market was located near the fortress. It was brimming with people out shopping and haggling loudly to get a good bargain. The adults chatted excitedly with one another about the Passover and all that had happened since they had last seen each other. Jeshua sneaked off to look at the market stalls. He was bored with all the talking.

In front of the entrance to the Roman fortress, a legionnaire approached Jeshua, looking down at him with a friendly smile.

«Hallo, young lad, out all alone? What's your name?» asked the huge soldier.

«Jeshua!» he answered and smiled back at him.

«Jeshua, eh?» repeated the legionnaire, stroking his chin. «I'm willing to bet you'd love to see inside our fortress, wouldn't you?»

Jeshua beamed. «Oh yes please!» he replied in Latin. This promised to be more exciting than all the talking! He turned to look back at his parents, but they were still deep in conversation. A quick look at the fortress surely would not do any harm …

«Come on,» said the legionnaire, beckoning to Jeshua, «we'll go in together, then you'll be safe!»

Jeshua followed the soldier's long strides with his short legs and looked around wide-eyed at the pentagonal inner courtyard, the two watchtowers and the colourful flags flapping in the wind.

«Just wait here a moment, Jeshua,» ordered the legionnaire, «I need to speak to my men over there for a second …» He went over to two men at the edge of the courtyard and spoke to them in a low voice. Now and then he looked over towards Jeshua, pointing at him. Jeshua suddenly began to feel uncomfortable in the fortress. The men seemed to be discussing something quite excitedly. One of them pointed up at the tower, and the legionnaire looked up at it briefly.

At that moment, Jeshua heard a voice in his head saying: «Run! Run away quickly!» He did not hesitate for one second. Before the men had even turned back from the tower, he ran like the wind through the gates. He found himself in a side street. There was a large wooden crate in front of one of the houses, behind which he hid himself; just in time, as he heard the three men running out of the gates. Jeshua crept round the crate as the men walked on, in order to stay out of their sight.

«Where's he gone?» asked the legionnaire in Latin, which Jeshua had learned with Merit. «It's got to be that Jesus[31] of Nazareth who's wanted by the Judaean Tetrarch, Herod! We must grab him. Gaius,

---

[31] Jesus is the Latin form of the Hebrew name Jeshua

you go to the left, Flavius, you go right, and I'll go straight on. He's so small, he can't have got far!»

Jeshua heard the men walking away. He lifted the lid of the crate and looked inside. He was in luck – it was empty! He climbed nimbly into it and pulled the lid over himself. Inside it stank dreadfully, but he did not mind that. Luckily it had a knothole through which he was able to peep out. He would stay here until the men returned. That seemed to take forever, but eventually he heard steps. Gaius had returned, and soon Flavius also came back together with the legionnaire who had spoken with Jeshua. They were not looking happy – that was good!

Jeshua waited until the three men had gone into the fortress, then he counted to a hundred before cautiously lifting the lid and peering out. No-one was there. He climbed out of the crate, pushed the lid back onto it and ran as fast as his feet would carry him back to Gershon and Esther's house.

In the meantime, the family had returned from the market with Esther. They had become very worried and had been looking everywhere for Jeshua.

«Jeshua!» shouted Mariam, «Thank God! For heaven's sake, wherever have you been?»

«Imma, Abba[32], They saw me! They wanted to capture me!» he cried, beside himself with agitation.

«Who saw you?» asked Jossef.

«The Roman soldiers!» exclaimed Jeshua. «They asked me my name, and a nice soldier said I

---

[32] Aramaic for dad

could look at the fortress, but they really wanted to capture me!»

«Are you sure?» asked Mariam.

«Yes! He said I must be Jesus of Nazareth who's wanted by Herod! The men talked to each other, then they pointed up at the tower – that's when I ran away and hid!»

The adults looked at each other anxiously. That did indeed sound bad.

«What do we do now?» asked Mariam. «Do you think they'll find us here, Esther?»

«I guess it's only a matter of time,» answered Esther sadly. «I regret to say, I think you'll need to leave Babylon. You certainly won't be safe here now.»

«Listen,» suggested Jossef, «it's important that we put as much distance as possible between ourselves and the fortress. We mustn't delay. If we go to the pier at Ma'adi, we can cross by ferry and maybe find a ship travelling south.»

«I think you should wait a while until the excitement has died down,» suggested Gerschon. «The Romans will be checking the ferry today. Come with me, I'll show you a place where you can hide.»

The family followed Gershon into the garden, where he removed some wild plants with a thin layer of earth and pulled open a wooden trapdoor lying beneath. «It won't be very pleasant for you, but you could stay here for a few days until the coast is clear again,» he said

Esther joined them and said: «I'll bring food as often as I can. We'll call you when the situation improves and you can go to the ferry. But we'll tell our children you've gone away for the day, so that there's no danger of them accidentally giving you away.»

Esther gave Mariam an oil lamp, and the family climbed down into the damp underground limestone cave. Jeshua sidled up to his mother, shivering slightly from the cold. Esther and Gershon hurried back to the house, picked up the family's possessions and their mats and brought them to the cave. They took their leave of one another and Jossef heard the sound of earth and plants being pulled back over the trapdoor, then it was silent in their cave. Luckily, there were a few gaps and holes letting in a little air.

Neither Jossef nor Mariam scolded Jeshua for going off alone and talking to the legionnaire. The situation was too serious for scolding, and Jeshua already had a hangdog expression. He was well aware that it was due to his curiosity that they had to hide.

Mariam felt a little hand stealing into hers. She looked down at Jeshua, who now had tears in his eyes, took him in her arms and gave him a hug.

«My darling!» she said, much moved, «The Lord has looked after us thus far, and He will continue to protect us!»

Hours passed. They lost all sense of time, only realizing night had fallen when the holes and gaps could no longer be seen. Jeshua was already sleeping, rolled into their mat, when Mariam and Jossef, who had by now become very thirsty, at last heard the trapdoor opening.

Esther's face appeared in the entrance, lit by an oil-lamp. «Here you are!» she said, «here's some water, vegetables and bread.»

Mariam took the jug and the basket from their friend, and Esther climbed down to them into the cave.

«It was just as we feared,» she told them. «A Roman soldier went to the synagogue this afternoon and asked around whether anyone knew anything about you. Unfortunately, I wasn't there to warn them. Someone directed the soldier round here, and he already turned up on our doorstep this evening, so it was a really good thing you were able to hide. We told him you'd already left, going north towards Leontopolis. I hope he believed us. Stay down there in the cave for another day or two. By that time, we should know whether they're still searching for you in Babylon or not.»

The family ate and drank gratefully, then they slept. Next day, Esther came twice and Gershon came once, telling them that all was quiet and that they would probably be able to risk taking the ferry next day. The hours crept by, but before the holes and gaps were lit by the dawn, Gershon came with Esther and their donkeys and advised them to leave.

Such a sudden departure was not at all what they had envisaged. Esther fetched the children who took their leave of their rather sleepy little friend with puzzled expressions. While Mariam packed up their belongings, Gershon explained to Jossef how they could get from the ferry jetty via Giza and the necropolis of Memphis to Maresi harbour. They loaded their baggage onto the donkeys, and sadly said goodbye to their friendly hosts.

Jossef offered Gershon a generous payment for their prolonged stay, but he refused, saying: «You'll need that for your fares on the ship! It was a pleasure and an honour to accommodate you. You're our friends now! Go with God, peace be with you!»

«Peace be with you too!» called Mariam, Jossef and Jeshua as they set off for Ma'adi which was about half an hour's walk towards the south.

Was this real, or were they dreaming? The sudden departure seemed quite surreal to them. Here they were, alone again without any forewarning.

At sunrise, the family climbed down the steep steps to Ma'adi pier and crossed the Nile by ferry. On the other side, they soon found the main road to Giza. Jossef took Jeshua up in front of him on his donkey. The two donkeys trotted along at a good pace, their little hooves hammering on the broad, paved Roman road. The pyramids could be seen from afar, and as they got nearer, they also saw that there was a row of three smaller pyramids in front of them which were almost covered by sand. Each pyramid was faced with a layer of white, polished lime which was crumbling away in some places. There were still traces of the gold leaf which had once graced the tips.

When they arrived at the foot of the pyramids, they were amazed at the incredible size of these buildings: The foremost, largest pyramid, the Cheops pyramid, was all of 450 feet high! Behind it, the Chepren pyramid, although a little smaller, seemed larger as it stood on a 30-foot stone slab. After two days cooped up in hiding, Jeshua was longing to make the most of their newly-won freedom and said he would like to walk around one of the pyramids – he chose the middle Chepren pyramid – and they slowly encircled it, standing still now and then to admire the majesty of this masterpiece of human construction. Jeshua would have liked to have entered one of the pyramids, but Jossef explained that they had been walled up long ago and could not be entered. It took them quite a while to walk around this one pyramid, as each side measured about 700 feet!

As the sun came out between the clouds, Jeshua looked up and sketched the form of the rays with his hands. «The pyramids are like the sun!» he said.

Jossef smiled. «That's true!» he replied, impressed, «They really are built like the rays of the sun!»

Jeshua discovered the huge sphinx squatting majestically below the pyramids facing east, its long forepaws and its haunches almost covered by sand. Half-lion and half-human, the statue seemed to hold a magical attraction for the boy. Jeshua ran over to it and looked up into its human face.

«it looks as though it knows a secret!» Jeshua called out to his parents as they slowly came down to join him by the sphinx.

«There's something to be said for that, Jeshua,» agreed Mariam. «What secret do you think that might be?»

«This is Pharaoh, so it's an Egyptian god who knows everything, including the secrets of life and death,» answered Jeshua pensively.

«Well, maybe,» said Mariam, wishing she had not asked.

Esther had given the family a packed lunch, which they ate in the shade of the great pyramids, before riding south along the dusty path towards Memphis. Soon they saw the white walls of the temples, one or two smaller sphinxes and the monumental statues of Ramses ahead. They dismounted from their donkeys and walked around between the many temples of the necropolis. They were feeling rather nervous, and Jossef kept his eyes open for any Roman soldiers who might be patrolling. The Temple of Ptah, the god of craftsmen, particularly interested him, as the wall paintings showed some Egyptian building methods, including the building of the pyramids Jossef explained some of the processes for Jeshua to better understand what the paintings depicted.

In the temple forecourt, a group of musicians were playing a curious melody with unusual intervals upon tall, slender, brightly painted harps in the form of crescent moons, accompanied by long pipes, as well as small and large drums. Jeshua found the music rather sad.

The sun was already sinking towards the horizon when they arrived in Maresi. They went straight to the harbour, where they found a large ship with the sailors busy on deck preparing to set sail. Jossef spoke to the captain who was standing on the pier, who explained that the ship would be leaving at sunrise for Beni Suef. Jossef asked whether the captain had room for them and their animals as far as Beni Suef.

«Yes, you can come along!» the captain replied, «but it'll cost you.»

«Of course, no problem,» Jossef assured him, and accompanied by the captain, they embarked with their donkeys across the gangway.

Jeshua was excited at being on a large sailing ship again. He ran about the deck before approaching the captain.

«I've been on the sea!» he told the captain.

«Oho, so you're an experienced sailor, are you?» the captain grinned. «Good to have you on board, little man! What's your name?»

But somehow, Jeshua had no desire to tell him!

33

The family were allocated room below one of the latticed deckhouses. Jossef removed the baggage from the donkeys and tethered them to a railing. Mariam rolled out their mat below deck ready for night. But they only dared to move freely about on deck once night had fallen. Jeshua went round chatting to all the sailors, but he never told them his name. He had learned an important lesson.

Jossef took Jeshua with him when he went to talk to the captain, who now had plenty of time for a chat, as all had been made shipshape. Jossef introduced himself, and the captain told him his name was Nechti. Nechti said he hoped for a good wind from the north next morning, even though there was not even a breeze that evening. Providing there was enough wind, they should reach Beni Suef within two days, and if the wind was strong, in half that time.

«Wow! That's very fast!» marvelled Jossef.

Nechti winked. «It's a large ship, and the longer the ship, the better the speed!»

«What takes you to Beni Suef, Nechti?» asked Jossef.

«We're carrying grain,» he replied. «See that hold there? It's filled with three tons of grain.» Nechti briefly opened the hold, and Jeshua peered inside, but it was too dark to see much.

«Will we find a guesthouse at Beni Suef?» asked Jossef.

«You're better carrying on to Heracleopolis Magna to stay the night. There are far more options there and it's also more interesting for you travellers. It's not at all far, not even an hour from Beni Suef on foot.»

Jossef thanked Nechti and went down with Jeshua to join Mariam below deck. The three of them snuggled up together and were soon rocked to sleep by the slight swaying of the moored ship.

The raised voices of the sailors woke them at the first light of the new day. Nechti was calling out orders in all directions, and his crew were occupied with final preparations before setting sail. Jossef rolled up their mat, and they went on deck with Jeshua. The wind had freshened. They would indeed make good headway.

All three went and stood at the prow to watch the activity. As the sun rose, Jeshua looked back towards the north-west and pointed to the tips of the pyramids of Giza illuminated deep red by the low morning sun. Mariam put her arm on Jeshua's shoulder and kissed the top of his head.

«Beautiful, isn't it?» she said, «and I believe we'll soon see more pyramids, but only from a distance.»

The ropes were cast off, and the rowers brought the ship into the middle channel of the river, where the sails were hoisted. The thick red canvas flapped loudly in the wind, and then, like a horse given its head, the ship suddenly gathered way. Jeshua crowed with pleasure! The voyage could not be long enough for him.

It was more diverting to travel the Nile by ship than on foot. They passed many islands, upon which fields of vegetables had been planted. Fertility was all around them. After about two miles, the landscape of the east bank became sparse and stony. In the distance, they could see as far as the eastern mountains. The west bank was still green and fertile. On the banks of the river, there were palm trees and bushes behind which they could see freshly sprouting tender green shoots in the fields of grain. Other fields contained pumpkins, onions and chickpeas. By June, there would be a rich harvest.

Close by in the west, they saw the broad, lime-washed, stepped pyramid of Sakkarah. Jeshua pointed to it and shouted: «That looks like a cake!» They all laughed, as it really did look rather like one.

A few hours later, the sails were struck, and the ship approached its berth for the night. The family was now quite hungry. They crossed the gangway and went to the nearest village where they were able to buy bread and vegetables. They stretched their legs walking around the village, then they found a good spot on the riverbank and sat down to enjoy their meal, while watching the last boats returning to the village. The constant wind had tired them, and they felt themselves relaxing as they moved further away from Babylon. Only now did they fully realise how tense they had become after the shock of Jeshua's discovery by the Romans.

«Will we ever be able to live in safety again?» asked Mariam anxiously. «I hope the Romans aren't able to pick up our trail! Now they know we're near, I'm convinced they won't give up until they find us.»

«You're quite right, my love,» agreed Jossef, «we really are in great danger. But I believe we need to take each day as it comes and always be ready to react quickly when necessary – just as we did in Babylon!»

«Yes, that's true, we did react well,» said Mariam. «On the ship I feel completely safe. It's like a small separate world in which we're inviolable. But once we're travelling on land again, I know I'm going to be looking behind me all the time to check whether we're being followed!»

«All the more important to use this time on the ship to conserve our strength,» said Jossef.

In silence, they watched the water of the Nile flowing past; the dark, swirling waters soothed and reassured them. In a contented mood, they returned to the ship for the night.

The trip to Beni Suef did indeed take almost two days and did the family a world of good, particularly Jeshua who had been on deck all day, closely observing the landscapes and people on the banks of the Nile. On the second day they saw more pyramids at Dahshur in the west, some of which had odd shapes, especially the Bent Pyramid which appeared to have gone a bit wrong – the ancient Egyptians had obviously still needed some practice at that point! The Nile did not always follow a straight course. Especially after the second day, it meandered widely and was bordered on both sides by fertile fields.

By midday of the second day, they had already arrived at Beni Suef, a pretty harbour in a very fertile region.

Mariam, Jossef and Jeshua took their leave of Nechti and his crew, Jossef paid their fares and they and their donkeys disembarked over the gangway, thankful to have plenty of time for finding their way to Heracleopolis magna before evening.

Outside Beni Suef, they found their road almost immediately. Grapevines were growing on both sides of the road, but the grapes were still too small to eat. Below the grapevines, cucumbers and pumpkins had been planted. At the roadside, under the first row of grapevines, there was a lush strip of grass upon which the donkeys grazed and the family ate a light snack. They all walked along the grass verge in the shadow of the grapevines; it was pleasantly cool, and easy on their feet.

Heracleopolis was located on the main road to Fayyum, an important oasis of the western desert. The town itself was very green, as it was watered by a tributary of the Nile. Grapevines were also growing here, and a beautiful park with palm trees and acacias looked inviting, but the family walked on, in search of accommodation for two nights. They almost forgot their fear in the beauty of the place, but as they approached the first guesthouse, they looked around to see whether they could see any Roman soldiers nearby. However, the few people out in the streets did not look at all suspicious, so they went inside and asked for a room. Unfortunately, the house was full, but the landlord directed them to a simple guesthouse two streets further on, which would presumably have rooms. The house in the west of the town did indeed have one room free, so they accepted the plain room with thanks.

In the evening, the landlord told them what there was to see in Heracleopolis: the Tomb of Neferkau and his wife, Sat-Behetep were not far from the guesthouse, and also in the same direction they would find the Temple of Heryshef, near which there had once been a lake which was mentioned as the lake of cleansing in the Egyptian Book of the Dead.

When they were alone again, Jossef said: «I have absolutely no desire to do any sight-seeing. It's just too dangerous.»

However, Jeshua objected strongly to this: «Oh please, Abba! I want to see the tomb and the temple!»

So the family decided after all to visit these sites next day. Now they needed something to eat, so they found an inn where they enjoyed vegetable pancakes with a tankard of beer.

When they returned to their room, Jossef was frowning and said: «We've so far lived quite well on our journey, Mariam. But now our funds are getting low. The ship was a good idea and speeded up our escape, but it set us back a fair amount of money. From now on, we'll have to tighten our belts.»

«I suppose that was to be expected,» replied Mariam. «After all, money doesn't last forever! If we avoid staying in guesthouses from now on, it'll have the additional advantage that we'll be more difficult to find.»

«That's true. I wonder how long they've already been searching for us without our knowing?» said Jossef «So far, we've been lucky they've never come across us. But in Babylon, our luck was out.»

«Oh come on, Jossef,» consoled Mariam, «We're still in God's hands. He'll continue to protect us! But if I'm honest, I must say this threat is also making me quite anxious.»

«Let's just hope we can always stay one step ahead of them!» said Jossef.

Towards midday of the following day, they wandered westwards and soon found the tomb near a rocky area at the edge of the desert. Jossef was on his guard, continually looking around to see whether there were any soldiers. But Jeshua remained unconcerned. Fascinated, he looked at a detailed relief on the outer wall of Sat-Behetep's tomb showing slaves bringing wine, a cornucopia and food offerings to the tomb. He glanced over to his mother and said: «These foods are to strengthen Sat-Behetep's Ka soul on its journey to Earu, Imma! That's what Merit told me.»

Jeshua walked on to look at the next relief. Mariam looked at Jossef with a frown and said: «I'm not sure it was a good thing that Merit told Jeshua all those things. Do you think he's beginning to believe them?»

«No, Mariam,» replied Jossef, «I think Jeshua is quite able to differentiate. I rather think he looks on all those stories as myths.»

It was only quarter of an hour on foot from the tombs to the Temple of Heryshef, but there was no longer any sign of the lakes, they had disappeared long since. The temple was in good condition. They entered the huge vestibule which was bordered by two side passages lined with columns. The columns were incredibly tall and thick – they made them feel tiny! The family went along the passage on the right to the back of the vestibule.

They walked between a double row of palm columns into the main hall where there was a long staircase on either side. They climbed the right-hand staircase to a gallery which was built over the side passage and afforded them a view down to the vestibule.

With a shock Jossef noticed two Roman soldiers down below, who had just entered and were walking through the vestibule casting a glance in all directions.

«Get back, quickly!» whispered Jossef to Mariam and Jeshua, who promptly pressed themselves against the back wall of the gallery. «There are a couple of soldiers downstairs. Perhaps they're searching for us!»

«What do we do now?» asked Mariam, also in a whisper.

Jeshua crept forward to the balustrade. He was small enough not to be seen from below. He peered down at the two soldiers between the uprights of the balustrade, then he turned to his parents.

«They're going into the main hall,» he whispered to them.

Jossef beckoned to Mariam and Jeshua to follow him. They squatted behind a post at the top of the staircase. Jeshua peered over the banister and whispered to them that the two soldiers were now approaching the left staircase.

Jossef breathed a first sigh of relief. «What now? Are they climbing the stairs?» he asked his son.

«Yes,» replied Jeshua.

«Both of them?»

«I think so, yes, both of them!»

«Right, listen: as soon as both of them reach the gallery, we'll run softly down this staircase, through the side passage of the vestibule, then straight outside and home without stopping!» ordered Jossef. «But keep near the wall of the side passage, otherwise they may see us.» Mariam and Jeshua nodded.

At last, Jeshua saw the two men appear on the gallery. He nodded to his parents. All three scurried softly down the stairs, through the side passage to the exit, and they were off like lightning to the guest-house. Jossef kept glancing back over his shoulder, but it appeared they had not been seen. That was close!

After that, they stayed in their room recovering from the shock, and did not risk going back to the inn for another meal.

«Maybe those two soldiers weren't even look-ing for us,» said Mariam, in an attempt to calm her own nerves.

«Maybe not, but maybe they were,» countered Jossef. «They were certainly looking for someone. We've been lucky again!»

«You see?» said Mariam, «God's with us! He won't allow us to fall into Herod's hands.»

«I think I'll pay for our room straight away, then we can leave really early tomorrow morning to avoid meeting any soldiers,» recommended Jossef.

«While you're paying, I'll go to the market quickly and get some provisions,» said Mariam. Je-shua would have liked to accompany her, but Mariam did not want to have him along, in case there were any soldiers there.

Jossef took Jeshua with him and went to find the landlord, who wanted to know whether they had visited the temple.

«Oh yes, it was very exciting!» replied Jossef, as he counted coins into the landlord's hand – it had, in fact, been far more exciting than the landlord could have imagined!

34

Travelling south, the family followed the course of the tributary which was named Joseph after the vizier Joseph from the Book of Genesis – the family found this very apt! The road from Heracleopolis to the south remained near this river, so they had no problem finding water.

After a while, Mariam had to call a halt as she was feeling quite unwell. She drank some water and soon felt a little better, so that they could move on again.

The verdant land was flat, and the path was not difficult to find. They saw no one other than a few farmers on their way to their fields and began to relax. By evening, both the river and the road took a western turn to the edge of the desert. A stone bridge had been built over the River Joseph, and they spotted hill crags in the rocky desert on the horizon. They crossed the river in the hope of finding a suitable cave for the night amongst these crags. Although there turned out to be no caves, the rocks at least gave them sufficient protection against curious eyes. The family set up camp, Jossef lit a fire, and they ate a light meal, as Mariam was too tired to cook. She could not even find the energy to sing Jeshua a lullaby, falling asleep as soon as they had eaten.

Mariam was luckily feeling stronger next morning. They breakfasted shortly after sunrise, returned over the bridge to the east bank of the river and found the southbound road again. The river meandered in wide curves between fields and small villages. After an hour they reached the village of Dishashah, where a friendly villager offered them a mint tea which they drank in front of her house. The woman told them that they were now between Lower and Upper Egypt.

«Did you know that Heracleopolis magna used to be the capital of Upper Egypt?» she asked the travellers. They said no, they had not known this, and the woman, who was a widow, glad of company and the opportunity to pass on her knowledge, told them a little about the eventful history of Lower and Upper Egypt which had sometimes been united and at other times divided.

«But the waters of the Nile unite us, no matter how those in power divide up our country!» commented the widow with a toothless smile.

The family took their leave of her and thanked her for the tea and the history lesson. They needed to get on, hoping to make good headway that day. The friendly widow gave them cakes sweetened with honey, but when Jossef attempted to pay her, she refused and wished them a good journey.

«If only everyone was so kind! …,» said Mariam, as the woman waved to them.

«Oh I don't know, we've met so many friendly people on our journey,» amended Jossef, and Mariam smiled sheepishly.

«Yes, you're right! I'm feeling rather negative ever since that shock in Heracleopolis. I'm gradually getting really fed up with this eternal travelling, always packing up and going on, never settling any-where, always in danger!»

«Chin up, love!» encouraged Jossef. «I'm sure better times are just around the corner!»

«Ah, but when, Jossef? When are things finally going to get better?»

Mariam was very despondent; her husband hardly knew her. He took her in his arms, kissed her tenderly and just held her close for a while. He felt responsible for his little family and only wished he could offer them more security. He too would have preferred life to be different than it was at present.

«Mariam, my love, I believe it would be good to cover a large stretch by ship again,» suggested Jossef. «This land travel is too slow, and you appear to be very tired. Expensive or not: let's return to the Nile! I'm sure we can find another ship travelling south. What do you say?»

«Quite honestly, I'd be really glad to!» nodded Mariam gratefully. «Even though we have no set des-tination, I just have this feeling we'll be safer in the south.»

«Yes,» agreed Jossef, «I have exactly the same feeling – great minds think alike!»

Shortly afterwards, the River Joseph flowed even further west, and they had to leave the river to return to the Nile, so they took the path to the south east which would bring them to the village of Ishnin Nasarah by evening.

«Nasarah!» exclaimed Mariam wistfully with tears in her eyes, «that sounds like Nazareth!»

«It does indeed,» agreed Jossef, «and I believe we'll need to sleep here, as we won't make it to the Nile before night falls.»

They traversed the village, filled their water skins at the well and walked on a little until they had found a good spot for a camp in an orchard. Jossef did not light a fire as they were too near the village. The donkeys grazed peacefully beneath the fruit trees, and Mariam distributed bread and nuts to the family. Jossef managed to find a few apricots under the trees which provided a sustaining meal together with the widow's honey cakes.

Before they slept, Mariam sang Jeshua a rather melancholy lullaby which brought tears to her own eyes. Once Jeshua had fallen asleep, Jossef asked her: «Mariam, you seem to be very sensitive at the moment, and you haven't been feeling well. What's up with you? Are you ill?»

«Oh, darling, I don't know,» replied Mariam and cried even more, «it's just all become too much for me! I can't go on like this. I want to go home! I feel so homesick for Nazareth and for my mother!»

Jossef took her in his arms and rocked her back and forth for a while. «Darling, if only I could conjure us back to our beautiful home in Nazareth! But is it possible there's another reason for your sensitivity? Are you expecting a child?»

Mariam looked deeply into her husband's eyes and nodded slowly. «I've been wondering the same thing. It is possible. And if that were the case, I don't know whether to feel happy or concerned.»

«Well, I'd be thrilled!» exclaimed Jossef beaming.

«Yes, of course. But we're so far from home, and it's difficult when we're travelling. Do you remember how difficult it was on the way to Bethlehem?»

«It was a little difficult, but we managed.»

«My sweet, you didn't have to carry the baby in your belly – I did! I remember very well what a weight it was!»

«Nevertheless, it would be just wonderful!» said Jossef and cuddled up to his wife, who stared into the darkness with wistful eyes and continued to brood.

Early in the morning, before first light, Mariam had to get up to be sick. When she returned, Jossef grinned and said he reckoned they now had confirmation.

Mariam smiled too. «It certainly looks like it!» It had been good to share her suspicion that she may be pregnant, and Jossef was right: Together, they would cope with this. Mariam lay down again and dreamed of life with two children. As dawn broke, they set off towards the Nile.

They had not been going for half an hour, when Jossef stopped abruptly, gazing into the distance. About one mile away there appeared to be a gathering of people, between whom he spotted the gleam of metal. He suddenly had a feeling of foreboding.

«Mariam, hold the donkeys quickly. I'm just going to walk on a bit, to try and see what's going on down there. Stay here, please!»

Jossef ran along the path until he came to a slight incline, which he climbed up to get a better view. He strained his eyes; it was difficult to tell, but there appeared to be a military unit of about twenty men standing in three rows. In front of them stood a man, presumably an officer, who was giving them orders. Jossef quickly ran back to his family.

«Soldiers!» he shouted. «We must go back quickly, and as far as possible! Mariam, we'll have to ride. I'll take Jeshua up in front of me. Come on, let's go, no time to lose!»

They mounted their donkeys awkwardly, as they were fully loaded with the baggage, and drove them on at a trot. The beasts seemed to sense the urgency of the situation, for they were almost galloping despite their heavy load. They kept up this pace for about half an hour. After this they began to tire, falling back into a slower trot, then a walk. Finally, they stood still and refused to walk another step. They had managed to travel a good five miles to the west.

«Right,» said Jossef, «I believe that'll do for now, we can lead the donkeys again. We've managed to outdistance the Romans for the time being.»

They dismounted and moved on, leading their tired beasts behind them. Just before reaching the small hamlet of Baysus they came to a well.

«We must water the donkeys,» said Jossef, leading his beast to the well, where he lowered the bucket.

Mariam was just about to do the same when a sharp pain pierced her belly. She doubled up, groaning, and fell to the ground.

«Mariam!» shouted Jossef.

«Imma!» shouted Jeshua.

Jossef hurried over to his wife, while Jeshua climbed down from the donkey and followed him. Mariam was bleeding and had turned very pale. Jossef gave her some water, then he carried his wife away from the well into the shade of a tree. He brought a bucket of water with which he bathed her forehead and stayed with her until she had recovered a little.

«Oh, Jossef,» sighed Mariam, with one hand on her belly, «our child's left us again,» and she began to weep bitterly.

Jeshua crept up to her. «But I'm here, Imma!» he said, mystified.

«Yes, my darling, I know,» replied Mariam and wept even harder.

Jeshua placed his little hand on his mother's belly. Slowly, the cramps ebbed away, and the bleeding stopped. Mariam fell back with a huge sigh and closed her eyes.

Jeshua looked up at his father enquiringly. Jossef took his son onto his lap, tenderly stroking his hair.

«You see,» he explained carefully, «we thought you were going to have a little brother or a sister.»

Jeshua looked at his mother lying in a pool of blood. Mariam lifted her head, took Jeshua's hand and said:

«Please go with your father to the well and fetch me another bucket of water. Then you two go for a walk for a while. In that time, I can clean myself up. I'll soon be feeling better!»

Jossef went with Jeshua to the well, where he also cleaned his robe of Mariam's blood, before pulling up another bucket of water for his wife.

«Abba, won't I have any brothers or sisters now?» asked Jeshua haltingly.

«Oh yes, Jeshua!» exclaimed Jossef, giving his son a hug. «You'll have brothers and sisters later, but not this time.»

They took the bucket to Mariam and left her alone to clean up in her own good time. While she did so, her tears flowed like streams. No doubt it was better this way, but it pained her nevertheless that a child had left her womb.

After quarter of an hour, Jossef came back with Jeshua and asked how Mariam was feeling.

«A little better,» replied Mariam.

«My darling, I'd love to give you more time, but I'm afraid we have to carry on, as we still don't know whether the soldiers are close on our heels or not.»

«Of course,» answered Mariam, «I'm alright again now, but maybe I'm not quite up to a full gallop!»

The family now needed to feel each other's company. Jossef and Mariam took Jeshua by the hand, and they walked slowly and pensively along the wide road south.

«Jossef,» said Mariam, «I can't sleep out tonight. Will we soon be reaching a town?»

«I can just make out a village about a mile from here,» replied Jossef. «It's at the edge of the desert, but it looks large enough that it probably has a guesthouse. Shall we try there?»

«Yes, please,» answered Mariam in relief.

They reached the village of Bahnasa at sundown. Thirsty as they were, they had already emptied their water skins, so they refilled them at the well near the entrance to the village, where their path met the River Joseph again. They sat in the shade of a tree and slaked their thirst.

Bahnasa was quite a large village, but there was unfortunately no guesthouse, so Jossef asked around for accommodation and was directed to a farm at the South-Eastern edge of the village. As they approached the house, the farmer was just returning with his heavily laden donkey. Jossef explained that they were looking for accommodation for the night, and the farmer offered them a room with a friendly smile. He told them he had just come from his fields where he had been harvesting cabbages.

There was cabbage soup thickened with wheat for supper, together with a tankard of beer. Jossef explained that they were on their way south and would like to travel on the Nile, but no longer had much money left.

The farmer grinned and winked with a crafty eye. «Aye, well I know just the thing for you!» he said. «My brother lives and works in Cynopolis, that's the ancient city of dogs. My brother's a cunning dog, too!» He laughed loudly at some private joke and coughed even more loudly. «Paneb's got to go to our sister in Hermopolis. He's a goldsmith and has to bring her her wedding jewellery. But Hermopolis is upstream, so he needs a second man to row with him. You could be that second man!»

«Ah, I understand – yes, certainly I could do that!» said Jossef, who had sometimes rowed on the Sea of Galilee. He had marked on his hand-drawn map that there was a Jewish community at Hermopolis and could hardly believe their luck.

«He'll ask a small fare of you, but not much …» – another cough – «'cause otherwise, he'd have to take one of his workers as second rower, and that man would be missing from work.»

«Yes, I understand, and that's absolutely fine!» placated Jossef, «and I assume your brother can row back by himself, as he'll be returning downstream, is that right?»

The farmer tapped the side of his nose with his finger. «Yeah, you've got it! That's it! My, you're a bright one!» – another cough.

Mariam smiled at this conversation and thought to herself that this sister must be quite a bit younger if she was just getting married. The farmer looked at least sixty, but that might be deceptive.

Jossef asked how to find Paneb in Cynopolis and the farmer gave him directions to his goldsmith's workshop. He told them it was at least twenty miles from Bahnasah to Cynopolis, so they would need to stay the night with his brother before setting off on the Nile.

«I'd like to give you something to take along for Paneb, save me a trip – oh, and remind me to fill your water skins before you go,» said the farmer, but Jossef shook his head.

«Thank you, and we can willingly take something along for you, but we only just filled our water skins at the well coming into Bahnasah, so we won't need any more water yet.»

«That old well? That's been dried up for years! You can't have got water from that!» exclaimed the astonished farmer.

«Oh yes, we did!» said Jossef. «It was working alright!»

«That's a strange thing, now!» said the farmer, his brows raised. «At any rate, you'll be tired and wanting your beds. I'll just show you to your room.»

Mariam was surprised to see that the room was nice and clean, and contained a proper comfortable bed, even though the farmer himself looked rather unkempt. She sank onto the bed with a sigh of relief.

«Jossef, love, I'm going straight to sleep! But you feel free to go and have a chat with the farmer.

I'm sure he'd love that. Perhaps Jeshua would like to come too.»

However, Jeshua was too tired and cuddled up to his mother, who was rather glad he was staying with her.

Jossef spent a merry evening in the farmer's living room over another tankard of beer. He learned quite a bit about the villagers of Bahnasa, about the farmer's family, Paneb and his sister Tuja in Hermopolis, and also about the situation in Middle Egypt under Roman rule. The farmer had a simple mind, but he was friendly and amusing, and Jossef laughed politely at his rather bawdy jokes

35

It was a large basket of cabbage heads that the farmer wanted the family to take with them to Paneb. In exchange, he asked nothing for board and lodging. However, with the additional weight of the cabbages on Jossef's donkey, they really did take the whole day to reach Cynopolis. Mariam mostly rode her donkey as she was still feeling weak.

Jeshua, on the other hand, was full of energy and looking forward to the river trip on a smaller boat. He ran ahead, throwing sticks at the birds and chattering away nineteen to the dozen. But when they caught their first glimpse of Cynopolis, he stared in silence at the Hellenistic town which was built over both banks and also on a long island near the west bank of the river. There were only the ruins of the walls and a few alabaster statues left of the Anubis temple on the east bank.

On their way into the town, they found a well and watered their tired, thirsty donkeys. Then they went straight to Paneb's workshop on the west bank, a large, obviously prosperous business employing ten goldsmiths who were presently tidying their work-benches for the night.

Jossef and Mariam introduced themselves and explained their situation. Paneb was pleased with the cabbage heads they had brought for him.

«My, you had a heavy load to carry!» he said with a broad smile. «If you wait a while, I'll be finished here and I can take you to my house. You're welcome to stay the night there. My brother did me a great service in sending you to me!»

Jossef tethered the two donkeys outside the workshop, and the family strolled through the lanes of the town for about half an hour. There were workshops for many different crafts located there, including a weaver, a baker, and a boatbuilder for papyrus boats which particularly interested Jossef.

When they returned, Paneb was standing in front of his workshop, shutting it up for the night. It was now becoming quiet in this part of town, as all the businesses had closed for the evening. Paneb led them through narrow lanes down to the pier at the water's edge where he asked them to take their places in his own papyrus boat with the typical Egyptian raised, banded prow and stern. Jossef led the two donkeys on board and tethered them in the middle of the boat, while Mariam and Jeshua boarded. Paneb rowed around the island where water birds were calling in the evening air. The oars splashed softly in the water, as Paneb skilfully manoeuvred the boat around the pointed northern end of the island and set a course for the east bank. As he rowed, he told the family there used to be a dogs' cemetery on the east bank. The mummified dogs were still buried there. The citizens of the old city of Cynopolis had previously worshipped dogs and the dog-headed god Anubis, and certain elderly inhabitants of Cynopolis still considered dogs to be sacred animals.

«Right, Jeshua,» warned Mariam, «Hands off the puppies, remember?»

Jeshua giggled and promised not to pick up any puppies. The memory of the cats in Bubastis and the threat of their worshippers was still a sufficient warning to him!

«As you see, there's not much left of the old city of Cynopolis now,» explained Paneb, «as it was almost completely destroyed during a civil war. We have the Ptolemy to thank for our present town.»

«Yes, you can see the Hellenistic influence,» added Jossef, while Paneb manoeuvred the boat to the pier where he jumped out. Jossef threw him the rope, and the boat was moored. Jossef and Mariam led the animals carefully onto solid ground. They followed Paneb up a steep incline to his villa, surrounded by palm trees and beautiful flower beds. A young dog came bounding up to them, barking merrily. It jumped up at Paneb, licking his face.

«Hey! Down, Busha!» laughed Paneb, «where are your manners? You can touch this dog, because she belongs to me. By the way, what's your name, lad?»

Jeshua hid behind his father's legs, and no one told Paneb the boy's name. Paneb just shrugged and said: «Come on, you can stroke Busha, look!»

Jeshua cautiously stretched out a hand towards the sand-coloured bitch, which sniffed at it and laid a large paw on his shoulder. He stroked Busha's head and beamed happily.

The boy and the dog ran playfully over the wide lawn, while the adults first went to stable the donkeys, then took their baggage to the house.

«I've got a bathhouse,» Paneb told them, «you're welcome to take a bath before we eat, there's plenty of time. Now I'll take these cabbage heads to the kitchen – thanks a lot for the transport, by the way! My brother will have been pleased you took on that task for him, and I'm also very grateful!»

Paneb left them, disappearing into the eastern wing of the large house with the cabbages. Jossef and Mariam unpacked their few things and made themselves comfortable in the luxurious room with a soft, comfortable bed.

«Oh Jossef, I feel rather squalid in these rich surroundings!» said Mariam despondently. «The farmer at Bahnasah never said anything about his brother being so rich. But Paneb's nice and doesn't seem to have any airs and graces.»

«No, he doesn't,» agreed Jossef, «but the difference between Paneb and his brother couldn't be greater! One so dapper – he looks a bit like a Greek! – and the other so poor and scruffy. You can see a slight similarity in their faces if you look carefully, but the difference is so great that one can hardly believe they're related!»

«However can Paneb allow his brother to live in such poverty, when he himself is so rich?» wondered Mariam.

«Maybe his brother doesn't want to live any other way? We don't know, and anyway it's none of our business.»

«Mm, yes – no. I'm not sure.»

Jeshua came charging in and told them Busha had been able to catch a small leather ball in the air. Jeshua still held the ball in his hand. His parents made the right noises, then told him to get ready, as they were now going to bathe. Jeshua crowed with joy! The family made their way to the bathhouse, where they spent a pleasant hour in the warm water.

Afterwards, a rich meal was served in an elegant dining room with a large table and reclining eating couches. Paneb's servants brought a hors d'oeuvre of mussels, a main course of two different meats, vegetables and grain and a dessert of fruit, all served with a fine wine. Paneb obviously had an excellent cook, for the dishes were delicious, and the family gave way to temptation, greatly overindulging.

«We'll be leaving tomorrow morning early,» said Paneb, after they had talked for a while. «I'll call you when it's time to get ready. We'll have to make one stop between here and Hermopolis; we can stay the night with friends of mine in Gebel el-Teir. Now you'll need your sleep. I wish you a very good night!»

The family dragged themselves to their room with heavy stomachs. Digestive problems disturbed their sleep, but the comfortable bed was exquisite!

***

Shortly after sunrise, a servant came to wake the family and invite them to take breakfast in the terrace room which provided a wonderful view over the Nile. Paneb was already sitting at the table. He greeted them with a smile. Dressed in a simple linen tunic, with his hair brushed instead of set in curls on top of his head, he was hardly recognisable. Now the likeness to his brother was slightly more evident.

«Sleep well?» he asked.

«Thank you,» answered Jossef vaguely and diplomatically, «and you?»

«Yes, very well, thanks! We'll leave as soon as we've eaten, so that we don't arrive too late at my friend's place in Gebel el-Teir.»

After their delicious breakfast, Jossef loaded their donkeys, Jeshua said goodbye to his four-legged friend Busha, then they all went down to the pier, took the donkeys on board and tethered them in the middle of the boat. Paneb asked Jossef to take his place on the second thwart. Mariam and Jeshua sat on the middle seat near the beasts.

Paneb cast off, climbed on board and took his place on the remaining thwart. With a few skilful strokes of his oars, he steered the boat to the middle of the river.

«And now – pull along with me!» he ordered Jossef, who immediately took up his oars and rowed with strong strokes, adopting Paneb's rhythm. They were travelling upstream, but the boat swiftly gathered way – the two strong men were a good team. Jeshua shouted for joy, and Jossef enjoyed using his full strength for a meaningful purpose. Paneb relaxed and smiled at Jossef – with his help, they would accomplish the stretch in good time. He was most satisfied with his unexpected additional oarsman.

Mariam was looking happy once more. She struck up a song which exactly matched the rhythm of the oar strokes. Jeshua sang along with the chorus, and soon all four of them were singing along animatedly, giving the men's rowing even more thrust! Paneb laughed, feeling glad that he had taken these strangers on board. It made the journey much more enjoyable!

The landscape of the east bank had changed. Now, the Nile flowed under high rock faces, with only a small strip of arable land between. Jeshua looked up, blinking against the sun, and saw a large raptor circling high above on a thermic current of air. It landed in the rock face, fed its brood sitting on the nest and flew off again in search of further prey for its young.

By this time, the sun was high in the sky. Paneb made for a spot on the west bank in the shade of a few trees and allowed the boat to run up onto a small sandy beach. He conjured up a large basket in which he had packed ample provisions. Jossef had become very hungry from the strenuous rowing, and he partook eagerly of the food. Mariam was still feeling full from the previous evening's meal and ate little of the delicacies Paneb had provided for them. However, they all drank thirstily, as it was hot, and they had had no protection from the sun on the water.

After their snack, Paneb allowed time for his second oarsman and himself to recover, as it was the hottest part of the day and pointless to continue rowing yet. During this break, he showed the family the beautiful gold jewellery he had made for his sister's wedding: a necklace decorated with lapis lazuli which was draped over neck and shoulders; a headdress in the same style with a lapis diadem for the forehead; matching earrings and two rings. Mariam went into raptures over it. Paneb passed her the jewellery and told her to try it on. Under Paneb's instruction, Jossef helped his wife to put on the jewellery around her neck and head. Soon she was looking like an Egyptian bride!

«Pretty, Imma!» exclaimed Jeshua.

«Yes, isn't she?» said Jossef, «I'd marry your mother as an Egyptian bride too!»

Mariam leaned cautiously over the edge of the boat to see her image reflected in the water – the headdress nearly slipped into the water! She gasped and just managed to save it. Paneb's eyes widened, and he turned a little pale.

«Oh I'm so sorry, Paneb!» she said sheepishly. «I'd better give it all back to you before something happens to it!»

Very carefully, she passed the costly pieces over to Paneb, who wrapped them in a cloth and put them away in the basket with a serious expression. «Well, it was my own fault for boasting about my work!» he admitted.

«The jewellery is beautiful, Paneb!» said Jossef. «You're very talented, and your sister's bound to be thrilled with it!»

«Yes,» agreed Paneb, «I do believe she'll like it – providing it arrives in one piece!» and he winked at Mariam with a smile.

36

As soon as the worst of the heat was over, they all took their places, and the two oarsmen pulled together again. Jossef could now feel his arm muscles after the break, and it was a relief when two hours later, Paneb told them they would reach Gebel el-Teir on the east bank in just one more mile. Mariam and Jeshua looked in that direction and saw a small village lying in a gap in the rock face where a Wadi led into the hinterland – a desert village, were it not for the Nile; sandy, dusty, and dry.

Paneb moored the boat at the pier and the donkeys were taken ashore. They all walked into the village, a collection of simple mud-brick dwellings. Paneb, who was carrying another large, heavy basket, pointed towards the right-hand cliff-top and told them a Roman temple had been built up there a couple of years earlier. He then led the way to his friend who lived in an old mud-brick house at the top of the village where it was even drier, with an old well in front of the house.

They were simple but very friendly people. Mariam and Jossef were amazed to see how Paneb seemed just as much at home in these surroundings as he had done in his luxurious villa. Paneb had brought gifts for his friend and his family: fresh vegetables, cakes, and two large pitchers of wine. Their host left the travellers plenty of time to stretch their legs and to rest before the evening meal. Mariam and Jossef went with Jeshua to the rock face at the edge of the Wadi. They found steps hewn almost vertically leading upwards in an audacious curve to the top of the cliff. Of course, Jeshua wanted to climb to the top. Jossef was too tired from rowing, so Mariam set off slowly up the steps with her son.

«Be careful!» called Jossef from below.

«We will!» the two climbers replied, setting each step cautiously, Mariam always looking upwards, as the rockface was very steep. The last few steps took all Mariam's strength, but Jeshua was still full of energy. They found the temple close by the steps and sauntered around between the columns. It was not a large temple, but it had an attractive, symmetrical layout. Wandering in the cool of the late afternoon, they slowly recovered from their climb. After a while, Roman priests arrived to celebrate a ritual sacrifice, so Mariam and Jeshua returned to the top of the steps and admired the breathtaking view from the clifftop over the verdant banks of the Nile.

The descent was considerably more difficult than the ascent. Dusk was falling, and they had to place each foot very carefully. To keep herself from feeling dizzy, Mariam stopped now and then to lean against the rockface and look upwards. Jossef was waiting for them at the bottom of the steps, where Mariam threw herself into his arms and breathed a sigh of relief.

Once Jeshua reached the bottom, he gazed up the rock face they had just descended. He nearly lost his balance and put out his hand out to support himself on the rock surface. Small lumps of sandstone crumbled and rolled from the rock face where his hand had laid.

«Oh!» exclaimed Jossef, «this stone's very soft and loose! We'd better keep a good distance from the cliffs!»

Jeshua looked up again and discovered a nest in the upper third of the rock face. He asked his father what birds were nesting there. Jossef explained that they were falcons.

«Merit told me the god Horus has a falcon's head,» said Jeshua. «and now I've seen a real falcon!»

He caught sight of an even stranger bird with a horn above its thick bill[33] hammering a hole in the soft rock. He pointed it out to his father, who shared his amazement at the strange creature but was unable to tell him what bird it was.

***

It turned out to be a most enjoyable evening at Paneb's friends house, and it was also a very long evening. In the end, Jossef was so physically exhausted that he retired to their room and lay down, to allow his aching limbs to recuperate.

Next day, he was surprised to note that the pain had all but disappeared, and he was able to row just as strongly as the previous day. They continued to make good headway. There were still cliffs to their left on the east bank. The strip of arable land between river and cliffs sometimes became wider and in other

---

[33] Hornbill

places it was quite narrow, whereas the west bank was always green and fertile.

Jeshua's eyes were fixed mostly upon the rock face. He saw many falcons nesting and was fascinated by the birds.

There came a point where the rock face rose vertically from the bank of the Nile, which wound around the cliff in a sharp left curve. They had almost circumnavigated the curve and were just rowing past the steepest spot when Jeshua shouted: «Stop!»

It was such an emphatic shout, that the two oarsmen immediately stopped rowing and allowed the boat to be pulled back by the flow of the river.

«What's up, lad?» asked Paneb, irritated.

At that moment, a huge boulder thundered down from the highest point of the cliff face and landed with a loud splash in the water not far from the prow of their boat. Mariam screamed, and the two donkeys started to bray as the boat rocked perilously, almost throwing them off their hooves. Jossef and Paneb stared unbelievingly at the spot where the boulder had hit the water – if they had continued rowing, their boat would have been struck by that huge lump of rock!

Jeshua attempted to calm the donkeys. Paneb tried to counteract the rocking of the boat with his oar, and Mariam bailed water out of the boat using a pot. Slowly, the boat stopped rocking. They calmed down but were still trembling from shock, all except Jeshua who had remained completely calm.

«The gods be praised that you always kept your eyes on the rock face, my lad!» exclaimed Paneb. «Well done! You saved our lives!»

As the two men began to row again, Mariam laid her arm over Jeshua's shoulder and asked him quietly: «Did you see the rock start to split up in the rock face, Jeshua?»

«Not really, Imma,» replied Jeshua. «I looked up there and saw how it got like this …» and Jeshua tensed both his fists until they trembled. «That's when I shouted 'Stop'. The rock only split and fell down afterwards.»

«Could you see the tension in the rocks?» she asked.

«It wasn't really seeing, like I'm seeing you. It was more like knowing something was about to happen,» Jeshua attempted to describe what he had experienced.

«At any rate, it's a very, very marvellous thing that you were able to do that, my darling!» said Mariam, hugging Jeshua to her side. He smiled up at her.

The rest of the journey continued without further mishap. In the late afternoon, beyond another curve of the Nile, they saw the old city of Amarna far ahead on the east bank: the town of the pharaoh Echnaton. On the west bank, there was a small harbour.

«This is the harbour for Hermopolis,» said Paneb. «From here, it's only a short walk into town. It's one of the largest towns in Egypt.»

He pointed to the south-west where they could see the tall buildings and temples of the city.

«Do you see that fort there?» asked Paneb, pointing to a large fortress on the bank of the Nile to the south, opposite Amarna. «That's the customs office. If you want to continue upstream, you have to pay, and it's not cheap!»

«In that case, it's a good thing we're disembarking here!» smiled Jossef.

«Exactly!» laughed Paneb and helped the family coax their donkeys off the boat. The two beasts were quite shaken by the rockfall, and it took some patience before they were finally on solid ground again.

«I hope you'll stay here for a few days!» said Paneb, while he moored the boat. «My sister's wedding is in one week – you'll be welcome to join in the celebrations, if you want!»

«After I almost dropped her jewellery into the Nile?» said Mariam with a wink.

«Look at it this way: Your son saved our lives,» replied Paneb, «otherwise I wouldn't even be here now, let alone the jewellery, so I reckon we're about quits!»

They laughed, but Jossef said they would not be joining in the celebrations as they did not belong to the family. However, they would be pleased to stay a few days, and if they could help with the wedding preparations in any way, they would be only too pleased to do so.

Paneb led the way from the harbour along a busy street directly into the town centre. The family looked in amazement at the number of people in the streets, the height of the houses, some of which were up to seven stories high, and the elegance of the town. In the town centre, all houses were built in the same Hellenistic style, giving it an aesthetic and homogeneous appearance. The streets were laid out at right-angles to one another on a grid. Paneb went right, then left, and after a few hundred yards right again.

«Oh,» sighed Jossef, «all the streets look the same here! I'm not sure we'll find the way on our own!»

«It takes some getting used to, that's true, but you'll soon get the hang of it!» commented Paneb encouragingly. «To be on the safe side, I'll draw you a plan of the town.»

Paneb's sister Tuja lived on the top floor of a six-storey building. Once they had stabled their donkeys, they mounted the circular staircase in the centre of the house behind Paneb, who opened the door of the apartment.

Tuja came to meet them, beaming. She was a beautiful, slightly plump woman, no longer in the first flower of youth, probably about 25 years of age, certainly younger than Paneb or his brother. She was wearing her black hair in two long plaits.

Paneb explained that Jossef had taking on the rowing with him, then he introduced everyone. Jeshua stayed in the background, attempting to make himself invisible, and indeed no one asked him his name. Tuja showed the family to their room and gave them time to freshen up.

«We'll eat in one hour!» Tuja told them. «On the bottom floor, there's a bath if you wish to use it.»

They did indeed wish to, particularly Jossef who appreciated the warmth of the water to relax his tense muscles.

As in Paneb's house, it was an opulent meal. Paneb and the family had worked up an appetite during the adventurous boat trip, and they ate hungrily. This time, no digestive issues disturbed their sleep since they were completely exhausted from the events of the last few days. They slept almost as soon as their heads touched their pillows.

37

There was only one topic at breakfast next morning: the wedding! About 160 guests had been invited, among whom there would be several Roman legionnaires. They were friends of the bridegroom, and although they were not likely to show any interest in a small boy at a wedding, Mariam was still glad Jossef had refused the invitation.

Tuja and Paneb's parents were no longer alive, so the organisation of the wedding was all down to the couple themselves and the bridegroom's parents. As they were wealthy people, no one needed to worry about the cost. The bridegroom and his parents lived in the same house as Tuja, so the married couple would simply take over an additional floor, meaning that the family would own almost the whole house.

There appeared to be nothing for Jossef and Mariam to help with in preparation for the wedding, so the family went into town. After only one day, they were already getting the hang of the street system and were now finding their way around this lively city.

They wandered through the gate of a clay brick perimeter wall and over to the Thoth temple which had begun to be called the Hermes temple, as Thoth, being the god of script, communication, and magic, was synonymous with Hermes. The temple was located on a small hill in the centre of the perimeter wall. There was a magnificent portal at the entrance to the temple, with reliefs of Thoth's sacred animals, the ibis and the baboon. There were also reliefs of hares, since Thoth's consort was the hare goddess, Unut. Hermopolis was situated in the 'hare nome', the 15th land division of Upper Egypt. The portal was flanked by two even larger tracts known as pylons. Its columns were painted with alternating bands of red, blue, and yellow.

Inside the portal stood a large obelisk of black siltstone, a type of stone to be found in the flood-plains of the Nile. Jeshua was just able to make out the hieroglyphs for 'Pharaoh Nectanebo II' on the obelisk, but he got no further. It was too difficult, and he lost interest. He had all but forgotten Merit's hieroglyph lessons.

Inside the temple, there were two rows of thirty-foot-high columns with Corinthian capitals decorated with finely chiselled leaves. The stones appeared to be sprouting, it was very lifelike and cleverly done. Monumental statues of Thoth, of baboons and of ibises decorated the hall. There was also a statue of the god Seth; it seemed that he was worshipped here too. At the back of the hall, a group of live baboons had settled down to groom one another.

The family were tired, so they returned to Tuja's apartment, where a busy chaos still reigned. The dressmaker had brought Tuja's robe for the final fitting. The robe was made of expensive gold brocade, fitting tightly at the bust and falling to a full, floor-length hem. The dressmaker had also brought Tuja a gold blouse of gauze to go under the dress, and there was a long train made of the same gold gauze, which fell from the shoulders to the floor. Tuja looked stunning in the robe, and she knew it!

After a light supper, Jeshua went straight to their room as he did not wish to draw attention to himself, which absolutely suited his parents. Paneb told everyone about the incident with the jewellery and also about the rock fall, but he only mentioned Jeshua in passing, so his name did not crop up.

There was a comfortable atmosphere in Tuja's household with this friendly brother and sister, but Jossef was nevertheless on his guard lest their identity and that of their son should somehow be made public. However, the four days they spent in Hermopolis went by without the dreaded exposure occurring. Indeed, it almost seemed to Jossef that Paneb was purposely steering the conversation away from the subject. He appeared to have caught on to the fact that they had something to hide, and to be protecting them. Whatever! Jossef was very grateful for Paneb's intuitive discretion.

The family went to find the Jewish community at Hermopolis. They were able to spend the evening of the Day of Preparation in the company of a Jewish family and to visit the synagogue on the Sabbath. However, they did not accept the invitation to stay with the family for their remaining days in Hermopolis, as they did not wish to insult Tuja's hospitality.

When they took their leave of Tuja and Paneb on the morning of the fifth day, Paneb said to Jossef: «I can tell you're righteous people, Jossef. Of course, I've noticed that you're hiding something, but I'm quite sure it's nothing criminal, so I won't force the issue. It's entirely your business! May the gods go with you, and if ever you should return to Cynopolis, please don't hesitate to look in on me again!»

The two men embraced warmly. «Thank you, Paneb! You're a very understanding man, and I much appreciate it! Certainly we'll visit you again, if our fate should ever bring us back to Cynopolis – we'd love to!»

Mariam wished Tuja all the best for her wedding and for her future life with her husband. She embraced her hostess, and the family set off.

Their next destination was the town of Mallaui, after which they would continue southwards. In the meantime, the donkeys had recovered from their shock and trotted willingly along.

As they were leaving the town they passed the Thoth temple. Jeshua was eager to go inside, as he could hear the baboons in there, calling and howling in the early morning air, greeting the rising sun. The animals were regarded by the priests as the harbingers of their god, and therefore sacred. Jossef accompanied Jeshua through the gate and into the temple, while Mariam waited outside the perimeter wall with the donkeys.

Jeshua went up to one of the baboons, and as he did so, Jossef saw that one of the priests was observing him critically from behind the colonnade. Suddenly, the large baboon went for Jeshua, who screamed and stepped backwards, knocking over one of the smaller baboon statues, which went crashing against a large ibis statue, bringing it down with it. Both statues were shattered to a thousand pieces.

The priest immediately rushed over to Jeshua.

«What on earth do you think you're doing?» shouted the priest. «I don't believe it! Out of here!»

«I'm so sorry,» Jossef attempted to placate the priest, while Jeshua just stood there wide-eyed, «the boy was afraid of the monkey.»

«And to top it all, you're foreigners!» chafed the priest. «You've no business being in here at all! Out of here, get out, both of you!» and he went at the two of them with a threatening fist.

Jossef grabbed Jeshua's hand, racing out of the temple and through the gate. The priest called some colleagues, and they all came running out after them with the intention of punishing them.

A Roman soldier, who had become aware of the rumpus, appeared from the road to the south. The family were now standing at a crossroads, between the priests and the soldier. The priests called out to the soldier, explaining what was going on. The soldier asked the family what they were doing there, but before he could come any nearer, Jossef grabbed his son and mounted his donkey. Mariam mounted hers, and the family disappeared at a fast trot along the road to the east before the soldier could catch them.

They rode on until they reached the Nile, where a ferry happened to be waiting. They embarked and were rowed over to the east bank, after which they continued at a fast pace in an easterly direction until they felt the danger had been averted for the time being.

The donkeys were tiring and very thirsty, but they only had the water in their skins. Otherwise, there was not a drop of water in sight. Mariam filled her pan with the water from their skins and gave it to the donkeys. There was not much left for themselves. The region was dry and treeless, offering no shade. Once they had drunk the last drop of water, they sat in the sun, allowing their donkeys to get their breath and considering what to do next.

Jeshua wandered over to a spot behind a large boulder. He looked down at the ground, removed one of his father's tools from a bag and began to scrabble in the earth with it.

Jossef came over to him. «What are you doing, Jeshua?» he asked.

Jeshua continued to dig without answering. As he dug deeper, the soil was damp, and suddenly water sprang to the surface!

«Oh, Jeshua, that's amazing!» shouted Jossef. «Come over here, Mariam, and have a look at what our son's found!»

Mariam hurried over and was just as amazed as her husband. Mariam and Jossef began to fill the water skins. The water was flowing ever more strongly. Mariam led the donkeys over, so that they could drink their fill. The water was fresh, tasting better to the travellers than the best wine!

Mariam slowly climbed up to the top of a rocky hill to observe the lie of the land and to see whether they were being followed, which did not appear to be the case. She sat on a stone, looking over towards the city of Hermopolis where the elegant houses reached up towards the sky. The portal of the temple could be clearly seen, but there were no agitated crowds gathered there, nor could she see any soldiers or signs of a chase. Things appeared to have calmed down again. Jeshua clambered up the hill and sat beside his mother.

«Lovely!» he commented on the view of the fertile land to the west.

«Yes,» agreed Mariam, «it really is lovely, and now I believe we can relax. But that was close again!»

«I'm sorry, Imma,» said Jeshua contritely.

«You couldn't help it, Jeshua,» Mariam consoled him. «Of course, it would have been better if you hadn't approached the monkey, but you weren't to know how it would react. These animal idols are really getting you into hot water, aren't they?» Mariam smiled encouragingly at her son, who returned her smile gratefully. «And now you've found water again! You little treasure!» she said and planted a big kiss on her son's cheek.

The two of them climbed down from the hill and told Jossef all was quiet in Hermopolis. He suggested they had now better take the ferry back to the west bank, then walk along the Nile to the south. Later they could turn westwards towards Mallaui and thus avoid going anywhere near Hermopolis.

It was not so very far, and they met no further problems, arriving in late afternoon at the market town of Mallaui which was surrounded by smallholdings. They asked around for accommodation and were directed to a widow who was glad of the money for herself and her autistic son. She was not very sociable, but that was all the better for the family who did not wish to be conspicuous.

The widow did not offer them a meal, so they took some of their provisions outside and ate them at a pleasant spot under a group of palm trees beside the River Joseph, which here created the boundary between the necropolis and the town of the living. Towards evening, the wind freshened, sending the palm fronds swishing and dancing. It had been another eventful day, and the soothing evening atmosphere helped them to relax and forget all its dangers. Ever since Babylon, life had been fraught with danger and problems, and the family hoped beyond hope that those had been the last!

After a peaceful night and a refreshing sleep, Jossef paid the widow – the coins were dwindling, so he could not give her much – and the family set off again towards the south.

They had not even gone a hundred yards when they heard a strange voice behind them coming ever nearer and calling incessantly: «Meee-rit! Meee-rit!»

All three froze and listened. How was that possible? Was someone here named Merit too?

They turned towards the voice and saw that it was the widow's son following them. The widow stood in her doorway observing things from afar.

In a weird, artifical-sounding voice, the boy shouted again and again: «Meee-rit! Merit lo-ove!! Meee-rit! Merit lo-ove!!»

Jeshua's eyes narrowed. This was directed at him! For a brief instant, he had seen a grotesque-looking goblin sitting on the boy's shoulder.

«Come along, Jeshua, just keep walking!» said Jossef, «if we ignore him, he'll go away again.»

But instead, Jeshua walked up to the boy, stood in front of him and repeated: «No! Leave him!» just as many times as the boy shouted «Merit love». It was like a duel.

Suddenly, Jeshua raised his face to the heavens and cried: «Abba, help him! Abba, Abba, please help him!»

At that moment, the boy collapsed in a heap, like a puppet whose strings had been cut, and lay motionless on the ground

Jossef hurried over to the boy, placed a finger on his neck and felt for a pulse. He looked at Mariam and slowly shook his head.

Now the widow came running up. «What have you done? You've killed my poor boy! You devils!» she spat at them.

But Jeshua looked at his father, who was still kneeling next to the boy, and said: «No, he's not dead! He's only sleeping, Abba!»

Jossef pulled Jeshua along with him, and Mariam hurried after them, while the widow took her son in her arms and continued to wail loudly: «You've killed my boy!»

However, before the family had even reached the next bend in the path, Jossef looked back and saw the boy sit up, shake himself and rub his eyes. Otherwise he seemed to be unharmed.

«That's incredible!» exclaimed Jossef. «He had no pulse, he really appeared to be dead, but now he's alive again, and as right as rain!»

«Abba, he wasn't dead!» repeated Jeshua. «He was only sleeping.»

«Thanks be to God!» shouted Mariam. «But now let's get out of here! We've attracted quite enough attention!»

PART VII:

Moshe's Cave in the Hills

38

The road south followed an irrigation canal through fertile fields of chickpeas, grain, and cotton. Between each field were small irrigation channels leading off from the canal, which the family crossed by means of simple plank bridges.

It would soon be harvest time. Everywhere, the farmers were preparing for the harvest, sharpening their sickles, cleaning the granaries, and organising accommodation for the seasonal labourers. The family would be lucky to find a place to stay that evening. On the other hand, the hectic preparations would detract attention from them. They would just be one more foreign family looking for lodgings.

By evening, they reach the village of Sanabuh, where their luck was in. They were allocated a place in a simple workers' hostel. The evening meal was served in a large hall. The workers and their families sat on the floor around a long, low table, upon which simple dishes such as chickpea stew, hummus and flatbread were placed. There were also large jugs of water and beer in the middle of the table. Many of the seasonal workers knew each other from previous harvests, and many had brought their wives and children along. Conversation was lively and loud, centring on such topics as politics and economics. Just as they had hoped, no one paid any particular attention to them here.

After the main course, the women and children went outside, where the children played together, and the women grouped to chat.

The menfolk stayed sitting in the hall and were served cheap liquor. Jossef learned from the man next to him that most of them worked as builders during the rainy season. Sometimes though, when there was no employment to be had on large construction sites, they worked in quarries. This work was dangerous and exhausting, as they had to work hard in great heat. Many were killed in accidents.

Slightly tipsy from the strong liquor, Jossef went outside to air his heavy head and to search for his family.

«Ah, there y'are!» he said, upon finding Mariam and Jeshua leaning against the house wall, in conversation with a very dark-skinned woman from Upper Egypt.

«Pooh, Jossef, your breath smells terrible!» exclaimed Mariam, and the Egyptian woman laughed. «Come on, let's get off to bed, Jeshua and I are tired.»

«Me too!» said Jossef with a watery-eyed smile at his wife. «Le's go't sleep!»

«Good night!» said Mariam to the Egyptian woman, rolling her eyes. The woman grinned, said goodnight, and went to find her child who was still playing with his little friends.

Jossef awoke next morning with a splitting headache. Mariam said it served him right, but he stood up for his behaviour, saying that he could not have refused the hospitality or acted differently to the other workers without drawing attention to himself.

«It's all a question of moderation,» commented Mariam.

«Yeah, yeah, yeah!» groaned Jossef and went to load the donkeys. The family left without breakfast as the workers had already had theirs hours ago and had left for the first day of the harvest

They continued to follow the canal, making a short halt in the shade of a group of acacia trees for a sparse breakfast. The donkeys tore contentedly at the long, lush grass beneath the trees.

After only three miles they caught sight of the town of Cusae ahead of them on the southern horizon. They decided to take a brief look at the town before moving on. Cusae was not far from the Nile, less than a mile from the water. Walking into the town from the north-east, Jossef discovered to his surprise that there was a boatbuilder there! Why not directly on the Nile? – Jossef asked himself. He also asked this of the boatbuilder, who had just been chatting to an official outside his workshop.

«Ah, good question!» replied the owner. «You see, we'll be right on the water's edge here, once the floodwater rises!»

«What about during the dry season?» continued Jossef with interest.

«I've got another workshop over there on the Nile,» replied the boatbuilder. «We're just starting to build a number of boats which will be ready when the flood's at it's highest. In this way, we can work throughout the year!»

«That's a good plan!» said Jossef, explaining that he had worked in a boat and shipbuilders' yard in Ashkelon himself.

«Oh, in that case: Welcome, colleague!» said the owner, adding that he would be pleased to show him round the workshop, which he and Jeshua promptly took him up on. The boats were built of papyrus, but wood was also used for the floor, the benches, and the oar-brackets.

«If you're ever looking for work: I could use an additional man,» suggested the owner.

But Jossef explained that they were on their way south. The family took their leave of the boatbuilder and went to look at the town, which was quite large but had nothing of particular interest except a small Hathor temple.

Just as they were leaving the town, they noticed with alarm that a Roman legion was setting up camp to the south of the town, so they quickly decided to make a detour to the west, in order to skirt around the Roman camp at a great distance.

They turned off to the west and walked over the plain towards the rocky area marking the border between the Nile valley and the desert. Leaving the last villages behind them in the plain, they climbed a path to a stony hill where they hoped to find a cave for the night.

The stone was of a similar type to that of the caves near Beit Guvrin. Just like those caves shortly before Ashkelon, these also seemed to have almost organic forms. As they threaded their way between rocks and stones, Jeshua noticed a cave which had debris and wooden beams scattered in front of it. He pointed at it and called out to his parents: «Imma, Abba, what's that?»

Mariam and Jossef followed their son to the cave, leading the donkeys behind them.

«What was that, is more like it,» answered Jossef. «Someone once made themselves a real home out of this cave, with walls, doors and everything! But it must have fallen to ruin a long time ago.»

They walked on a little, and could hardly believe their eyes when an old man suddenly appeared from out of one of the caves, staring at them in surprise!

«I'm so sorry!» called Jossef, «we didn't mean to disturb you!»

«Ah,» said the old man, «with that accent, you must be foreigners like me! Where do you come from?»

«We're from Israel,» replied Jossef.

The old man's eyes nearly popped out of his head.

«From Israel!» he breathed respectfully. «I'm from Israel too!»

«You don't say!» exclaimed Mariam and Jossef, changing to Aramaic. «Peace be with you!»

«And with you,» answered the old man. «If you'd like to, please come into my cave. It's very simple and I can't offer you much, but since the Lord has sent you to me ...»

«Thank you,» said Jossef, «we'd love to!»

The family followed the old man into his cave where a small fire was crackling away, with a pan of water boiling upon it.

«Just right for a cup of tea!» said the old man, placing mint leaves into three clay beakers and pouring boiling water over them. Once he had placed a beaker of fragrant tea on the ground in front of each visitor, he squatted on his heels and looked intently into the face of each visitor. His eyes rested long upon Jeshua, then he said to him: «Youngster, come over here to me, please!»

Jeshua glanced at his parents who nodded encouragingly. He rose, went over to the old man and sat in front of him on the earth. The old man stretched out his hands to touch Jeshua's head. He stayed for a while in this position, then he asked: «What's your name, lad?»

«Jeshua,» he replied without a moment's hesitation.

«Ah, yes! I do believe you're the one!» said the old man slowly and softly. All of them heard the soft rushing of wind and beating of wings that accompanied his words. He began to recite:

«*Lord, creator of the world, now I can enter your kingdom,*
For I have seen the Blessed One whom you have sent to save all people;
Your light shines through him, showing your glory for the people of Israel and for all men.»

Jossef and Mariam were amazed at these prophetic words about Jeshua, as the old man genuinely seemed to realise whom he had sitting in front of him!

The old man explained that his name was Moshe and that he had once been a priest in the temple at Jerusalem. However, he had been here in this cave for many decades now. He had married an Egyptian woman of Jewish decent and had followed her back to her home country. They had lived together in Thebes for some time. When his wife died, he had wanted to return to Jerusalem, but he had ended up staying here, as the Lord had commanded him to wait in this cave until the Messiah came to him.

Moshe raised his hands and blessed the family, then he turned to Mariam and said in a chanting, prophetic voice:

«Behold, this child will become a stumbling block for many in Israel, for they will oppose him. Some, however, will stand straight again. But for you, mother of this child, it will be as if a sword pierced your own soul, when he causes the thoughts of the hearts of men to be revealed, both good and bad.»

Mariam felt quite shaken by the words, for old Moshe had spoken an uncomfortable prophecy.

In his normal voice, he said to Jossef: «Please return to my cave tomorrow, if you can. Tonight I'll meditate on what exactly my task is to be.»

«Certainly, we'll do that. By the way, my name's Jossef, and this is my wife, Mariam.»

«Pleased to meet you!» Moshe replied with a toothless smile. «and now I wish you a good night!»

«Goodnight, Moshe, and peace be with you!» the three of them said as they rose and left Moshe's cave.

They returned the way they had come and stood in front of the cave with the ruined walls. There was even an old well opposite the cave. Perhaps that would be a good place to spend the night. They tethered the donkeys to a wooden beam and unloaded their baggage. They were able to make the cave quite comfortable, and there was a cosy atmosphere, as if good people had once lived here.

As they sat around their own fire and discussed the amazing encounter with Moshe, they were all in agreement that they felt a blind trust towards this man. They had all heard the beating wings and rushing wind which had accompanied his words, and they were astonished how similar his words had been to those of the angel, both to Mariam and to Jossef, prior to Jeshua's birth.

«I like him!» concluded Jeshua, «and I'm glad we're going back to his cave tomorrow!»

39

The family did not return to Moshe's cave until midday. Mariam brought him some hummus and bread from their provisions, but Moshe refused the gift, saying:

«Thank you very much for the gift, Mariam! It's kind of you, but for years now, I've only eaten herbs and sometimes a few berries. My old stomach can no longer cope with such heavy food.»

Once again, they sat around Moshe's fire and were given a beaker of mint tea. When they had finished it, Moshe said ceremoniously:

«During the night, the Lord showed me my task with Jeshua. The boy is to stay here and to come to me. I can teach him many things which will be of help to him on his further path The Lord also showed me that King Herod is aiming to kill the child.»

Jossef and Mariam looked at one another. «It's true, Moshe. Herod really is searching for Jeshua. But if he's to stay here, ... we'll have to stay too,» said Mariam slowly.

«That will be necessary, yes,» replied Moshe. «You spent last night in Joah's cave.»

«Oh, so the man who used to live there was named Joah?» asked Jossef, wondering how the old man knew they had stayed there.

«When I arrived here, Joah was living with his family in that enlarged cave,» explained Moshe. «They were a happy, generous family and used to bring me food to begin with. At that time, I still believed I would only be staying here for a while before travelling back to Jerusalem. But the Lord commanded me to remain here and to eat nothing but herbs. Three years later, their youngest child was bitten by a cobra and died, so the family moved away from here. Understandable! They wanted safety for their other children.»

«That is sad,» said Mariam, «yet the cave has a good atmosphere, as if the happy times had remained, rather than the sad.»

«That's true,» agreed Moshe, «I can feel that too, and I do believe the family is happy now, wherever they've gone. But you never lose the sadness that comes from the loss of a child.» Moshe seemed to slip back into the past; his eyes had a faraway look, and he was silent for a long time. Then he turned back to Jossef and Mariam.

«If Jeshua can come to me at least every second day at around this time, that would be very good. If he wishes to come every day, that's even better.»

«What do you think, Jeshua?» asked Jossef, «Do you want to come to Moshe every second day, so that you can learn from him?»

Jeshua was already beaming at Moshe's last words, and he said joyfully: «Yes, I'd like to! Thank you, Moshe!»

«We thank you too, Moshe,» said Jossef. «If the Lord plans to do great things through our son, and that appears to be the case, he'll need to be spiritually equipped for his task. As to us, we will indeed settle in Joah's cave. With all that building material out front, I should be able to reconstruct it and make it homely for us.»

«In that case, we're now neighbours!» said Moshe and laughed gaily. The family laughed with him and began to look forward to their new life here in the stony desert behind Cusae.

They returned to Joah's cave, Jossef lit a fire and they began to discuss their new situation.

«Jossef, to be honest, I'm really glad to be staying here,» admitted Mariam. «All this travelling is so tiring, and I long for a home again. It also appears to be fairly safe here. But whatever will we live from?»

«That's a problem we would also have had if we had continued to travel,» commented Jossef. «We've now got hardly any money left.»

They sat for a while in front of the crackling fire, staring into the flames and searching for inspiration. Jossef suddenly jumped up.

«I've got it!» he shouted enthusiastically. «On my own, I can go to Cusae any time with no problem. As long as Jeshua's not with us, there's no danger. I could ride in and work at the boatbuilders' every day, coming home in the evenings! What do you think? Wouldn't that be a good solution?»

Mariam raised her brows. «Well, I suppose that's not a bad idea, and it would do you good. Yes, I think you should give that a try!»

Jossef stroked his wife's silky, dark-brown hair. «This is a new phase in our life. I'll go to work, Jeshua will have his schooling with Moshe – and you, Mariam? Won't the days be rather long for you?»

«I'll make us a lovely home here!» enthused Mariam. «Jeshua will still be with me a lot. I can continue to teach him the scriptures. Don't worry, I'll soon find ways to occupy myself! Trips down to the nearest village shouldn't be too dangerous, even if I take Jeshua with me.»

«So it's agreed!» exclaimed Jossef joyfully. «Tomorrow, I'll ride to the boatbuilder and ensure I can get employment with him … mm, I wonder how those papyrus boats are made! Do they create a wooden framework under the floor to support the papyrus? …» and Jossef was lost in thoughts of boatbuilding, while Mariam told Jeshua a bedtime story. Family life had found its way back into Joah's cave again.

***

Of course, Jossef was given the job. The boatbuilder was pleased to see him the next day and thrilled that he had come back for the job after all.

«I'm Khufu!» said the boatbuilder. «Welcome to my workshop!»

«My name's Jossef,» he replied, «and if you don't mind, I've got a suggestion to make about my terms of employment. I'd be satisfied with a very small wage if you'd allow me to build my own papyrus boat in my own spare time, but with materials from your workshop. And as an additional payment for that material, I can offer you some salt from Wadi Natrun.»

«Considering the fact that you still have to learn to work with papyrus, I think that's actually a reasonable suggestion,» answered Khufu content-edly. The two men agreed upon the terms of employment, and Khufu got one of his workers to immediately start showing Jossef the techniques of working with papyrus. Jossef, for his part, was able to make some suggestions from his experience in Daniel's workshop. These made good sense to Khufu, so that Jossef quickly gained recognition in the workshop.

It was a very contented husband and father who returned to Mariam and Jeshua that evening! Jossef told his family of the agreement he had come to with Khufu.

Jeshua jumped up and down with glee! «Yippee, We're going to have a boat!» he shouted and hugged his father's legs impetuously.

«Hey, mind out, lad, you'll knock me over» laughed Jossef and ran his fingers through Jeshua's dark curls. «Yes, we're going to have a boat, but it'll take a while, because I can only work on it in the evenings, and I've also got our cave to rebuild.»

Jossef rather suspected he may have taken on too much. On the other hand, after such a long period of unemployment he was raring to go. In fact, he started on the construction work that same evening, while Mariam cooked the supper.

40

Jeshua went to Moshe's cave next day and found Moshe awaiting him at the entrance. He laid his hands on Jeshua's head and spoke a blessing before they both entered the cave. That blessing soon became a ritual for them both, as did many other aspects of Moshe's teaching.

They both sat down behind the fire, looking out from the cave. Moshe said nothing for a long while, nor did he move. Jeshua glanced over at him.

«Can you sit quietly, Jeshua, doing nothing, without thinking, just being here?» asked Moshe.

«Not very well,» admitted Jeshua, «I get fidgety. My arms and legs start itching to move.»

«That's quite normal, especially at your age,» said Moshe. «At my age, it all comes quite naturally. But that's going to be a part of our meetings, just sitting for a while, not doing anything, not thinking anything, not saying anything. It's an exercise which will stand you in good stead later in life when things get hard, believe you me!

But as soon as you leave my cave, I want you to forget everything you learn from me. Life should be fun for you. At your age, you should be enjoying yourself. The difficult times will come for you soon enough.»

«What difficult times?» asked Jeshua somewhat anxiously.

«Sit opposite me, Jeshua, come nearer – that's it!» commanded Moshe. He laid his hands upon Jeshua's head and went into a trance, during which he kept murmuring: «Hmmm ... yeeess ... oooh ...»

He removed his hands from Jeshua's head and looked him in the eye with great intensity.

«Jeshua, you do understand, don't you, that we all have to die?»

«Ye-es ...»

«Every person dies a different death. Some people die in bed during their sleep, others have an accident or are killed in wars. There are those who suffer from terrible diseases and die in great pain. You'll not die peacefully in your bed, Jeshua, and you won't live to see your children and grandchildren gathered around you. But your life, and also your death, will be very important for many people. The world will become wider than it is today. And in this wider world, there will be people in all parts of the earth who will remember your life and your death for all time, finding in this their salvation. Through your life and your death many will reach the Kingdom of God.»

Jeshua's eyes widened as Moshe voiced this prophecy about his life. Moshe continued:

«Do you sometimes feel that you're particularly close to the Heavenly Father, Jeshua?»

«Not often. Sometimes a little bit, when my mother reads from the scriptures or sings psalms. But once, when a met a boy, I did feel it.»

Moshe laid his hands upon Jeshua's head once more and made his trance noises: «Aaah ... hmmm ... yeeess ...,» then he continued:

«Jeshua, what you saw was real. There really was a demon on the shoulder of that boy. The boy had a sickness of the spirit which allowed the demon to take possession of him. And what did you call out, so that the demon left him?»

«Um, I called out: Abba, help him! Abba, Abba, help him!»

«Exactly, Abba – Father!» replied Moshe with a soft smile. «We're all sons and daughters of God, but you're a son of God in a very special way, because you were conceived of the Spirit. You're God's beloved son, and he'll never let you fall, even if it sometimes feels as if he has. And so that you're well-armed for those times when you can't really sense your Heavenly Father's presence, we're going to continue these exercises of sitting still without thinking of anything and without moving. After that, we're going to recite some prayers together. Then you're to go home to your mother and really let off steam! Have lots of fun, Jeshua, and enjoy life with your dear parents! Right, now sit on your heels, lay your hands lightly in your lap and leave your eyes open just a crack, completely relaxed. Now breath in – and out – and in – and out, just feeling that you're in God's presence. If your thoughts go wandering off, bring them gently back time and time again, back to the in – and out – of your breath.»

Moshe and Jeshua sat still for some time. Jeshua glanced over to Moshe and his fingers began to pluck at his clothes.

«Just a few more minutes, Jeshua! Compel your spirit to be quiet again!» reminded Moshe. After another five minutes, release finally came, as Moshe moved slightly and said: «Now we'll pray together.»

«Oh Moshe, it's so hard!» complained Jeshua.

«Don't give up, Jeshua, everything's difficult to begin with! You'll soon master it, you'll see.»

Moshe stood up, raised his eyes and hands to heaven and said: «Heavenly Father, you have sent your Son Jeshua to me. Your spirit lives in him, your strength leads him. He is to be the way, the truth, and the life for many people. Father, teach him where to find the water of life, for his life will be the source of that water for many people.»

Moshe laid his hands upon Jeshua's head again, spoke a blessing over him and said: «There you go, Jeshua, now run home and enjoy life! Forget all I've said until you come back to me the day after tomorrow!»

Jeshua thanked Moshe and left the cave, jumping and hopping from one stone to another. Now and then, he took a stone in his hand and sent it hurtling into the sky. He arrived at Joah's cave quite out of breath.

«Hello Jeshua,» his mother greeted him, putting aside an item of clothing she had been mending. «How was it with Moshe?»

«It was difficult, Imma,» said Jeshua, «I can't sit still!»

«Hah! You've got ants in your pants, Jeshua! You're such a fidgety Phil! I can well believe you found that difficult. Come on, let's go for a walk, that'll do me good too!»

Mariam took her son by the hand and together they walked back to the place where they had climbed up the narrow path from the valley on their first day.

The nearest village, Muharraq, was not far away. Mother and son strolled between the green fields in the light of the late afternoon sun and came upon a young woman sitting in front of one of the first houses in the village, topping and tailing beans into an apron on her lap, while her small son played next to her on the path. They both looked up as Mariam and Jeshua approached. The young woman smiled warmly.

«Hello!» she called out, «enjoying the evening air too?»

«Good day,» greeted Mariam in her turn, «yes, lovely isn't it! How old's your little one?»

«He'll soon be three,» she replied.

«My boy's turned three already,» said Mariam. «We've moved into Joah's old cave, my name's Mariam, by the way.»

«Ah, that's wonderful! Joah and his family would be pleased to know their cave is being used again. My name's Anchesenpepi, but you can call me Pepi!»

«Phew, glad to hear it, Pepi! I don't think I could remember that long name.»

«You're not Egyptian, are you?»

«No, we're from Israel. My husband works at the boatbuilder's in Cusae,» said Mariam proudly.

«Ah, for Khufu!»

«Do you know him?»

«Not personally, but I know of him, and I know where his workshop is.»

Pepi fetched some sweet juice and moved over to make room for Mariam next to her, while Jeshua went to play a cat's cradle game with the little boy. Mariam asked for a knife and an apron, and helped Pepi to top and tail the beans. The two women and their two children thus spent a pleasant couple of hours, enjoying each other's company.

«Hello, Mariam, found a new friend?» they heard Jossef calling from afar. Jossef rode up to them, dismounted from his donkey and kissed his wife's cheek.

«Hello, love! This is Pepi,» answered Mariam. «Pepi, my husband, Jossef. We'll come on up with you, my love. It was really nice to meet you, Pepi!»

«Indeed it was, Mariam,» she replied, «have a nice evening!»

«Jeshua!» called Mariam, «We're off now!»

«Coming!» they heard him call from the other side of the house. Jeshua came running round the corner, straight into his father.

«Abba!» he shouted and jumped up into his father's arms.

«Hello, you cheeky monkey! Shall we go home now?» He put his son on his donkey, and the family slowly climbed back up the path, while Jossef told his family about his day at work.

Life was worth living again. They finally had a home and a daily routine with a real meaning, which they had sorely missed for so long. In their cave, they were able to celebrate the Sabbath properly and in peace, although there was no synagogue there. They were also able to celebrate the Feast of New Year, the Day of Atonement, and the Feast of Booths – Sukkot or Harvest Thanksgiving, but for these feasts they did miss the fellowship of a Jewish community.

Jossef went happily to Khufu's workshop every day. The work was satisfying, and he was contented. This gave him the energy to stay longer at the workshop in the evenings, working on his own boat. He was also working on rebuilding the cave each evening. The construction work was coming along nicely. From the material lying around, Jossef soon understood just how Joah had built the extension. He was making a similar construction, and he had managed to mend the old well in front of their cave.

Mariam was also playing her part. She had once accompanied Jossef to Cusae while Jeshua was with Moshe. She had bought two cheap carpets and new clothes for the whole family. The carpets immediately made the cave look more homely, and new clothes felt like a real luxury after more than two years in the same old things. She tore up the old clothes and made wall hangings out of them.

Jossef had brought some wood stain from the workshop with which Mariam painted the wood of the extension, to make it more durable. She suggested painting the wood with colour, so Jossef brought two pots of paint from Cusae the following week, one a cheerful red and the other a warm ochre. Jeshua helped his mother with the painting, and their cave dwelling was soon looking even better than it had in Joah's time.

Jeshua continued to visit Moshe every second day, and each time, Moshe reminded him to forget everything he had told him as soon as he left his cave, to let off steam and to enjoy life. Moshe was very much aware that the boy was still very young for such teachings, but fate had sent him to him now, and not later, so it seemed it was meant to be this way.

Jeshua no longer found sitting still quite so difficult. Constant practice had brought the desired results, and he sometimes even found a deep sense of peace whilst sitting.

Moshe extended the exercise as soon as he noticed that Jeshua had found this peace.

«Once you're completely still and you've found inner peace, Jeshua, you can start to open yourself to the presence of the spirit. Speak to your Heavenly Father from the bottom of your heart. He wants you to turn to him with your whole heart. Hold nothing back, Jeshua! He's waiting for you!»

«What should I say to my Heavenly Father, Moshe?»

«You can start like this: *Abba, Father, Holy One, I am here, and I will listen when you tell me your will.*

Keep it light and relaxed, like when you're sitting still, and expect nothing. This step will also take time.»

Moshe and Jeshua practiced this step for a few weeks, and to begin with Jeshua did not have the impression that anything was really happening. He felt nothing in particular and could hear no voice telling him what the will of the Father was.

But it was as it had been with sitting still. Gradually, Jeshua could feel the closeness of his Heavenly Father. He had already attained a strong concentration and could now abide in the presence of the Father for much longer. Moshe had never directly praised Jeshua, but now he said to him: «You're making good progress, Jeshua! You're allowing God's spirit to reside in you, that's excellent. Can you now also sense how much your Heavenly Father loves you?»

«Yes,» replied Jeshua without hesitation, «I can feel that now. Do you think my Heavenly Father's glad, Moshe?»

« He's very glad, Jeshua! He's been waiting.»

Moshe gave his little pupil the usual blessing and sent him off home to his parents.

He watched Jeshua skipping home over the stones in the last rays of the sinking sun and marvelled at the fact that in his old age, he had been given this great honour of becoming mentor to the future Messiah.

41

Everywhere, the harvest had now been gathered in. It had been a good year and a rich harvest. Now, the countryside rested in peace and quiet. The granaries were full; everyone could relax.

Jossef had expected the rains to start soon, as they had done in the North of Egypt. But now he noticed that the waters of the Nile had begun to rise without one drop of rain falling! He asked Khufu how this could be.

«Ah, of course you've only been in the north, Jossef» explained Khufu, «so you can't know. Here in the south there's hardly ever any rain, but the Nile still rises and we also have flooding, though not as much as in the north. The rain doesn't fall here, but in the upper reaches of the Nile on the Ethiopian Highlands, near the Atbara Spring. There'll be a real monsoon up there right now, with unbelievable amounts of rain falling in a very short time! And we get to profit from it too. Isn't that wonderful?»

«It certainly is! Amazing, I hadn't realised that!» answered Jossef, impressed.

The boats in the workshop were now half finished, and Jossef's own boat was also progressing nicely. By the time the waters reached the workshop, all boats would be finished and ready for launching.

Jeshua had become very impatient to see their own boat finished and to take it out on the river. Jossef therefore suggested to the family that they could take a trip south for a few days as soon as it had been launched – as a maiden voyage. They could leave the boat in Asyut and explore the surrounding area.

«Jeshua, you can give our boat a name!» suggested Jossef, so Jeshua immediately began to think about it.

He had found the name before the boat was even finished: «Gabriel!» he said to his father. «The boat's to be named Gabriel – Strength from God, because our boat's got to be strong!»

«Like the angel!» said Jossef, «That's a very good name, Jeshua! Mariam, I take it you agree?»

«Oh yes,» she said, «that's an excellent name! Let's just hope our boat really is strong!»

«Woman, do you doubt my skill?» ranted Jossef, acting the tyrant.

«Far be it from me, good spouse!» trilled Mariam sweetly. Jossef and Jeshua laughed.

However, Jeshua had to wait a while before he could finally board the 'Gabriel'. As the waters rose, pressure also increased to finish the commissioned boats, and Jossef no longer found enough time to work on his boat every evening.

In the first days of August, the water had finally risen to a level directly in front of the workshop, meaning that Khufu's pier had the ideal position. The customers came to collect their boats, and Khufu's coffers filled up from day to day.

At last, Jossef was able to tell his family to prepare for the trip south with the 'Gabriel'. While Mariam and Jossef packed the necessary provisions for the journey, Jeshua ran over to Moshe and informed him that the family were travelling south for a few days, so he would not be able to come for his teachings. Moshe blessed Jeshua and told him he would be awaiting his return.

In the evening, Jossef asked: «Mariam, will you be able to help me with the rowing? It's not far to Asyut, but it's upstream, and if I have to row alone, we won't get anywhere.»

«I want to help with rowing too!» exclaimed Jeshua.

«Let's wait and see, my lad,» said Jossef doubtfully, «I'm not sure you're strong enough! We'll see, alright?» he repeated. «Mariam, what do you think?»

«I'll do my best,» she replied, «perhaps it'll be better than nothing!»

The donkeys could sense they were off on their travels again as they were loaded up next morning. They brayed excitedly. Jeshua was also jumping around like a puppy. Mariam glanced back into the cave to check that they had not forgotten anything, and the family set off the way they had come through Muharraq three months ago.

It was good to be travelling with the knowledge that they would soon be returning home – quite a different experience from being permanently on the road with no fixed abode and living in constant fear of discovery. Obviously, they still needed to remain cautious and ensure that Jeshua was not found, but this was unlikely as long as they were on the water.

Jossef had moored the boat further upstream from Khufu's pier. When Jeshua saw the lovely craft with the name 'Gabriel' painted in demotic script upon narrow strips of wood on the prow, he shouted: «Our beautiful Gabriel!»

He climbed aboard, followed by Mariam and Jossef who carefully led the donkeys aboard and tethered them in the middle of the boat, as they had done in Paneb's craft. Jossef and Mariam each took their places upon one of the thwarts.

«If you want to try and row too, Jeshua, sit on your mother's lap,» recommended Jossef. «It'll be easiest for you to pull along with her!»

He did not really believe Jeshua would be able to help, but at least it would give him the feeling that he had rowed too.

Due to the flood, the Nile was now almost three times as wide as it was in the dry season, and the water was still flowing quite strongly. There was also a fair southerly wind. To begin with, the course of the river was reasonably straight, bordered on the east bank by cliffs down to the water's edge. Then the river meandered off to the west, leaving the cliffs behind. Although Asyut was not far from Cusae, it was farther than Jossef had thought due to the many curves in the river. Would they make it in one day?

But Jeshua hung onto his mother's oars and gave all his little body could give. Mariam was also rowing with all her strength. However, towards midday she shouted: «Oh Jossef! I can't go on! Can we take a break soon?»

Jossef, remembering the long lunchbreak Paneb had given them in the shade of the trees, sought a good place to moor the boat for lunch. They found a suitable spot shortly before the village of Hawatka. It even had a pier by a small clump of trees. Jossef rowed the boat to the pier with a few skillful strokes of his oars and moored the 'Gabriel'.

Jossef and Mariam led the donkeys ashore and let them graze the grass beneath the trees. The family ate a snack and drank copiously from their water skins, then they lay down in the shade and slept until the midday heat had passed.

Fairly well rested, they took the donkeys back on board and set off again. At least the south wind had abated. Towards evening Jossef knew they would make it. As the sun sank behind the western mountains, they saw the town of Asyut ahead.

«We've arrived!» rejoiced Jossef, and Mariam and Jeshua cheered. It had been a long, hard day. Jossef was proud of his family for rowing so stalwartly, and Mariam was proud of her husband for building such a wonderful boat.

They found a berth in the large harbour on the west bank and moored the boat. The donkeys were taken ashore, and the family set off immediately to find a place to camp, as they did not want to risk being discovered by any officials.

By the light of the moon, they made for the cliffs to the south-west of the town. After walking for a few miles, they found a suitable cave. Jossef lit a fire, and Mariam cooked a vegetable stew. As soon as they had eaten, all three slept soundly, and dreamt of rowing.

They discovered next morning that they had a wonderful view over the floodplains of the Nile from their cave. They saw how the agricultural areas in the valley had been separated up into flood basins with banks in between, each served by influx and outlet channels. During the highest flood levels, the basins were now flooded. For about six weeks they would remain closed so that the silt could settle and soak the ground below.

Asyut was built far enough from the Nile so as not to become flooded during the high-water periods, as indeed were all large towns on the Nile. Because the town held a strategically important position, the Ancient Egyptians had named it 'Sentinel'. This name still appeared to suit the place, as the family spotted the camp of a Roman legion to the south of the town to protect it from any threats from that direction, like the camp near Cusae. Flags fluttered in the rising sun, and the metal tips of the masts gleamed. Having now seen the camp, they were very glad they had gone straight to the mountains and not stayed the night in the town.

They left the cave, loaded up the donkeys and continued southwards along the base of the cliff. The dry southerly wind had freshened again, raising dust and sand to swirl about them.

After rounding the head of a rock face, the path took a south-western course. Now they saw the upper reaches of the Nile and the lands of the south, whereas Asyut had disappeared behind the cliffs. The limestone rock face towered above them, making them feel very small.

Towards the southeast they saw the impressive rock-cut tombs of Qau in the distance on the east bank of the Nile. Three of the huge rock tombs had a lower temple with a colonnaded forecourt. A covered pathway led up the mountain to a large upper temple cut into the rock. The fourth rock tomb consisted only of an upper temple. This view gave the family their one and only impression of the landscape of Upper Egypt. They would not travel there, as it was too far.

In the early evening, they found themselves a cave which looked suitable for the night. Jeshua ran ahead towards the cave entrance, then he stopped abruptly.

At the cave entrance sat a lioness, watching the approach of the boy with her head lowered. She growled a soft warning. Jossef and Mariam stood stock-still, stiffening in panic, and taking the donkeys on a short rein. Mariam slipped her trembling hand cautiously into that of her husband. They did not dare move or come any closer.

In slow motion, Jeshua lowered himself to the ground and squatted on his heels, with his face always towards the lioness. For a long time, he sat motionless and silent in front of the beast.

Suddenly, the lioness rose. Jossef's hand grabbed his wife's as he tensed every muscle of his body, ready to intervene.

But then, something incredible occurred. Growling softly in the back of her throat, the lioness slowly walked away from the cave and disappeared round a rock spur.

Mariam ran straight up to her child and clasped him to her. «Jeshua! Oh, my boy! I really thought we'd lose you!» she exclaimed, crying from relief. Jossef also ran up and hugged his son.

«Jeshua, however did you do that?» he asked. «I also thought the lioness was bound to attack!»

«Imma, Abba, it wasn't so bad!» answered Jeshua, «Moshe's taught me how to talk to wild animals. He said if I'm going to live in the desert, I need to be able to do that.»

«You spoke to the lioness?» asked Mariam, amazed. «But how?»

«Moshe told me I have to look just to the side of the animal, not straight into its eyes. First I have to feel its soul. After that, I can send a request from my soul directly to its soul.»

«That's what you did?» asked Jossef, just as amazed as his wife.

«Yes, and Moshe always says I have to do it with authority and respect, otherwise it won't work. My wishes must never harm the world of the animal.»

«Moshe taught you a very practical lesson there!» added Jossef. «I'll be eternally grateful to the old man. But isn't that difficult?»

«It was easy with the lioness,» replied Jeshua, «but Moshe got me to practice with more difficult creatures such as spiders, cobras and scorpions.»

«Why is it easy with the lioness but more difficult with the smaller creatures?» asked Mariam.

«It has nothing to do with the size, Imma,» replied Jeshua. «The souls of the spider, the cobra and the scorpion are very different from our souls, but the soul of the lioness is more similar to ours.»

«At any rate, it's wonderful that Moshe taught you that,» said Mariam. «He's a very wise man.»

Together they entered the cave which was now in complete darkness, as the evening sun had disappeared behind the mountains.

After Jossef had lit a fire, they saw just how huge the cave was – it was at least thirty feet wide and extremely deep. The ceiling was completely blackened by soot, showing that at some point people must have lived there. Mariam cooked a wheat soup, and Jossef went to the back of the cave with Jeshua to lay out their mat for the night. Jeshua gazed at the back wall.

«Look, Abba, there are drawings on the wall!» he exclaimed, pointing at a large red painting.

Jossef lit a thin taper of wood, brought it over to the wall and illuminated the rock painting with it.

«Who's the goddess painted there, Jeshua? Do you know?» asked Jossef.

«Um, could be Isis. No, wait a minute, it says here: Hat ... Hathor! It's Hathor, the goddess of love and of motherhood! She also has cow's horns with the disc of the sun between them, like Isis!» Jeshua declared, having studied the hieroglyphs and paintings. «She looks like a cow,» he added.

Jossef examined the whole length of the painting which covered the entire back wall of the cave. It appeared to be very old. There were images of women dancing. In one picture, Hathor stood with a staff in hand and accompanied by a lioness, looking towards the dog-headed god Anubis. Jossef tapped Jeshua on the shoulder, pointing to the lioness.

«Our lioness!» exclaimed Jeshua joyfully.

After they had finished their soup, Mariam also came over to look at the wall painting. The depicted women were all beautiful. Some of the pictures were very sensuous, even lascivious. This was unusual in Egyptian art which was generally stylised and formal.

«Well, my darling,» whispered Jossef in his wife's ear, whilst lovingly stroking her hair, «as we happen to have landed in the cave of the goddess of love ...» and his mouth sought Mariam's lips. She responded to the kiss, while he gently drew the garment off her shoulder and traced its curve with his finger. A wave of pleasure gripped Mariam, then they were in each other's arms abandoning themselves to passion, while the goddess of love looked down from the wall upon the couple in approval.

Jeshua had wandered outside to see whether the lioness was still around anywhere. He sat in the cave entrance, playing with twigs and stones and softly humming a melody he had often heard his mother sing.

42

The next day, they descended from the mountains and returned to Asyut, where the 'Gabriel' was still safely moored at the pier. Jossef suggested that Mariam and Jeshua should now act as coxswains instead of rowing.

«We'll be travelling downstream, so we'll be fast, even if I row on my own. That's why I'll need your help steering around other craft on the river.»

Jeshua was amazed how much faster they were travelling than on the outward journey.

«Abba, you're so strong!» he exclaimed.

«That's the river pulling us along!» explained Jossef.

Long before midday, they spotted the place where they had taken a break under the trees with Paneb, but this time they carried on, as they did not yet require a break and were keen to get home. The 'Gabriel' had well proved its worth; Jossef was satisfied with his craft. Next day he would be returning to work.

By the ninth hour, they were already within sight of Cusae. Jossef rowed up to Khufu's pier, moored the 'Gabriel' and helped Mariam to lead the donkeys ashore.

One of Jossef's colleagues was just leaving the workshop. He spotted Jossef and asked: «So how did your boat perform in the water, Jossef?»

«It was fine! The boat's good, everything's in order. I'll no doubt take it on another trip with the family. My wife even helped me with the rowing, you know!»

«Oh, I'm impressed! Well, see you tomorrow, Jossef and have a good evening, all!»

«You too, thanks!» called Jossef, as the family walked away towards Muharraq.

Pepi and her little boy waved to them as they walked past her house.

«Did you have a good time?» asked Pepi.

«Yes thank you, Pepi! The boat really proved its worth!» replied Mariam.

«Have you got anything to eat at home? Or would you like some vegetables from my garden?»

«Oh, we'd love some, please, Pepi!» said Mariam, disappearing with her friend into her garden and returning a few minutes later with fresh herbs and vegetables.

«Pepi, I'll bring you some salt from Wadi Natrun if you want,» offered Jossef.

«Yes please, that would be great!» nodded Pepi, before the family took their leave and climbed the path back to their cave.

It was a true homecoming. Their beautiful, cosy cave welcomed them, and they felt a great warmth and a sense of well-being. But Mariam still often thought of her real home and her mother. Was Hannah still alive? Was she well? Had she been able to find out anything about her family's fate? Mariam's yearning was still just as strong; even their lovely cave did not entirely compensate for it.

The Nile floods were slowly receding. Every day, Jossef checked to see that the 'Gabriel' was still afloat. Khufu's workers were now occupied with clearing the workshop before moving back to the other one near the Nile bed.

On the way home from work, Jossef noticed that the flood basins had now been opened, allowing the water to flow into the lower lying fields and en-suring that these were also irrigated. After four quiet months of the floods, everywhere was now a hive of activity.

Now and then, Mariam went down to visit Pepi while Jeshua was having his teachings. Sometimes, Jeshua came down afterwards to play with Pepi's boy until Jossef joined them after work, and the family of-ten walked up to the cave together. Those were days of comfortable routine which strengthened their family bond. They had lived in the cave for almost half a year, and it had become a real home to them.

Jeshua had now started to visit Moshe every day. He felt driven to do this, as if they no longer had much time together.

One day, Moshe met Jeshua at the cave mouth with the words: «Jeshua, last night I had another vi-sion. I saw that it would not only be your life and death which would be important for the salvation of the people, but also and above all your resurrection from the dead! I saw that you would be raised from the dead and would appear to many people – I couldn't exactly see how this would happen. But this vision has given me a deep certainty that I will also live on after death in the Kingdom of God. So you're not to mourn after I'm dead, Jeshua, as we will meet again on the other side!»

He proceeded to teach Jeshua as he had done every day, and Jesua went hopping and skipping home as he had always done after the blessing, which on that day was rather more prolonged and portentous than usual.

When Jeshua arrived at his mentor's cave next day, Moshe was not waiting in front of it as he usually did. Jeshua stopped short, looking around to see whether Moshe was somewhere outside, then he entered the cave hesitantly. The fire had gone out. The cave was in darkness, but there seemed to be a slight golden shimmer in the air. Jeshua clearly heard the beating of wings and rushing of wind. Then he caught sight of Moshe, sitting up against the back wall of the cave, his eyes slightly open and a peaceful smile frozen in death upon his lips.

Jeshua had never seen a dead person before. He gasped in shock, then he slowly went up to Moshe and squatted on his heels in front of him. He sensed that he was not alone in the cave with his deceased mentor. There were thousands of good souls here with him to attend Moshe's passing. There was a cheerful, very peaceful atmosphere. Indeed, Jeshua could feel no sadness. Rather, he was pleased that his mentor was clearly now in such a good place.

«Thank you for everything, Moshe!» breathed Jeshua respectfully. He rose and went slowly back to his parents to tell them that Moshe had died.

Jossef and Mariam followed their son to Moshe's cave and approached the old man's corpse. All three stood in silent prayer before him for a while. Then Jossef said: «I believe we ought to dig a grave and bury him before he becomes the prey of some wild animal.»

Jossef went down to Muharraq to borrow a spade from Pepi. By evening, Moshe's grave was ready. They wrapped him in a sheet and laid him in the open grave, lighting four candles at the corners. They brought out Moshe's ceremonial objects, laid them with the body and covered the grave with earth.

Jeshua and Mariam stood beside Jossef as he recited the Mourning Kaddish[34], accompanied by the strong sound of beating wings and rushing wind:

> «Exalted and hallowed be his great Name.
> In the world which he will create anew,
> where he will revive the dead, construct his
> temple, deliver life, and rebuild the city of Jeru-
> salem,
> and uproot foreign idol worship from his land,
> and restore the holy service of Heaven to its
> place,
> along with his radiance, splendour and
> Shechinah,
> may he bring forth his redemption and hasten
> the coming of his Messiah,

---

[34] Kaddish is the sanctification of the name of God and is spoken substitutionally for the deceased.

in your lifetime and in your days and in the life-
time of the entire House of Israel,
speedily and soon.
May his great Name be blessed forever and to
all eternity.
Blessed and praised, glorified,
exalted and extolled,
honoured, adored and lauded be the name of
the Holy One, blessed be he.
Beyond all the blessings, hymns, praises and
consolations that are uttered in the world;
May there be abundant peace from heaven,
and a good life for us and for all Israel;
He Who makes peace in his heavens, may he
make peace for us and for all Israel;
and say, Amen.»

«Amen!» answered Mariam and Jeshua.

They proceeded to clear out Moshe's cave before returning slowly to their own cave.

***

That night, Jossef had a dream. He saw the angel who had visited him after Jeshua's conception with the command to remain with his wife and to give the child the name of Jeshua.

This same angel was looking lovingly at him from the cave entrance, saying: *«Rise, Jossef! Take the child and his mother and return to the land of Israel, for those who sought the child's life are dead.[35]»*

---

[35] Matthew 2, 19-20

PART VIII:

Homeward Bound

43

Jossef awoke excitedly from this dream and was aware of the sounds of beating wings and rushing wind slowly fading away. Mariam also awoke, sensing her husband's restlessness. She too heard the unmistakable signs of the presence of God's spirit.

«I had a dream,» Jossef told his wife in a voice still slurred from sleep, «but it was more than a dream, it was a message. In this dream, I saw the face of an angel standing in the cave entrance, telling me that Herod and his confederates are dead. It means that now, no one's after Jeshua's life. The angel also told us to return to Israel!»

«Home!» shouted Mariam loudly and happily.

That woke Jeshua, who asked what was up.

«Jeshua!» she exclaimed. «We're going home! The evil ones are dead and are no longer searching for you! We can return to Nazareth!»

«What!» exclaimed Jeshua.

«Yes, my pet, we're going home, at last! Oh, I'm so happy, I could dance!»

She not only could, but she stood up and did so! Soon Jossef and Jeshua joined her in a rumbustious jig, hooting and squealing as they danced, and Mariam joyfully sang a song of praise and delight.

These had been days full of strong emotion, starting with Moshe's death and burial, and now this joy. They were too excited to eat breakfast. Instead, they immediately began to plan the homeward journey. Luckily, they now had the 'Gabriel'!

Mariam suggested they visit Paneb on their way, as they could now tell him, without any risk, their reasons for keeping Jeshua's name from him.

«We can also stay a few days with Gershon and Esther in Babylon,» suggested Jossef.

« I'll cock a snook at the Roman soldiers in front of the fortress!» exclaimed Jeshua, and they all laughed.

«Yes, you do that, you scallywag!» said Jossef, amused. «But then, Jeshua, I'm afraid we'll have to sell our 'Gabriel'.»

«Oh no, Abba!» shouted Jeshua, aghast.

«Oh yes, my boy, we can't travel over land with a boat, and we'll need the money for our journey home. Perhaps we can sell the boat to someone in the community at Babylon.»

«Gershon might want our boat ...» mused Jeshua, somewhat reconciled.

«I'd like to visit Leontopolis and the Jewish Onias temple we heard about in Belbeis, as I'd like to sacrifice a pair of turtle doves in thanks for our deliverance from danger, and also for our precious son!» said Mariam.

«Oh yes,» agreed Jossef readily, «we'll do that. Most Egyptian Jews apparently prefer to make the journey to Jerusalem rather than sacrificing here, particularly at Passover. But the Onias temple is more or less on our way.

From Leontopolis, we can easily travel on to Belbeis, so I hope we can stay with Ahab and Dinah again. We can reach the Israeli border via Wadi Tumilat and Pelusium and return to Ashkelon, as I definitely want to visit Leah and Daniel again, and discover what happened after we left.»

The day was spent in sharing memories of their outward journey more than a year ago. But Jeshua's suggestion to visit Merit on the coast met with a flat refusal, as that would take them too far out of their way. Jeshua pouted and became a little morose, but in the end he accepted the decision.

The next day, all three went to Pepi to take their leave of her. Mariam became rather emotional, as she had grown very fond of Pepi. They explained that their cave would now be free in case any other newcomers to Muharraq wished to use it.

They went to Cusae, where Jossef explained to Khufu that he would no longer be making the move to the other workshop with them. Khufu was rather disappointed at losing a good worker so suddenly, but he did understand that the family wished to return to Israel and wished them all the best.

«All the best to you too, Khufu, and thank you very much for the great employment and the chance to build my own craft for the return journey!» said Jossef.

«Be honest now, Jossef,» said Khufu, «when you asked to be allowed to build your own boat, did you already know you would soon be returning home?»

«No!» Jossef defended himself, «I had absolutely no idea! We honestly thought we'd be staying here for a long time!»

«But we did hope so,» added Mariam, «we always hoped so.»

«Well anyway, I hope you'll be very happy back in your home country!» repeated Khufu.

They said goodbye and walked into the town, which Jeshua had not yet seen properly. With unaccustomed confidence, they also walked to the south of the town, where they stood outside the camp of the second legion, looking up at the wooden watchtowers, the flags, and the legionnaires going about their daily business.

Jeshua stood at the bottom of one of the towers and mischievously called up to the guard: «My name's Jeshua, what's yours?»

The guard laughed good-naturedly and called down: «Hallo, you little rascal! My name's Antonius!»

Afterwards, Mariam went to the market and bought provisions for the journey. The family walked home for the last time, climbing the path to their cave which they would be leaving behind them for ever. There was nothing to keep them here now Moshe had passed away.

***

Once the donkeys were loaded and standing in front of the cave, Mariam cast a last glance inside. Despite the joy of returning home, tears filled her eyes.

«Ah, Jossef,» she sighed, «we invested so many hours of work in our cave, and we've made a beautiful home out of it! I hope someone else will come and appreciate it as much as we have!»

«Yes, I must say, I've got quite a lump in my throat too!» admitted Jossef, as they led the donkeys away, turning back to look one last time upon their beloved cave.

Jeshua was as flexible and unattached as ever and was merely looking forward to the trip with their 'Gabriel'. A permanent home was still unfamiliar to him. During the last few weeks, he had begun to feel restless from the long period of living in one place. Only his teachings with Moshe had been able to calm him. He was now glad to be on the road again. Jossef sometimes asked himself how his son would cope with being settled in Nazareth!

They waved again to Pepi as they passed by, calling out last farewells, then they walked down to Khufu's pier in Cusae, said farewell to Jossef's fellow workers, and climbed aboard the 'Gabriel'. The donkeys were tethered in the middle of the boat as usual, Jossef dipped the oars into the water of the river, which was now much narrower – the Nile had returned to its original bed – and manoeuvred the boat into the middle channel. Mariam and Jeshua acted as coxswains again, and with a following wind from the south, the boat quickly gathered way for Cynopolis.

It was quite different to navigating in flood time. There was far more traffic, and small boats were crossing between the banks as their owners went about their daily business. There were also ships travelling north and south along the river. Mariam and Jeshua really had to keep their eyes peeled in all directions, to ensure that Jossef was able to row safely between all the traffic. They admired Paneb all the more for having travelled back alone from Hermopolis, all those months ago.

Although they were making good headway thanks to the south wind, the family would not be able to accomplish the whole stretch to Cynopolis in one day, so they decided to spend the night at Tuja's house in Hermopolis once more.

Tuja was now three months pregnant and was pleased to welcome her Jewish friends again. She told them all about the wedding and asked them to take one of her wedding earrings to Paneb for repair. The earring had been torn off during the general hubbub of the wedding feast, and a piece of lapis was now missing. Jossef took the earring into safe keeping.

In the evening, the family visited the Jewish community with which they had celebrated the Sabbath half a year previously. Passing through the town, they marvelled once again at the elegance of the buildings, but they gave the Thoth temple a wide berth, in case the angry priests happened to remember Jeshua from his encounter with the baboon.

The south wind had become stronger overnight. As they went to board the 'Gabriel' next day, the Nile was unsettled, the wind whipping the surface into waves. The donkeys did not embark willingly, but eventually they were tethered safely in the middle of the boat. Jossef cast off and jumped aboard before the boat could be pulled away by the current, while Mariam attempted to stabilise it with one oar.

The 'Gabriel' soon gathered even more speed than the day before. The wind was obviously keeping many people from the water, as there was far less traffic than the previous day, and not one ship came towards them from the north.

Mariam and Jeshua both looked up at the place where the boulder had come crashing down in front of Paneb's boat on the outward journey, but this time their wild ride on the waves around the headland was not interrupted by rockfall.

Shortly afterwards, they caught sight of the village of Gebel el-Teir on the east bank where they had spent the night with Paneb's friends, and once again, there were falcons dancing on the wind in front of the rock face. The breathtaking pace continued all the way to Cynopolis. Three hours later, they were already mooring the 'Gabriel' next to Paneb's boat at his pier. They disembarked on rather wobbly legs.

«Phew!» said Mariam, «God be praised, we've arrived here safely! That was a little too wild for my liking!»

«Oh, I thought it was great!» commented Jeshua.

«I'm sure you did, you little madcap! The wilder the better for you, eh?» smiled Jossef, running his fingers through his son's windblown locks. «You'll need to comb your hair a little before we go and meet Paneb.»

Jeshua dragged his fingers through his knotted curls – that would have to do.

They led the donkeys up the stone pathway to Paneb's villa. Busha had got wind of their arrival and came lolloping over to greet them with a loud bark. Five little puppies came scuttling after her.

«Oh, how cute!» cried Jeshua, taking one of the puppies in his hands. The puppy thanked him by licking his face. Busha placed her paws on Jeshua's shoulders, wanting him to greet her too, so he put down the puppy and stroked the mother's head, who obviously remembered him.

Paneb, hearing Busha's loud greeting, came out of the house, raised his hands and shouted joyfully: «You're back! Come on in, my dear friends!»

Mariam and Jeshua followed Paneb into the house, while Jossef stabled the donkeys. There was an elegant young gentleman sitting in the large living room. Like Paneb, he also had his hair dressed in the Hellenistic style, but the curls on top of his head were blonde, not dark like Paneb's.

«Mariam, Jeshua, may I introduce my friend, Sinuhe?» said Paneb. «He's now living with me. Ah, and here's Jossef! Jossef – my friend, Sinuhe.»

«Pleased to meet you!» they all replied. Sinuhe had a warm, friendly smile, which became even warmer whenever he looked at Paneb. The two men appeared to get on extremely well together.

Jossef unpacked Tuja's earring and told Paneb about the mishap at the wedding feast, to ensure it did not get forgotten.

«Oh!» said Paneb, «it's strange I didn't notice that during the feast!»

«I believe she only noticed it herself after the feast was over,» explained Mariam.

«Well anyway, thank you very much for bringing the earring along with you – you appear to be turning into my own private transport unit!» smiled Paneb. «More than half a year ago, Jossef brought me a huge basket of cabbage heads from my brother in Bahnasah, Sinuhe. He also acted as my second rower on the way to Hermopolis before Tuja's wedding.»

«Of course,» laughed Sinuhe, «Paneb's family always knows how to wrap their fellow men around their finger!»

Jossef laughed, but stood up for Paneb: «Well, Sinuhe, I must say we also profited from this deal, as we were wined and dined like kings and were also able to reach our destination.»

«Oh yes,» nodded Sinuhe, «Paneb certainly knows how to treat his guests!»

«On that note,» said Paneb. «would you like to bathe before dinner? I'm sure you've had a challenging time on the river with this wind.»

«We certainly have!» replied Jossef, «and we'd love to bathe, please.»

They left Paneb and Sinuhe and went off to the bathhouse to shed the exertions of the last few hours in the warm water.

During dinner, an exquisite creation of fish, Paneb asked cautiously: «Where were you heading after Hermopolis, Jossef?»

«Ah, now, first we owe you an explanation,» answered Jossef. «As you guessed when we were taking our leave of you, we did indeed have a secret. The secret was our son, whose name is Jeshua, by the way.»

Jeshua smiled broadly at Paneb, who briefly bowed his head to him.

«Jeshua was wanted by Herod, the tetrarch of Galilee, Peraea and Judaea,» continued Jossef. «Herod had developed a real thing about our son; he thought Jeshua might make a claim to his throne.»

Paneb raised his brows and whistled through his teeth. «Why did he think that, Jossef?» he asked pensively.

«Astrologers first put the idea into his head, then his scribes confirmed it by means of prophetic scripture. Herod couldn't get that out of his mind. He was searching everywhere for Jeshua. In Babylon, Roman legionnaires once almost caught him at Herod's behest. But Jeshua was crafty enough to escape from under their noses, so to speak.»

«Wow! Jeshua, that's some feat!» interjected Paneb.

«It really was, yes!» continued Jossef, smiling at his son with pride. «We've now been on the run for three and a half years, and presumably we've always been just a few steps ahead of danger!»

«And – excuse me for asking – why do you now feel you can talk openly to us about all this?»

«Because apparently, Herod has now died, meaning that the danger has passed!» Jossef beamed with relief at being able to say this at last.

«Oh, I see!» exclaimed Paneb. «That's wonderful! So now you can return home!»

«Exactly,» interjected Mariam, «at last we're on our way home! And I can't tell you what a relief that is! But before we leave, we wish to visit a few friends who've shown us great kindness on our way: In Babylon, in Belbeis, and last but not least: you, Paneb!»

«,We particularly wanted to speak openly with you at last,» added Jossef. «It's important to us that you understand why we had to keep Jeshua's name from you.»

«Thank you,» said Paneb, moved by their honesty.

Sinuhe interjected: «I'd heard that this Herod had died – I believe it was only about two weeks ago. Apparently, he caught some terrible disease. By all accounts, he must have been quite a tyrant!»

«That's true,» said Jossef, «he even had members of his own family killed, among others his own children. So we quite believed him capable of killing our son without a qualm.»

«What a dreadful situation, but it's all over now. The gods have obviously protected you,» said Paneb. «So now, let's forget the bad times and turn our attention to creature comforts!»

Sinuhe winked at Paneb, raised his glass and said: «To better times!»

They all took up the toast and applied themselves to the delicious dishes with a healthy appetite.

44

Next morning, Paneb told them Sinuhe had already left for work and that he sent his regards. He explained that his friend worked in an office on the east bank, not far from Paneb's villa.

The travellers had slept late, but Paneb stayed to eat breakfast with them in the terrace room. While they ate, Jossef explained that he had worked for half a year as a boatbuilder in Cusae, which was why he was now the proud owner of a papyrus boat, at present moored next to Paneb's boat at his pier.

«Oh, I'm most impressed!» said Paneb. «When you leave, I'll come with you and take a look at this boat of yours.»

«It's called 'Gabriel'!» said Jeshua, «and on our way south, I helped with the rowing!»

«Really?» marvelled Paneb. «You did that, Jeshua? My, what a strong lad you are, to be sure! Where did you go after Cusae, Jossef?»

«We only took a trip down to Asyut,» explained Jossef, «as the maiden voyage of the 'Gabriel'. Jeshua did indeed do some rowing with Mariam when we were travelling upstream. From Asyut, we climbed up to the mountains and stayed the night in a cave. We got a good view of the rock-cut tombs from there. Then we returned to Cusae.»

«The rock-cut tombs of Qau!» commented Paneb. «They're quite something, aren't they?»

«Yes they are, but we didn't want to travel any further south. That was enough for us,» explained

Jossef. «Right! I think it's time we were on our way! Many thanks for your hospitality, Paneb!»

«You're very welcome,» he replied, «and as I said, I'm coming down to the pier with you. I have to take Tuja's earring over to the workshop anyway.»

While Jossef fetched the donkeys, Mariam and Jeshua took the baggage outside. As they were leaving, Busha came bounding over to bark a loud good-bye, with the five woolly little balls of cuteness trailing behind.

«Paneb,» asked Jeshua shyly, «are you going to keep Busha's babies?»

«No,» answered Paneb, «I'll be giving them away. Someone's always in need of a watchdog.»

«Abba,» Jeshua begged his father, «aren't we in need of a watchdog? Couldn't we take one of the little dogs? Please!»

«Oh Jeshua!» replied Jossef, «that would only make the journey home more difficult! When we're back home, we can find a dog for you.»

«But Abba, I want to have one of Busha's! Please, ple-ease!»

Paneb laughed and looked from Jossef to Mariam. He could tell they were on the verge of giving in to Jeshua's wish.

«It is a good breed, very patient, obedient and intelligent,» he said, with a wink at Jeshua.

«Oh very well,» said Mariam, «go on, choose yourself one. But you must promise to teach the creature some manners and always to keep an eye on it when we're travelling.»

«Would you like a male or a female?» asked Paneb.

«A female, like Busha,» replied Jeshua, «and I'm going to call her Busha too!»

Paneb picked up the two female puppies and held them out to Jeshua, who chose the sand-coloured one like Busha, but with a black patch over her right eye and ear. Jeshua tucked the puppy inside his shirt while they climbed aboard the boat. Paneb was impressed with the 'Gabriel' and proclaimed that Jossef had not wasted his time in Egypt. While Jossef rowed their boat around the island, Paneb stood on the riverbank waving to them, before climbing into his own boat and rowing over to the west bank.

The south wind had dropped. Now that there was more traffic, the family did not make such good headway. Soon, Jossef realised they would need to spend the night somewhere between Cynopolis and Beni Suef. They found a village on the east bank which, at this point, was as green and fertile as the west bank. A farmer took them in for a small fee and some salt from Wadi Natrun.

On the second evening, they reached Beni Suef, moored the 'Gabriel' and walked into Heracleopolis, where they were able to stay in the same guesthouse as they had on the outward journey. They laughed as they remembered their adventure in the temple, when they had had to flee from the Roman soldiers – in retrospect, even such scary situations had a certain entertainment value!

Jeshua and Busha were already inseparable. Whenever they were in the boat, Busha usually balanced on a ledge around the prow, looking into the water. Once, she even fell into the Nile, but she knew by instinct how to swim, and Jossef managed to manoeuvre the boat so that he was able to fish her out of the water. She shook herself vigorously – everybody got wet! But on the whole, Jossef had to admit that Busha gave more cause for smiles than for trouble.

After four more days, the family reached Maresi. They passed the large harbour where they had embarked on Nechti's ship, rowing on to a small pier at Ma'adi. They moored the 'Gabriel', led their donkeys ashore and went straight on to Babylon. Gershon and Esther welcomed them with open arms.

«Have you heard the news?» called Gershon. «King Herod's dead!»

«Yes,» answered Mariam and Jossef in unison, «we know. That's why we're on our way home!»

«But you will stay with us for a while, won't you?» asked Esther.

«For a few days, but we want to get on to Leontopolis,» said Jossef, «and then home!»

«Know what?» said Gershon, «we also need to go to Leontopolis soon, as I have something to discuss with the priest there. We could go together.»

Jossef told Gershon that they were now the owners of a boat, which they were thinking of selling. Gershon beamed and glanced over at Esther.

«That's such a coincidence, Jossef! We were actually thinking of buying a boat! How big is yours?» asked Esther.

«Come with us, and we'll show it to you!» suggested Jossef.

Gershon and Esther found the 'Gabriel' ideal for their purposes. It occurred to Jossef that they could all travel together to Leontopolis in the 'Gabriel', where Jossef, Mariam and Jeshua would continue on foot, while Gershon and Esther could travel home to Babylon in their boat. Everything was falling into place nicely, as if it had been thus planned from the beginning.

But first they spent a few pleasant days with their Jewish friends, also celebrating the Sabbath, and of course, the children were crazy about Busha!

Gershon described the route to Leontopolis to Jossef that evening, after which they talked about their onward journey to the Jewish community at Belbeis.

«Belbeis!» said Gershon pensively. «After you had left, we attempted to find out who it was in Belbeis that had betrayed you.»

«But do we know for a fact that the information about our being in Egypt came from Belbeis?» asked Jossef.

«Oh sorry, of course, you can't know that! The Roman soldier who came to us when you were in the underground cave, confirmed that the information had come from Belbeis.»

«Really?» exclaimed Jossef, agitatedly. «But who was it? Surely not Ahab and Dinah.»

«No, it wasn't them. We travelled to Belbeis and had a long conversation with them. It seems Herod had heard about an earthquake at Bubastis, and that a small child from Israel had been there. So he sent a spy to find out more. We went to the synagogue and asked around. At first, everyone pretended not to have any idea what we were talking about, but in the end they told us a man had come to the community asking about a child. The description of the man sounded pretty much like that stranger I tried to welcome at our synagogue last time you were here, do you remember?»

«Vaguely, yes, but I don't remember what he looked like,» answered Jossef.

«Anyway, it turned out it was the caretaker of the community who betrayed you to this man, against payment!»

«What?» shouted Jossef in horror, «that nice old Jehuda? I don't believe it! He was always so friendly to Jeshua! He really liked him.»

«Later, he said the Romans had not told him why they were looking for you. But that's a poor excuse! If Roman officials are looking for someone, you can be pretty sure nothing pleasant is going to come out of it!»

«Indeed!» said Jossef. He brooded for a long time about why Jehuda had betrayed them. It was enough to make him lose his faith in humanity, like the time in Kalya when they had learned that the parents of the He-He-He had sold their own children.

It was terrible, and he was no longer sure he wanted to visit Belbeis at all now. On the other hand, he would like to see Ahab and Dinah again, and it was not their fault. Maybe they would be able to give him further details which would make the whole affair more understandable.

That evening, Mariam gave her husband some news that made him forget his brooding – she now had one more reason to make a sacrifice in the temple at Leontopolis, for she was pregnant again!

45

When Mariam told Gershon and Esther next morning that she was expecting her second child, Gershon considered that required a celebration! He said he would invite a few friends from the community for a feast.

Jeshua opened his eyes wide when he heard the news and asked: «Imma, will I get a brother or a sister now?»

«Yes, pet, you will!» announced Mariam happily.

«Will it be a boy or a girl?»

«We don't know yet, Jeshua.»

«If I can choose, I'd much prefer a brother!»

They all laughed, and Mariam explained to her son: «We don't get to decide that, Jeshua! It's all in God's hand.»

Esther discussed with her pregnant friend what to cook for the feast, and the two women went off to the market together to buy the required vegetables. Gershon asked a farmer friend to bring him a calf, which they would roast on a spit in the garden.

The feast was the more pleasurable for Mariam and Jossef because they knew they would soon be home in Nazareth. They were euphoric! A new beginning – a new baby, what more could one want?

Mariam's only great wish was that Hannah would still be alive to see her two grandchildren. She really would take good care of herself so that God willing, this wish could be fulfilled.

Both families and their friends celebrated until late at night. They ate outside in the garden at a long table. Gershon cut slices of tender calf-meat from the roast and distributed it to the guests. Afterwards, Esther served some delicious cakes with tea, for which they moved into the living room. The children were allowed to stay up, but soon their eyes fell shut, so they went to lie down in a corner of the living room and slept despite the loud voices of the adults laughing and singing. Busha also slept, curled up in Jeshua's arms.

The families spent the next day clearing up after the feast, and then came the Sabbath. In the end, they had already spent a good week in Babylon as they finally set off for the pier and their 'Gabriel'. After an emotional scene with Tirza and Benni who had to stay behind with their grandmother, they were finally able to embark and row north.

Gershon acted as coxswain since navigation was tricky here. After passing Heliopolis on the east bank, he steered them through the first branching of the Nile and safely into the central fork. A few miles further on at the next branch, they took the right-hand, Pelusian fork of the Nile. Shortly before they reached their destination, the river branched one last time, and again they had to take the right fork. At the tenth hour, they finally caught sight of the 'Lion's Town', Leontopolis, ahead.

The new town was situated nearer to the river than the old town. On a hill at the back of the town, they could see the walled fortress with its high tower and the long building of the Onias temple to the right of this. The temple looked nothing like the Jerusalem temple from the outside, but Gershon told them that the Holiest of Holies and the sacrificial altar were exact copies of those in Jerusalem. He explained that it had been built about 150 years earlier by the priest Onias with the support of the Ptolemies, purely for the sake of the Jewish legionnaires stationed at Leontopolis. Gershon suggested he first go and discuss his concerns with the priest, who was sure to know where they could find lodgings with a Jewish host.

The 'Gabriel' was moored at the pier. The two families walked through the new Hellenistic town and climbed up to the fortress behind it, taking a look at the temple courtyard on the way. The town had been busy, as the salesmen were closing their shops for the evening, but up here by the fortress, all was quiet. The hill afforded them a good view of the surrounding districts as far as the last branch of the river they had circumnavigated shortly before. The broad, 180-foot stone tower narrowed towards the top, with a gabled roof surrounded by a small wooden gallery.

«If someone up on the tower looked down at us, we'd look just like ants!» said Jeshua.

«Quite so,» agreed Gershon, before going through the gates into the temple enclosure. The family sat down with Esther in the forecourt to rest and take a drink.

They walked around the fortress wall and looked down from the other side of the hill towards the east. They looked for Bubastis and Belbeis, but those towns were still too far away to be seen from here. Another gate led into the old fortress court, where they were able to admire the fortified buildings from outside but were not permitted to enter. The ancient walls smelt damp and musty. In the shadow of those high walls, it was very cool, so they returned to the temple gate and waited there for Gershon, who reappeared after half an hour with a satisfied expression.

«Our conversation went just as I had hoped,» he said, «I was able to clarify all our community's questions, and he gave me the address of a Jewish guesthouse in the new town where we can stay. Shall we make our way there now?»

They descended from the fortress hill and went back to the new town. On the way they passed the Sachmet temple. There was not much left of it, only a couple of seated lioness statues which reminded Jeshua of 'his' lioness in the mountains to the south of Asyut.

After searching for a while, they found the guesthouse, where they were welcomed heartily by their hosts. They were given a good supper, and Busha was also given a bowl of meat. Jeshua and Busha played in the garden until they were both nice and sleepy.

Gershon had made an appointment with the priest for Jossef and Mariam to sacrifice on the following day. First, they went with Jeshua to the tradesmen to buy a pair of turtle doves. At the appointed time, they went to the forecourt and gave the doves to the priest who ritually sacrificed them. While he carried out this ritual, Mariam, Jossef and Jeshua sang words of praise and thanks from the Psalms:

> «I will offer to you the sacrifice of thanksgiving and call on the name of the Lord.
> I will pay my vows to the Lord in the presence of all his people,
> in the courts of the house of the Lord, in your midst, O Jerusalem. Allelujah! [36]
> Oh give thanks to the Lord, for he is good; for his steadfast love endures forever!
> Let Israel say: ‹His steadfast love endures forever.›
> Let the house of Aaron say: ‹His steadfast love endures forever.›
> Out of my distress I called on the Lord; the Lord answered me and set me free.
> The Lord is on my side; I will not fear. What can man do to me?
> Open to me the gates of righteousness, that I may enter through them and give thanks to the Lord.
> This is the gate of the Lord; the righteous shall enter through it.
> I thank you that you have answered me and have become my salvation.
> The Lord is God, and he has made his light to shine upon us.

---

[36] Excerpt from Psalm 116

*Bind the festal sacrifice with cords, up to the
horns of the altar!
You are my God, and I will give thanks to you;
you are my God; I will extol you.
Oh give thanks to the Lord, for he is good; for
his steadfast love endures forever!* [37]
Amen.»

They looked at one another joyfully. During the last few years, they had been through a lot and gone without most comforts. In the end, and with the help of some miracles, they had conquered all the blows which fate had attempted to throw at them. Indeed, the Lord had been with them and had protected them.

Mariam laid a hand on her belly. He would also protect this child, who would play with Jeshua and grow up in a safe home, not having to live in fear. It was a miracle that none of the dangers they had encountered, nor their nomadic lifestyle, appeared to have left any negative mark on Jeshua. Mariam also thanked God for this.

Hand in hand, and deeply moved, they walked down from the temple into the town. They met Gershon and Esther standing outside the guesthouse and told them about the sacrifice and their gratefulness for having come safely through all danger.

They stayed one more night with their friends in Leontopolis. Gershon slipped a very generous payment for the 'Gabriel' into Jossef's hand that evening.

---

[37] Excerpts from Psalm 118

«That much?!» exclaimed Jossef.

«It's to make your homeward journey a little easier,» said Gershon, patting Jossef on the shoulder. «You've put your whole heart into that boat, Jossef. Don't think I haven't noticed how hard it is for you to part from it!»

Next morning, the path of the friends parted at the pier for ever. It was not only Jossef who found it hard to relinquish their boat and to say goodbye to their friends. Jeshua shed a few tears as he watched Gershon and Esther rowing away to the south in their 'Gabriel', slowly becoming smaller in the distance.

The family turned east, skirting the town, and setting off for Belbeis with mixed feelings, as it was a place which held many good memories, but also the place of their betrayal.

46

By evening, they could feel every muscle in their legs! The family had got out of the habit of walking long distances, so their bodies first had to adapt again. They walked for three days before reaching Belbeis, during which time they always slept outdoors. They could now really have used a bath, but there were no baths here. Giving Bubastis a wide berth as they had done two years ago on their way north, they did not pass the fort coming into Belbeis, but entered the town through the west gate instead.

They made straight for Ahab and Dinah's guesthouse. The couple were out in the garden, and when Jossef put his head through the gate, Ahab exclaimed: «I don't believe it! Our friends from Israel! Peace be with you! Welcome! Come on in, friends!»

Dinah smothered Jeshua in a big hug. «Little Jeshua! My sweet child! And my, how you've grown! How long has it been?»

«Almost three years, Dinah,» replied Mariam.

«You will stay with us for a few days, won't you?» asked Ahab.

Jossef nodded. «We'd love to,» he replied.

Stabling the donkeys, Mariam and Jossef felt it was only yesterday that they had last done that here. They were given the same comfortable room and immediately felt at home there.

Mariam helped Dinah to prepare supper and spoke gaily about the fact that she would soon be home in Nazareth again, saying she hoped so much that her mother would still be alive to see her two grandchildren.

«Two?» said Dinah.

«Yes, Dinah,» answered Mariam with a dignified smile, «I'm expecting again!»

«Oh Mariam!» exclaimed Dinah, «how wonderful! Congratulations! Yes, I do hope your mother lives to see them. Does she even know where you are?»

«No, she doesn't,» sighed Mariam, «it would have been too dangerous to contact her. I have no idea whether she even knew we were wanted by Herod. But we'll tell you all about that when we're together this evening.»

«Yes, we only heard about it when Gershon visited us trying to find out why Herod had started to search for you in Egypt. We had no idea!»

Sitting together after supper, Jossef and Mariam told the whole story of their flight to Egypt and how close they had repeatedly come to being caught by Roman soldiers. Gershon and Dinah wondered at all the trials their friends had been through.

«And when I think that they would probably never have looked for you in Egypt if Jehuda hadn't said anything!» said Dinah.

«Yes,» agreed Jossef, «it causes me great pain to think Jehuda betrayed us like that. At first, I could hardly believe it. Gershon told us the Romans hadn't informed Jehuda why they were after us, but that doesn't really make matters better.»

Ahab and Dinah looked at one another sheepishly. «I admit it's bad that he told the Romans about you,» said Ahab. «They approached Jehuda because the members of our congregation told them Jehuda knows everybody. At first, he denied ever having seen you. But I'm not sure why, they just wouldn't believe him! They kept coming back and interrogating him again and again. They tried subterfuge, cajolery, bribery and in the end, they were rough with him. At that point, he gave in and told them you had been here. That was all they wanted; they just required confirmation that you were in Egypt and not elsewhere, and also that you were in contact with Jewish communities here. After that, they were as polite as you like, gave him money for the information, and finally left him in peace. They didn't tell him Jeshua's life was in danger, but it still left Jehuda no peace that he had betrayed you. He donated the entire sum of money to the community coffers, and he's suffered terribly ever since.»

«To be honest,» said Jossef indignantly, «I really think it serves him right! Sorry, but I'll never be able to forgive him for endangering our son's life like that!»

«Jossef,» countered Dinah, «Jehuda's a broken man. He's aged twenty years since then. I sometimes wonder whether his bad conscience is going to send him to an early grave. Speak to him, Jossef! Please!»

«I'm sorry, Dinah,» replied Jossef stiffly, «there's no question of that! I can't and I won't do it. You're asking too much of me.»

Dinah shook her head with a worried frown, but she realised Jossef was not to be moved at present.

Maybe he would soften later. She changed the subject and went into the kitchen to make some tea. Afterwards, everybody went off to bed, but no one could really sleep after that unsettling conversation.

***

Only Jeshua had slept well. An hour before sunrise, Busha woke him by poking her wet nose into his neck.

«Come on, Busha!» said Jeshua cheerfully, «let's go for a walk!»

It was cool out. The air smelt fresh, and the first birds had begun their dawn chorus in the surrounding trees. Jeshua strolled through the sleeping streets with Busha at his side, whistling a merry tune through his teeth.

As they passed the synagogue, Jehuda was standing in the forecourt sweeping the ground with a brushwood broom. He looked up, saw Jeshua and stood still. Jeshua came over and greeted him.

«Hello, Jeshua,» said Jehuda meekly. «I can't sleep, that's why I'm up so early. Would you please come in and sit with me? There's something I'd like to talk to you about.»

Jeshua went willingly into the vestibule with the old man and sat next to him on a bench.

«How you've grown, Jeshua. Are you well?»

«Yes, thank you, Jehuda. We've often been in danger, but God has always protected us.»

«Praise be to God! Jeshua, my mind's very heavy because I told the Romans you were in Egypt.

Ever since, I've worried day and night that you might be suffering under those Romans.»

The old man's hands were shaking. He had tears in his eyes. With a weak voice, he continued: «And since then I always have the same dream. An angel appears to me. He lays hot coals on my head with a large pair of tongs. I can feel the heat and smell my scorched hair in the dream! The angel tells me that you're the Messiah. But the fact that I actually betrayed the Messiah just makes everything far worse for me. Nothing happened to you, but the thought that it might have done plagues me all day long. It would have been my fault if they had killed you. Jeshua, I believe I'm losing my mind. I see shadows rushing past me and hear jeering voices in my head.»

Jehuda put his head in his hands and rocked from side to side. He sobbed and groaned, then he grabbed Jeshua's wrist. Busha snarled softly.

«Jeshua!» exclaimed Jehuda desperately, «please bless me! Please say you forgive me! Otherwise I can't go on living!»

Remembering Moshe's daily blessings in front of the cave, Jeshua stood up and laid his little hands upon Jehuda's head. His head was indeed very hot and smelt singed. Jeshua spoke quietly and assuredly:

> *«Jehuda, the Lord bless you and keep you;*
> *the Lord make His face to shine upon you and*
> *be gracious unto you;*

*the Lord lift up the light of His countenance
upon you and grant you peace.*[38]

I forgive you, Jehuda.»

Jeshua embraced the old man, whose body was wracked with sobs. Jeshua stayed with him until his sobbing ceased.

«Now you're feeling better,» said Jeshua; it was not a question, it was a simple fact.

«Yes, Jeshua, thank you!» said Jehuda. «I believe I'll go and lie down on my bed now. I think I'll sleep peacefully for the first time in many months. God bless you, Jeshua, my Lord! God bless your life's work!»

«God will bless you too now, Jehuda. Peace be with you.»

«And with you, Jeshua,» said Jehuda, smiling for the first time since his conversation with the Romans.

The streets were beginning to awaken as Jeshua returned with Busha to Ahab and Dinah's house. When he arrived, the two families were already at breakfast.

«Where have you been, Jeshua?» asked Mariam.

«Out walking Busha,» replied Jeshua.

After breakfast, Dinah made another attempt to convince Jossef to speak with Jehuda, but Jossef adhered firmly to his refusal to do so.

---

[38] Numbers 6, 24-26 – the Aaronic blessing

Jeshua casually mentioned that he had met Jehuda on his morning walk and had spoken to him.

Jossef's jaw dropped. «You spoke to Jehuda?» he asked, dumbfounded.

«Yes,» answered Jeshua, «he was upset, but now he feels better because I've forgiven him for betraying me.»

Dinah beamed! The son appeared to be far more empathetic than his father! She resolved to go to Jehuda sometime that day and ask him about his conversation with Jeshua.

In the afternoon, Jossef and Mariam began to plan the next steps of their journey. They would stay two more days with Ahab and Dinah until after the Sabbath. Then they would travel through Wadi Tumilat as quickly as possible, this time keeping to the canal to ensure a water supply, avoiding the rocky area to the north and the cave where Jossef had been so ill.

On the Sabbath day, both families went to the synagogue together. Jehuda stood at the entrance and greeted Dinah and Ahab with a smile. Jeshua smiled at Jehuda, but Jossef looked the other way, acting as though his attention was entirely upon another couple they knew well. He went over to the couple and spoke to them, completely ignoring Jehuda. Dinah shrugged sadly. Then they all went inside for the Sabbath service.

Afterwards, Jossef said he wanted to go home immediately to start packing, but it was clear he just wished to avoid Jehuda. Jossef remained as stubborn as a mule, whereas Jeshua went over to Jehuda and took his leave of him warmly. Mariam also went and said goodbye to the old caretaker.

There was a cloud of tension over the Sabbath meal, which should really have been a celebration of peace. Jossef was unable to overcome his negativity. His son had demonstrated magnitude in forgiving Jehuda, thus making his father look even more petty. Yet Jossef's only concern had been for his son. He felt doubly deceived and became even more taciturn, until in the end everyone was longing for them to leave, just so that the tension could be relieved.

Parting from Ahab and Dinah was therefore not as warm as it should have been. But Dinah was very grateful to Jeshua for forgiving Jehuda. She pulled him into a firm hug, saying: «Thank you, Jeshua. You did well! Thanks to you, Jehuda's now feeling much better! You're a little love!»

47

The days spent in Belbeis had given their feet and legs a chance to recover. When the travellers set off again, all three felt fit and were soon back in the rhythm of their daily marches. After a few miles, Jossef was finally able to relinquish his bad mood.

Coming from the other direction almost three years ago, they had passed by to the north to find a cave in which Jossef could recover from his sickness, so they saw the canal in Wadi Tumilat for the first time. It had been built by a pharaoh in times gone by, to connect the Nile with the Red Sea, and was impressive, stretching in a long, straight line across the landscape. The proximity of the canal made finding water easy.

On the first night, they stayed at a farm. The friendly farmer gave them a bag of fresh, juicy figs for the journey. The second night they spent outdoors. On the third day they had already reached Lake Timsah, but they quickly passed it by and continued to the eastern desert, remembering the mosquitoes which had led to Jossef's malaria. In the desert, they slept in a cave during the day and set off again in the late afternoon once the sun had lost its heat. They had to spend one more night outdoors near the Ballah Lakes before arriving at Pelusium the following day.

Once again, their luck was in, and they were able to stay at the same guesthouse with the attached thermal bath they had stayed in on their outward journey. Jossef and Jeshua pampered their tired limbs in the warm water and enjoyed the feeling of being clean again.

After a delicious supper, they spent the evening in the lush atrium, enjoying the cool air and listening to the splashing fountain. Their thoughts circled around all the adventures they had experienced in Egypt, and they shared memories, grateful that all had turned out well in the end.

***

Next day was the Sabbath, so they remained in Pelusium. On the following day, they passed the Serbonian salt lake, walking as far as Rhinocolura. Mariam remembered the game of cutting off noses Merit had played with Jeshua, but Jeshua had forgotten it – he had still been very small at the time, just over six months old.

Two days later at the Brook of Egypt, they crossed the border between Egypt and Israel. They were back in their own country, yet no longer needed to fear anyone or anything! Once they were out of sight of the border guards, they sang and danced merrily together in celebration of this special day. They decided to treat themselves to a slightly better guesthouse in Raphia.

The guesthouse they had chosen was elegant, and some of the guests were clearly Romans. The family were still not accustomed to feeling relaxed in the company of Roman officials! Raphia had once been an important fortress, and even at that time it still had military importance as a border town.

The house had its own bath which Jossef and Jeshua used before the family went into town to find an inn. As they stepped out of the guesthouse onto the street, Mariam and Jossef gasped as they saw a Roman centurion passing by who looked the spitting image of Lucius. They did a double take.

«Just like Lucius!» they both said at the same time.

Jeshua looked closely at the centurion. Merit had not often talked about Lucius, but when she did, it was with such longing that he was interested to see what Merit's beloved Lucius had looked like. Obviously, he hardly had any memory of the time in Ashkelon and none at all of Lucius, whom he had only seen four or five times.

On the way to Gaza next day, they came to the beach where Jeshua had played with Merit, building dams of sand to block the rivulets.

Jeshua shouted happily: «I remember! I can remember this, Imma!»

They stayed one last night in Gaza, before starting on the last leg of their long journey. Jossef was excited about seeing his sister Leah again, and Jeshua was also looking forward to seeing his aunt. although he could no longer remember her.

Approaching Ashkelon from the south, they came round the corner where they had chatted with Leah's neighbour outside her house, then – at long last! – they saw Daniel and Leah's house ahead. For now, their journey was over. What a wonderful feeling!

Leah was alone at home. Jossef entered the house first. He took his beloved sister in his arms and hugged her, not wanting to let her go.

«Leah!» he said, «we're back at last!»

«Jossef!» sighed Leah contentedly, «what a wonderful surprise! And Mariam – I see you're expecting again!»

«Hello, Leah!» said Mariam, embracing her. «Yes, you're right! And you must have a very good eye, because it's not really visible yet.»

«Oh yes it is, Mariam!» answered Leah with a smile, «I can certainly see it!»

«Jeshua, do you remember Aunt Leah now?» asked Jossef.

«N-no,» admitted Jeshua, shyly stepping into his aunt's fervent embrace.

The donkeys were led to the familiar stable, and the family took their baggage to the same room they had occupied more than three years ago. Soon the family was sitting at the living room table, and it was like old times again. So much had happened in the meantime, that they hardly knew where to begin.

But one subject was foremost in Jossef's mind: «Leah, what happened here after we left for Egypt?»

«Oh, that is indeed the most important thing,» replied Leah. «It didn't take long for Herod's officials to turn up here, asking where you were.»

«Who was it who betrayed us in Nazareth? Do you know?» asked Jossef sullenly.

«Yes, Jossef, we know that now,» replied Leah, «but you need to understand that Herod's spy was able to keep his identity secret in Nazareth. No one knew who he was. He was just one more seasonal worker at Rivka's olive grove.»

«So it was at Rivka's!» exclaimed Jossef. «In that case, it's my own fault to some degree, as I mentioned to Rivka and Mordechai that I have a sister in Ashkelon.»

«Well, after all, you weren't to know how things were going to turn out, were you? Anyway, somehow the spy unobtrusively steered the conversation onto the subject of you and your relatives, Jossef. No one thought anything of it when Rivka told him about your sister in Ashkelon, and he didn't even show a reaction to this information, although it was exactly what he had been waiting for. He stayed for the whole harvest period rather than disappearing once he'd got what he was after, so he didn't arouse any suspicion at all. Apparently, he was a really nice person, and no one suspected him!»

«How do you know all this, Leah?» asked Jossef.

«Ah, now, when the officials turned up here the first time, wanting to know where you were – well, I just had to find out. I went to Nazareth myself. I visited your mother, Mariam, then I asked around in the village.»

«My mother!» exclaimed Mariam, «how is she? Is she still alive?»

«Yes, Mariam, she is still alive, but she's not at all well. It's damaged her health worrying about what happened to you. She's aged terribly. I was unable to tell her where you were, much as I'd have loved to!»

«Imma!» said Mariam in despair, «If only she can hold out until we get home! It would be so wonderful if she could see her two grandchildren!»

«It certainly would,» said Leah, «but I suppose that means you'll not be staying with us for long now, right?»

«I'm afraid so,» admitted Jossef. «We really would like to leave for Nazareth as soon as possible.»

«But if you went by ship, you'd be able to travel to Ptolemais in just one day,» suggested Leah in the hope of keeping her brother with her a little longer. «You could spend that week here, instead of on the road.»

«That's certainly an idea, Leah, yes,» agreed Jossef. «We'd be home much quicker by ship. But we won't delay our departure by more than three days. As Mariam says, we want to get home, if only for Hannah's sake. I'll go to the harbour tomorrow and find out when there's a ship sailing for Ptolemais.»

Daniel arrived home from work and was amazed to see their unexpected guests.

«Jossef, Mariam, and little Jeshua! Oh, how wonderful! Welcome, my dear brother-in-law!» he exclaimed, embracing Jossef.

Then he looked at Jeshua. «Such a big boy now, Jeshua! How time must have flown, eh?» Daniel gave Jeshua a hug and asked him whether he would like to come to the workshop next day.

«Yes please, Uncle Daniel!» cried Jeshua enthusiastically.

Leah served supper, as her husband was hungry after a hard day at work. After the meal they sat in the living room discussing all that had happened in Israel while Mariam, Jossef and Jeshua had been in Egypt.

«Leah, you told us that Rivka accidentally told Herod's spy about you and your being related to us,» said Jossef, «but what I'd like to know is: how come Herod even got the idea we could have gone to Egypt?»

«Ah well,» interjected Daniel, «that was actually an unlucky coincidence. When the officials turned up here a second time wanting to know where you were, we told them you had only just left for Nazareth. At first they believed us, but when they realised you had never arrived there, they came back a third time and asked again. We just said that was all you had told us, and that we couldn't tell them more than that. We suggested you may have met with an accident on the way back to Nazareth ...»

«Yes,» interjected Leah, «but then they didn't believe us any more. I'm pretty certain they would have come back again and may even have resorted to more extreme methods, had they not happened upon one of our neighbours just round the corner from here, when they were leaving our house. The officials questioned her and she readily told them all she knew, as she's always up for a chat with anyone. But of course, she had no idea of the importance of their questions. This neighbour knew both you and Merit of course and had happened to see you passing by on the afternoon of your departure. She told the officials Merit had said you were on your way to Gaza. They asked her how much baggage you had with you, and the neighbour commented that it had indeed seemed rather a lot of baggage for a day trip to Gaza. The officials drew their own conclusions as to your real destination.»

«I'll give that old gossip a piece of my mind!» said Jossef angrily. «If she'd kept her mouth shut, we might never have been discovered. And as to that old tale-bearer in Belbeis …»

«Heavens, Jossef!» commented Leah, «don't be like that! You know very well what these officials are like. They would have kept on interrogating people and would have found out in the end anyway!»

«No, I don't agree!» countered Jossef. «If only people had shown a little integrity and constancy, the officials would never have found out where we were!»

«But Jossef, don't forget they were rough with Jehuda,» said Mariam, «and I'd like to see how constant you'd be, if you were tortured by officials or soldiers to squeeze information out of you about someone you didn't even know that well!»

«I would stand up to them, Mariam,» said Jossef severely. «I would never betray anyone, however much they tortured me!»

«Hey, Jossef!» shouted Leah angrily. «You're so stubborn! You've always been like that! Come down off your high horse, will you? How do you know how you'd react in such a situation? I only hope you'll never have to prove it!»

Mariam was pleased to hear someone give Jossef a piece of her mind, and Leah was quite right. But the siblings were fighting out an old quarrel, and Jossef did not back down from his point of view. He really could be as stubborn as a mule!

48

To Mariam's great relief, the subject was dropped next day. Leah and Jossef were once again the devoted brother and sister they had been before their quarrel. After breakfast, Daniel took Jeshua with him to his boatbuilding workshop accompanied by an excited Busha, and Jeshua told his uncle all about their boat, the 'Gabriel', with which they had rowed through Egypt from south to north. Daniel was impressed that his brother-in-law had built his own boat out of papyrus; he would ask Jossef that evening how such boats were constructed.

In the meantime, Jossef had been to the harbour and reserved a place for himself, his family and his donkeys on a large trading ship that would be leaving for Ptolemais in four days' time. When he told them the date of their departure that evening, Leah was thrilled to hear that in the end, she would have had her brother with her for five days after all.

The Sabbath day came round before their departure, and the two families went to the synagogue together. Mariam remembered the last time she had stood there with Merit. She became nostalgic thinking of Merit, and mentioned it to Leah.

«I still miss Merit to this day,» said Leah, «but it was such a relief when we heard that the culprits had been caught, exonerating Merit of all guilt.»

«We accompanied Merit all the way to her home,» recounted Mariam. «Her family had been questioned by Roman officials and soldiers long before we arrived. It was a good thing Merit's family knew nothing about it all. Their shock was so obviously genuine when the officials told them about the attack on Lucius and the search for Merit, that they henceforth left them alone. By the time we arrived there, Merit's innocence had already been proven.»

«Oh my! That could have turned out very differently if the culprits had never been caught!» groaned Leah. «A bit of luck, that!»

«It certainly was! Time after time, we had so much luck on our journey, or rather: we were in God's hands. He protected us and is doing so still.»

«His name be praised!» exclaimed Leah reverently. «You certainly have been through so many adventures and always came out unscathed. I suppose we only know a fraction of what happened to you.»

«Yes, I do believe we'd have to stay here at least a month to tell you about all our adventures!» laughed Mariam.

«Know what, Mariam? I've got an idea: Why don't we all meet up in Jerusalem for the next Feast of the Passover?» suggested Leah.

«Next year in Jerusalem!» cried Mariam gaily. «Providing my mother's condition allows for it ...» she added ponderously.

The men and women congregated in the vestibule of the synagogue after the service, and Leah told her brother about their decision to meet up in Jerusalem for next year's Passover. They all agreed upon this as Daniel also loved the idea of next year's meeting.

The prospect lessened the pain of yet another farewell, which moved all four adults to tears two days later at Ashkelon harbour. Only Jeshua remained cheerful and lighthearted as he proudly went ahead of them, climbing the gangway to the great sailing ship 'Orion' with Busha safely tucked into his shirt, although she was rather too large for that now. There was a gusty wind and dark clouds were looming on the western horizon. Jossef and Mariam followed their son up the gangway and tethered the two donkeys to a wooden bar with the other animals on board. The family went and stood at the railing, waving to Daniel and Leah.

«I hope it won't be stormy!» Daniel called up from the harbour.

Jossef had been thinking the same thing, but he tried to look unconcerned for Mariam and Jeshua's sake, so as not to alarm them.

The ropes were cast off. With much creaking and groaning, the ship moved away from the harbour wall. The sails were set, and as the 'Orion' gathered way, the two families waved one last time to each other.

Out on the open sea, the swell was far more perceptible. Jeshua stood at the railing, holding Busha firmly in his shirt and gazing out at the coastline.

«That town there is Ashdod!» explained his father, shouting against the wind. The sailors turned the main sail, the ship came about and put out to sea. Soon the coast was a mere strip on the horizon. The

'Orion' came about again and sailed north, parallel to the coast.

Now the black clouds were immediately above the ship, and the wind became ever stronger. The ship dipped steeply forwards; it lifted again and dipped backwards, tossed upon the boiling sea like a cork. Mariam's face had taken on a slightly green colour. Jossef tried to be strong for her sake, but soon he was also feeling ill. When Mariam had to vomit, Jossef held her headscarf away from her face, but then he also had to vomit.

A sailor brought ropes and asked them to tie themselves to the railing, as it was about to become rather stormy.

«Good heavens, what's it been like up to now?» Jossef called back to him, but the sailor just laughed.

He had been right, the wind did indeed become even stronger, and the waves were so large that they were now breaking over the deck, drenching everyone to the skin. The animals howled with fear, stumbling and sliding about on the slippery wooden deck, some even tumbling over on the heaving surface.

Jeshua had seen the fear in the eyes of his suffering parents. He called out to them that he was going to the prow, but they could not hear him above the wind and only lifted their heads to vomit again.

So Jeshua made his way laboriously forward, holding on tight to anything within grasp with one hand and clasping Busha firmly in his shirt with the other.

Upon reaching the prow, he climbed onto a deck box, grabbed the railing and looked up at the sky which had turned a threatening yellowish grey. Less than a mile away he spotted a huge waterspout coming straight towards the 'Orion'. Jeshua turned his face to heaven and called out desperately: «Abba, Abba, help us! Please help us!»

Just then, a mammoth wave caught the ship and sent the prow dipping steeply downwards. Jeshua held onto the railing with all his might, so as not to be thrown into the sea. But in doing so, he lost his hold on Busha, who fell out of Jeshua's shirt and flew through the air over the railing, landing far below in the sea!

«Busha!» screamed Jeshua, panic-stricken. «Busha, Busha!» He peered over the railing. Far down in the water, Busha was bravely attempting to swim, but then Jeshua watched helplessly as she was caught by the ship and pulled underneath it.

He ran as quickly as he could to the stern – he failed to notice that the storm had suddenly abated and that the ship was now sailing on calmly, without rolling at all. The sky was also getting lighter.

At the stern, he climbed onto a ledge and looked down again into the water, calling desperately for Busha, but she did not reappear. Deeply shocked, he walked back to his parents who were now sitting up, but still had very pale faces.

Mariam saw her son's hollow eyes and his look of despair and asked: «Jeshua, where were you? Whatever's wrong?»

«Busha!» he sobbed, «I lost Busha overboard! She fell out of my shirt when the biggest wave hit the ship!»

Jeshua wept inconsolably. Mariam took him on her lap, stroking his head.

«Oh my poor darling! That's terrible!» she said. «Poor little Busha!»

She held her son in a tight embrace and rocked his little body, which was wracked with sobs.

«At least the storm's abated,» said Jossef. «I was beginning to fear the ship would capsize. I'll go to the donkeys and see whether they've suffered any injuries.»

Mariam's donkey's weak leg had indeed become inflamed after it had fallen on the wet deck. Walking to Nazareth would be difficult for it now. Jossef sighed. Might he have to leave the donkey in Ptolemais and pick it up later, or would he even have to put it down? Once they were ashore, he would have to look at the leg again and see.

Because of the storm, the trip to Ptolemais had taken much longer than scheduled. No one had felt like looking at the view of the coastal towns. Mariam had been too busy comforting poor Jeshua, and Jossef had been thinking what to do about the injured donkey. This was not at all the happy arrival they had envisaged! It was already pitch-dark when the lights of the town finally came into sight. Whether they liked it or not, they would now have to spend the night in Ptolemais.

The sea was completely calm as the ship slipped slowly into harbour and was moored at the quayside. The clear night sky was full of stars. It was hard to believe that only a few hours previously, they had been through such a bad storm!

After paying the captain for the turbulent trip, there was still enough 'Gabriel' money left for a night in a comfortable guesthouse. They urgently needed to rest and recover before starting for Nazareth.

It was a sad little group that finally disembarked from the 'Orion' with a lame donkey and a small boy inconsolably and unremittingly weeping – hardly the picture of a family returning home from exile!

Of course, for Jeshua, it was not a return home at all, but an arrival in a foreign country which he did not know. He would be exchanging a nomadic lifestyle for a settled one, to which he would first have accustom himself. And now he had to accomplish this without his trusty friend Busha! At that moment, life seemed to him especially harsh.

Immediately opposite the harbour, they found a large guesthouse. It was rather loud there, but they did not wish to spend too long searching and were given an acceptable room. Mariam and Jeshua carried their baggage to the room, while Jossef went to stable the donkeys, warning them that he would take longer than usual as he wanted to make a compress for the donkey's lame leg.

Neither Jeshua nor Mariam had any appetite – Jeshua because of the shock, and Mariam after her seasickness. But at least the child in her womb did not appear to have suffered any damage!

Mariam bedded Jeshua down next to her and sang a psalm of comfort to a slow folk tune with a wistful oriental melody:

> *«God is our refuge and strength, a very present help in trouble.*
> *Therefore we will not fear though the earth gives way, though the mountains be moved into the heart of the sea,*
> *though its waters roar and foam, though the mountains tremble at its swelling.*
> *There is a river whose streams make glad the city of God, the holy habitation of the Most High.*
> *God is in the midst of her; she shall not be moved; God will help her when morning dawns.*
> *The nations rage, the kingdoms totter; he utters his voice, the earth melts.*
> *The Lord of hosts is with us; the God of Jacob is our fortress.[39]»*

Jeshua cried to begin with, but he soon slept from exhaustion and was relieved of his sorrow for a while. Mariam thought Jeshua was probably finding this similar to the loss of Merit – a beloved friend had suddenly been torn from him. At least this time, he

---

[39] Psalm 46, 1-7

had not shut himself off from his mother but was seeking her comfort.

By the time Jossef returned from the stable, mother and son were fast asleep in a close embrace. Jossef lay down next to them and slept almost immediately.

49

Next morning, Mariam's donkey's leg was still swollen, and the creature was very jumpy, not letting Jossef get anywhere near the leg to change the compress. Jossef discussed with Mariam whether to leave the donkey in Ptolemais and fetch it later, whether it could attempt the uphill journey to Nazareth or whether to put it down straight away. However, Jeshua put up such resistance to the first and last of these options that they decided to try taking it along with them. Losing another animal right now would have been just too much for Jeshua to bear.

However, the final decision was taken by the donkey itself. As Mariam tried to lead it out of the stable, it braced itself against this with its three healthy legs and was not to be moved! Even Jeshua now appreciated that the remaining stretch of the journey would have to be undertaken without it.

Jossef went with Jeshua to speak to the landlord about their situation. The landlord turned out to be an animal lover who said he knew just what needed to be done for such a leg injury. Jossef could leave the donkey with him without any qualms and pick it up again later. They agreed upon a price for the service, and with this Jeshua had to be satisfied. Mariam and Jossef also favoured this solution since the donkey had served them loyally during their years in Egypt and did not deserve either further suffering or death.

Mariam went with Jeshua to the donkey. She laid her forehead against the creature's forehead, stroking it fondly and saying thank you to it for all its hard toil. Jeshua did the same, weeping again while he did so.

Only the few possessions they really needed were loaded onto Jossef's donkey. The rest was disposed of in Ptolemais, to lighten the load. They set off up the zig-zag path with their remaining donkey, climbing higher and higher until they were well up in the Galilean hills.

Mariam sniffed the air, savouring the familiar scents of her homeland. Her heart became even lighter as she heard people speaking in their own Galilean dialect, and she greeted them joyfully. The long journey was finally coming to an end.

It took them two days to walk across the Galilean highlands – with Mariam's donkey they would no doubt have taken at least four – and at midday of the third day, they finally saw the houses of Nazareth upon the crest of the hill above them. Mariam cheered loudly. Jossef took his wife in his arms, kissed her and said: «We're home, my darling, God be praised and thanked!»

Jeshua looked up with interest at the unknown mountain village above them. So that was to be his home. Should he be feeling something? He could not, not yet. But he had heard so much about the place: his parents' beautiful house, Rivka's olive grove, his father's workshop and specially his grandmother, that he did feel a slight joyful expectation somewhere deep inside.

Jossef and Mariam did not want to go to their own house until they had found out what had happened to it. Maybe someone else was living there now. Was the house even still standing?

First and foremost, they wanted to see Hannah. Mariam could hardly wait to see her mother again, but she felt anxious that they may already be too late.

They walked up to Hannah's house, the house of Mariam's childhood. Everything looked just the same, as if time had stood still. Jossef and Jeshua hung back, allowing Mariam to enter first.

Mariam cautiously opened the door and entered the familiar living room. There was an uncanny silence. Nothing moved.

Then she heard a thin voice calling from Hannah's bedroom: «Who's there?»

Mariam raced into the bedroom and fell to her knees before her mother, who had become so thin that she hardly recognised her. Hannah smiled up at Mariam and asked: «Daughter, is it really you? Or am I dreaming?»

«It's really me, Imma! I'm home!» Mariam cautiously embraced her mother so as not to hurt her, kissing her gently.

«Ah, Mariam!» said Hannah. «I've been so worried about you and your child! Are you all well, all here?»

«Yes, Imma,» replied Mariam, «we're all well, and we're all here. In fact, there will soon be one more of us, for I'm expecting another child!»

«Oh Mariam, how wonderful,» said Hannah smiling, «I thought I would never see you again. Now I'm so happy!»

«Ah, Imma, I also thought I'd never see you again. Thank you for still being here, for waiting for me.»

«And now, Mariam, bring little Jeshua to me, please! I want to see my grandchild.»

Mariam went out and fetched Jeshua and Jossef into Hannah's bedroom. Jossef stayed in the background while Mariam led Jeshua to his grand-mother's bedside.

«Jeshua,» said Hannah in a thin, but happy voice, «you're a good-looking lad! You look a bit like your mother. Turn to face the side – yes, you really do look like her. Welcome to Nazareth, my little one!»

«Thank you, Savtah[40],» said Jeshua politely.

Then Jossef also approached the bed. «Peace be with you, Hannah!» he said, kissing her on the cheek, which felt like paper. «It's wonderful to be back!»

«Did you take good care of my daughter, Jossef?» asked Hannah

---

[40] Hebrew for Grandma

«Yes, he did, Imma,» replied Mariam with a smile, «he looked after both of us very well, didn't he, Jeshua?» Jeshua nodded.

«And you, Hannah?» asked Jossef. «How are you?»

«I've become very weak. I can no longer eat much. When you disappeared, I lost my appetite and never found it again. So many months of not knowing what had happened to you. That took it out of me. I've become an old woman, Jossef, very old; much older than my actual age, and I'll not be much longer for this world. But now I've met my grandson, I can leave the world in peace.»

«If you can hold out a bit, you can see another grandchild too, Hannah!» said Jossef.

«Yes, Mariam already told me. How long have you got to go, Mariam?»

«A few more months yet, Imma, I should imagine,» answered Mariam.

«Well, I'm going to have to find my appetite so that I can hold on, aren't I?» smiled Hannah, and the family laughed with her. «Children, I need some sleep now. Please stay here. It's good to know you're in the house!»

«Yes, Imma, we'll stay here,» said Mariam.

They left the room softly and sat in the living room. Jossef suggested he could make a quick visit to Rivka and Mordechai. Jeshua wanted to come too, as the atmosphere in his grandmother's house was rather heavy for an energetic boy. But first Jossef unloaded the baggage from the donkey, carried it into the house and stabled the donkey, giving the tired beast some well-earned water and hay.

In the early evening light, Jossef and Jeshua walked over the meadow at the edge of the village towards Rivka's olive grove, while Mariam, blissfully content, began to unpack their possessions and to put them away in the old familiar cupboard. She lit the oil lamps and made a fire in the hearth.

50

The little olive grove had grown and was now a proper olive plantation! Rivka and Mordechai had obviously been working hard to increase their crop.

Jossef took Jeshua by the hand and walked towards Rivka's house between the olive trees. The trees had grown much larger since Jossef had last seen them. On the north side of the house, Rivka had built an extension – the olive business appeared to be flourishing!

Jossef had just begun to describe to Jeshua how much smaller the olive grove had previously been, when Rivka, hearing his voice, came out from behind the house.

«Jossef!» shouted Rivka joyfully. «Welcome home to Nazareth!»

«Peace be with you, Rivka!» answered Jossef with a smile. «Thank you! It's wonderful to be back after all this time.»

«How's Hannah?» asked Rivka with a worried frown. «I've been going over to her every day to take care of her, ever since you failed to return from Bethlehem. She hasn't been well, Jossef.»

«I know, Rivka, and thank you. She's suffered greatly from our disappearance. She's grown weak: she tells us she hardly eats anything now.»

«That's right. I brought her food every day, but she hardly touched it.»

«When we arrived yesterday evening, we told her Mariam's expecting again. Maybe that'll encourage her to regain strength.»

«To be quite honest, I'm not sure that's possible now, Jossef. But let's hope for the best! Wonderful news that Mariam's going to have another child, though. And who's this?» asked Rivka, looking at Jeshua.

«This is our son Jeshua!» said Jossef, and Jeshua politely greeted Rivka.

«Jeshua! You will have grown, and now you're seeing your home for the first time, aren't you?» said Rivka with a broad smile.

«Your olive grove has grown too! It's a real plantation now!» said Jossef, glancing towards the trees.

«Ah yes, that was Mordechai. He's really promoting the business, seeing to it that we don't rest on our laurels, or rather on our olives! He's married now, that's why we've built an extension.»

«What are you saying about me?» asked a deep male voice, as Mordechai came towards them from the house extension. He had developed into a strong, mature man. There was no trace now of his angular adolescent frame and his previous insecurity. «Peace be with you, Jossef!» he said.

«And with you, Mordechai! It's wonderful that your business is doing so well!»

«Yes, we're happy with it,» responded Mordechai. «That's why we've had to start employing seasonal workers to help with the harvest. But we shan't start on the subject of seasonal workers, shall we? I'm sure you want to get back home before midnight! Come over for lunch tomorrow in the new house, then you can meet my wife, Tamar.»

«We'd love to, Mordechai, thank you! Well good night, and good night, Rivka!»

Jossef and Jeshua returned to Hanna's house. The house lay in silence once more, as Mariam had already gone to sleep.

However, Jossef and Jeshua were not yet tired enough for sleep, so Jossef went out with his son again. They strolled through the darkening streets. Jossef showed Jeshua where the synagogue was, where the market was held, and he also showed him the steep street where the craftsmen had their workshops. But he still avoided going anywhere near their own house and his workshop, for fear that they could have been taken over by someone else. There was plenty of time for that later.

***

Mariam got up twice in the night to go to her mother, as she thought she heard her calling. Jossef was also a little unsettled, as he was worried about the house and workshop.

At breakfast, Jossef told Mariam about Rivka's olive plantation now being three times as large as it had been before they had left for Bethlehem. He passed on the invitation to lunch with Mordechai and his new wife, Tamar.

Mariam brought Hannah a little thin porridge for breakfast and explained that they would be going over to Mordechai and Tamar's for a few hours.

«Will you manage without us, Imma? » she asked.

«Mariam, love!» said Hannah slowly and softly, but with a cheeky smile, «I've managed without you for almost four years; I'm sure I'll survive a few more hours! Don't fuss like a mother hen, now.»

Mariam tried giving her mother a few spoonsful of porridge, but Hannah turned her head away. «I'll eat it later, Mariam. Please, go with your family to Mordechai. Later you can tell me what you talked about.»

«Alright, Imma, if you're sure. But you really will eat it, won't you?»

«Yes, yes! You're a dear daughter, but I'm not hungry yet.»

The family made their way to Mordechai and Tamar's new house. Rivka was also there, and Tamar had decorated the table for the occasion. She had roasted a young goat in olive oil from their own production, seasoned with fresh herbs. During the meal, Mordechai and Tamar told them the latest Nazarene gossip which caused plenty of laughs. After the meal, they sat in front of the house in the shade of a pergola covered with climbing grapevines.

Jossef asked: « Rivka, will you please tell us all about this spy you had working for you?»

«Certainly,» said Rivka, making herself comfortable with a cushion at her back. «The man came to us together with a whole group of seasonal workers from Judaea. They all seemed to know each other from other harvest work. The spy – his name was Joachim – was a very pleasant man! No one would ever have suspected him of having ulterior motives! He was charming, witty and also an excellent worker. His questions were never conspicuous. They seemed completely natural, the way one does ask questions amongst fellow workers. How could someone seem so nice, and at the same time be so deceptive?»

«Mind you,» interjected Mordechai, «a spy would obviously need to have charm and friendly ways, ex officio so to speak, otherwise no one would confide in him! But it certainly was amazing how well he played his role! He seemed completely natural and trustworthy.»

«When we heard he was a spy,» continued Rivka, «and that his mission had been to find out whether you had relatives anywhere – well, to begin with, we really had to think hard whether we had ever mentioned relatives of yours! I suddenly remembered that we did discuss, in a general context, the importance of family at a wedding, when we were talking about Mordechai and Tamar's wedding. I casually said what a pity it was that Jossef's sister had been unable to be present at Jossefs wedding. Mordechai asked me – Mordechai, mark you, not Joachim! – where Jossef's sister lived, and I explained that she was married to a boatbuilder in Ashkelon and presently engaged in organising her own daughter's wedding. You see, Joachim didn't even need to make an effort! We more or less served him up the information on a platter!»

«Ah, I understand, Rivka! The crafty so-and-so! Herod obviously knows how to pick his henchmen. No one would suspect anything, you're right,» agreed Jossef. «The craziest thing of all is that we actually heard in Ashkelon that Herod had infiltrated your plantation with a spy, and you'll never believe who told us!»

«No, who was it, Jossef?» asked Rivka.

«A Roman centurion!» answered Jossef with a grin.

Jossef told them the whole story of Merit and her relationship with Lucius, and how he had told them of camp gossip that a spy had been planted in Nazareth by Herod, to find out whether Mariam or Jossef had relatives anywhere. He also told them of the attack upon Lucius and how Merit had been accused of his murder. He explained that they had escaped over the border into Egypt together with Merit and had taken her to her home, also mentioning how hard it had been for Jeshua to part from her. Their friends were amazed at all the adventures the family had experienced in Egypt.

«Yes,» concluded Jossef, «life taught Jeshua a few hard lessons in Egypt, and it'll no doubt take him time to settle down here. By the way,» said Jossef, attempting to sound casual, «how are things with our house and my workshop?»

Mordechai and Rivka smiled and looked at one another. «We stood up for your house, Jossef,» said

Mordechai. «We've always believed you'd come back someday, so we saw to it that no one took your house away from you. The same goes for your workshop. Of course both house and workshop are now a little dusty in places, but at least they still belong to you!»

Mariam and Jossef cheered loudly. «Actually, I was almost afraid to ask!» said Jossef. «You've done us a great service there, thank you, Rivka!»

«However,» added Mariam, «at present, we'll still be living with my mother, because obviously she needs us now.»

«Of course,» said Rivka, «but your house is there when you need it.»

Mordechai rose. «I must go and see to the dogs. They need feeding.»

Jeshua pricked up his ears. «Can I come too, Mordechai?» he asked.

«Of course, come on,» said Mordechai, and the two of them disappeared in the direction of the stable. In the meantime, Mariam told the tragic story of Busha's death in the sea.

«Our bitch has recently had puppies,» said Tamar, «so maybe it would be a comfort for Jeshua to have one of them?»

«Oh Tamar, I believe that would really help Jeshua feel at home here in Nazareth!» answered Mariam enthusiastically.

After a while, Mordechai and Jeshua appeared with a puppy which was almost the size Busha had been when she died, but with a much more slender frame.

«Mordechai's given me a puppy!» shouted Jeshua, «It's not Busha, and it's not quite as intelligent as she was, but it's also a girl like Busha, and I'm going to call her 'Zipporah'.»

Tamar smiled with satisfaction. She invited them all back into her living room for tea and dates, as the enlightening afternoon slowly came to an end.

51

Jeshua ran ahead with Zipporah in his arms; he could hardly wait to show his grandmother his new dog!

As he walked into her bedroom, he called out: «Savtah look, I've got a new do ...», then he came to a sudden halt. His grandmother lay motionless with her mouth open and contorted, her face as white as putty.

Mariam went up to her, laid her head next to Hannah's and listened. She could just about hear her thin, very slow breathing.

«Imma,» said Mariam softly, «we're home.»

Hannah laboriously sucked in a breath through her contorted mouth, then with great difficulty, she managed to say: «Mariam, I don't think I'll be able to see my second grandchild after all. I'm sorry. Please pray for me now, that my sins may be forgiven!»

Mariam beckoned Jossef over, and he spoke the words of Reconciliation for the Dying:

> *«May the words of my mouth and the meditation of my heart be pleasing to you, O Lord, my rock and my redeemer.*
> *Forgive us, our Father, for we have sinned;*
> *pardon us, our King, for we have rebelled;*
> *for you are a pardoner and a forgiver.*
> *Blessed are you, Lord, the gracious One who abundantly forgives.»*

He recited the Kaddish[41], as he had done two months previously for Moshe, and at the end Mariam, Jeshua and Hannah responded: «Amen!»

Hannah looked up at her daughter with eyes growing dim, then breathed her last.

Mariam pulled off her headscarf, tore her garment, fell upon her mother's body and wept bitterly. Jossef closed Hannah's eyes, laid a white cloth upon her face and placed a burning candle at her head. He brought Jeshua, with Zipporah still in his arms, over to his grandmother's bed, and the family stood by Hannah's body in silent prayer.

***

Jossef left Mariam and Jeshua at Hannah's deathbed to keep the vigil and hurried away, first seeking out Rivka.

«Rivka!» he shouted, «Hannah's just passed away!»

«Ah,» replied Rivka, «I thought it wouldn't be long. You see? She only waited for you.»

«It looks like it, yes,» agreed Jossef. «Rivka, I'm off to find the cantor. Can you please call all our nearest friends together, so that we can hold the burial in front of our house tomorrow morning?»

«Of course, Jossef, I'll be pleased to!» assented Rivka. «Afterwards I'll go and help Mariam wash the body. »

---

[41] See page 336

«Thank you!» called Jossef as he hurried away to the cantor's house.

Once Rivka had arrived, she helped Mariam and Jeshua to lay the body on the floor, where they washed it and ritually poured water over it. Then they wrapped it in a white shroud.

When Jossef returned, he said another prayer, after which the door of the house was opened so that Hannah's soul could pass out. During the night, the family kept death watch by the body.

Next morning, the Rabbi, the cantor and all their friends appeared for the burial. The simple service took place in front of Hannah's house. Mariam wept and keened throughout the ritual. She was inconsolable. Now her mother would never get to see and hold the child that was growing inside her womb!

Hannah was lowered into the grave. When all those present had sprinkled earth into the grave, the Rabbi spoke the concluding words: «*The Lord gives, the Lord takes away, praised be the name of the Lord.*»

After the burial, all their friends entered Hannah's house with the food they had brought with them. They seated themselves on the floor and distributed the food amongst those present. The older villagers remembered when Hannah had come to Nazareth from Bethany as a young bride, to join her husband and start a new life there. The memories of times gone by were comforting and brough Hannah close for them all. That evening, Jeshua learnt a lot about the people of his new home, sensing their warmth and geniality, while Zipporah played in front of Rivka's house with her own mother and her siblings once more.

Rivka offered to help tidy Hannah's house, together with Tamar.

«What are you going to do with the house, Mariam?» asked Rivka diffidently.

Mariam's eyes filled with tears. «Oh, Rivka! I suppose I'll have to sell it; without my mother, it's not a home anymore! You told us yesterday we still have our own lovely house. We don't need two houses.»

«In that case, we'll also help you with clearing the house when the time comes,» offered Rivka, and Tamar nodded vigorously.

«You're such kind neighbours, Rivka! Thank you!» said Mariam, much moved.

The company stayed together until the evening, when their friends and neighbours returned to their homes. For the first seven days of the period of mourning Jossef, Mariam and Jeshua remained at Hannah's house, where Mariam was leaving behind so many memories from her own childhood and also from the time of Jeshua's conception.

**

On the eighth day, the family once again took possession of their own beautiful home. There was indeed a lot of dust, but otherwise all was just as they had left it when they had departed for the census in Bethlehem more than three years ago – with no idea that it would be so long before they returned!

Jeshua wandered slowly around the house. His parents had already prepared a room for him, which he could now call his own. It was strange to think that he had already been here in his mother's womb! He liked the house very much, and obviously Zipporah did too, for she was sniffing around in all the corners and had already reserved a place next to the hearth for herself.

As soon as they had everything in the house to their satisfaction, Jossef was itching to visit his work-shop.

«Want to come too?» he asked Jeshua, who eagerly picked up Zipporah and walked with his father the short distance to the limewashed cob building with the wooden doorway – his father's workshop. Jeshua put Zippora down as they entered, and she jumped merrily around their feet. As she had done in the house, she sniffed in all the corners, until she started to sneeze from the dust and the sawdust. Jeshua laughed, picked her up and kissed her dusty nose. Jossef inhaled the familiar, much-loved smell of wood and looked forward to getting back to work again at last.

In the meantime, Mariam climbed the steep street where all the craftsmen had their workshops, to buy a few pretty oil lamps at the potter's shop, thinking of Merit as she looked around the shop. At the top of the village, she bought fresh beans and flour at the market, as she wanted to make a festive meal for the family that evening and to make the house look nice, in gratefulness for their safe homecoming. She went home over the fields to buy a lamb from the shepherd, who slaughtered and prepared it for her, so that she only needed to roast it over the open fire that evening. Soon Jossef would be working again at Galilean building sites and bringing some money home. The family could afford to treat themselves.

When she got home, Mariam carried all the carpets outside and beat out the dust. By the time Jossef and Jeshua returned from the workshop, the house was already looking more homely. She told them she had bought a lamb as a reminder of their first supper near Beit Guvrin, shortly before arriving in Ashkelon. At that time, they still had no idea that they were going to have to flee over the border into Egypt.

While Jossef skewered the lamb ready for roasting, Mariam told Jeshua about the evening in Beit Guvrin, and how she had sung him a lullaby while the meat was roasting on the fire.

«Imma, will you sing that lullaby for me now, please?» begged Jeshua.

«Yes of course, come and sit by me, Jeshua!» answered Mariam gladly.

Jeshua grabbed Zipporah and made himself comfortable, leaning happily against his mother as she began to sing:

«When you lie down, you will not be afraid;

when you lie down, your sleep will be sweet.[42]»

Whenever Mariam paused for breath, the silence was broken only by the spitting of lamb fat in the open fire. Zipporah and Jeshua both sighed in contentment.

Jeshua wistfully remembered what Merit used to say at the end of her Egyptian myths: It has come to a good end.

---

[42] See page 57

List of Persons in the order of appearance:

Mariam (Mary), mother of Jeshua

Jeshua (Jesus), her son

Jossef (Joseph), carpenter, Mariam's husband

Elisheva (Elisabeth), mother of Jochanan (John) in Bethany

Zechariah (Zachariah), Elisheva's husband, priest in the Jerusalem temple and father of Jochanan

Sarah and Shimon, and their children Martha, Elazar (Lazarus) and little Mariam (Mary), neighbours of Elisheva in Bethany

Makahn, Kamran and Behnam, three learned astrologers from Persia, and their apprentice, Aftab

Herod the Great, Tetrarch (King by the grace of Rome) of Galilee, Judaea and Peraea

Enosh, official, spy for the High Priests and for Herod

Tabitha, owner of the stable in Bethlehem where Jeshua was born

Yitzhak, her son

Salome, a midwife in Bethlehem, and Mariam's half-sister

Leah, Jossef's sister in Ashkelon

Daniel, Leahs husband, boatbuilder in Ashkelon

Merit, the Egyptian friend of Leah in Ashkelon

Lucius Antonius Cicero, centurion, Merit's lover in Ashkelon

Kulom, Sarah and Amunet, a family living north of Bubastis (today Zagazig) who helped the travellers

Ahab and Dinah, Jewish owners of the guesthouse in Belbeis

Jehuda, caretaker at the synagogue in Belbeis

Hemire, Hesire and Hepire, young slaves and later potters from Kalya, west of Wadi Natrun

Meketre, Merit's father, an Egyptian potter in Baltim

Judith, Jewish wife of Meketre, Merit's mother, in Baltim

Gershon and Esther, Jewish owners of the guest-house in Babylon (today Old Cairo), and their children Tirza and Benni

Nechti, captain of the Nile ship from Maresi to Beni Suef

Paneb, goldsmith in Cynopolis (today el-Qays)

Tuja, Paneb's sister in Hermopolis magna (today el-Ashmunein)

Moshe, Jewish prophet in the stone desert near Muharraq

Khufu, boatbuilder in Cusae

Anchesenpepi, (Pepi for short), friend of Mariam in Muharraq

Sinuhe, friend of Paneb in Cynopolis

Hannah, Mariam's mother and Jeshua's grandmother

Rivka, owner of the olive plantation in Nazareth

Mordechai and Tamar, son and daughter-in-law of Rivka in Nazareth

Bibliography:

Steve Mason: Flavius Josephus and the New Testament, Translation into German: Manuel Vogel, Francke Verlag, München, 2000

Othmar Keel and Max Küchler: Orte und Landschaften der Bibel, Benziger/Vandenhoeck & Ruprecht, Zürich und Göttingen, 1982, Band 2: Der Süden

Otto F.A. Meinardus[43]: The Itinerary of the Holy Family in Egypt, Studia orientalia Christiana: Collectionea, 1962, Vol. 7; and: The Holy Family in Egypt, 6th Edition, 2000, based on Coptic sources, sermons and traditions

Ancient Egyptian Love Songs with Myths and Love Stories, (Altägyptische Liebeslieder mit Märchen und Liebesgeschichten), Artemis Verlag, Zürich, 1950

Günther Hölbl: Altägypten im Römischen Reich: Der römische Pharao und seine Tempel, Verlag Philipp von Zabern, Mainz am Rhein, 2005, Band I und III

Katja Lembke, Cäcilia Fluck & Günter Vittmann: Ägyptens späte Blüte: Die Römer am Nil, Verlag Philipp von Zabern, Mainz am Rhein, 2004

Alfred Bertholet: Wörterbuch der Religionen, Alfred Kröner Verlag, Stuttgart, 1985

---

[43] Philosopher and Coptic theologian

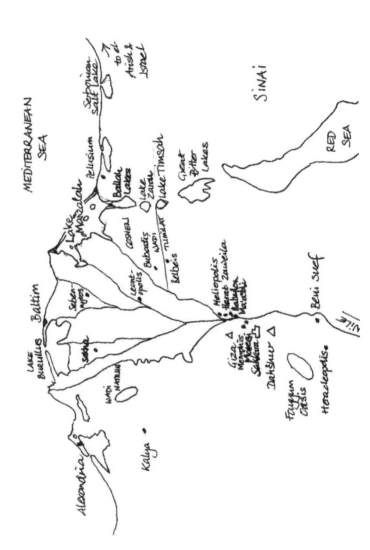

416

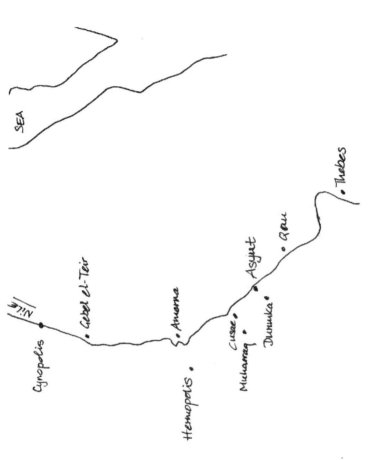

SEA

Nile

Cynopolis

Gebel el-Teir

Amarna

Hermopolis

Cusae

Muhamaq

Asyut

Dunuka

Qau

Thebes

Afterword

The characters in this story are all fictitious, apart from Jeshua, Mariam, Jossef, Hannah, Elisheva, Zechariah, Jochanan, Salome, Martha, Elazar and little Mariam – oh, and of course Herod!

Many details are taken from the legends of Coptic tradition, such as the *springs* which were found at all the respective locations and were said to have been blessed by the infant Jesus[44] and are therefore curative. The *dried-up well at Bahnasah*, from which the Holy Family was able to obtain water, is also mentioned in Coptic legend. And according to legend, Jesus drove out a devil from a child near *Mallaui*. The Coptic tradition has also preserved the story of the inhabitants of *Bubastis* refusing the Holy Family water – according to this tradition, the town was destroyed for this reason – and the inhabitants were indeed worshippers of the cat idol Bastet. The story is told of a couple named *Kulom and Sarah* who helped the Holy Family near Bubastis in their time of need, and that Jesus healed Sarah. Interestingly, *Salome* is shown in some icons and mosaics in Egypt and mentioned in some legends of the Holy Family, and in others she is not, so I have only included her in my story as far as Ashkelon. The following two stories are also to be found in Coptic legend: a *boulder* falls from the cliffs above the Nile, and thanks to the intervention of Jesus, narrowly misses hitting the Holy Family; and when the Holy Family visits the temple at *Hermopolis*, the idols fall down and the family are chased by the priests. There is also a legend which says that Jesus placed his hand on the rock in Gebel el-Teir, and the rock split open, enabling the Holy Family to hide in it from the priests. Finally, the following elements are also owed to Coptic legend: The *granite bowl* given to Mary by the women of Sebennytos (Samanoud); water gushing forth under Jesus' feet in *Sakha*; *Mary's hill* on the eastern bank of the Nile upon which she sits, looking across at

---

[44] Jesus is the Graeco-Latin form of the Hebrew name Jeshua, which is the shortened form of Jehoshua

Hermopolis; the tree and the spring at *Matariya*; a holy man named *Musa* or *Yusha* from Jerusalem who was in close contact with the Holy Family at Muharraq and was buried there; and last, but not least: *four young people* who were travelling together with the Holy Family.

In most of the places mentioned, as well as in Durunka (where, in my book, the *cave of the lioness* is situated), Coptic churches, chapels and monasteries are to be found today. Apart from Kalya (fictitious), Fayyum and Thebes, all the places shown on the map (pages 416-417) are said to have been visited by the Holy Family.

It occurred to me while writing that Jesus also lived a nomadic life during the time of his ministry. Possibly, this lack of attachment, this readiness to move around, with *nowhere to lay his head* [45], had its roots in the nomadic life the family led in Egypt during his early childhood.

My imagination was stimulated and fired as much by the Coptic legends as it was by the stories in the Bible, and so I decided to write this book. When I began researching, I had no idea how much information had been preserved by the Coptic church, and later, I was lucky enough to be able to visit the places mentioned in my book. My travel guide, Dalal el-Asser (a Muslim), and the many Coptic Christians, priests, monks and nuns we met, told me these and other stories, enabling me to comprehend the Flight to Egypt in a new light. My deepest thanks go to Dalal and to all these acquaintances for a deep spiritual experience which I will never forget.

My thanks go to my sister, Annette Atkins, who diligently proof-read and corrected this book.

Stephanie Meier

---

[45] Matthew 8, 19–20; Luke 9, 57–58

Stephanie Meier: **Visiting Elisheva**

A short story about the visit of Mariam to her Aunt Elisheva. Both women are pregnant with their sons Jeshua and Jochanan. I have related the story as it is told in the Bible, also adding fictional elements.

First published in Autumn 2018 by Books on Demand

.